"Do you always stare? Thorne gritted out, her gray eyes flashing.

Dev grinned belatedly, walking over and sliding his arms around her. Thorne stiffened. "When something's worth looking at, yes. Relax, will you? I'm not going to bite."

Thorne pouted, crossing her arms protectively across her breasts as Dev lifted her easily into his arms. She was heatedly aware of his warmth and that beguiling twinkle in his eyes. "Since when do brigands keep their word?"

Dev enjoyed her spirit. "There is honor among thieves, my lady. Although," he drawled, "you wouldn't know that. You've been hidden away in your manor at Somerset, no doubt."

Thorne snapped her mouth shut, fighting off the dizziness that flared through her. "You're enjoying this too much, Captain."

He deposited her on a blanket near the fire. "God forgive me, Gypsy, but I am."

Dear Reader,

This month we are happy to bring you *Rogue's Honor*, a new book from DeLoras Scott. Those of you who have followed DeLoras's career since her first book, *Bittersweet*, will be delighted by this tale of the Oklahoma land rush and of partners each with their own dark pasts.

With *Heaven's Gate*, the writing team of Erin Yorke has created the dramatic story of a wayward English countess and the renegade Irish lord who is determined to force her surrender.

Lindsay McKenna's *King of Swords* is a sequel to her January title, *Lord of Shadowhawk*. Abducted and held for ransom, Thorne Somerset learns to love the bitter soldier who holds her fate in his hands.

A fugitive Union officer and a troubled Rebel girl overcome seemingly insurmountable odds to find happiness in *The Prisoner*. Set at the close of the Civil War, this tender story is the first historical by popular contemporary author Cheryl Reavis.

Next month look for titles by Maura Seger, Julie Tetel, Lucy Elliot and Elizabeth August from Harlequin Historicals, and rediscover the romance of the past.

Sincerely,

The Editors

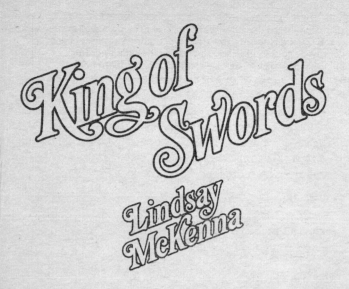

King of Swords

Lindsay McKenna

Harlequin Books

TORONTO • NEW YORK • LONDON
AMSTERDAM • PARIS • SYDNEY • HAMBURG
STOCKHOLM • ATHENS • TOKYO • MILAN
MADRID • WARSAW • BUDAPEST • AUCKLAND

Harlequin Historicals first edition May 1992

ISBN 0-373-28725-9

KING OF SWORDS

Books by Lindsay McKenna

Harlequin Historicals

Sun Woman #71
Lord of Shadowhawk #108
King of Swords #125

LINDSAY McKENNA's

Native American background spurred her interest in history, which she feels is a reflection of what goes on in the present and an indication of what the future will be like. Most interesting to Lindsay are the women of history. She feels their strength of spirit can be an inspiration to the women of today. Her three favorite historical periods are the Old West, medieval times and the Roman era.

Lindsay, an avid rock hound and hiker, lives with her husband of fifteen years in Arizona.

To some of my dedicated, caring and loyal readers:
Jennifer Gilman, Debra McCune, Dinah Bryant
Rushing, Amy Bottke, Diane Spigonardo, Bevereley
Mercer, Barbara Kieffer, Yvonne Hering, June Ply,
Coreen Atkins-Sheldrick (Canada), Carley Martin,
Margaret M. Battersby (England), Rose Albea,
Grace Baskin, Pat Diehl, Donna Jo Wagner and
Midge Wagner

"The highest courage is to dare
to appear what one is."
—John Lancaster Spaulding

Prologue

March, 1798, near Wexford, Ireland

"Dev... *help!*"

Shannon's shriek carried over musket fire, screams of men and whinnies of horses as the British cavalry thundered down upon the beleaguered Irish rebels that surrounded him. Dev chanced a glance, jerking his head to the left as he raised his sword to parry an oncoming blow by a redcoat who was charging him across the broken barricade of overturned carts. To his horror, he saw his wife of two years and his sister, Alyssa, being captured and dragged away by the British.

No! God have mercy, no! Desperately, Dev parried as a grim-faced soldier leapt down off a broken cart to engage him. Steel clashed with steel. Dev felt the savage vibration of the swords biting into each other all the way up his bloodied arm.

Tired. He was so exhausted, everything was a blur around him except for Shannon's frightened plea. He had to help her! He had to escape the surge of enemy soldiers pouring through the breach to kill the Irish who had dared to defy them. Sweat stung his eyes, his dark, auburn hair clinging to his skull as he fended off the next thrust. There! With a flick of his wrist, he disarmed the soldier and lunged forward. A look of surprise and then horror washed across the enemy's face as Dev felt his blade sink deeply into the redcoat's body.

Momentary triumph soared through him as he wrested the bloodied blade free. Shannon! He had to stop them from taking Shannon and Alyssa as prisoners of war! Men around him were retreating; the ragged army of Irish in the garb of farmers was bent and then mangled beneath the wave of cavalry now funneling through the broken barricade. Dev was jerked backward, thrown off balance as his brother, Gavin, hauled him out of the fray. Dev tried to wrench free.

"No, Dev," Gavin cried out, "too many! You can't help them!" They were swept along the slippery, bloodied earth. Dev strove to break free and save his wife. *Sweet Jesus, let me get to her! Shannon! No!* With the fury of a madman bent upon destruction of everything in his path, Dev tried to rally his beaten men. The British swallowed up the pitiful Irish contingent.

His last glance was of Shannon and his sister being hauled up into an awaiting cart, surrounded by the enemy. Their hands were bound, their eyes wide with unadulterated fear.

Shannon! he screamed. *I love you! No! I can't lose you... I can't....*

Chapter One

March 1803, Spain

"Shannon! No..."

Dev's screams echoed off the walls of his haunted mind. He saw Shannon crying his name, although he was too far away to actually hear her. They were taking her away in a wooden cart toward the quay where the British ships were anchored in Wexford Bay. *God, no!* He moaned, watching as his wife disappeared into the bloodred haze that always ended his nightmare.

Dead... His beautiful wife of two years was dead. She had been captured and put aboard a four-masted sailing ship bound for Newgate prison in London. Captain Vaughn Trayhern, the second son of an English earl, had tortured and killed Shannon while aboard that ship.

Groaning, Dev turned restlessly onto his back. Shannon's clear, laughing features danced before him. Her eyes were the color of his beloved Ireland, her hair a lustrous ginger shot through with strands of gold and copper. She was beautiful, and innocent.

In his sleep, Dev automatically clenched his fists. Sweat stood out on the tightened planes of his square face as all the anguish fraught with hatred entwined into the hellish morass that embraced him.

"Cap'n Kyle? Dev?"

Dev fought to pull himself from the insidious clutches of the nightmare. He felt the grip of a friendly hand on his shoulder, shaking him one more time, and recognized Lieutenant Niall Scanlon's low voice.

"I'm awake," he muttered, sitting up. Automatically, Dev pushed several strands of hair off his damp brow. He glanced around. A bare thread of gray light over the hills heralded the beginning of dawn in the province of Catalonia. The March morning was fragrant with the rich odor of the earth beneath him and the scent of pine mixed with the salt of the Mediterranean nearby. The sound of horses eating the succulent grass relaxed him. He raised his head, looking over at his lieutenant, who squatted before him.

Scanlon, a fellow Irishman, offered him a vague hint of a smile. He and the rest of Dev's French squadron were disguised as peasants in order not to draw suspicion from the Spanish people.

"All's quiet? No patrols from the Gerona garrison in Barcelona?"

"Nothing."

Dev grunted, rubbing his face tiredly. That was unusual. During their travel to Barcelona from France they had dodged patrols with great frequency. "We'll start running into them soon."

Scanlon nodded, looking beyond him as if trying to pierce the darkness. From the east they could smell the briny scent of the Mediterranean, less than four miles away.

"I have Sergeant Terebenev and Corporal Erhard riding within a five-mile radius of our camp to ensure no surprise Spanish patrols."

"Terebenev and Erhard get along like oil and water," Dev muttered as he rose. The cossack, Terebenev, hated the last moment German replacement, Wolfe Erhard. Dev had tried to tell the Count de Lasalle, his commander, that he wanted no national rivalries in his handpicked cavalry unit, but he had lost the argument. Erhard stayed. Instead of his soldiers being wolves on the battlefields across Europe, they were now foxes, ordered to become Napoleon's eyes and ears to gauge the peasants' unrest and the readiness of their military machine against the Spanish monarchy's.

Scanlon walked with him toward the fire. "I told Erhard to follow Terebenev's orders."

"Or else," Dev grumbled, crouching before the coals. A small tin of boiled tea sat to one side of the embers. He chose a battered cup from nearby, pouring the brownish liquid into it. Today they would ride near the sea. There was less chance of being seen there by the Spanish peasants who tilled the rich, fertile soil farther inland.

"Get the men up," he told Scanlon quietly. It was time to begin their day.

Dev remained by the coals and watched as Niall nudged each man with the toe of his worn leather boot. Something gnawed at him, but he couldn't pinpoint the unsettled feeling. Every time he'd experienced that uneasy sensation in his gut, something went wrong. He grimly pressed his lips into a single line, his blue eyes narrowing as his mind ran through the list of possibilities.

The most obvious threat was that of running into a Spanish patrol. The Count de Lasalle had given him strict orders not to engage them at any cost, but simply to scatter like leaves before the wind and try to outrun them and hide. He flicked a glance toward the hobbled horses who ate around them. They were good animals, all of them battle tested—musket ball or saber scars were scattered over their lean bodies.

"They're up," Scanlon said.

"Good. Send Cassidy out to bring in the patrol."

Dev looked down at himself as he rose. His white peasant shirt was creased with dust and in dire need of a washing. The dark blue wool breeches he wore were stuffed inside his badly scarred black boots. The leather bandoliers that crossed his broad shoulders and draped down across his chest warned everyone he was a man of war, not peace.

Once he stood, he could feel the knots he'd gained during sleep slowly begin to dissolve. The horizon was now a

pale wash of pink, and activity was beginning to stir around
him.

The horses lifted their heads, ears pricked forward.
Terebenev rode in, his bearded face thundercloud black.
Not far behind him was Wolfe Erhard. His meaty face was
made fiercer looking with the thick black mustache that
draped below his full lips. The Russian sergeant guided his
bay gelding toward Dev, snarling something over his
shoulder at the German hussar.

Dev watched the hulking Russian dismount from his
steppe pony, which was dwarfed by his owner's size. Dev
had learned to respect the ponies caught and tamed by the
Russians. They were captured from the Mongolian desert
and were as tough as the Arabian mare he owned. No horse
could keep up with his gray mare, Ghazeia, except for
Terebenev's hardy mount. And the six-foot, five-inch cossack was as rugged as his steppe pony.

"Kyle," Terebenev growled in his rumbling voice.

"Find anything out there, Ivan?"

The Russian touched his thick, wiry black beard, his eyes
a fierce ebony color. "No, sir, but that hussar bastard will
cause us trouble." Ivan hunkered down.

"What happened?"

"We spotted a small pueblo about five miles south of
here," Ivan grunted, pouring himself some tea into the
same cup Dev had just drunk from. "Erhard wanted to go
find himself a woman. Any woman. I told him he'd attack
a mare if there wasn't the two-legged kind available." Ivan
grinned, showing his chipped and yellowed teeth as he rose
to stand next to his leader.

Dev swallowed a smile. "Did you let him?"

"Told him if he wanted to bed something so badly, he
could take on your mare." And then Ivan's bushy brows
drew together. "We don't have time for women right now."

"War is for men, not women or children," Dev agreed
absently.

Ivan's rounded cheeks increased to the size of apples as
his smile deepened. "Erhard's like all the rest of Napoleon's legions—they steal what they can along the way.

Don't matter whether it's food, a woman or a girl. I told him he'd better forget women while he's with us or you'd take your knife and geld him."

A dry smile shadowed Dev's face. "I hope you told him to leave my mare alone, too."

Ivan matched his smile. "I told him you'd kill anyone who touched that mare." His eyes took on a twinkle. "Ghazeia's a prize," he enthused, waving his hand to emphasize his words. "Better even than my steppe pony. Tougher."

"And better looking. Your pony has the ears of a mule."

"But he hears like a Russian wolf!"

"I'll give him that. Sure he isn't part dog?"

Ivan's booming laughter rolled across the salmon-tinted landscape. "As long as he doesn't lift up his leg to pee, then we have nothing to worry about."

Dev clapped him on his heavy, powerful shoulder. "It's time to go. Let's mount up."

"Yes, sir."

The men fell into the routine. Normally, they would mount and ride two by two, with Dev leading the column. But on this mission they rode loosely, without any apparent sense of formation. Settling the wide-brimmed straw hats on their heads, they continued in a southerly direction. They followed the curve of Spain's coast, catching sight of the blue of the Mediterranean every now and then.

"You feel anything?" Dev asked Niall as he rode up.

Niall studied him for a moment, his narrow face unreadable as he digested Dev's question. "No. What's bothering you? Erhard?"

With a snort, Dev leaned down, running his long, large-knuckled fingers through Ghazeia's silver mane. The mare arched her neck a little more, responding to his touch. "Erhard will always be a problem. No, my gut's tight."

Scanlon blinked once, his green eyes thoughtful. "Then there's trouble ahead."

Dev nodded. "The question is, what? And when . . . ?"

"Thorne, *mi corazón,* what are you doing out here?"

Thorne lifted her head from the sleek neck of Angela, the

bay mare. Her gray eyes were dark with pain as she met her aunt's kindly brown gaze. Her lips, once thinned with anguish, pulled into a slight smile of apology.

"I'm sorry, Aunt Maria. I—I had to..." Her husky voice fell into silence. Thorne turned toward her petite aunt, who entered the stall.

"To escape?" Aunt Maria coaxed, lifting her voluminous silk skirts of sky blue as she walked up to her. She placed her arm across Thorne's shoulders, pulling her close for a moment and giving her a hug. *"Mi corazón,"* she whispered. "My heart, what am I going to do with you? You've been at our villa for one week now, and I find you hiding out here in the stable with our animals."

Thorne, who stood a head taller than her aunt, forced a smile she did not feel. "I'm sorry, Aunt Maria." She stood back, absently petting the Andalusian mare's silky neck. "I—just feel better out here. I can't explain it." And then a pained look fled across her heart-shaped face. "Why can't I go riding like I did at home? The beach is only a mile away and I long to be by myself. Just for a little while, Auntie."

Maria's oblong face was set off by dark, intelligent brown eyes. She gave her niece a patient look. *"Mi corazón,* a young lady of Spain never rides by herself. She must have an escort. The very handsome Captain Eneas Garcia has called for you every day to go riding with him." Maria gave her a sad look. "And you refuse."

The rich, sweet smell of the straw enveloped Thorne's nostrils and she leaned against the mare, closing her eyes. "I can't, Auntie. I just want to be alone, to remember Mama... I can't carry on conversation and be polite when I feel as if I'm being torn apart inside." She opened her eyes, revealing their dove gray color, fringed by thick black lashes. "Is it wrong to feel hurt? To feel the loss of Mama?" she asked, her voice growing hoarse. "It's only been a month since her death. Father's stroke has left him addled, barely a ghost of himself. When Mama died, a large part of him died with her. I'm sorry I haven't been a better guest—''

"Nonsense, *mi corazón!*" Maria patted her hand warmly. "You were right in coming to tell me of my sister's death." She shuddered. "Thank God you did not send a letter instead. I would have died of shock. It was you who absorbed my grief, tears, and comforted me. You've been so strong. First for your father, and now for me." She gave Thorne a tender smile. "And her Gypsy blood you carry has brought you home. Did Rosa tell you that during our youth as Gypsies, we traveled throughout Spain and France?" Maria's thin lips drew into a sad line. "And you're so very much like her." Maria touched the scarab amulet that Thorne wore about her slender neck on a thin gold chain. "Come, let's leave this stall. I have fresh lemon and water waiting for us on the portico."

Maria reached out, clasping Thorne's long, shapely hand. She noticed that she wore no other adornment except for her mother's amethyst ring and the scarab necklace that lay at the base of her throat. The Gypsy blood ran richly through Thorne, and Maria saw a great resemblance between her and her now departed sister. She had Rosa's large, almost tilted eyes, her straight, clean nose and full, blossoming lips—red lips that needed no cosmetics to bring out their natural pomegranate color. Maria smiled to herself; Thorne was an English version of Rosa. She had picked up her beautiful white skin from her doting father, John, and his hawklike gray eyes. She wished color would once again flood Thorne's gaunt cheeks, and that she would regain the weight she had lost because of her grief.

Sighing, Maria realized Thorne would soon be leaving for England. In two more days she was going home to take care of her ailing father, the Earl of Somerset. John was close to sixty, an invalid now after the shock of his wife's unexpected passing.

"I think you are more Gypsy than you ever guessed, Thorne," she said as they walked along a tiled path toward the portico.

Thorne, who had been thinking of walking along the ocean's sparkling sand, turned her attention back to her aunt. She longed to feel the warmth of the water on her bare feet. "What do you mean?"

"How much did Rosa tell you of our heritage?"

"She had many stories to tell me. I used to love to sit and listen to her tales of how you two grew up here."

"She told you how we crossed from France, through the great Pyrenees into the hot desert of Spain?"

Thorne nodded. "Yes."

"Did you know what a rebellious young lady your mother was? Like all Gypsy women, she rode astride a horse, never sidesaddle as ladies of England are taught." Maria laughed softly. "Rosa was a hellion by English standards."

Thorne's gray eyes widened. "She never told me about that!"

Chuckling, Maria said, "Of course she wouldn't. She wanted the very best for you, Thorne. Rosa wanted you to have advantages and privileges, wanted you raised as the lady you are, trained in all the arts and ready to take your place in the *ton*. Something that she could not do, because the *ton* treated her as an outcast."

"Because she was a Gypsy," Thorne agreed, bitterness leaking into her voice. She touched her hair, which had been coiffed into soft curls on her head. "I always knew Mother was hurt by the fact that few of the *ton* offered us invitations to parties and balls."

"Ah, but when your father presented you to society, that all changed."

Thorne shrugged. "I never cared for the *ton*. They're elegant fops parading around like circus clowns, so pretentious." She frowned. "I like honest conversation, Aunt Maria. Real people."

Maria chuckled. "Spoken like a true Rom. You've the soil of the earth goddess, Ceres, in your soul. The quicksilver of the full moon for your emotions, which ebb and flow daily with passion and fervency. Yes, you are more

Gypsy than you realize. You have your mother's soul, Thorne.''

"I know that," she whispered, her tone raspy with tears. "Mama often told me I inherited her love of plants and animals." Thorne held out her hands, splaying them outward. "I long to sink my fingers into the earth and feel her rich warmth. I want to walk along that ocean and allow the unseen feeling of the water to pass through me. I long to be one with things that are not considered proper in English society."

Maria's heart twisted with compassion as she heard the ache within Thorne's voice. If only she could comfort her in some way. A twinkle came to her eyes. "If my husband, Juan, would allow it, would you like to ride Angela on the beach this evening? Providing you stay within sight of our villa?"

Hope leapt to life in Thorne's gray eyes. Her cheeks flushed with the vibrant pink of excitement and she clasped her hands together. "Oh, Auntie, if I only could. If—"

"Listen to me, young one. Have the maid, Francesca, find you a suitable riding habit and then go rest. I'll bring you news of Juan's decision later. Now go! No more sadness in those lovely eyes of yours."

"Yes! Oh, yes, I will, Auntie. I promise I will." Thorne turned, unable to contain her excitement. Oh, to ride a horse once again! To pound along the surf, in union with the sea, sky and earth! Thorne reached out, hugging her aunt effusively. "I love you so much, Auntie. Thank you for understanding!"

"The heart of a gypsy you have, Thorne. Just like your mother. God forgive the man who takes you as his wife. I hope he realizes how very special and how unlike other women you are."

Thorne barely heard Maria's parting comment as she flew through the portico toward her room. Freedom, at last! Sweet mother earth, how she missed horseback riding!

If Aunt Maria or Uncle Juan ever discovered the black riding boots, buckskin breeches and white peasant blouse she had hidden in her traveling trunk, they would die of shock, Thorne thought wryly. Only her mama knew of her midnight and early morning rides in boy's costume. With her thick ebony hair coaxed into a single braid, she would tear across the moonlit countryside or dew-soaked morning grass without fear of discovery. If someone saw her, they would think it was a young lad on horseback instead of a well-bred young woman who was supposed to be married at her age.

Unable to remain still and realizing it would be hours before Maria could persuade Juan to allow her to go riding, Thorne pulled out the tarot cards that her mother had taught her how to read. She pressed her fingers against the scarab. It had been given to her mother by the old woman who had been the *Drabnari,* or doctor, for the Gypsy band; a sign that her mother would be the next healer in the encampment. The ability to heal had been passed on to Thorne.

Thorne closed her eyes and pressed her hand against her throat, feeling the warmth of the scarab beneath her fingers. Her mother had taught her the properties of plants, how to lay her hands upon sick animals and people and heal them. The sting of tears struck her eyes, and Thorne released a soft sob, remembering the wonderful times she and her mother had spent together. All she had left were memories, the scarab and a deck of well-worn tarot cards. Automatically, Thorne shuffled them and then laid them out in the Celtic spread.

Her heart pounded once to underscore the importance of the first card she laid down—the Death card. Swallowing hard, Thorne turned over the next one, the King of Swords. Her hand trembled as she placed it across the Death card. The day was hot, as usual, but Thorne felt suddenly chilled. The cards never lied. The day her mother had died, the Death card had turned up in her morning reading.

Trying to mollify her fear, Thorne concentrated on the King of Swords. That would symbolize a leader, a man in charge. But he would be a warrior, someone who was used to living or dying by his own aggression. She knit her arched brows. Who was this man coming into her life to transform it? Perhaps the tarot weren't working properly because her grief interfered, altering the sensitivity of the cards. Thorne quickly gathered up the deck, tucking it back into the silk pouch. She couldn't face any more tragedy; she was too emotionally fragile to deal with it. She didn't want to know what the rest of the spread would ordain.

Afterward, she sat pondering the King of Swords. Did the cards speak of Vaughn Trayhern, who wanted her hand in marriage? He was an ex-cavalry officer who had been a hero in the Irish rebellion.

No, Thorne told herself. The man she dreamed of in the innermost recesses of her heart was sensitive, like herself. She had confided to her mother that she longed for a man who knew how to give, to reach out in affection and to touch in return. Vaughn Trayhern, a proper English gentlemen, was the second son of the Earl of Trayhern. He was handsome and rich, but Thorne did not want him as her husband. He was the rage of the *ton* and one of its most eligible bachelors. She had met him only twice, briefly, because she usually fled society parties, feeling uncomfortably out of place. Why had Papa entertained the match? Her mother had opposed it. If it hadn't been for her mother's death, she would be engaged by now. With her father's mind barely functioning anymore, he seemed to have forgotten the match. Thorne prayed he had—forever.

Chapter Two

"My Juan! Sometimes I do not think he makes proper decisions," Maria began, sweeping into Thorne's room. Her sky blue silk gown emphasized Maria's beautiful olive skin and heightened her flashing brown eyes.

Thorne felt her heart drop. She sat on a chair near the open doors to a small patio that led off her bedroom. "What do you mean, Aunt Maria?"

"*Mi corazón*, my *burro* of a husband doesn't want you riding down by the beach! His friend, the colonel from Gerona's garrison, says that because we sit so close to the French border, there is always a risk of spies from Napoleon's army nearby."

"What? That's impossible, Aunt Maria! The Pyrenees stop everything. And everyone! I've never seen mountains so high. Spies!" Thorne snorted in a most unladylike manner. Her gray eyes flashed with indignation. "I'm seven and ten, Auntie. I'm old enough to be married and have children. How can Uncle Juan do this to me? All I want to do is ride. I promise I'll stay close to the villa, in sight of you and the servants."

Maria reached out, touching Thorne's arm. "I'm sorry. I thought my Juan would approve of you riding. Dinner will be at ten tonight."

"At ten," Thorne answered absently. When Maria left in a swish of silk, Thorne went to the heavily carved walnut door and locked it. It was seven o'clock. In another hour, it would be dark. She would have two hours before dinner. One hour for the maid to dress her and curl her hair. That left an hour free. Thorne smiled, a thread of excitement beginning to course through her. Moving to the trunk, she opened the yawning lid. Quickly, Thorne pulled out her male riding clothes, including the well-worn black boots that fit snugly up to her knees.

She shrugged into the white peasant shirt. Because she had small breasts, she never had to worry about them interfering in her riding activities. The buckskin breeches hung sadly on her. She had indeed lost weight, she noted, running her hands down her legs. She would have to buckle the belt up more tightly at the waist so they wouldn't fall off! The boots fit perfectly, and as Thorne turned to look at herself in the mirror, a smile blossomed on her lips. She gathered up her mane of hair and loosely plaited it into a single braid. Then she waited for the cloak of dusk to descend, to cover her escape to the stable and beyond.

Andalusians were known for their fieriness, but Angela walked quietly behind her. Smiling, Thorne hugged the mare effusively once they were out of the stable and standing on the warm earth outside the gates of the villa. She turned, suddenly realizing that for the next hour she was free. Thorne allowed all of her cloistered senses to open up and bloom in the balmy night. A thin slice of moon gave her just enough light and the Mediterranean beckoned her.

"Come," she whispered, swinging up on the large animal in one graceful motion. Thorne sighed. Just the act of hugging her legs to the quivering sides of a horse once again made her blood sing with unparalleled joy. Free! She was free! Taking up the reins, she barely pressed her right calf against the sensitive Andalusian and headed for the beach a mile away.

They wove in and around the small sand dunes, which were tufted with strong strands of salt grass. In the darkness, the hills looked like perfectly rounded mounds, and as Thorne got to know Angela better, she took the eager mare up and over a few of them.

Attacking a third hill, one that was much larger and harder to scale, Thorne threw her weight forward, giving Angela her head. The horse grunted, flinging herself up the vertical face of the hill. Thorne laughed, calling encouragement to her horse. One wrong move by Angela, and they could twist sideways and fall over backward. But Thorne had been born to the saddle and knew horses as intimately as she knew herself. They crested the top of the hill, Angela flying off the summit, her legs straight out in front of her to act as cushioning springs when they hit the earth once again.

Before Thorne could pull on the reins, it was too late. As her mare skimmed the hill and plunged downward at a dizzying speed, Thorne's stomach knotted. There, nestled between the two mammoth hills, was a group of poorly dressed men. Men who were stripped almost naked and washing their clothes in the ocean. A group of horses was hobbled nearby. The glittering array of weapons that lay around them sent a chill through her. Thorne clenched her teeth. All of her aunt's warnings slammed back into her memory. She saw a man with dark auburn hair swing around, his naked chest powerful looking as he pinned her with a savage glare.

Thorne wanted to scream. She wanted to cry. But it was too late. Angela plunged down the hill, sending sand flying like a transparent veil around them as her hooves sank deeply into the earth. They were heading directly into the small encampment. Terror surged through Thorne as she heard the same man shout a warning in French. He pulled a sword from the scabbard lying on the ground near him. He was going to kill her! The savagery on his face as he ran toward her shocked Thorne. There was no way she could stop Angela. She gripped the mare hard with her long thighs as the horse jolted and twisted to keep from sliding sideways and falling. Thorne threw the reins forward, giving the mare her head. My God, they were on a collision course! The soldier loped easily toward them like a lean, wild animal.

Thorne's eyes widened and a scream rose to her lips. The soldier snarled something as he raised his hand to try to grab at the mare's reins. Instinctively, Thorne tore her boot from the stirrup and kicked out at his face. Boot met the hard flesh of his shoulder. Thorne gasped, almost knocked out of the saddle from the impact. Angela grunted and spun to the right, away from the man. Cries and shouts suddenly erupted behind her. Thorne threw her arms around the neck of the mare as Angela sped off, melting back into the darkness.

Fear throbbed through Thorne, robbing her of coherent thought. She risked a glance across her shoulder. Dread washed over her. At least five of the solders had mounted and were thundering in her direction. Why hadn't she listened to Aunt Maria! Her mouth was dry with terror. She hunched down, face pressed against the horse's mane as she tried to decide how to escape the pursuing soldiers. She had never ventured this far away from the villa before. Was there a road near? Should she stay on the beach? Could Angela outrun them?

To her left were darkened hills and mounds of sand. Could she possibly lose the soldiers among them? Or should she circle back, getting close enough to the villa to call for help? Gripping Angela's mane, she called out pleadingly to the horse. The mare valiantly responded, placing more distance between them and the soldiers. What would happen to her if they captured her? Thorne had heard the leader explode in French, giving orders. They were enemies to England! And to her. Memories of her brother, James, being killed by another enemy to her country slammed back into her mind. He had died in May of 1978, near Wexford, Ireland. She had loved James fiercely.

Just as she whipped the mare around the base of one hill, Thorne felt the horse falter badly. Angela grunted, plunging down into a huge depression that had appeared unexpectedly. With a gasp, Thorne threw the reins away, leaning back, trying to help the mare regain her lost balance. Impossible! The force of her mount slamming into the sand catapulted Thorne completely out of the saddle. Her hair, once plaited, now tore free as she sailed through the air. She had lost her race for freedom.

Thorne landed heavily on the sand. She let out a low gasp of pain, the wind knocked from her. From years of riding experience, she remained relaxed and rolled end over end, hair falling like a coverlet across her shoulders. Finally, Thorne staggered to her feet. She saw the horseman come down the hill, his gray mare's nostrils wide and flared. Spinning around, Thorne ran toward Angela, who had just shakily gotten to her feet.

She was within inches of reaching Angela's reins when a blow between her shoulder blades sent her sprawling. Thorne slammed into the unforgiving sand, vaguely aware of dancing hooves close to her head. Sand sprayed upward through her hair and into her eyes, momentarily blinding her. She had to escape! Gasping, she scrambled to her knees. A hand reached out, grasping the thick sheets of her hair and hauling her back down on the ground.

Thorne cried out once, red-hot pain radiating from her scalp. She raised her hands to protect herself as she lay beneath her attacker. Eyes of dark obsidian observed her, glittering like a feral animal's. His face was tense and glistening with sweat as he placed his knee on her shoulder so she could not rise. She gasped, staring up at his chest, which was covered with dark hair, awed by the powerful play of muscles she saw.

Thorne's breast heaved and her lips parted in a silent scream. He was an animal, a savage, naked animal capable of killing her. Her eyes bulged as he pulled the knife from its sheath. Throwing her one arm across her face, she stiffened, waiting to feel the blade twist into her taut body.

"Scream and you're dead," he snarled.

Thorne blinked, feeling pain drift up her shoulder, where he had pinned her. His nostrils flared; he smelled of sweat and musk. The scent was not unpleasing, and at the same time, it excited her senses for no discernible reason. She heard the pounding of hooves and realized the other men were drawing near.

"Who are you?"

Thorne felt him relax his grip on her hair, and she gulped for breath. "I—I'm Thorne Somerset."

"You're English."

"And you're Irish!"

A tight smile slashed across his well-shaped mouth. "Natural enemies." And then he frowned, apparently searching his memory. "Somerset? The earl of Somerset?"

Did she dare tell the truth? Thorne choked back a cry as he tightened his grip on her hair. "Ow...yes! Let me up, you—you—"

With a curse, Dev released her hair and threw his leg across her middle. The look of fear mixed with outrage that crossed the woman's heart-shaped face almost made him laugh. Her large gray eyes narrowed and she knotted her fists, pounding futilely against his hard torso.

"Let me go!" she shrieked, bucking and twisting beneath him. Her heart hammered wildly. Thorne struggled, her black hair falling around her. She hated him for smiling. He was Irish. He was her enemy! And he could kill her.

Dev slammed her backward into the sand, his large hand splayed between her breasts. He could feel the birdlike beat of her heart beneath his palm, the softness of her breast. She was soft and womanly, despite the male clothes she wore. Heat began to uncoil in his loins as she continued to struggle beneath him. English. She was English. Somerset...he remembered the name well. A Captain James Somerset had fought at the battle of Wexford. He had helped round up the Irish prisoners, and Captain Vaughn Trayhern had shipped them back to England.

He glared down at the girl, tasting hate. He jerked her hands above her head, watching as fear glazed her eyes. Good, she should be frightened.

"Are you the earl of Somerset's wife?"

"No! Let me up! I swear, I'll—"

Dev nodded to the four men who rode up. They dismounted, making a semicircle around him. Dev took the knife, pressing it to the tender flesh of the Englishwoman's glistening throat. He forced the steel blade down, drawing a fine, thin line of blood like a necklace about her throat. "His sister, then!" he ground out, forcing her to look at him. Damn her! He saw the abject terror in her eyes. But he also saw silver flecks of defiance. Her mouth was so near to his, full and beckoning to be captured and tamed.

Thorne sobbed once, the cold blade making her freeze in horror. He was going to slit her throat. She closed her eyes, her thick black lashes sweeping down across her cheeks. Uncle Juan would find her raped and dead in the morning. Already she could feel the male hardness of his body pressing into her belly, and it left her feeling weak and confused. "Daughter," she rasped, trying to swallow.

"And Captain James Somerset?" he demanded.

"My—my brother. He's dead now!"

"A just end," Dev said harshly, smiling.

He released her hair, sitting triumphantly on her small, thin body. He eased the blade just slightly, enough to let her know he wasn't going to slit her throat. Not yet. "Who's riding with you?"

Thorne opened her eyes, dragging in sharp, jagged breaths. "No one!"

Dev glanced up. "Scanlon, take two men. Go back and search the area she came from."

"Yes, sir." Niall gave him an apologetic look. The military way of life and vernacular were instilled too strongly in him. In the heat of the chase, even he had forgotten that they were disguised as peasants.

"Let me go with them, Cap'n," Erhard begged, coming forward.

Dev scowled up at the hussar. "Quiet! You stay here."

Thorne's gaze moved from the hulking, black-bearded giant back to the man sitting astride her. Captain? He was their leader? He had spoken French earlier. But he was Irish. Perplexed, Thorne glared up at him.

Under any other circumstances, her captor would have turned the head of many a woman. His face was square, with an uncompromising jaw, sensual lips, a broken but aristocratic nose and high cheekbones. But his midnight eyes, flecked with intelligence, were what mesmerized Thorne. She saw the ugly white of a scar that ran across his left cheek and noticed the burgundy color of his short hair. Croppy... he was a croppy. Thorne's blood chilled. This man with the scarred face, who looked terrifyingly handsome in a sense, was part of the Irish uprising five years ago at Wexford, in Ireland.

The cold blade remained at her throat, and Thorne knew she was going to die. Hot tears stung the backs of her eyelids, but she refused to allow any of the men to see her cry. Closing her lips into a grim line, she ceased to struggle, lying still beneath him. It was only a matter of time. *God, please let them kill me swiftly. Don't let him torture me, as I've heard the Irish do to English prisoners.*

Suddenly, Thorne wanted to live more than ever before in her life. But one look up into the captain's grim features, wreathed with hatred, and she knew she wouldn't live to see another dawn. The tarot spread came back to her; he was the King of Swords, and the blade he held at her throat would transform her life to death.

"If you're going to kill me," she croaked, "make it quick."

Dev looked down at her. Why did she have such large, doelike eyes? Even in the moonlight, he could see their soft gray color. And why did she have to look so damned innocent when she was not? He saw the thin trickle of red blood where he had pressed the knife against her throat, suddenly contrite for having scarred her perfect white flesh. Despite her disheveled appearance, she reminded him of a pristine white rose, edged in the pink color that flamed in her cheeks.

Dev got off her, remaining on one knee at her side. "Sit up," he ordered.

Shakily, Thorne did as he instructed. Her abundant black hair tumbled across her shoulders and she pushed several strands away from her face. Horses stamped and snorted restlessly around them. The men were wary, as if trying to ferret out sounds hidden in the darkness.

"Why were you riding out here in these clothes?" Dev demanded.

A small bit of her dread dissolved when she saw him place his knife back into the scabbard. Thorne had never seen a man naked to the waist before, and she was in awe of his beauty. He wasn't pretty. No, the captain reminded her of a powerful stallion. Supple sets of muscles blended smoothly into others with each economical movement he took. Thorne swallowed against the dryness in her throat as he lifted his head, his cobalt gaze burning into her. Automatically, she covered her breast with her hand, trying to still her pounding heart.

"My uncle, Juan de Vega, wouldn't allow me to go riding, and I wanted to. I wore the men's clothes so no one would realize it was me."

Dev held her unsure gray gaze. Sweet Jesus, she looked so vulnerable. Why couldn't she be a hard-looking bitch like so many of the other Englishwomen he had seen? Right now, his dislike of the English warred with his protective instinct to shield any woman or child from the ravages of war. "You should have listened to him, damn it."

Thorne lifted her chin, stung by his low snarl.

"Cap'n, what are we going to do with her? If she's English, she'll run back to wherever she came from and tell them we're here." Jan Vermeer, the Dutch corporal, came forward. He was the smallest man in the unit and had blond hair and pale blue eyes.

Thorne stared at the Dutch soldier, her lips parting. His face was scarred far worse than that of the captain who knelt at her side.

"I say let's keep her," Erhard spoke up, rubbing his hand over his crotch. "I've been needing a slut anyway, Cap'n."

Vermeer shot Erhard a venomous look. "You're Germany's finest? I doubt that! You idiot! She'll slow us down. And then we'll have to stand guard to make sure she doesn't escape. How did you get sawdust for brains? Did your mother breed with a tree?"

"Enough," Dev ordered, his voice whiplike. Both soldiers glared at each other, but obeyed. Dev stared down at

Thorne. "You're like the spear that was thrust in the side of Christ to me."

She lowered her lashes, biting back a barrage of heated retorts. To engage his Irish temper would be foolish. "Let me go. I promise I won't say anything to anyone."

Dev's laugh was low and taunting. The woman's head snapped up and her gray eyes blazed with fury. So, she had some backbone. But that had been obvious from the moment she had kicked him in the shoulder to stop him from grabbing the reins. Hate overrode his momentary admiration for her. "You're the daughter of the earl of Somerset?"

"So what if I am?"

Erhard chuckled. "A laydee, Cap'n. Let her sample some real men. Bet she's never been laid yet. A virgin, she is."

Heat flowed into Thorne's face and she bowed her head, tasting humility. "I give you my word as an English-woman, I won't tell anyone you're here," she ground out.

Dev swung his head to the left, glaring at Erhard. "Keep your mouth shut or I'll cut that damn tongue out of your head, Erhard."

Erhard glared down at the officer. Although Kyle was taller, Erhard outweighed him. He itched to wrap his hands around the Irish officer's throat. "Anything you say...sir."

Scanlon galloped back to them, dismounting and walking quickly over to Dev. He glanced down at Thorne, then devoted his attention to the captain.

"We found a villa two miles from here. So far, no activity around it. We were able to trace the trail of her horse back to the gate she came out of."

"No escort?"

Scanlon shook his head, wiping the sweat from his brow. "None. She's alone."

"In more ways than she knows," Dev growled, rising. He glanced at Vermeer. "Guard her, Jan."

Scanlon followed Dev as they walked out of earshot of the group. Pushing his fingers through his short hair, Dev studied his friend of five years.

"What are you going to do with her?" Scanlon asked quietly.

Dev threw his hands on his hips. "I'd like to slit her English throat."

A vague smile crossed Scanlon's taut features. "You've never hurt a woman before."

"This is different. She's English."

"It appears she stole an hour or two to go riding behind her hosts' back."

Dev studied Niall grimly. "I've got two choices. Kill her now and get it over with, or let her go."

"The second choice is no choice."

"If we take her along, we risk discovery. She could scream for help. Or try to escape in the night. It would mean posting a guard on her. And someone will mount an effort to find her. She's an earl's daughter."

"That's what worries me. There's that garrison in Barcelona. If she's Somerset's daughter, they'll have soldiers scouring the countryside for her," Niall warned.

Dev stared out across the glasslike mirror of the Mediterranean. His brows moved upward. "Wait...what if we demand a trade-off? My brother, Gavin, rots at Newgate prison." A savage gleam lingered in Dev's narrowed eyes as a plan formulated rapidly in his head. "My brother for her," he muttered. "It's a fair exchange and perhaps the only way to free Gavin."

"Kidnap her?"

"Why not? Send Ivan with a note telling them to bring Gavin to Madrid." Dev gave him a cutting smile. "This way, I get my brother and the earl can have his precious daughter back."

"But the burden will be on us."

Dev looked over his shoulder toward his men and the girl. She looked incredibly fragile and pale sitting tensely among them. "On me."

"Then you'll take her to Madrid with you?"

"Yes. We'll pose as husband and wife. Better cover."

Niall grimaced. "She doesn't look the sort to go along willingly with your plan."

"I can't kill her," he said, remembering vividly the time when Shannon was dragged off to the cart by the British redcoat.

"You may want to when you see the trouble she causes, Dev."

Thorne cringed inwardly when the man they called Captain Kyle came back. She was awed by his height and magnificent build. Even in his buckskin breeches, which molded his long thighs, and the scarred black boots, he was someone to beware of. The hair on the back of her neck rose as his gaze settled on her. During her struggles, the shirt she wore had been torn, exposing the curved flesh of her breasts. Erhard's glittering black eyes had made her grip the pieces of cloth tightly together with her hand. She could feel her heart pounding hard as the captain studied her.

"Jan, go get her horse. And fetch a piece of rope from my saddle."

Her lips parted. "Wh—what are you going to do with me?"

Dev squatted down before her. Damn her soul to hell for being so beautiful. She was dirty from their struggle, her hair in wild abandon around her face, and yet she looked ravishing. His mouth compressed. "We're kidnapping you, Miss Somerset."

Thorne gasped. "You can't! You—"

Kyle gave her a bloodless smile. "You're going to free my brother, who rots in Newgate. We'll trade you for him. I think that's fair. We're going to instruct your father to have Gavin brought alive to Madrid and then an exchange will be made. If Gavin doesn't show up, you're dead."

Her face drained of color as the implications sunk in. Her father was sick and grieving over her mother's death. She shut her eyes tightly. What about Aunt Maria? Oh, God, she would faint. Uncle Juan would be furious with her and embarrassed. As she sat there in those ensuing minutes, Thorne considered only the devastating effects her foolish ride would have on others. Later, when Scanlon rode up and dismounted, she watched Captain Kyle shrug into his wet peasant shirt, quickly buttoning it up and shoving the extra material down inside the waistband of his breeches.

He and Scanlon knelt down on either side of Thorne. Niall held the quill and small piece of parchment ready. "Who gets this note?"

"My uncle. Juan de Vega."

"You're not full-blooded English, then," Dev said.

Thorne shook her head, unable to hold his virulent glare.

"Spaniard? Castilian, more than likely," he prodded savagely.

She snapped her head up, daring to meet his hard, merciless eyes. "My mother was a Gypsy, from Spain, if you must know!"

One brow rose, and surprise was mirrored in Dev's eyes for a brief moment. "Do you hear that, Scanlon? An English rose with the tainted blood of a Gypsy in her. Interesting combination, eh?"

Niall said nothing, noting the hurt on the woman's drawn features.

"What do you care?" she spat.

A wide-eyed cat with claws, Dev thought. He smiled, but it didn't reach his eyes. "Your life depends on me knowing everything about you. Is your uncle from your mother's side?"

Trying to choke back her sudden anger, Thorne felt herself becoming shaky in the aftermath of her chase and capture. "My mother's sister, Aunt Maria, is married to a Spanish nobleman."

"And your mother married the earl of Somerset? A titled lord lowering himself to marry a woman of Gypsy blood?" His hand captured her chin between his thumb and forefinger, forcing her to look at him. "If you think your beauty is going to sway me from knowing a lie when I hear one, then you're mistaken, English."

Thorne wrenched free, almost falling backward. She scrambled to her knees, watching him tense, getting ready to seize her. "I told you the truth!" she cried hoarsely.

"Sit down before I knock you down."

Breathing in ragged gasps, Thorne sat. "I'm half English and half Gypsy. Look at this if you don't believe me!" She held up the scarab that encircled her neck. "I know the Irish are backward, but even *they* know the sign of the Gypsies."

Dev wanted to slap her for her arrogance. One moment she could be a petulant child, the next a shrieking harpy. He examined the scarab, aware of the pulse throbbing wildly at the base of her throat, a throat that should be worshiped with butterfly kisses and made to moan with pleasure. He pushed away those torrid thoughts, surprised at the turn of his feelings. Normally, no woman caught him off guard. But this one had.

"It's the English blood in you that's gotten you into this trouble," he growled. "Are you engaged?"

"No!"

"Who would want a part Gypsy?"

Thorne's eyes grew dark with hurt, but she said nothing, all too aware that he was right. Gypsies were distrusted even more than the Irish were. "My father's allowing me the choice of the man I want to marry," she hurled back, lying.

Dev grinned, enjoying her spirit. "Probably because no family in their right, blue-blooded mind would have you tainting their stock."

Thorne uttered a cry and tried to slap his laughing face. He caught her hand easily and she watched in horror as his long, tapered fingers curled around her wrist like a snake squeezing its prey.

"Bastard!" she hissed.

He chuckled, holding her arm in midair. "No more than you. At least I'm pure Irish." His smile disappeared. Dev released her, as if scalded by the contact with her flesh. "At best you're a bitch. Are you the same way in heat?"

Mortification swept through her, and Thorne stared openmouthed up at him. "You're rude and insufferable, Captain. A blackguard without a heart or a soul!"

Dev rubbed his sandpapery jaw. "The English murdered my heart, Miss Somerset, and I sold my soul to the devil to get back what they took from me."

Her eyes blazed. "Took what from you?"

"My wife," he told her in an emotionless tone. "My brother is in prison, my father is dead. The only one who has survived is my younger sister, thank God." He looked down at his scarred sword hand, studying it darkly. "And I'll avenge my family any way I can."

"By using me! You hide behind the skirts of an Englishwoman, Captain? That's not very courageous. But then," she sneered, "I'd expect cowardice from a croppy!"

Niall tensed. He saw Kyle's face go pale, his eyes narrowing with such hatred that Niall braced himself for the upcoming explosion. Croppies were Irishmen who fought for the liberation of their country from England. They showed their allegiance to Ireland by cutting their hair shorter than was deemed correct. And Dev's hair was shorn so short that even his ears showed.

Rage consumed Dev. He allowed his hand to settle on the hilt of his knife. Slowly, he pulled it from the scabbard, his eyes never leaving her frightened ones. He reached out, jerking her over to him.

"Niall, hold her hands."

Thorne gave Scanlon a pleading look as he gripped her hands tightly. What was the captain going to do? She cringed away from Kyle as he lifted the knife upward, the blade glittering in the moonlight. He grabbed a fistful of her hair. "All right, Miss Somerset," he told her in a deadly quiet voice, "you hate croppies so much, we'll make you look like one."

A sob tore from Thorne's lips as she saw him lower the blade against her black hair. "No...please...no, not my hair," she quavered softly.

Dev laid the blade against the silken tresses, hypnotized by the tears in her gray eyes. For a split second, he succumbed to her cry. And then he remembered Shannon. And the English. His mouth turned downward. He gripped the hilt more firmly, sawing through the tresses, watching as they curled and fell on his white-knuckled fist. He blocked out her sobs and pleas, savagely finishing the job he had begun. When he was done, her hair barely covered her delicate ears, the ends shorn and hacked in odd lengths against her skull. He threw the last of the hair down into her lap.

"Now you're a croppy," he snarled. "Just like me. Never forget it."

Chapter Three

They traveled through the heat of the next afternoon. Thorne was grateful when Ivan gave her his broad-brimmed straw hat to wear; she was certain her face was growing red from the sun. The Catalonian landscape consisted of gentle hills and valleys of tilled soil. To her anguish, they were moving inland, toward the hot desert that inhabited the central part of Spain. Thorne had heard of the desert area but had never seen it, because she had traveled by ship from London to the port of Barcelona.

Opportunities to study Devlin Kyle were few but each time she was able to stare at him without getting caught, she found one more feature of his face she liked instead of hated. His mouth drew her gaze again and again. A strong mouth, with a full lower lip. A mouth used to giving orders and having them carried out. What would he be like to kiss? Thorne's eyes widened in shock. A young lady simply didn't entertain such thoughts! Especially toward her captor. She tried to recall the times she had been kissed before. Sometimes, there had been quick, stolen kisses at a masked ball, or a warmer kiss to her hand by one of her few admirers. No man had been allowed to chastely kiss her lips. None had possessed a mouth molded of fire and tempered steel as Devlin Kyle did, either. Thorne dragged her gaze from his mouth, a rush of guilt flooding her. Only a mistress or harlot would think such torrid thoughts.

Her study of the men had made the afternoon bearable. It had also kept her mind off her aching, protesting thighs.

When they finally stopped beneath a grove of fragrant pine, Thorne saw her opportunity to escape. The men were all tired, and so were the horses. She reached down, pretending to run her fingers through Angela's silken mane as Vermeer dismounted. The Dutch soldier dropped the reins and they fell to the ground, beneath the mare's head.

Thorne had been watching. Kyle had entered the lush valley through a small pass between two wooded hills. She had spied a *pueblo* ten miles to the south. It was a sizable village composed of adobe huts, and there was a good chance that there would be a detachment of Spanish soldiers in the town. If she could ride fast enough and guide Angela in and out of the groves of oak and pine, she might make good her escape.

Dev turned just in time to see the girl bend down and with startling agility, catch up the reins to her mare.

"Corporal!" he shouted.

Vermeer stiffened and whirled around. Too late!

With a rich curse, Dev spurred Ghazeia forward. He saw the girl lean forward, slashing the leather to her bay mare. Even in the explosion of his anger, he admired her riding skills and bravery. Bobbing low on the Andalusian, she looked like a jockey. He pursued her down the meadow toward the main road that cut through the valley toward the village in the hazy distance.

Dev's eyes narrowed. The Andalusian was tiring rapidly. As much as he wanted to throttle Thorne, he wasn't going to risk her life by trying to stop her on the hard road. Eventually the horse would slow sufficiently for him to make a safe approach. He watched as she used her hands and arms to coax every ounce out of her mare. The Andalusian was responding to her, despite her exhaustion. Perhaps it was Thorne's wild Gypsy blood that gave her the magical quality to rally a horse that was so fatigued it could barely lift its legs.

Thorne saw a small cloud of dust no more than two miles away from them. Did her eyes deceive her? Did she see the blue and white of the Spanish uniforms? Hope sprang to life in her heaving breast as she yanked Angela off to the right, aiming her directly at the unit of soldiers. Oh God, please let her escape! Let her—

The Andalusian mare grunted heavily as she plunged down a small embankment off the road. Her front legs caught on a low hedge of brush, and she was unable to lift them high enough to clear the unexpected obstacle. In seconds, the animal plowed into the white, dusty earth, throwing her rider. The horse cartwheeled end over end.

A cry of warning died in Dev's throat. He threw out his hand the instant he realized the mare was going to be unable to negotiate the jump, and terror twisted in his chest as he saw Thorne thrown over the horse's head. Ghazeia swerved sharply to miss the hurtling Andalusian. Dev jerked his horse to a stop, dismounted and ran to where the girl lay unmoving in the brush.

Thorne lay like a rag doll sprawled on her back, as if someone had carelessly thrown her away. Breathing hard, sweat dribbling down his tightened jaw, Dev knelt at her side. He kept one ear keyed to the Spanish patrol, wondering if they had been spotted, and the other for his men, who were not far behind. Scanlon would have seen the patrol and would know what action to take. Right now, Dev had to see if Thorne was still alive.

He stretched his fingers outward to press against the slender expanse of her neck. Her white peasant shirt had been torn open by the fall, the swell of her breasts visible from beneath her silk chemise. Dev cared nothing for the view, gulping for breath as he willed a pulse to fluctuate beneath his fingertips. Thorne was colorless; her lips were parted, as if in a cry that had never left her throat. Her fingers were slightly curled and her closed eyes unmoving.

"Come on . . . breathe, damn you . . . breathe!"

He heard the thunder of hooves coming from two different directions. His mare lifted her head, ears pricked forward, an unmoving statue above them. Desperately, Dev searched for a pulse. She couldn't be dead. No, she was too lovely, too innocent . . . There! One beat . . . two . . . He closed his eyes momentarily, feeling a rush of thankfulness. Thorne was still alive.

There was no time to check her over for broken bones. In one fluid movement, he scooped her limp form up into his arms. He mounted his Arabian and then drew Thorne across his lap, holding her tightly against him. Glancing to the left, he saw Scanlon leading the five-man Spanish patrol on a merry chase to the west of them. He and Thorne would be safe. Turning Ghazeia around, Dev rode past the unmoving Andalusian mare. The horse had broken its neck. It was fortunate her mistress hadn't done the same thing. He tried to ignore the fact that Thorne felt like a bag of bones in his arms. Her head lolled against his shoulder, blood tricking from her nose.

"Damn you," he snarled softly, glaring at her. "Live, you hear? Live to regret this folly."

Dev sat near Thorne's shoulder, occasionally glancing down at her. Night had fallen four hours ago. Around him, his men were snoring heavily, trying to catch up on badly needed sleep which had evaded them since the girl's capture.

He got to his knees and leaned over Thorne, his face very close to hers. Her large eyes were open, and Dev saw life in their depths again. A ribbon of gratefulness wound through him as he watched her in the ensuing silence. She licked her lips, and he found himself wanting to press his mouth to them to take away the pain that marred her expression.

"Thorne?" His voice was gruff, unsure.

She stared up at him, her heart beginning a skipping beat. Why couldn't she hate him? In that moment the impenetrable mask was ripped aside, and she saw the man beneath. He took her breath away. The man she saw held anxiousness as well as kindness in his eyes. Captain Kyle, kind? Impossible! Thorne's fear melted the instant he laid his hand on her head in a protective gesture when she didn't answer right away. An overwhelming tidal wave of care surged through her and she closed her eyes, afraid that he might see how much his touch affected her.

"Are you all right? Answer me, my Gypsy."

His Gypsy. Thorne swallowed against the lump forming in her throat. The roughened care in his voice vibrated through her, tearing away all her defenses, leaving her vulnerable to him as a man, not her captor. Shaken, she murmured, "I'm thirsty, Captain. But my head hurts so much, I fear I can't sit up."

His laugh expressed relief as he gathered her into his arms after filling a tin with water. "Just thank God you woke up. That's enough."

Each time her gray eyes rose to meet his, Dev felt his heart contract with some undefined emotion. He pressed the cup to her lips and she drank thirstily. A few drops of liquid trickled from the corner of her mouth and followed the slender curve of her throat.

"You had me worried. That was quite a spill you took," he told her huskily, placing the tin cup on the ground. Gently, Dev laid her back on the blanket, making sure she was covered. He caressed her hair.

Thorne frowned. When he placed his hand on her hair, her headache eased. Irritated that he should have such a profound effect on her, Thorne tried to ignore him. "I had to try to escape, Captain."

He sat down, drawing up his knees, suddenly awake and happy. "I've decided it was your Gypsy blood that made you do something so reckless and foolhardy."

Thorne opened her eyes, glaring up at him. "That Spanish squadron will be back. I know my uncle. He won't rest until you're caught and hanged."

"Easy, Gypsy, you're spitting fire and showing your claws. Don't upset yourself. You've been unconscious a long time, and that's not a good sign."

Thorne opened her mouth to deliver a barrage of less than flattering adjectives at him. But as she continued to see the real Devlin Kyle, for once without that mask he wore like armor, she swallowed the response. "Please," Thorne begged, "just let me go. I feel as if my head will split. I don't even know if I can ride, it hurts so much."

Dev scowled, torn by her plea. Sweet God, but she could reach inside him and touch his heart. How? Since Shannon's death, he'd felt nothing except the cold fury of hatred. Until now. Automatically, he reached out, soothing the wrinkles from her brow. "You're too young to get lines on your face yet, Gypsy. Close your eyes and sleep. It's five hours until dawn." He slid down beside her, pulling the blanket across him. He lay no more than a few inches from her.

Thorne sucked in a breath at his daring maneuver. She could feel the heat from his powerful body and blinked once, afraid of what he might do next. When one corner of his mouth lifted, she relaxed slightly.

"Are all Gypsies as wary as you?" he asked, his voice slurred with exhaustion.

"What do you mean?"

"You act as if I'm going to attack you."

"I wouldn't doubt it."

Dev smiled and closed his eyes. "Go to sleep, Gypsy. The men under my command know better than to touch a woman. Even you. Even if you are English."

Her head hurt too much to argue with him. Nausea began stalking her, and as she tried to move, she found every bone in her body ached from the violent fall. Turning onto her side, using the hard leather of a saddle for a pillow, she quickly spiraled into sleep. Just knowing more about her uncertain future gave her a measure of solace. Despite Kyle's hatred of her, he wouldn't kill her. But Thorne didn't believe him for an instant when he said he'd leave her alone. No, the hungry look in his dark blue eyes triggered a primal female knowing in her.

Thorne heard the murmur of men's voices and she feigned sleep, listening in on the conversation.

"Ivan, you and Jan continue toward the province of Andalusia."

"Yes, sir. What about *malenki ptitsa*?"

"She'll go with me. Wolfe will ride ahead to Madrid and meet me there." He tapped the map with a twig that lay at his feet. "Does anyone have any questions? We'll meet in

Madrid at the agreed-upon time and then ride back to France together.''

There were no questions.

The sun was barely above the horizon and the morning was cool, with beads of dew like miniature diamonds on the stalks of grass beneath the oak grove. Dev looked at the face of each of his men. They were good soldiers. Reliable, except for Wolfe, who was an unknown factor. Dev scooped up the map and refolded it. He rested his hands on the nicked leather belt that girded his hips. ''Ride safe, men. And remember, we're the Sparrowhawk squadron. Strike swiftly, silently, and then disappear.'' He raised his hand, releasing them to their new set of orders. Farewells were exchanged among them. Dev watched his men mount up and ride in six different directions. He glanced over his shoulder. Thorne was still sleeping, and he had no intention of going anywhere today unless a Spanish squadron forced them to move.

The meadow fell silent except for the gurgle of the brook nearby. Dev walked down to the water and stripped off his shirt, breeches and boots, wading out to the clear depths.

Thorne bit back a gasp when she opened her eyes and saw Kyle standing naked, washing himself in the knee-deep water. She'd never seen a man unclothed. A strange, twisting sensation began in her lower body. Despite the ache in her head and the nausea, she stared, fascinated. If there was such a thing as male beauty, then Devlin Kyle possessed it. The sun's slanting rays struck his hard, limber body, caressing him with golden tones. The interplay of each grouping of muscles was sheer poetry in her eyes. The dark hair on his broad chest narrowed down across his flat torso, only to fan out once again. Thorne felt a rush of heat up her cheeks as she observed his manhood. Suddenly frightened, she drew the blanket over her head and turned away, mortified.

How long Thorne lay there, she had no idea. She had no wish to confront the captain while he was dressing. Only the faint odor of smoke from a fire forced her to turn over and struggle to a sitting position.

Dev raised his head, his dark hair plastered against his skull. He placed the small teakettle on a branch above the licking flames.

"How do you feel?" he asked, coming over and crouching down at her side. His recently washed white peasant shirt clung to his upper body, outlining his shoulders and chest.

Thorne placed her hand to her forehead, trying to control a wave of sudden dizziness. She placed her other hand out on the ground to steady herself. "Dizzy," she muttered.

Dev twisted around and casually threw a few more twigs onto the fire before returning his attention to Thorne. "You've got color again," he noted.

If only he knew why! Thorne avoided his gaze, at a loss for words.

A slight smile played on Dev's mouth as he removed her hand from her brow and looked deeply into her gray eyes. The pupils were dilated, even though sunlight was streaming across the land and striking them. "Your eyes don't look right."

Thorne quickly pulled her hand away from his long, callused fingers. His grip had been firm but gentle. And why was he being so friendly with her? Addled, she mumbled, "I don't feel right, either."

"Can you stand?"

"I don't know, Captain."

He sighed. "Stop calling me that. From now on, call me Dev."

Thorne raised her head, a quizzical look on her face. "Why?"

"Because I said so."

"That's not good enough, Captain."

Dev saw the petulant set of her lips. The little vixen. Somehow she knew he wasn't going to reprimand her when she was obviously injured. "Are you only this contrary when you're sick, or are you like this all the time, Gypsy?"

Thorne flushed scarlet at the intimate tone in his voice when he called her Gypsy. "If you expect me to be civil after you've kidnapped me and nearly broken my neck—"

"You were the one who tried to break your own neck in the escape yesterday."

She chewed on her lower lip, refusing to meet his cobalt gaze. "And I shall again and again. You have no right to hold me prisoner, Captain. No right. What have I done to you? I can't be held responsible for all the sins of the British Empire, can I?"

Grimly, Dev got up. "You're going to try, Miss Somerset. Now, if you want to attend to your toilet, I suggest you do so. I've got a fresh rabbit that one of the men caught to roast. I suggest you get up and get moving now. There are no servants here to do your bidding."

Anger dulled some of Thorne's pain and dizziness. Throwing off the blanket, she realized with a sinking feeling that someone had dressed her in a different shirt. The garment she now wore hung loosely about her shoulders. Her hand went to her breasts, which the shirt just barely concealed.

"What is this?" she demanded, pushing the shirt up closer to her throat. There had to be some way of making it stop hanging so provocatively, exposing the cleavage of her breasts.

Dev looked up from skinning the rabbit. "That's one of Ivan's shirts."

"But—"

"The shirt you were wearing, Miss Somerset, was torn, and the buttons were ripped off when you were thrown from your horse. I couldn't have you going around looking like a woman of the streets, could I?"

Her lips parted in protest. If she hadn't felt so miserable, she would have responded. As it was, she placed both her hands against her breast. Her voice came out in a strangled whisper. "Then who undressed me?"

"Ivan and myself. Would you have rather had Wolfe do it instead, Miss Somerset?"

The man was hateful! Thorne's eyes went dark with humiliation and anger. "You're a blackguard, Captain Kyle! You have no honor. No integrity as an officer and a gentleman!" she sputtered.

Dev grinned and went to the fire, throwing some loose tea into the kettle of boiling water. "Use some of that anger to get up and about," he ordered.

The very idea that he had seen her naked made Thorne turn crimson. She wanted to slap that grin off his stubbled features. If she had known a few choice curse words, she would have used them. And when she had trouble trying to get to her feet, she grew even angrier because he remained crouched, watching her efforts. He was laughing at her! Mocking her with his dark blue eyes. She felt like a newly born foal who had never walked before, the dizziness making it impossible for her to stand.

Thorne was prepared to crawl on her hands and knees to the stream, if necessary, when Dev uncoiled from his squatting position and ambled over to her. As he reached down, wrapping his fingers around her upper arm, Thorne jerked out of his grasp.

"Don't touch me!" she rasped, glaring up at him.

Dev's mouth flattened into a thin line. "Stop behaving like the child you are and let me help you. Or do you want to sit right here in front of me and complete your toilet?"

She hated him for having undressed her. For having seen her when no man had ever been allowed that privilege. Her anger ballooned tenfold, and she sat there, hands gripped tightly together in her lap, realizing escape was impossible. "I'm not a child!"

"Then quit acting like one," Dev snarled, gripping her by the arm and pulling her up. Up and into his arms.

Thorne gasped as she fell against the hard planes of Dev's body. She pushed herself back, both hands splayed against his chest. She would have fallen if he hadn't held on to her. Dizziness washed over her, and she uttered a cry of frustration, hating to lean on him. Her heart pounded madly in her breast as Dev slipped his arm around her waist. He patiently led her to the bank of the stream, to the safety of a grove of low brush where she could have privacy.

"I hate you," she gritted out between clenched teeth.

"It's mutual, Miss Somerset, I assure you." Dev halted and allowed her to sit near an oak. He stood there uncertainly for a moment, hands on hips, watching her. Thorne had grown pale again, except for two bright red spots on her cheeks. Small dots of perspiration clung to her upper lip. He tried to lessen the harshness in his voice. "Don't be so foolish as to think you can run away again."

Thorne stared angrily at the gurgling stream. "Don't worry, Captain, I won't. I'm not that stupid."

"You're just naive, Miss Somerset, not stupid. Call me when you're done or I'll be forced to come over here and check up on you after a certain amount of time. Don't dawdle like most women do with their toilet."

"You—you animal!"

Dev bowed mockingly. "And your jailer. Never forget that. Ever."

Thorne attended to the most immediate necessities of her new existence. She knelt by the stream, doing the best she could to cleanse herself. She longed to strip the clothes from her body and bathe. Oh, for a hot, fragrant tub of water! She had taken so much for granted, having maids at hand. As she splashed water over her hair and scrubbed it clean, she knew she would never take anything for granted again. She sat up and looked around. Kyle had busied himself at the fire. Quickly, Thorne shed the shirt. She winced, taking note of the huge purple bruise on her shoulder and arm. It hurt to raise her arm, but she was able to take a partial bath.

Dev was beginning to get worried and stood, looking toward the brush where Thorne was supposed to be. Had she tried to run off again? Earlier, he had heard the splash of water. Now the grove was silent.

"If you're still there, Gypsy, you'd better say something," he warned.

"I haven't run away, Captain!" came the tart reply.

"Are you clean enough to come and join me for a meal?" His mouth drew up in a sour grin. He shouldn't tease her, but she needed to be taught that she couldn't be a headstrong, spoiled brat, either.

"You may come and get me, Captain."

Dev moved the kettle aside and walked to the bank. He rounded the brush and stopped. Thorne looked like a drowned rat with her short hair clinging wetly against her small, perfectly shaped skull. His gaze traveled down from her ebony hair, which shone with blue highlights, to her ripe red lips. His body hardened and he frowned. The white shirt draped over her like a sack of flour, many times too large for her. Nevertheless, her small breasts thrust proudly against the fabric, and he vividly recalled their shape, size and tempting color.

"Do you always stare?" Thorne gritted out, her gray eyes flashing.

Dev grinned belatedly, walking over and sliding his arms around her. She stiffened. "When it's worth looking at, yes. Why? I'd think someone of your beauty would be used to stares by the men of the *ton*. Relax, will you? I'm not going to bite."

Thorne pouted, crossing her arms protectively across her breasts as he lifted her easily into his arms. She was heatedly aware of his warmth and that beguiling twinkle in his eyes. "Since when do brigands keep their word?"

Dev enjoyed her spirit. "There is honor among thieves, my lady. Although," he drawled, "you wouldn't know that. You've been protected from the ugliness and truth of life. Hidden away in your manor at Somerset, no doubt."

Thorne snapped her mouth shut, fighting off the dizziness that flared through her. "You're enjoying this too much, Captain."

He deposited her on a blanket near the fire. "God forgive me, Gypsy, but I am," he admitted, sitting down next to her. Dev wanted to reach out and smooth several strands of hair that were twisted and in need of taming. Instead, he reached for the kettle, stirring the contents inside before placing it between them on the ground.

Thorne looked around. She saw Kyle's gray mare grazing down along the bank near the stream. "Where's Angela?"

"Angela?"

"Yes, my horse."

Dev handed her a spoon. "Dead. Died of a broken neck when you took that fall." When he saw her eyes suddenly fill with tears, he added gruffly, "I'm sorry."

Angela was dead, because of her own folly. Thorne felt the hotness of tears and turned away, not wanting Dev to see her cry. She gripped the spoon tightly in her hands, fighting back a sob. "It's your fault!" she cried. "All of this is your fault!"

"If you would have stopped and thought first before you went riding pell-mell over the countryside, you could have saved everyone from trouble. Including that Andalusian mare of yours."

Thorne gasped, twisting around. Her face was waxen, flesh drawn tautly across her cheekbones. Tears splattered across her cheeks. "You're the devil's own spawn!" she cried.

"Do you always wound those around you, like that name of yours?" he countered, his eyes narrowing.

Thorne sat there, staring at him. Her knuckles whitened on the spoon and she wanted to throw it at him. But something cautioned her not to. Even he had his limits of patience with her, and Thorne saw anger flaring in the depths of his thundercloud blue eyes. She sobbed twice more before choking down all her grief and pain over Angela's demise. "That horse was innocent," she whispered.

"And so was I, once. The moment you're born is the only time you're innocent, Gypsy. Now, forget the horse. You made a decision. Live with it." He shoved the small tin cup of tea into her hands. "Drink. You're looking worse."

Thorne took a ragged breath, wincing beneath the whiplash of his hard voice. God, how cruel he was, and callous. She stared down at the brownish-looking liquid. Nausea rose in her throat, and she dropped the cup, turning and gagging.

With a curse, Dev got to his knees, holding Thorne as she vomited. He placed his arm beneath her breasts and his other across her damp brow. She sagged into his arms afterward, unable to hold her head up. He swallowed all his anger when he realized how weak she had become. Taking a cloth, he wiped her mouth and nose. His heart wrenched when she gripped his arms with her trembling fingers, trying to sit up on her own.

"I—I'm sorry..." she rasped, her head lolling back on his shoulder as he turned her around.

"Hush, Gypsy." He carried her back beneath the spreading oak, laying her down and covering her up with the blanket. His instinct not to travel today had been right. Thorne's pallor frightened him. He pushed back several damp strands of black hair off her brow as he watched her fight to control her tears. He squeezed her shoulder. "I'll bring you water."

She didn't want anything. One moment Kyle could be so gentle that it brought tears to her eyes. The next, an animal without heart or soul. Thorne closed her eyes, her hand resting across her stomach, confused. He didn't have to hold her when she got violently ill. He could have let her lie stretched out on the ground, fouling herself with her own vomit. But he hadn't. He'd moved instantly to help her. Thorne opened her eyes as she heard him approach. Worry was evident in his expression as he knelt beside her.

"This will stay down," Dev promised her quietly, sliding his arm beneath her shoulders and drawing her upward.

Thorne wasn't so sure. Nausea and dizziness were attacking her again. He must have read the uncertainty in her eyes because he said, "Trust me, Gypsy." She closed her eyes as he pressed the cup to her lips and drank without protest, trusting him.

Chapter Four

The succulent odor of rabbit being roasted awoke Thorne much later. The sun had changed position drastically since she had fallen asleep after drinking the water Dev had given her. Thorne went through a mental assessment of how she felt before she slowly sat up. Her head ached, but not as fiercely, and her stomach, at least for now, was docile once again. Thank God. It was pleasantly warm and the leaves overhead moved languidly with the mid-afternoon breeze. She pushed the blanket aside.

"Good, you're awake."

Thorne turned her head to the right, finding Captain Kyle sitting with his back against the oak she rested beneath, studying her. He held a bridle in his hand and was making a repair to it. Her mouth was gummy and she found her voice little more than a croak. "I slept a long time?"

"Yes, you did." He reached over and handed her a cup of water.

Thorne slid her fingers around the tin and managed a slight smile of gratitude. She wanted to ask Dev why he could be so kind one minute and a coldhearted brigand the next. Every time he called her Gypsy, it was as if he had reached out and physically caressed her. Thorne handed him the emptied cup.

"Thank you."

Dev set the bridle aside and got up. He crouched down beside Thorne, studying her intently. "How are you feeling?"

"Better."

"Dizzy?"

She nodded her head very slightly.

"As a Gypsy, you must know about herbs," he said. "Are there any around here that might help your head? I can gather them for you."

Thorne squinted her eyes, searching the grassy banks. "I see coltsfoot and plantain, but they won't help me."

Dev liked the huskiness in Thorne's voice upon awakening. There was an unshielded simplicity about her. A sharp memory of Shannon slowly coming awake in his arms almost made him wince. He missed marriage more than he ever could have known. More important, Dev missed the company of a woman. But not any woman. She had to be special. Like Thorne Somerset. His brows dipped when he realized what he had just admitted to himself. Grudgingly, Dev ignored his feelings, slamming the door shut on his heart. Now was not the time to get emotionally involved with a woman, especially her. She was English.

"No...I don't see anything," Thorne said apologetically, turning to meet—and melt beneath—his cobalt gaze. The breath was gently stolen from her as their eyes met and held. In that swirling moment, Thorne felt the full impact of Dev's emotions toward her. She blinked once to assimilate that heady warmth entwined with heated desire. And then, just as quickly, a veil dropped over his guarded expression and he was nothing more than a hardened soldier once again. Disappointment registered in her gray eyes and she tried to offer him a semblance of a smile. "Will we be passing any village? Perhaps there will be someone there who dries and sells herbs."

He nodded. "There's a small village we'll be passing through tomorrow afternoon. We'll stop then. Feel like standing? The rabbit is ready to be eaten."

Her stomach growled loudly. Thorne saw the beginnings of a smile in his eyes and she shared it with him. "It smells wonderful."

Dev held out his hand to her. "I don't imagine you've eaten too many meals outside your manor or villa."

She stared at his proffered hand. A hand with many scars and calluses. "More than you know," she said in defense, sliding her fingers into his opened palm. A tingle went through her as his hand closed around hers.

"Oh?" Dev teased. "Picnics between ladies and gentlemen? Those don't count." He gently pulled Thorne to her feet, watching her closely. She was petite, the bones of her wrists small and birdlike. Ivan had named her well, "little bird," *malenki ptitsa*. Automatically, Thorne placed her hand against his arm to steady herself. Dev waited. "Dizzy?"

Thorne tried to shrug and found the movement excruciating, the corners of her mouth drawing inward with pain. "Not as much. Give me a moment, Captain."

Dev stood patiently, his hand firm on her elbow. He tried not to react to her butterfly touch, willing his hardening body back beneath his control. "Dev," he reminded her. "From here on, call me Dev. I can't afford to have you call me captain in a village or within earshot of a peasant."

Thorne lifted her head, drowning in the midnight blue of his eyes. "I'll call you that when necessary." Her balance wasn't good and he felt her tremble. Despite how she felt, she made it to the log that Dev had pulled up for her to sit on.

He dismissed her defiant attitude. "Just don't forget when to use my first name," he warned Thorne darkly. Dev took the roasted rabbit off the spit. He caught a bit of grease from the rabbit and sucked it off his fingers. "I'm surprised you haven't been promised in marriage to some count or viscount. Isn't that the aim of women in your stratum, to marry at or above your station? Much like a matador collecting ears off the bulls he kills in the arena?"

Thorne's mouth thinned. "I don't care for your parallel, Captain. I do not 'collect' male admirers like many single women of the *ton*."

"Why not?" he goaded, holding her luminous gray eyes, which glimmered with life. Dev found himself admiring her spirit and honesty.

Thorne pushed dirt around with the toe of her boot. "I don't know," she admitted. "Most of the men I know are taught to say just the right thing at the right time. There's—" she hesitated, groping for the correct words. "Why can't men and women have honest, searching conversations? Why must they always play these word games with one another?" She sighed and looked over at him. "Men always think women incapable of any intelligence. I pride myself in knowing a great deal about the various countries of Europe. I would, for once, like to discuss the issues of those countries with a man instead of just being a—a bauble to be seen and envied on his arm!"

Dev traded a wry look with her, a half smile lingering at the corners of his mouth. "It sounds as if you were bored with your own kind, Miss Somerset," he said blandly, pulling the rabbit apart and setting it down between them on the log.

"My kind? I treat everyone I know with equal honesty and fairness, Captain. I don't make a distinction of class the way you do."

Dev gingerly tore the steaming hare into smaller pieces, handing one to Thorne. "Well, we're going to find out just how well you get along with the working class." He sank his teeth into the firm, juicy flesh of the rabbit. "For the next few weeks you're going to live with me and off the land. You'll have the sky for a roof and the earth as your bed." The glitter in his eyes deepened as he watched her daintily pick at the rabbit without use of utensils. "No silverware, no maid to dress and undress you and no servants. Let's see how well you survive in your new surroundings."

Thorne carefully held up the meat, trying to decide the best way to attack the dripping, juicy flesh. She shot the captain a wry look over her portion. "My mother always said Gypsies were closest to the land. I'm sure I'll get along without cutlery and servants."

"We'll see," Dev said, swallowing a smile. "We'll see...."

The rabbit was salty and delicious, but Thorne's stomach began to roll after a few bites. Reluctantly, she placed the meat back on the log and looked for something to wipe her hands on. Finding nothing, she wiped them on the breeches she wore. The smudges of grease were repugnant to her. She hated the look and smell of dirty, soiled clothing.

"Finish that," Dev told her, pointing to the uneaten rabbit.

"I'm sick to my stomach again."

He frowned and offered her a cup of tea. "Go ahead, drink some. It will settle your stomach." The sun filtered through the leaves overhead, bringing out the blue highlights in Thorne's short black hair. A moment of regret sliced through Dev. She looked more like a young boy at first glance than a woman, although one look at those provocative red lips and thick lashes and anyone would know differently. Still, each time she unconsciously touched her shorn hair, Dev was needled by guilt.

Thorne finished the tea and placed the tin cup between them. "Thank you."

He said nothing, simply meeting her frank gray eyes. "I want you to try to eat some more meat, Gypsy. I know you're not feeling well, but you've got to try and get some food into you."

His coaxing tone made her try once more. Thorne took the offered morsel, nibbling on it. For a moment, she relaxed in Dev's presence. Was it because he called her by the pet name of Gypsy? The word rolled of his tongue in such a caressing fashion that Thorne felt herself responding helplessly to him somewhere deep within her heart.

Dev stripped off another portion of rabbit, handing it to Thorne. He was pleased to see that she wasn't going to be stubborn. "Are all Gypsies like you, trusting of others?"

"Gypsies are known for their clannish ways," she pointed out. "Other people distrust us."

"Then why are you being so docile and trusting?"

Thorne grimaced. "The tea didn't kill me earlier, Captain, so I know you don't want me to die. It's not a matter of trust as much as realizing you want to keep me alive."

Dev smiled sourly, giving her another chunk of the dark meat, which tasted similar to chicken. "How have the fops reacted to your defiance?"

Thorne was going to argue with his choice of words until she saw a glimmer of humor in his eyes. "I'm afraid I shocked the few who showed an interest in me, Captain. When they realized I was more than an empty-headed doll, they quickly drifted off to some other woman who was trained in the art of proper conversation."

A slight smile hovered around Dev's mouth as he continued to give Thorne tidbits of the rabbit. She ate them without any obvious problem.

"So, you were an outcast in your own class, Miss Somerset? A Gypsy beneath the veneer of your English upbringing?" he taunted softly.

Thorne chewed on her lower lip, avoiding Dev's teasing expression. "Yes, that's correct, Captain. My mother was disdained and shunned because she was thought by the *ton* to be of the lower class. My father married her anyway." She lifted her chin, pride in her eyes. "He married her because he loved her."

"Go on."

Thorne took the last shred of meat from his fingertips, grateful that he cared enough to want her to eat. Then she remembered that Dev needed her alive and not dead, and she tempered her reaction to his gallant gesture. "Father was in Spain when he met my mother. He was staying in Madrid, trying to negotiate with King Phillip for some shipping rights to the East Indies. The King had invited the Gypsies to come and perform for the royal court." Her voice grew softer and she closed her eyes, recalling her mother telling the story so many times before, when Thorne was a small child on her knee. "My mother, Rosa, was the premier dancer of her time. She wore a red dress and her black hair was so long that it almost reached her hips. The instant my father saw her dance, he fell in love with her. He tried to gain her attention that night, but like all gypsies, my mother would have nothing to do with him. He was a *gorgio*, an outsider.

"My father has a fine sense about people. He knew that if he offered gold to see her, the Gypsies would take insult." She opened her eyes, amusement in them. "He paid a fortune for a pure white Andalusian stallion and had it delivered the next morning to the leader of the camp. My father's servant then gave Rosa's father a message, saying that he would gladly buy him the largest herd of white horses he desired, if he would only grant him permission to see his lovely daughter."

Dev met her smiling eyes, thinking how strikingly beautiful Thorne was in that moment. "Your father was an intelligent man, bargaining with something the Gypsies cherish."

She sobered slightly, running her hand over the grass at her side. "My father is a fair man, Captain. I know you've suffered misfortune with the English, but John Somerset is a gentleman. He has honor and integrity. And when he met my mother, he treated her with the same deference as he would the Queen of England. He didn't care that she was a Gypsy from Spain. To him, strata of class don't exist. He spent a month with the Gypsies and fell hopelessly in love with my mother."

"It sounds like a fairy tale," Dev grumbled.

"Not all of life is harsh, Captain. My mother agreed to come to England after they were married. James, my brother, was born first. And then, four years later, I came along. My mother always would tell me how happy she was with my father." Her eyes darkened in fond remembrance. "They weren't like so many other couples I've had an opportunity to observe."

"Your mother sounds almost magical," Dev grunted.

Thorne felt the hotness of tears brimming her eyes. She turned away, feeling them dribble down her cheeks. "Sh-she's dead now...."

Dev's mouth tightened as he watched the tears roll down her face. Why did Thorne have to be so easily touched. "Recently?" he growled. Tears always made him uncomfortable.

Thorne sniffed, wiping the tears away with the back of her sleeve. "Y-yes. Two months ago. We were in a carriage when highwaymen attacked us. The coach overturned and Mama died of a broken neck."

"What about you?" Dev asked.

"I had some bruises, that's all," she quavered. And then Thorne gave him a trembling smile. "I didn't mean to talk about my mother. That's why I was here, in Spain. After the coach wreck, my father suffered a stroke. He was going to come to Spain to tell my mother's sister of her death, but I chose to come instead."

Dev exhaled and stared past the stream of the lush countryside. Damn it, why couldn't she be like any other prissy Englishwoman he'd seen before? They were cold, their long, skinny noses stuck up in the air. He chanced a look at her. Thorne had closed her eyes, resting her head on her drawn-up knees. In that instant, he wanted to reach out and comfort her for all the pain he'd heard in her voice. Reminding himself of what the English had done to his wife and family, he was able to suppress the tenderness coming to life in his heart.

"How did you come to be named Thorne?" he asked, thinking a change in topic would ease her grief.

"It's not uncommon for Gypsies to name their children after a flower, plant or tree."

"But a thorn? Something that can wound you?"

She held his curious gaze. "My full name is Whitethorne."

"Another name for the hawthorn bush," Dev murmured, searching his memory. "Why name you after the hawthorn?"

A sad smile crossed her mouth. "My mother was a herbalist. In the *ton*, they whispered that she was a witch, but that wasn't true. She loved plants and flowers...all of nature. The hawthorn bush is a heart remedy, Captain. The berries it produces are crushed and used as a tincture to soothe hearts that have suffered injury."

Dev met her smile, his eyes thawing and becoming warm. "So you were your mother and father's remedy for their heart?"

"Yes. Mama always said I brought them nothing but happiness."

"Did your friends make comments about your name?"

Thorne nodded and closed her eyes, her headache gradually receding. Was it the tea? Or perhaps that Dev had finally gotten her to eat? Or was it his presence? She didn't want to look too closely for the answer. "As you can guess, I was accused of being a thorn in many people's side."

"And I'm sure you've wounded many a young man's heart with your beauty," he murmured.

"Don't be fooled, Captain. I'm not recognized as properly blooded material by those of the *ton*." Thorne shrugged. "I didn't care about that, anyway. I told Father I wanted a man who could find joy in plowing the warm earth or holding our child. And—" she avoided his intense stare "—loving me." She took a deep breath. "I'm sure you'll laugh at my idealism, Captain. But I believe two people can marry for reasons of love and not just convenience."

Dev rose in a abrupt motion, his mouth set against the deluge of feelings her honesty had released. Every moment spent with Thorne was becoming like a spear piercing his heart. "Lie down and rest some more," he said gruffly as he turned and walked away, leaving her alone.

Perplexed by Dev's behaviour, Thorne took his advice. As she nestled her head into the crook of her arm, the fragrance of grass encircled her, and she laughed at herself. *I belong nowhere,* Thorne decided tiredly, closing her eyes, allowing the babble of the stream to lull her back into a healing sleep. *The* ton *laughs behind my back, discussing my lineage like the bloodlines of one of Father's horses. And Devlin Kyle judges me because he thinks I'm one of the* ton. A softened sigh escaped Thorne as she gave in to slumber, allowing the warm earth to cradle her. The earth made no judgment upon her; all it did was receive her, and she felt a new kinship with her surroundings, finding a corner of peace where she thought none had existed before.

Chapter Five

A sense of well-being cradled Thorne. A small sigh escaped her parted lips as she burrowed more deeply into the folds of the cotton shirt, her nostrils dilating, taking in an unfamiliar, although not unpleasant, scent. Drugged with sleep, she stirred, her hand sliding up a warm, hard expanse, coming to rest near her cheek. Contentment flowed through her, and vaguely she heard the cheery call of birds. Then her waking mind took over and an overwhelming amount of information flooded her groggy state. Arms were holding her. Strong arms wrapped around her, pressing her against the unyielding planes of a man's body.

Thorne's lashes flew open, her gray eyes dazed with confusion. At the same instant, she pushed herself away from Dev and sat up, facing him.

Thorne's face grew hot with mortification when she realized Dev was fully awake and watching her. Cheeks burning fiercely, she glared down at him. She was about to hurl a stinging comment at him when she saw the shadowed look in his cobalt eyes. A tingle raced through her; somehow she sensed that he had found holding her just as enjoyable as she had. And then his roughened voice broke through the shocked silence.

"You slept like a babe in my arms last night."

Shyly, Thorne hung her head, at a loss for words. The fact that she hadn't even been aware of him coming to her bed in the first place stunned her. Rubbing her brow, she muttered, "I don't think this is necessary, Captain. I didn't try to escape. I won't try to escape." She turned, her features distraught. "It isn't proper for me to share my bed with you...." she began lamely.

Dev roused himself, feeling incredibly well rested. "You're going to find out there are many things in life that aren't proper, so you might as well adjust to that fact." He turned, drinking in the pale yellow sunrise coloring the horizon. There was a chill in the air and he saw Thorne wrap her arms around herself. The thin cotton shirt wouldn't shield her from the dampness, so he got up and placed the wool blanket about her shoulders. She looked up at him, lips parted in surprise, her huge gray eyes like soft diamonds that he could drown in.

"I'll get a fire started," he said gruffly. "When you're done with your toilet, come over and get warm."

Later, Dev shared deer jerky and a hard biscuit with Thorne. Despite the male clothes she wore and her short hair, she was breathtakingly feminine. He scowled, watching how gracefully she reached over to pour herself some tea into his battered tin cup. Every motion was like poetry. He grimaced, wishing she weren't part Gypsy.

After breakfast, Dev saddled up his mare and looked at Thorne.

"Ready, Miss Somerset?"

"For what?" Thorne demanded, wary of him.

"Would you prefer to walk beside me rather than ride?"

"Yes, I would."

Dev grinned and slipped his hands around her narrow waist. She weighed next to nothing as he placed her in the saddle. Before she could struggle, he had released her, placing his foot in the stirrup and pulling himself up behind her. "I'm sure you would, but we have to get to Madrid and walking isn't preferable," he told her, his mouth near her ear. He smiled as Thorne stiffened because of his closeness. Taking the reins in his right hand, he placed his other hand on his thigh. She sat with her back ramrod straight, trying not to allow the sway of the horse to cause her to brush up against him. Dev slid his arm around

Thorne's waist, forcing her to lean back on him. She struggled to pull away.

"Let me go!" she cried.

"Don't fight me," he warned her in a vibrating tone, pulling her back against him. "You're still recovering from that fall. If you're stupid enough to fall off this horse instead of leaning against me for support, then you deserve to be held."

Thorne gritted her teeth, her skin burning hotly where he touched her. He was so hard and strong, and she felt so weak. "Damn you," she rasped, "damn you to hell, Captain!"

Dev kept his arm around her waist as she reluctantly gave in. "I've already been to hell, Miss Somerset. So there's no sense in damning me to it again with your very limited vocabulary."

Thorne tried to put her arms someplace where they didn't have to rest against him. It was impossible. *He* was impossible. "Tell me, do you always bully women? It's a wonder any female in her right mind would marry the likes of you!"

Dev swung Ghazeia up and over a crest that would take them out of the valley. A series of hills rose like welts out of the fabric of the earth, covered with the green of spring grass. He glanced down sharply at Thorne, stung by her retort.

"My wife, Miss Somerset, was a woman who made the sun burn brightly in my life by day and made my nights a series of dreams I thought only existed in men's imaginations." His voice lowered. "She was my life. My happiness, Miss Somerset. When she smiled, I felt close to tears. I saw joy in her eyes when she came willingly into my arms. What we shared was a miracle of love, something that men would die for." Ghazeia danced nervously beneath his hand, feeling his taut anger. He jerked hard on the reins to quiet the mare, immediately sorry that he had hurt her sensitive mouth.

Thorne gnawed on her lower lip, her eyes downcast, shame flowing through her. She felt his anger. But more, she felt his anguish and grief. "I—I'm sorry, Dev."

He dug his heels into the mare, sending her into a trot down the gentle slope of the hill. Dev wanted to punish Thorne for her unthinking remark, knowing that the jar of the trot would be uncomfortable for her. He wanted to throttle her. Damn her callous English attitude!

They traveled until noon at either a trot or slow canter, weaving in and around hills and moving easily through valleys strewn with flowers and grass. Thorne took a shaky breath, exhausted by the hard riding. She clung to the saddle, head bowed as Dev dismounted, leaving her alone. The anger that radiated from him was ominous and dark.

"Get down," he ordered her tersely.

Thorne obeyed. The instant her feet touched the ground, her knees buckled. If it weren't for her grip on the saddle pommel, she would have fallen like a sack of grain to the grassy ground. Pain throbbed through her temples as she fought to regain her balance. She licked her dry, chapped lips. Riding for hours in the hot sun without any protection had burned her skin a dull red. Gritting her teeth, she forced her legs to hold her and she turned, clutching at the saddle, meeting Kyle's black eyes.

"I told you, I'm sorry, Captain." She forced the words out in a quavering voice. "Haven't you punished me enough for my transgression?"

"You're just beginning to pay for what the English have taken from me, Miss Somerset."

Her gray eyes widened with confusion. "If I'm going to pay, then at least give me the satisfaction of knowing what I'm paying for!"

Dev gripped the reins until his knuckles whitened. "My wife was murdered by one of the King's own. He dragged her up on the deck of a ship bound for London, a ship full of innocent Irish civilians caught in the jaws of the uprising in Ireland. My father had already been tortured and refused to give the officer information on where the rest of the gunpowder and supplies were hidden. So the English bastard figured if my father wouldn't talk, he could make him do it by torturing my wife."

Thorne cringed against the horse, horror in her eyes. "Oh, my God, no..."

Dev's breathing grew labored. "Don't feign surprise, Miss Somerset. When it comes to outright cruelty, no one is better suited to the task than an Englishman. He had my wife stripped naked to the waist in front of the ship's company and, by his own hand, began to peel back her flesh with a cat-o'-nine-tails."

Thorne pressed her hand across her mouth to stop the cry of anguish knotting in her throat. "I—I didn't know...I'm sorry... so sorry...."

Dev threw the reins down and began to walk. After a few paces, he spun around on his heel. "Shannon had more courage than any ten men," he rasped. "She refused to tell the redcoat where the supplies were located. The secret died on her lips." He drew himself up, barely able to contain the grief that threatened to overwhelm him. "The English have destroyed my family. My brother is in Newgate and, by God, you're going to get him released." His shoulders slumped and Dev felt all the anger draining from him. "How would you like to have your family slaughtered like animals?"

He stalked off to gather wood for a fire, relieved to have such a mundane task to take his mind off the past. All he wanted to do was resume traveling just as soon as possible.

Waves of heat covered the valley like a shimmering curtain. The ground was drying out rapidly beneath the rays of the sun. A small *pueblo* of thirty or so adobe homes appeared out of the haze and heat in the distance. Thorne was parched. She felt the Arabian mare begin to favor her leg as they drew near the village in the early evening. Thorne wished she could lean her aching head against Dev's chest, and she longed for a bath to get rid of the gritty dust that clung to her perspiring skin.

Dev pulled to a halt half a mile from the *pueblo*. Around it was land under cultivation, with most of the men working until almost sundown in the fields. He spotted a village square and a well nearby. It wouldn't hurt to spend a night in a clean room, eat decent food and lie in a bed. The last thought made him look down at Thorne. He was worried about her. She was flushed and her eyes were narrowed in pain. Guilt nagged at him. She hadn't deserved his anger earlier.

"We're going to find an inn for the night," he told her, watching Thorne's lips part in surprise. "Providing, Miss Somerset, that you keep your status a secret. The moment I hear you scream for help or try to tell someone you're kidnapped, I'll head us back out into the countryside."

She licked her dry lips. "Don't worry, I want a bath and bed too much to say anything."

Dev nodded grimly. She had common sense, another point in her favor. As they entered the village, children who were playing stopped to stare at them. Chickens clucked and squawked, diving out of their way. A few dogs, all mangy and underfed, barked a few times and then went to lie back down in the shade provided by the roofs of the adobe homes. Dismounting at the square, Dev gave Ghazeia and themselves a long, cool drink of water. Several slender olive trees provided shade around them.

Thorne splashed water over her face, groaning because it felt wonderful, the rivulets escaping and running down her neck and soaking into her shirt. When she turned, she was met by two inquiring brown eyes. Smiling, she knelt down, meeting the bold little boy at eye level.

"Hello," she said softly in Spanish.

The boy smiled shyly, his almond eyes sparkling. "Are you a *señorita?*"

Thorne touched her short hair. Of course, she looked more like a boy than the woman she was. *"Sí, muchacho."*

Dev watched stonily as Thorne spoke animatedly with the child. She had a way of disarming everyone she came in contact with. He spotted several cafés that would soon be filled with returning farm workers, who would sit and drink their coffee, sherry or wine and play cards before going home for the evening.

"Thorne?" He gestured for her to rise and follow him.

She smiled at the boy named Julio, then quickly fell into step behind Dev. Curious women and children watched as they tied their weary horse beneath one of the olive trees and walked to a café.

Dev chose a rough-hewn table that had two benches. Thorne sat down beside him. The owner came out, dressed in a white cotton shirt and black baggy pants.

"*Sí, señor?* Your order?"

Dev turned to her. "What do you want?"

She colored, realizing he was giving her a choice. "Some lemon and water?"

He looked over at the thin, kindly looking owner, whose face was deeply weathered and wrinkled. "Ale for me."

"*Sí, sí.*"

Thorne began to relax. She turned to Dev. "You're going to get us rooms?" The prospect of a bed to sleep in seemed an incredible luxury to her now. And to think she had taken beds for granted.

"A room for us," Dev said. He saw her eyes widen.

"But—but—" Thorne stammered, her voice lowering. "I told you I wouldn't try to escape! I can't room with you! It's not proper. Not right—"

"As far as everyone is concerned, you're my wife," he said, daring her to say a word against his decision.

Thorne's mouth dropped open, but she was unable to reply because the owner brought them their drinks. The cool lemon water tasted delicious and she listened to Dev talk to the proprietor. His Spanish was stilted and awkward at best. Thorne nearly choked on her drink when she heard what he was saying to the man.

"My wife is in need of new clothes. Perhaps your wife could bring her something more fitting to wear than these things," he said, gesturing to Thorne lazily. Then he turned to her. "As soon as his wife brings you clean clothes, get out of those trousers. There's no sense in your looking like a man."

Thorne automatically touched her short hair. Her beautiful, abundant tresses were gone. A hollow feeling of shame centered in her when she realized how grotesque and manly she must appear to him.

Dev saw all those feelings mirrored in Thorne's features. He reached out, brushing his knuckles against her cheek. She felt like a warm, ripe peach and he longed to continue the caress. When he noticed her shocked expression, however, he dropped his hand.

"You still look like a woman," he told her, his voice oddly strained, "with or without long hair."

A tingle of pleasure radiated from her cheek where he had given her the butterfly caress. Unconsciously, Thorne touched the same spot with her fingertips. Her gray eyes misted, making them again look like luminous, soft diamonds. Dev refused to look at her. In that moment, Thorne's heart blossomed with such fierce gratefulness that she reached out, resting her fingertips on the sun-hardened flesh of his lower arm.

"Thank you, Captain...."

He barely twisted his head, meeting her melting gaze. The hard line of his mouth momentarily eased. "Remember," he told her quietly, "call me Dev, not captain." He said it without rancor and he saw the miracle his change of tone had on Thorne. A tremulous smile touched her ripe lips.

"You have a heart after all," she whispered.

Dev lifted the mug of ale, feeling heat nettle his face. "Get Carlos, the proprietor, to take you to our room," he muttered. "His wife will prepare a bath for you. I'll join you later. I want to buy some supplies first." His blue eyes hardened. "And remember what I said. There's no place that I can't find you in this small village should you decide to try to escape, Thorne."

She got to her feet, smoothing out the fabric of the breeches across her long thighs. "I told you, I won't try to escape. I want to see my father as badly as you want your brother back."

Dev watched her turn and walk through the café with Carlos. Her shoulders were small and proudly thrown back. Despite the grueling days since her kidnapping, Thorne had mustered the spirit and courage it took to deal with the situation. Running his fingers through his auburn hair, Dev tried to shove all his newly awakened feelings toward her aside.

Chapter Six

"*Señor! Señor!*" Julio came racing up to Dev, tugging on his arm. "Your bath water is ready. The *señora* has already used it. Hurry or it will grow cold."

Dev wiped the sweat from his brow. He carried a sack of supplies from the small store. "I'll be right over, Julio. Here, take these to the stable and put them in the saddlebags."

The boy dipped his head, the bags nearly too large for his small arms to wrap around. "*Sí, sí.*"

At the inn, Carlos pointed out the first door on the left and Dev quietly opened it. The room was large, whitewashed and immaculately clean. He gaze roved from the copper tub sitting in the middle of the tiled floor to the bed, where Thorne lay asleep. He shut the door and walked over to her, his eyes growing shadowed. Thorne looked like a small lost kitten in the bed, her knees drawn up to her chest, hands against her breast. The thin white muslin dressing robe she wore around her naked form did little to hide her from his hungry inspection. She looked so clean and untouched in that moment, her lips slightly parted in sleep, her lashes ebony fans against the flush of her cheeks, her hair a blue black cap on her head.

A soft smile touched Dev's mouth. With a sigh, he turned and went to the only chair in the room, shedding his clothes. He dropped them outside the door so that Sophia, the proprietor's wife, could wash them. The water was lukewarm, but he didn't care, wanting to scrub the Spanish dust from his pores.

Later, hair dripping wet, Dev emerged from the tub. Thorne slept soundly through his bath and he began to grasp the depth of her exhaustion. He combed his fingers through his damp hair and wrapped a towel around his waist. As he stood there in the center of the room, his gaze moved back to Thorne. Dev needed to sleep. It was that simple. And he wanted Thorne in his arms. Already, at just the thought of drawing her to him, heat stirred his loins.

Thorne gave a sigh as he slid down beside her. Dev steeled himself in case she awoke. Instead, she simply burrowed her head deeply beneath his unshaven jaw, seeking his protection. Dev lay on his side with the Englishwoman in his arms. Thorne's hair was damp silk beneath his jaw, and the thin muslin was a flimsy barrier between his chest and her firm, young breasts. His nostrils flared as he slowly, deliciously, inhaled her female scent. A tremor of longing raced through Dev. So many of the senses he thought had been destroyed since Shannon's death suddenly ignited to life within him.

Closing his eyes, Dev shuddered slightly and tried to ignore the heated signals throbbing to life within him. God, Thorne felt so good, all curves and softness. Was she asleep? He stilled himself. Her breasts rose and fell slowly, and the beat of her heart was steady and constant. Sweet God, but she *was* a true thorn in his side! He wanted her, all of her, and she was his enemy. How could he want to bury himself in her warm, liquid depths? Enemy, Dev repeated groggily to himself. *She is my enemy....*

Dev jerked awake, his arm automatically tightening around Thorne. The quiet knock continued. Irritated and still partially asleep, he growled, "Come in."

Sophia smiled, bringing in their recently cleaned and dried clothes. "For you and the *señora*," she whispered, placing them on the dresser.

Thorne stirred, sleepily opening her eyes. She vaguely heard Sophia's voice and Dev's guttural response. She felt warm and safe.

"*Gracias,*" Dev said.

"Dinner will be ready shortly, *señor.* Please, come join us," Sophia urged, and shut the door behind her.

Dev directed his attention back to Thorne. He didn't try to keep her captive against him as she slowly awakened. The muslin dressing robe had no buttons and the material had parted during sleep, exposing her delicate collarbones and the valley between Thorne's small breasts. He saw her pink nipples harden as the material moved across them and fought the urge to lean down and draw one of them into his mouth and taste her natural sweetness. The scent of Thorne's body mixed with the sandalwood oil she had used after bathing. He inhaled deeply, watching her grow more aware of her surroundings. Her lips were parted, her eyes barely open as she focused on him. At first, Dev was sure Thorne wasn't wholly aware that she was in bed with him.

The sun had long ago changed position and the grayness of dusk now invaded the room. But even in the muted shadows, Dev watched the miracle he held in his arms awaken. There was no fear in Thorne's drowsy gray eyes, simply trust. He lay propped up on his elbow, his other hand resting on the curve of her hip. Dev knew from long experience that a person was most vulnerable upon waking. He held himself in tight check, wanting to lean down and taste the promise of her full, gently blossoming lips. Thorne's flesh was almost translucent and he reached up, taming a few stray strands of hair from her cheek.

"It's time to get up," he told her in a husky voice.

Thorne floated between sleep and dream. Lush tendrils of desire floated through her. She lay in Dev's arms, her hand resting on the dark, springy hair of his chest. The powerful beat of his heart thudded through her palm and Thorne took a long, shaky breath. She struggled to escape the silken webs that bound them quietly to each other in the silence of the room. Her eyes lifted upward, widening as she met and was consumed by the hungry fire that lingered in

Dev's gaze. Her mouth grew dry as she accurately read his desire for her. And then, fear gripped her. Thorne moved away from him, aware of the hurt mirrored in his eyes for a fleeting moment.

Pulling the muslin dressing robe tightly about her, she stared at him, realizing her compromising situation. Her slender fingers flew to the base of her throat as it dawned on Thorne that Dev was wearing nothing but a towel. Her heart beat traitorously. Dev was beautiful, Thorne realized, feeling herself go weak with an unaccustomed heat that was centered deep within her body. From the broad set of his shoulders and his deeply muscled chest to his flat, hard stomach and long, well-shaped thighs, he was achingly male. Her face grew crimson as she saw the beginnings of a smile pull at his mouth. Dev was not the least embarrassed by his near nakedness in front of her!

Thorne was about to sputter out something—anything—when she saw the white of a long scar that ran the length of his ribs. Her shyness fled in the wake of her discovery of so many scars on his body. Some were white and puckered. Others were pink, indicating that they were fairly recent. And one, located on his left outer thigh, was still red and angry looking, having just healed. Her gray eyes became soft. No wonder Dev was so hardened.

"You've been injured so many times," she whispered, an ache in her voice.

"Don't waste your care on me, Thorne."

Thorne leaned against the wall and tucked her legs beneath her. "Part of being a healer is feeling another's pain."

"Well," Dev drawled, running his finger lazily in an invisible pattern on the wool blanket between them, "I've given you enough pain already." He lifted his chin, staring darkly at her. "I've kidnapped you, cut your hair off and tarnished your reputation."

Thorne heard the regret in his voice. There was guilt etched in his eyes and she sensed his anguish over the act of cutting her hair off. Her throat constricting with sudden emotion, she said, "You've kidnapped me because you want your brother back. I don't know what his crimes against England are. I've tried to imagine what it would be like if someone I loved were in prison, and what I would do to try to free him." Thorne bowed her head. "There's nothing more important than family. I'd rather be kidnapped for that reason than for any other." She gave a hesitant laugh and ran her fingers through her dried ebony tresses. "My hair will grow back, although I'm sure much more slowly than I would like. I worry what my friends will say when they see me. Will they make more jokes about me...?" Her voice died away and she avoided Dev's intense look.

"What do you mean, jokes?"

Uncomfortable, Thorne muttered, "I mean nothing by my remark."

Dev rested against the oak headboard and made sure his towel remained in place around his waist. "Yes, you did. Who taunts you? And why?"

"Oh... just some of my friends."

"Friends never ridicule another friend," Dev corrected. "Are these the rich and spoiled of the *ton* you're talking about?"

Thorne nodded, giving him a half smile. "As I told you before, I'm not acceptable blood to the *ton*. They whisper behind my back that I'm a wild Gypsy by nature and garbed only in the raiments of my father's money and station as a guise."

"So?"

"I'm an outcast, Dev." Her eyes grew dark as she held his steady gaze. "When I get home to England and they find my hair shorn, then I shall have to bear all their veiled innuendos. They'll suggest that I was a witch and had my hair cut off in Spain as punishment. Spain is Catholic, as I am, and many of them dislike me because of my faith. They're Protestant and I'm not."

He stirred. Thorne was Catholic, as he was. Dev tried to conceal his shock but found it impossible, and Thorne laughed throatily.

"You'll find many contradictions about me," she said wryly. "I'm Catholic in a Protestant nation. I'm a Gypsy when I should be a blueblood—"

"And you wear your heart openly," Dev countered, catching her startled expression.

"Is there any other way?"

He snorted and sat up. "You're a ripe apple in the midst of hungry beggars, Gypsy."

Thorne watched Dev get off the bed, openly admiring his magnificent body, scars and all. She should be mortified, sitting on a bed next to him. And yet it was as if they were old friends meeting once again, relaxed and sharing each other's company. Dev walked to the dresser, picking up her clothes and handing them to her. "Here, wear these. And if you don't want to see me dress, then you'd best shut your eyes, Gypsy. Sophia is expecting us to dine with them shortly."

Thorne scrunched her eyelids tightly shut, gripping the soft cotton clothes between her hands. "They're shut," she said.

With clean shirt and breeches on, Dev felt better. He combed his hair and ran his hand across his stubbled face. He ought to shave. He laughed at himself. Since when had he worried about a few days' growth of beard? He looked at Thorne sitting on the bed, eyes shut lest she commit the ultimate sin. He turned to light a small lamp. Its yellow flame cast dancing light weakly through the room.

"It's safe now," he told her. A smile tugged at his mouth as he saw Thorne warily open first one eye and then another. She looked like a small child huddled on the bed. "Come to the café when you're dressed."

Thorne looked through the clothes, panic in her eyes. "But . . . I don't have any shoes . . . just my boots."

Dev opened the door, staring hungrily at her. "Then be like the rest of the good Spanish wives, walk barefoot."

"But that's improper! I mean, a lady never shows her ankle." Thorne's voice died in her throat as she realized he was regarding her with a tenderness that wrenched her heart.

"Gypsy, no matter what you do or don't wear, you're beautiful. No one will think anything of your going barefoot. I certainly won't." And then Dev grinned. "I'm not a gentleman, so how can I be offended by the turn of your delicate ankle?"

Grudgingly, Thorne accepted his reasoning.

"I'll be out in a few minutes," she said softly.

Dev nodded. "Would you like some sherry? Wine?"

She laughed, the sound silvery and nascent. "Do you want me to fall off the bench and slide beneath the table?"

He smiled, thinking that he'd like to have Thorne laugh like that more often. "Tonight we celebrate, Gypsy. A little wine isn't going to hurt you. Or me." Dev needed something to stop himself from taking the headlong plunge into liking Thorne far more than he dared.

When Thorne could eat no more and thought she would burst, Sophia produced spiced cakes and freshly made coffee for dessert. It was almost midnight before they retired to their room after thanking their hosts.

Thorne tried to still her nervousness as Dev closed the door to their room. She sat down on the bed.

"I've never eaten so much. And it was all so good."

Dev nodded and sat down on the chair, pulling off his boots and setting them aside. "Now you know what it's like to be a soldier. You begin to appreciate the small social amenities such as a bed to sleep on, good food and pleasant people."

She sobered, watching as he unbuttoned his white shirt, drew it off and exposed his magnificent chest. "Do you really think there are Gypsies nearby?" Hope rose in her tone. "Sophia said she saw a group pass through here a week ago."

He snorted softly, throwing the shirt over the back of the chair. "I'd rather run into Gypsies than those guerrillas Carlos talked about. They're the dangerous ones. I've come up against them before, and they're animals. Rape, murder and thieving are the least of their sins."

"They sound terrible," Thorne conceded softly, wondering what Dev was going to do about sleeping arrangements. The moon had risen, sending a pale wash of light through the window and across the bed where she sat. "Dev?"

"Hmm?"

"What—I mean . . . what about sleeping?" she asked in a strangled voice, vividly recalling her reaction to being held by him earlier.

Dev picked up her dressing robe and handed it to her. "I'll sit here and you go over there and get into this," he said, pointing to the opposite corner of the chamber.

She stared up at him. "You'll close your eyes?"

He ached to lean down and kiss her provocative lips. Did Thorne know how fragile and lovely she appeared to him in that instant? The white peasant blouse and wine-colored skirt she had borrowed from Sophia emphasized her womanly curves. "Do you want me to?" Dev taunted.

"Of course!"

"Very well. Go on. I'll lie here with my back to you."

Thorne was off the bed in an instant, gripping the dressing robe tightly. Her heart was beating erratically and her hands shook as she unbuttoned the blouse and then slid out of the skirt. She elected to keep her ivory chemise on, shrugging the robe across her shoulders and pulling it snugly around her. She licked her lips, unsure of what to do next. Spying the chair, she walked over to it and sat down.

"I—I think I shall sit here for a while."

Dev slowly rolled over. She looked like a deer tensed for flight from a hunter's musket. "And do what?" he taunted her softly.

"Well . . ." She glanced around, searching for something to do. "If I had a book, I could read."

"There's no book, Gypsy."

She clasped her hands tightly in her lap. "I'm not sleepy right now. I think I'll just stay up a bit longer."

Dev tried to control his smile for her sake. He patted the bed and moved over. "You don't want to be a bad guest and burn up all the good innkeeper's candles. Come on, we're going to need a good night's rest. Tomorrow we've got to leave.''

"But—"

"I'm not going to touch you," he promised in a low voice. "Now come over here. You can't sleep in that chair."

"Of course I can—"

"You'll fall off it, Thorne."

She shuffled to her feet, gripping the dressing robe. There was amusement in Dev's eyes as she cautiously sat on the edge of the bed. "You're laughing at me!" she accused. "That's not fair! If anyone finds out that I've slept with you, it will be my ruin!"

He reached out and slid his hand across her tensed shoulder. "I'm not laughing at you, Gypsy. And you're right, your reputation might be a bit wounded if this sleeping arrangement were known. But I'm not going to tell. And I don't think you will, either. Lie down here beside me. We need to sleep," he coaxed.

Thorne took a shaky breath and clung to the edge of the bed after she reluctantly lay down. With her back to Dev, she brought her knees up toward her chest, curling herself into a ball. Thankfully, the captain at least had the decency to wear his breeches to bed. Thorne closed her eyes, appalled by her wildly beating heart. After five minutes, she heard him speak in a soft voice.

"I'm going to buy another horse from Carlos tomorrow morning. I want you to ride Ghazeia."

Her eyes flew open. "I get a horse of my own?"

"You get Ghazeia," Dev repeated, his voice deepening with authority. "And you need to realize that if I whistle, that mare of mine will refuse to walk, trot or canter anywhere. So if you're thinking of escaping on her, be warned. She won't budge."

"You forget, I gave my word. Besides, I'm not daft, Captain. Don't you think I know she's got an injured leg?"

Dev placed his hands behind his head, staring up at the darkened ceiling. "I don't consider you daft at all. I think you're the most intelligent woman I've ever met. That's why I'm telling you the facts now, Miss Somerset. The mare is favoring that leg. You weigh the least, and right now she can do without the added stress of too much weight. I need her to heal.''

Thorne rolled over. Dev's profile was rugged and shadowed.

Sliding her hands up by her cheek, Thorne relaxed, realizing that Dev was not going to seduce her. Mere inches separated them and that was close enough for her.

Dev reached over, barely brushing her cheek. ''Why do you avoid speaking about yourself? What do you do at your father's estate if you're not attending parties?''

A tingle of pleasure radiated outward on her flesh where Dev had caressed her. Thorne didn't move, needing his touch. ''I work with the staffs of our two orphanage houses in London.''

He stared at her, disbelief flaring momentarily in his eyes. ''A few days a month?'' He had heard of some blue-blooded women giving the appearance of helping the less fortunate. But it was a sham and nothing more.

''Since completing finishing school two years ago, I've been working in London,'' Thorne admitted, avoiding his probing look. ''I manage the staff of both homes in the Soho district where the truly poor live.''

''I see.''

''I work with doctors, helping the sick and injured. That's what I wanted to be, a doctor. But they will never allow a woman to become one. So I use my skill and knowledge of herbs alongside the doctor we have employed, and we take care of the sick.''

The taste of bile coated Dev's mouth. He sighed and turned over, his back to Thorne. ''It's late,'' he growled, ''get some sleep.'' Anger surged through him. Helpless anger. And it was aimed at himself. Of all the people to hold for ransom! Why couldn't Thorne have been an arrogant blue-blood who slept until noon every day, had servants at her beck and call and went to parties constantly? He wanted to hold Thorne, to apologize for being such an ass to her.

Disgusted, Dev couldn't fall asleep for a long time. Sometime during the early morning hours, he turned over on his back and reached out to take the sleeping Thorne into his arms, her feminine scent and the sandalwood fragrance encircling his nostrils. It was only then that Dev slept, finding a shred of contentment in his violent world.

Chapter Seven

After paying Carlos for the lodging at the inn, Dev lifted Thorne onto Ghazeia's back. Her voluminous wine-colored skirt billowed out briefly, then settled back against her. The black boots she wore were knee-high and no part of her leg was exposed. Dev gave Thorne a smile and handed the reins to her.

Mounting the bay gelding that he had just purchased, Dev raised his hand in farewell to Carlos. They rode out of the *pueblo* as quietly as they had ridden in. Once, Thorne looked back, a wistful expression on her face. Dev rode beside her, their legs occasionally touching.

"Carlos and Sophia were wonderful to us," she said.

Dev nodded. "Part of it is the Spanish nature."

"And the other is their generosity of heart toward everyone. That's an uncommon virtue, one that I strongly applaud."

He smiled at her. "Just as you take starving and injured waifs into your orphanages?"

"Yes."

"Tell me what a day is like for you, Thorne."

She reached down, giving Ghazeia a gentle pat. The mare responded, flicking her ears. "Mama and I would come in by coach from the manor every day to help. Papa was busy at his London office with shipping interests. He's built a fleet of twenty ships over the years and has established a healthy trade with the New World. Sometimes he'll visit our orphanages, but not very often." Thorne gave him a sad smile. "All the children loved Mama. They didn't care if she was Gypsy. They loved her bright skirts and colorful blouses and forever admired her gold and silver bracelets, which jangled as she moved about. The babies would play with her necklaces and hoop earrings. The children always looked forward to her coming to visit. She would bring them sweets or little cakes, which she'd hide in one of the many pockets of her apron."

"Your mother didn't wear conventional clothes?" Dev asked, surprise evident in his eyes. No wonder they ridiculed Thorne, if her mother was seen in the gaudy, bright clothes of the Gypsies.

"When my father married her, it was one of the few times that the Roms approved of true blood marrying a *gorgio*, or non-Gypsy." She saw Dev's brows draw downward. "The Rom, or Gypsies, will tolerate a man marrying a *gorgio* woman so long as she takes on the ways of the Rom. But it's rare that a woman from the Gypsies is allowed to marry an outsider. In this case, my father went to great lengths to earn my grandfather's acceptance. There are many superstitions among the Rom, Dev. And the one that my grandfather made my father promise was to let my mama retain her Rom ways." She smiled warmly. "He kept that promise."

"So, did your mother dress you in Gypsy clothes? Is that why you were taunted by society?"

The sun felt good, Thorne thought, just as the conversation with Dev did. This morning he was more relaxed, the planes of his face free of tension. And she was euphoric because, finally, the barriers he had placed between them were no longer in evidence. It was as if they were friends, meeting after a long separation. "My mother taught me the ways of the Rom, even their language, but she never dressed me like herself."

"I wonder why?"

"Because she knew of the distrust the *gorgio* had toward us. *Gorgios* think we will curse them if we get angry."

"Can you?"

She smiled. "The Rom believe strongly in light and dark, purity and pollution. To them, there is a right way to live and a wrong way. Mama knew that some of her ways would appear to be strange. She also didn't want me to be a total outcast to my father's people. It happened, anyway. Mama knew I was getting teased at school because she wore Gypsy clothes. But she would not forsake her way. She tried to compromise by sending me to the proper schools, dressing me as a member of society, and having me accepted." Thorne gave a shrug. "It didn't work. I've gradually come to grips with it, Dev. I'm an outcast to the Rom and to the *gorgios.* I'm neither one nor the other. I live with a foot in each world, I suppose."

"If you had a choice, Thorne, which world would you live in?" he asked softly.

"The Rom, there is no question. I love their freedom, their laughter and their fierce love of life. They're free of stiff social conventions. But I will not forsake my father. He needs me, now that Mama is gone."

Thorne changed subjects, taking advantage of Dev's openness. "You mentioned the Earl of Trayhern before," she murmured, turning toward him. "I've met Tray and his wife, Alyssa."

Dev nodded, watching her expressive face light up with sudden pleasure. "What do you know of them?" Leaning over in the saddle, he plucked a small white daisy with a yellow center and handed it to her.

Thorne avoided his searching gaze, accepting the flower. It was such a small act, and yet it meant so much to her. "They came to London a year ago with their four children. Father has known Tray for quite some time, because he buys coal from him and has it shipped to London." Her voice dropped into a soft hush. "I love Alyssa and her children. They stayed at our manor for a week while Tray conducted business with his legal and accounting people. Plus, he and my father signed a lucrative coal contract between them."

A slight smile edged Dev's mouth. "Alyssa is my sister. Did you know that?"

Thorne lifted her chin, shock in her gray eyes. It took her several minutes before she could reply. "Well—I'd heard vicious rumors flying that Alyssa was a felon's daughter, but I never paid any mind to them. I knew Alyssa by her married name only."

"Her maiden name is Kyle," Dev confirmed. It shook him to realize that Thorne wasn't upset by that knowledge.

"She's so happy with her husband and children," Thorne babbled excitedly. "You could see it in the way she smiled and laughed. My mother and she got along wonderfully. And—" she gently touched the daisy "—I thought Alyssa was the most beautiful woman I've ever met. She was attractive outwardly, but she also shone through her heart. Everyone she brought into her circle of sunshine was better off for it." Thorne gave Dev a tentative smile, meeting his dark blue gaze. "If Alyssa is that loving and giving, then the rest of her family must be, also."

Dev held her steady, almost challenging gaze. "Well," he muttered, plucking another daisy and pulling the petals from it one at a time, "Lys always did have a soft heart."

"And a soft head?"

"I didn't say that."

"But you implied it."

"I don't know why she didn't end up hard and bitter like Gavin and me. Maybe it was Tray. Perhaps part of his understanding nature is based upon the fact that he was born with a clubfoot. Locals made fun of him, too. Perhaps he knew what it was like to be an outcast, like the Irish. He's a man with infinite patience, and an ability to look through someone to see what they're made of. Did Lys tell you how she came to Wales and how Tray took her in as a stray?"

Thorne shook her head. "We spent evenings together, Dev, but Alyssa never spoke of her past. She loves Tray. He's so kind to her and his children. They adore him."

"Lys deserves happiness after the hell she was put through by Vaughn Trayhern," he growled, snapping off the stalk of the daisy. He stared at her hard. "He was the one who raped my sister and killed my wife, Shannon."

Thorne blanched. Her head was spinning. Vaughn had killed Dev's loved ones! "My God...I didn't know. I'm sorry... he's destroyed so much of your family, Dev."

"Yes, he has. Did you ever meet him?" Dev asked tightly, thinking that Vaughn ran in the circle of the *ton*.

Her stomach knotted. Feeling faint, Thorne pressed her hand to her brow. "My God, he's asked for my hand in marriage."

The words exploded out of him. "What? You aren't serious? Doesn't anyone know that murderer for what he is?"

Thorne gave him a helpless look. "In the *ton*, Vaughn is considered a hero. He's very popular."

With a violent oath, Dev muttered, "He's penniless, Thorne! My brother-in-law, Tray, cut him off the moment Alyssa revealed that Vaughn had raped her." His eyes mirrored anxiety. "You aren't going to marry him, are you?"

Numbed by the revelations, Thorne shook her head. "Not now. Not after what I've learned about him. I never wanted to in the first place, but my father thought it would be a good match."

"If I ever meet him, he's a dead man. And he knows it."

Thorne had no doubt that Dev would kill Vaughn Trayhern. Her own emotions spun out of control. Vaughn had appeared to be such a gentleman. Women were flattered by his blond good looks. Men admired him for his brilliant war record before he had to retire with a permanent knee injury.

"When I first met Vaughn Trayhern, I was repelled by him," Thorne murmured. "And I didn't understand why I reacted that way toward him."

"Now you know. Cruelty comes as easily to Vaughn as kindness does to his half brother, Tray," Dev said tightly. His eyes flashed with concern. "Have your father drop him as a suitor, Thorne. He'll mistreat you the way he does anyone he has power over. Tray has told me Vaughn has two sides to himself. In public, he's a gentleman." His mouth tensed. "In private, he's a monster to servants and animals alike." Anguish rose in Dev as he wrestled with the idea of Thorne becoming Trayhern's property. "Whatever

you do, stay out of his clutches. You don't deserve any
further pain.''

"Father was considering the proposal, but then the carriage accident happened." Thorne grimaced. "Now, with
Papa's mental capacities affected by the stroke, I doubt he
even remembers his marriage plans for me. More important, I must stay at Somerset now and help Papa run the
shipping business. I think he will see that he needs me too
much to marry me off.''

"Be diligent," Dev warned. "Women aren't considered
ve capable in business. Your father may seek a match to
provide a son-in-law to run the business as well as a husband for you.''

Their intense conversation was interrupted when Dev
heard the pop of a musket being fired, followed by the
screams of women. He reined in his gelding, his face suddenly alert and tense. Jerking his head toward Thorne, he
growled, "Stay here.''

Ghazeia nickered plaintively, dancing beneath Thorne's
hand, wanting to follow the departing gelding. Thorne's
heart pounded wildly in her breast. How could she stay here
when Dev might need her help? Unable to stand the tension, she leaned forward, pushing the mare into a gallop.
The wind stung her eyes and whipped around her as they
quickly threaded between the brush. It took all her skill as
a horsewoman to stay astride the mare. When they hit the
level ground of the grass-laden valley, Thorne heard a blis-
tering volley of musket fire off to her left.

She urged the mare into an oak grove, toward the activity. Leaning low, they thundered on half a mile before suddenly coming upon a small meadow. There, Thorne saw
Gypsy women and children scattered about by an attacking band of four Spanish bandits. Horses skittered, wild-
eyed, through the melee. Children screamed. Pistol fire
popped around her and the acrid smell of cordite stung her
sensitive nostrils. She spotted Dev at the far end, engaged
in a furious battle with the enemy.

He had caught the guerrillas without their horses. Three
of the men were trying to hold up their unbuttoned pants,

running with swords drawn toward him. The other was trying to catch the horses. Dev was outnumbered! Thorne dug her heels into Ghazeia, flying through the meadow toward the man who was trying to mount the first panicked horse. She screamed shrilly, hoping to scare the horses even more. It worked. The animal reared and went over backward, carrying his rider with him to the ground. The other horses whirled around and fled deep into the oak grove. Thorne saw the guerrilla get up. His dark face was clouded with fury and his black eyes filled with rage as he drew his sword.

Thorne swerved her mare hard to the right as he lifted the sword. The blade whistled by, cutting very close to her left arm. Ghazeia stumbled, her injured leg giving out beneath the stress of the sudden movement. One moment Thorne was in the saddle, the next, sailing over the mare's head. She relaxed, hitting the ground and rolling. She had barely gotten to her knees, her skirts inhibiting her movement, when the black-mustached guerrilla charged her again. He held the sword high above his head. Panic set in, and Thorne scrambled to her feet. To her left, she saw a dead bandit with his sword still in his hand. Leaping over the body, she grabbed the weapon, gripping it with both hands.

Whirling around toward her pursuer, Thorne faced him. She had often watched her father fence with an épée. Was a sword any different? The guerrilla charged her. Screams, musket fire and shouts surrounded her. Thorne blocked all of it out, realizing that no one was going to be able to protect her. She saw the sword descend, aimed at her skull. It would cleave her in two. Out of instinct, Thorne raised her sword in a horizontal position above her head to deflect the blow. Metal bit into metal. The savage vibration jolted up her arms and into her shoulders as she absorbed the power of the blow.

Dev aimed his pistol at the guerrilla now facing him and fired. The enemy fell with a scream on his lips. Dev jerked his gelding to a halt. Thorne! He froze. He saw the bandit charging her with his sword. Whirling the gelding around, Dev dug his spurs deeply into the animal's heaving flanks.

Thorne! My God, she was going to get killed! Everything slowed as he charged toward her. He saw the terror on her face, but he also saw her courage. As she lifted that sword above her head, he was stunned by her move. It was a parry. How could she know about swordsmanship? A cry tore from him as he saw her take the full brunt of the blow meant to split her in half. Thorne staggered. The sword dropped from her hands as she fell backward, off balance. The guerrilla raced toward Thorne, his weapon raised to kill her.

With a shout, Dev drew the Spaniard's attention. He aimed the pistol, but it misfired. Dev knew he was in trouble. He had no time to draw his own sword as his horse hurtled between Thorne and the bandit. The blade of the enemy's sword came down. With a curse, Dev jerked the horse to the left. The animal swung into the Spaniard, knocking him down, but not before the sword point bit into Dev's thigh. The horse ran over the enemy, his hooves striking the man's head, killing him instantly.

Dev's lips drew away from his teeth as white-hot pain tore jaggedly up through his leg. Momentarily, he leaned forward, fighting off the blackness. One more shot was fired. He pulled the horse around, going back to finish off the last brigand.

Thorne shakily got to her feet, her hands pressed to her mouth as she saw Dev thundering toward the surviving enemy at the other end of the meadow. He had saved her life. A sob tore from her as she stood there, helpless to do anything but watch.

Dev expertly maneuvered the horse around, bringing his sword down upon the bearded Spaniard. Steel met steel, sparks flying. The guerrilla thrust his blade into Dev's horse in a cunning move. The animal screamed, staggered and then crumpled, taking Dev with him. Dev threw the reins away, leaping out of the saddle before the horse hit the earth.

The Spaniard grinned, knowing he now had the advantage. Dev risked rolling through the horse's flailing feet to escape his enemy. One leg caught him, striking him in the shoulder. With a groan, Dev fell to his knees and crawled away from the deadly hooves. He enemy circled the dying horse, his eyes gleaming with triumph as he lifted his sword to finish off Dev.

Making a supreme effort, Dev leapt to his feet, sword still in hand. Pain raced up his leg, and he staggered. Sweat stung his eyes as he turned to face the stalking guerrilla. Nostrils flared, Dev charged, sword uplifted. He saw the surprise in his enemy's eyes. The bandit hadn't expected an attack from him, only retreat. With a deft parry, Dev was able to get past the man's initial defense. But his quarry was a seasoned fighter, leaping back just as Dev's blade cut smoothly through his shirt, carving a bloody path across his chest. Both of them warily circled each other, breathing heavily. Dev had to finish him off quickly. He could feel the warm wetness of blood pumping down his leg. He would faint very soon, and if he did, he'd leave Thorne in the hands of his enemy. Dev pressed the attack.

Horses swirled around them, lifting the dust, momentarily blinding them. Dev reached to the side of his belt, drawing out a small dagger. Just as soon as the last horse galloped between them, he threw the blade. The man clutched at his chest, dropping the sword. His eyes rounded in disbelief as he crumpled to the dirt. Dev sobbed for breath, turning to make sure no one was stalking him from the rear.

Quiet suddenly invaded the bloody meadow. Dev leaned heavily on the sword to remain upright. Anxiously, he hunted for Thorne amongst the women and children who had survived the guerrilla attack. Four women had been injured and lay moaning on the ground. He saw three children bleeding and crying nearby. Wails filled the air. And then Dev spotted Thorne. She was tearing across the meadow, avoiding the fallen and wounded, skirts lifted. He saw the sheer terror on her pale face as she raced toward him; he also saw something else in her eyes that he couldn't quite interpret. Black dots danced before him, and he knew he was going to faint. Dropping the sword, he fell to his good knee, bending his head downward. Blackness started to claim him and Dev fell to the earth, rolling onto his back. He heard Thorne's cry.

She flew to his side and tore at the white petticoats beneath her skirt. With trembling hands, she tied a piece of the cloth above his leg wound, trying to stanch the bleeding.

"How bad?" Dev growled.

"I—I don't know yet," she gasped. "We need help."

Dev raised his head, staring at the women and children who were cautiously beginning to gather around them. "They're Gypsies?"

Thorne turned, her hand directly on Dev's sword wound to try to stop the bleeding. "Yes. Let me try to get their help. Don't move." She twisted her head in their direction. *"Rom!"* she cried out to the Gypsies, *"Mandel Angitrako Rom!"* She returned her attention to Dev.

"I told them I was an English Gypsy. They'll help their own kind." Or would they? She had lied, but that didn't matter. What mattered was that Dev's life be saved. Could she pass for a *tacho rat,* a true blood? "Dev, put your hand over the wound. I've got to talk to them or they're going to run away and we'll never find them. They'll have a camp, food and herbs so I can help you. Please..."

Thorne's hands were smeared with blood as she got to her feet. She singled out the oldest woman of the huddled group. Carnage surrounded them. She saw several children with wounds and women weeping inconsolably.

"Please," she begged in the Rom language to the old woman, "I am Rom. English Rom. We need your help. Will you take us in?"

The old hag stared up at her, her dark brown eyes narrowed. She clutched a dark purple cape to her stooped shoulders. "Rom?" she spat. "You have gray eyes, girl! You are *gorgio,* not a true blood!"

Desperation wound with fear as Thorne tore her attention from Dev, who lay waxen on the earth. "No, no, I am Rom. Look..." She pulled the scarab from beneath her blouse. "I am Rom."

The hag's eyes widened. *"Gitano inglés,"* she whispered, English Gypsy. And then she reached out, her arthritic fingers reverently touching the amulet Thorne wore. *Drabarni...drabarni..."* she croaked, tears suddenly coming to her eyes. "Doctor...you are a doctor!"

Thorne nodded, a smile coming to her tense features. "Yes, a doctor. And I have need of your help. My—my husband is wounded. Will you take us in? We can pay you. You have your own doctor to help these women and children?"

The hag's eyes rounded and she took a step back, as if struck by lightning. "Our *drabarni* died two months ago, *rawni.* We have great need of your skills. I am sorry I called you *gorgio* before. Your gray eyes... But that does not matter. Stay here! Our camp is far, but we will get help. We were out gathering wood when we were attacked by these despicable vultures."

Thorne reached out, barely touching the woman's shoulder. "Yes, send for help. Perhaps if you or someone else will take the gray horse?"

The hag nodded, her eyes already on Dev's mare. "I will send Maria. She is our best rider."

Taking a deep breath, Thorne nodded. The hag called shrilly to the Gypsy women and children, speaking in rapid Rom mixed with Spanish. The survivors stared at Thorne as if she were a saint suddenly appearing from heaven before them. The natural wariness in their eyes and faces melted into a look of relief. The younger women came forward, embracing Thorne, whispering their thanks for her help. They excitedly pointed to the scarab she wore at her throat. Dazed, Thorne looked around her. So much needed to be done for those who had been raped or wounded in the bandit's attack.

Chapter Eight

"*Rom San?*"

"No. *Raklo.*"

Dev frowned, pulled from unconsciousness by the whisper of women's voices. He felt pressure being applied to his left thigh, and white-hot pain arcing up through his hip. A groan tore from deep inside him. He dragged his eyes open. There, leaning over him, was Thorne. Dev blinked, stiffening as she took a knife and cut his breeches.

"Damn it, woman..." He sucked air between his clenched teeth, his fists digging into the bedding.

Thorne barely glanced up at him as she worked intently over the seeping leg wound. "I'm sorry," she choked. Strands of damp hair clung to her pale features. She pulled the torn breeches away from his injured thigh. The wound was a jagged puncture, which pearled with blood as she pressed around it. The injury was not grave, except that a great deal of blood had been lost, Thorne thought with relief.

Dev groaned again. Where were they? He saw a young girl of perhaps twelve standing next to Thorne, holding a bowl containing a green paste. She was dressed in a bright red skirt and a pink blouse. Her black hair was caught up in a silk scarf of yellow, and a single strand of silver coins adorned her neck. "Where—"

Thorne pulled over a basin of warm water. Manuela had drawn it from one of the many kettles that stood in the center of the Gypsy encampment. "The Gypsies you saved have brought us to their camp, Dev." Her gray eyes were large with fatigue. "You've been unconscious for almost an hour."

Thorne hesitated, trying to still her pounding heart. She bit on her lower lip as she concentrated on cleaning out the swollen wound. "The leader, Old Maximoff, is allowing us to stay here because of what you did to save their women and children." She glanced at the Gypsy girl, knowing she did not understand English. "I've lied and told them I'm pure Gypsy and that you're my *gorgio* husband. Right now, I'm the only doctor they have. Their *drabarni* died a few months ago and they need my services very badly."

Dev relaxed and stared up at the red cotton curtains that framed the small windows above the bed where he lay. The wooden caravan was cramped for space but filled with brilliant colors everywhere, from the gaudy curtains to the dark blue material draped above the bed like a transparent veil. Pain throbbed up and down his leg and he focused back on Thorne.

"Are you all right?" he asked in a hoarse voice.

"I'm fine. It's you I'm worried about." Thorne rinsed out the cloth and then scooped up a handful of the paste. "Grip the bed covers, this is going to hurt. I was hoping you'd still be unconscious so you wouldn't have to feel any more pain."

Dev managed a tight grin. "This is your chance to get even with me."

Thorne glared at him, her hand hovering over the wound. "I'm not like you, Dev. I've seen too much pain in this world already. I don't want to create more. Do you want a stick to clench between your teeth?"

He stared at her hand poised above his leg. "It's going to hurt that much?"

She nodded, her eyes luminous with exhaustion.

"No. Go ahead."

Thorne was as gentle as possible under the circumstances, pushing the paste deep into the wound. She tensed as Dev stiffened. Biting hard on her lower lip, she hurried to finish her task. Beads of sweat popped out on Dev's waxen features. Her throat tightened, as it had when she had ministered to the injured women. Swallowing a barrage of emotions that threatened to engulf her, Thorne wiped her hands on a towel. She took a silk bandage from Manuela to dress the wound. Dev had relaxed with a groan, his eyes shut. Sweat trickled in rivulets down the sides of his face.

"I'm sorry," she whispered, placing the dressing over the wound. "It's a paste of moldy bread crumbs, plantain and coltsfoot."

Dev managed a weak laugh. "Sounds like it will kill me."

"No, it will save your life. Puncture wounds are terrible to treat. I only hope I was able to get that paste to the bottom of it."

"I think you did, Gypsy." Dev felt a chill rack him. He opened his eyes, staring dazedly at Thorne as she worked over him. God, she was beautiful. And courageous. The battle came back to him and he frowned. "Why did you enter the fray? Why didn't you stay where I told you?"

"I couldn't stand hearing the screams for help, that's why!" She finished tying the knot in the bandage and lifted her chin. "Don't be angry with me. You're in no condition to be shouting at anyone. You need rest and sleep."

Dev stared at the Gypsy girl. "Does she know what we're talking about?"

"No. She knows Rom and some Spanish, is all."

"What about the rest?"

"None of them know English as far as I can tell."

Dev relaxed. "Now's your chance," he said harshly.

Thorne wiped her damp brow. "What are you mumbling about?"

"All you have to do is tell your Gypsy friends I've kidnapped you and you'll be free. They'll have my throat slit."

Swallowing hard, Thorne saw what the pain was doing to Dev. The corners of his mouth were turned in and his large hands were white knuckled as he knotted the bed covers. "No," she told him softly, "I won't do that."

He barely raised his lids, staring at her through the gloom. "Why?"

"Because..."

Dev released his grip on the covers and wrapped his fingers around her slender wrist. "Why? Any other English bitch would use this opportunity. Hell, anyone else would have left me to bleed to death in that meadow and made good their escape." His fevered blue eyes bored into hers. "Tell me why...."

Thorne remained motionless in his grasp. "Because you're like any other hurt animal, Captain. Just as I would never let a child die in a gutter in London, I wouldn't let you die, either, if I could help it."

Dev released her, disbelief burning in his gaze. "I'm your enemy."

"No," Thorne countered huskily, "you see me as your enemy. You've never been mine."

Pain surged through Dev in unbroken waves and he released Thorne from his grip. He clenched his teeth, fighting the agony. "When will I be able to ride? We have to get to Madrid."

Thorne stood, disbelief mirrored in her eyes. "A week. The wound is a puncture and did no major damage. The loss of blood will make you weak. That is what stops you from going to Madrid sooner." She walked quickly to the door of the caravan, the wood creaking beneath her feet. The Rom girl absently followed, holding the bowl of paste to her skinny form. Thorne stood in the doorway, the sunlight spilling into the gray depths, her heart pounding with anger. Damn him! Damn him to hell! One moment he could be as chivalrous as any knight, galloping to the rescue of those in need. In the next, all he could focus on was getting rid of her.

"Come," she coaxed the child, touching her shoulder.

As they walked down the three rickety wooden steps to the ground, Thorne wearily tried to gather her shredded emotions.

A candle sputtered nastily on the edge of the table in the caravan. Thorne shifted position, once again wringing out the cloth in cool water and gently wiping Dev's naked upper body. When she relieved Manuela earlier, Thorne had undressed him and placed several blankets over him. Between the needs of the injured Rom and her worry over Dev's condition, Thorne had eaten little throughout the remainder of the day. Manuela had come back bearing a plate of food and Thorne had forced herself to eat.

Even in the poor light, Thorne realized with a sinking feeling that Dev had lost a great deal of blood. His skin was colorless, with a gleam of perspiration beneath the auburn hair on his chest. In London, Thorne had treated only women and infant girls. The sight of Dev's naked body had shocked her at first, but she shook off the feeling. This was no time to stand on societal conventions.

As Thorne stared down at Dev, she no longer felt embarrassed. Exhaustion stalked her and she dabbed the cloth across his tense face. Old Maximoff had insisted that she keep Dev in the caravan and the family who owned it would sleep outdoors until he improved. But then, most Rom slept outside unless it was raining or snowing, so it wasn't a total inconvenience to the family.

A groan tore from Dev, and Thorne placed her hand upon his shoulder. She was wildly aware of the tensile strength of his powerfully built body. His lashes fluttered open, eyes bare slits beneath them.

"Dev?"

He stared at her a long moment, the silence stretching between them. He opened his mouth to speak, his voice cracking. "Shannon? Shannon, is that you?"

Thorne stirred and leaned over him, tenderly pushing several damp strands of hair off his fevered brow. "No, Dev. Shannon's dead, remember? This is Thorne."

Tears rolled from the corners of his eyes as he weakly grasped her arm. "No...no...you're my Shannon...my Shannon...."

Her heart wrenched as she saw his tears. "Oh, Dev... no...she's gone. I'm sorry."

A look of desperation crossed his features and his hand tightened painfully on Thorne's arm. "No...God, no! Shannon...please, I love you. I need you."

A sob rose in Thorne's aching throat as she allowed Dev to pull her across his chest. He was delirious, mumbling almost incoherently as he drew her down... down to meet his mouth. Panic gave way to the need to comfort him and the stirring of some unknown force within her. She had not realized the depth of Dev's feelings for the woman he loved beyond the grave. The fact that he held such a fierce, loyal love triggered Thorne's need to give it back to him, to try to atone for what the English had taken from him. His fingers were hot and fevered as he framed her face. She closed her eyes, allowing him to hold her against him.

As his mouth trembled against her lips, a small cry broke from Thorne. Their tears met and mingled where their mouths joined and he deepened the long, tender exploration of her.

"Shannon..." Dev breathed against her. "Beloved..." He tasted the lush softness of her lips beneath his mouth once again. Her flesh was velvet to him, her scent a heady drug as he drank more deeply of her shy offering. God, sweet God, Shannon was here with him, her body so pliant and comforting to his feverish state of uncertain fear. Dev drew back inches, looking into her luminous dove gray eyes. All the grief he had held for so long rose up within him and he sobbed raggedly, staring at her face surrounded by the darkness. "I've missed you so much, Shan—" he wept brokenly now "—and the child we never had. Oh God, I've been half a man since you left. Please, come back. Come back. I need you... need you..."

"Hush, beloved... everything will be all right. I'll always be here with you. Always."

His fingers tightened on her flesh and he kissed her hard, as if to convince himself that she was real, not a dream. She was here. She was his. "Promise, Shan?"

"I'll always be a part of your heart, Dev. Always."

Gradually, Dev released his grip and lay back, falling once again into a delirious state.

Thorne pressed her hand against her bruised lips to stop from sobbing. Tears glittered in her eyes as she stared down at the man who had changed her life in so many ways. He

was the King of Swords. He had cut off her hair. He had
humiliated her. He had shown her kindness and yes, even
tenderness on occasion through their stormy passage with
each other. But when he had kissed her, her world as she
knew it shattered. For those moments in time, Thorne had
felt what it was like to be loved fiercely by a man. And just
as shatteringly, in the moments afterward, she realized that
she loved Dev...with an equally growing force.

The gray light of dawn peeked through the drawn scarlet curtains as Dev awoke. He felt weakened and exhausted. Someone was lying next to him. He shifted his
limited attention. It was Thorne. Shock coursed through
him, momentarily erasing the throbbing pain in his leg.
What was she doing here? Dev felt the silk of her hair beneath his jaw, the warmth of her small hand on his chest,
her body tucked next to his in sleep. Reflexively, Dev
stroked her shoulder. A rooster crowed and he was vaguely
aware of people moving around outside the caravan.
Slowly, the events of yesterday seeped into his groggy mind.

The smell of an oak fire and the mouth-watering odor of
food reminded Dev that he was hungry. Thorne stirred, and
automatically he tightened his embrace, needing her nearness. His eyes darkened when he realized she could have
been killed yesterday. Regardless of her size, she was a
spitfire. Sometimes foolish but nevertheless courageous.
Dev felt a swell of unaccountable emotion sweep through
him. Last night... His brows drew together as he tried to
piece bits of his delirium together. Shannon? No, Thorne?
He had kissed one of them last night. Shannon was dead.
He twisted his head to look at Thorne. Despite the dark
smudges beneath her eyes, she was lovely. Had he kissed
her? God, he remembered the hot, sweet softness of a
woman's lips.

Thorne slowly awoke, feeling deliciously happy as she
moved through those mindless levels to wakefulness. The
scent of Dev surrounded her and she stretched like a feline
against him, glorying in those stolen seconds of bliss. She

knew he was awake when he embraced her gently in return, and she forced her eyes open.

"You're awake," Thorne murmured, dragging herself upright. Her blouse was stained with blood and her skirt badly wrinkled, but she didn't care. All of her attention focused upon Dev. Anxiously, Thorne searched his face for some telltale sign that he was better. She put her hand upon his brow. It was cool. Relief surged through her. "No fever," Thorne uttered thankfully.

Dev's blue gaze met and held her drowsy, dove gray eyes. Her hair was tousled and in need of a brushing, her eyes puffy and her mouth a lush reminder of what they had shared. "Last night," he began with an effort, his voice thick and scratchy. "Last night, did I kiss you?"

Thorne looked away, removing her hand from his brow. The silence magnified her raw emotions. "You were delirious," she whispered. "You were calling out for Shannon."

Dev heard the pain in Thorne's voice but did not understand it. She was shy with him, more than ever before. He searched his memory for more details that refused to come forth. "Did I—I mean, did I hurt you?"

She gave a shake of her head. "No."

"Thorne, look at me."

The tone of his voice went through her like the shaft of a sword. Hot tears filled her eyes and she refused to look at Dev, not wanting him to see her so emotional.

Dev reached out, his fingers trailing down her arm. "Thorne, please . . ."

Drawing a ragged breath, Thorne slowly turned her head toward him. Her throat constricted as she was once again privileged to see Devlin Kyle without his soldier's mask in place. "Wh-what?"

"I asked, did I hurt you? Your lips, they're swollen."

Thorne sucked in a breath as he lightly touched her lips with his fingertips. "Y-you didn't mean to. You thought I was Shannon and—you wanted to see her so badly that—"

Dev tightened his fingers on her upper arm, his eyes narrowing. "That what?"

"Don't do this to me, Dev. I've been through so much. Leave me a shred of dignity. Please..."

His mouth tightened as he read the anguish in Thorne's face. He had hurt her. She sat there, hands clasped in her lap, head bowed. There was anguish reflected in her eyes, and he felt like an animal. "I'm sorry," he muttered, releasing her. "I didn't mean to hurt you, Thorne. I was out of my head."

Dev didn't understand! Thorne swallowed her tears and held his stormy gaze. His kisses had inflamed her, triggered her young, untutored body to brilliant life. How could she tell him that his touch hadn't hurt, only exhilarated in a way she had never known existed before? "You miss her, Dev. And—you loved her deeply." A tender smile fled across her mouth. "I only hope that the man whom I marry one day will love me half as much as you loved Shannon. I'll be the most fortunate woman in the world."

Dev lay there, staring up at her. Thorne was bathed in the dawn light. At that instant, he knew this new feeling in his heart did not belong to Shannon, it centered around Thorne. Despite her shyness those huge, understanding gray eyes told him everything. And he wanted to open his arms and ask Thorne to come to him willingly to share what he felt for her. But as his gaze moved down to her swollen lips, he experienced Thorne's pain and tasted the bitterness of their reality. He could not make her his. Even if she consented, her reputation would be ruined forever if he gave in to such folly. She had to return to her English world and he to his own, with his freed brother. Something deep and primal within him wanted Thorne, all of her. Dev sensed a change in her, an unsureness that he read as fear of him, as a man, for what he had done to her.

"I—uh, didn't do anything else except kiss you, did I?"

Thorne shook her head. "No."

Dev swore softly, throwing an arm across his eyes. "I'm sorry, Thorne. I never meant to." Liar. He had been wanting to kiss her for quite a while, but not this way.

She slowly moved off the bed so she wouldn't disturb his wounded leg. "I'll have much to do this morning."

Dev didn't blame her for wanting to escape his presence. He turned his head toward her. Thorne looked like a Gypsy, he thought, except for her short hair. "Go ahead."

The sun was overhead when Thorne finished her rounds. She peeked in on Pilar and her baby, Juan. They were sleeping soundly. And, as always, Pilar's mother was there along with the two aunts, watching anxiously over the girl and her child. Thorne smiled to herself as she walked through the busy encampment. Rom women cared for their families with a fierce, protective loyalty. Did she feel any different about Dev?

Thorne slowed her step, digesting the emotions that Dev had brought unexpectedly to life in her by kissing her the night before. She touched her lips. They were still tender from the strength of his mouth, and unbidden desire simmered within her for no reasonable explanation.

As she opened the door to their caravan, Thorne saw that Dev was awake.

"You should be resting."

Dev turned his head toward her, hungrily taking in her form. Thorne looked ravishing in the white peasant blouse, which provocatively revealed the swell of her breasts. The bright green skirt and the string of gold coins around her neck made her appear a Gypsy in every respect. A glimmer of need burned in his eyes as he watched her plant her hand on her hips.

"Come over here, Gypsy."

Thorne didn't trust Dev. His voice was rich velvet in invitation, and a strange fluttering sensation began deep within her.

She walked to the bed. Dev had propped himself up with several pillows, the blankets in disarray around him. His injured thigh was exposed and Dev felt heat moving into her cheeks. "You shouldn't be sitting up," she muttered. "You need time to heal, time to—"

"Come here," Dev coaxed, reaching out and catching her hand, drawing her to the side of the bed. He searched her features. Gone was the child he had captured. Instead, he saw a very lovely woman. "Before you start worrying about others, you need to look at yourself."

Startled, her pulse leaping at the base of her throat, Thorne froze. "Wh-what are you talking about?"

Dev tugged her hand. "Sit, I won't bite you."

Reluctantly, Thorne sat and faced him. The sight of Dev naked to the waist sent strange and twisting signals throughout her. She could barely take her gaze form his mouth, heatedly recalling his kisses. Shaken, she clasped her hands in her lap. "I just came to see how you were."

"Now my Thorne is prickly," Dev teased. "Look at you. You've got dark circles beneath your eyes. Manuela's brother, Pablo, was in here just a while ago giving me some water, and he said you'd been working all morning." He picked up her chapped and reddened hand. "Shouldn't the doctor take her own advice and rest every once in a while?"

Thorne pulled her hand from his fingers. "Now you sound like my mother," she began irritably, and then she realized what she had said. Tears sprang to her eyes and she turned from Dev's sharpened gaze.

"Did you work like this in London, too?" he prodded quietly. "And your mother had to remind you to rest?"

Thorne nodded, biting down hard on her lower lip to stop from crying. There was so much about these new feelings that she didn't understand. God, how much she missed her mother. "How could I rest when a dying child was brought in?"

Dev felt suddenly weary. "Pablo told me that since we were brought to camp, you've been working and have hardly eaten a thing. How many people were hurt by the bandits?"

Thorne rubbed her face tiredly, excruciatingly aware of Dev's closeness. She was awed by the warmth that he was automatically able to establish with her. Had it been the kiss shared between them? Agonizing over her lack of experience in such matters, Thorne allowed the weighty question to be pushed aside. She got up and went to the cabinet opposite the bed, pulling out the clean dressing and bandages that Manuela had made for her the day before.

"Four women and three children," she answered, pulling the green paste out of the cupboard and setting it on the edge of the bed.

Dev watched her through half-closed eyes as she assembled the necessary items to change the dressing on his thigh. Thorne's fragility was apparent, her flesh drawn tautly across her cheeks. Was there any way to give her a reprieve from this ordeal? To allow her to rest from the responsibility suddenly piled on her small, broken shoulders? And yet she was strong, Dev acknowledged, in a way he'd not seen in a woman before. Despite Thorne's personal trauma, she was able to draw on an inner source of strength and give it unselfishly to others. There were so many things he suddenly wanted to discuss with her, but the time wasn't right.

"What about the women?" he asked, watching as she took a knife and slit the bandage around his leg. He inhaled sharply as air hit the wound.

Thorne glanced at Dev. His face was pale as she lifted the soaked dressing. The flesh around the wound was no longer red and angry looking. A pleased look came to her eyes. "The women are little more than young girls, Dev. Pilar, who is seventeen, was raped. She's—" Thorne swallowed hard, her hands trembling as she carefully began to remove the old paste "—she's in so much pain."

Dev tensed as he felt her cool fingers upon his flesh. His eyes flashed with anger. "I killed the bastard who did it to her. That's some consolation. I saw too many of our women in Ireland raped by the British, and I swore I'd never allow any of my men ever to hurt a woman or child while I was in charge of them."

She glanced up, meeting his eyes, which were filled with fury.

He snorted softly, fists digging into the bedding. "I broke my own rule with you, Thorne. I hurt you."

Thorne shuddered, Pilar's condition all too fresh in her memory. "At least you never allowed anyone to hurt me the way Pilar has been hurt, and for that I'm grateful."

Dev closed his eyes against the waves of pain now moving through him. Sweat beaded his brow and upper lip. "Any other Englishwoman would hate me for what I've done. Why don't you? I don't understand," he gritted out.

Thorne rubbed the sweat away from her forehead with the back of her arm, barely able to deal with Dev's probing questions as she changed the dressing. Every time he tensed, she felt as if a knife were being plunged through her heart. She always felt the pain of those she ministered to, but with Dev, she felt it even more. "Just a little longer," she begged him softly. "I'm sorry. I don't mean to hurt you, but the wound is looking much better."

His lips were drawn away from his teeth, flesh glistening as he managed a choked laugh. "The pain I'm experiencing is just payment for hurting you, Gypsy, believe me." And then he passed out.

Thorne managed a shaky sigh of relief and hurriedly finished. At least now Dev wouldn't feel the pain. Afterward, she gently drew the covers over him. The quiet of the early afternoon invaded the caravan and Thorne sat with her hand on his naked shoulder, simply needing Dev's presence. Despite the shortness of his auburn hair, he was devastatingly handsome in her eyes. Thorne wearily recalled when she had first seen him and how savage he had looked to her. Now, as her gaze lingered on his face, she saw, perhaps for the first time, his vulnerability as a human being. Not as a man who lived the role of a hard-bitten soldier, but a man with his own rules of compassion toward others.

Thorne leaned over and pressed a chaste kiss to his damp brow. The ache in her heart was growing deeper with each passing minute since that shattering kiss. The realization that she loved him didn't make her feel any better. He could never know of her feelings.

Thorne straightened the covers over Dev. A few days ago, she had thrown a blanket over her head in mortification when she had awakened to see him bathing naked in a stream. Now all his nakedness did was spur a hunger to life within her that she had never experienced before.

Thorne removed her slippers and moved quietly to the bed, hugging the edge of it in an effort not to touch Dev. God knew, she wanted to. She yearned simply to turn over and find her way into his strong, protective arms. As Thorne closed her eyes, giving in to exhaustion, she allowed love to suffuse her. Those fleeting feelings of joy would be the only thing she would ever be able to experience.

Chapter Nine

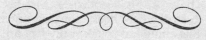

Dev stirred and opened his eyes. The pain in his leg had abated somewhat, and he felt better. He turned his head and his heart beat strongly in his chest. Thorne was in slumber, a mere six inches from him. His eyes widened in appreciation as he saw her withdraw slowly from the folds of sleep. She had tucked her hands against her breast, knees drawn upward. The thin cotton peasant blouse hid little of the swell of her breasts, and he watched in fascination as they rose and fell with each breath she took. The day was spent. A mauve-colored dusk now slanted through the small windows of the caravan, lending a pink quality to everything, including Thorne's translucent flesh. God, how he wanted to kiss her, to feel those ripe, sweet lips against his mouth once again.

Dev frowned, recalling his fevered dreams earlier of making love to Thorne. He slid his hand those few inches and gently stroked Thorne's rose-colored cheek. Her black lashes fluttered open, revealing slumberous gray eyes.

"Just lie there," he told her in a hushed voice as he continued to lightly stroke her cheek and the delicate line of her jaw. Thorne's lips parted, her eyes widening and focusing upon him. A slight smile pulled at the corners of Dev's mouth. "Your flesh is like a ripe peach, did you know that? A beautiful, smooth peach, and your eyes are the color of a mourning dove's breast." His gaze moved to her short hair. "And hair the color of a raven's wing with blue highlights. And lips... lips like a ripe red apple. Is there anything about you that hasn't been touched by nature? In my dreams of late, I wonder if you won't suddenly flee from me and sink back into the arms of nature and disappear forever. Will you, sweet Gypsy, who embraces those who hate or distrust you? Will you be like fog on a sunlit morning and disappear?"

Thorne closed her eyes, needing Dev's touch, needing the mesmerizing balm of his deep voice. She lay quietly, allowing him to stroke her cheek, soaking up each featherlight caress. She could not speak, only feel and absorb his trembling hand worship her face.

Dev's eyes darkened. "Look at me, Gypsy."

Slowly, Thorne lifted her lashes, meeting and melting beneath Dev's midnight blue eyes. Her heart blossomed fiercely with such a deluge of ripened emotions that she fell helplessly beneath the spell of his gaze. His face was tense and he stared hard at her, as if trying to look into her heart. "What is it?" she asked in a tremulous voice.

"I don't know...I can't explain it. At least not yet. You've changed."

A tender smile crossed Thorne's lips. "No...not me. You."

A frown furrowed Dev's brow as he reluctantly removed his hand. So few inches separated them, and yet it might as well have been miles. "That's impossible."

She stretched languidly, no longer afraid of him. "Wearing the clothes of a Gypsy hasn't changed me from what I was before, Dev."

He reached out, fingering the small necklace of gold coins around her slender neck. "Who gave you these?"

"Old Maximoff. Last night at dinner, he made a speech about how we had saved their families. In gratitude, he gave me the necklace. Really, he owes you even more. If you hadn't gone to help—"

A wry smile curved his mouth. "Did I have a choice with you along?" He allowed the necklace to fall against her flesh, watching her pulse beat rapidly at the base of her throat.

Thorne slipped her hands beneath her head, a dreamy expression in her half-closed eyes. "Yes. You could have been ruthless and not gone to help even though I wanted you to."

His scowl deepened. "Women and children deserve protection."

She reached out, her fingers resting on the back of his scarred hand. "That is one of the many things that I've come to like about you."

Dev hid his shock over her gesture. Her fingers were warm in comparison to the coolness of his. "I didn't think there was anything to like about me, Gypsy."

Thorne removed her hand, tucking it beneath her cheek once again. "Do you enjoy being a brigand, pretending you're without a heart, Captain? Because now I know differently. I've seen you care for me when you didn't have to. The time I vomited, you held me. And when I had nightmares, you came to my side. Despite your hate of me, you have tried to treat me fairly. You're not a blackguard without a soul as I first thought."

Dev took in a deep, ragged breath, lost in the warmth of her dove gray eyes. "I'm a criminal, Thorne," he began, his tone uncompromising. "I've hurt you more than I ever have any woman in my life. And for that, I can't forgive myself. You could have run from me and escaped here in the Rom camp, but you've stayed."

"Where would I have gone, Dev? I want to get home to my father. If I have to go to Madrid to do that, then I will." Her voice faltered. "I know you won't hurt me, I have nothing to fear from you. Before, I was afraid. I'm not now."

Dev slowly rolled onto his back, glaring up at the curtained ceiling. "Either you're a saint, Thorne, or a dream that will someday leave me."

"What do you mean, Dev?" She slowly rose into a sitting position, trying to tame her hair into some semblance of order.

What did he mean? Sweet Jesus, he'd never met a woman of such incredible tolerance and kindness. Didn't Thorne ever hold a grudge or experience hatred? Or anger so burning and deep that it left an indelible mark on her soul, as it had on his? He turned, looking at her in the dusk, feeling all his frustration melting away beneath her large, understanding eyes.

"Dreams are such fragile things, Thorne. You're a dream to me."

She offered him a soft smile. "Dreams are strong enough to hold the morrow's future, Dev. That's what Mama always told me. Without dreams we lose our hope, and then the will to live." With a shy laugh she added, "You're the first man to tell me I'm a dream. Although once a gentleman finds out that I work at orphanages in London and I'm part Gypsy, I may be responsible for some nightmares."

Dev reached over, capturing her small hand within his. "Don't let anyone tell you you're not a dream."

Thorne's smile dissolved as she drowned in the husky inference of his low voice. "Only if you'll believe me that dreams are strong enough to carry tomorrow's promise."

Squeezing her hand, Dev nodded. "All right, I'll accept that belief from you. You're my dream come true."

Thorne's heart fluttered in her breast and she avoided his warming look. "Shannon was your dream come true, Dev," she countered in an aching voice. "You loved her with your life."

Dev maintained a grip on her hand, holding her tender gaze. "The love I hold for Shannon will always be in my heart, Thorne. She was a wonderful woman in many ways, but she didn't have your depth of understanding or sensitivity."

Thorne stirred uncomfortably. What was he trying to say? He hated the English and therefore her. "It's almost dark. I'm going to have to see my patients. Do you want anything before I leave? A drink of water? Something to eat?"

He released her hand. "Just come back when you're done, Gypsy. That's all I want."

Dev watched her get up and leave. He felt oddly contented, a feeling reminiscent of the time when he was married. Thorne was apparently more rattled by their conversation. He saw the uncertainty in her expressive eyes and the slight tremble of her hands. He lay there long after she left, wondering what in hell he was doing. He had no right to lay claim to Thorne, regardless of how she responded to his touch and voice. He had seen smoldering desire in her gray eyes when he had run his fingers across her smooth, velvet flesh. Angry with himself, and caught in a trap between his emotions and what he knew must be done, Dev forced himself to go back to sleep and allow his body to mend. As he drifted off, he knew that every time Thorne came back to lie at his side, the temptation to take her would become greater and greater. And then what? He sank into a series of torrid dreams involving him and Thorne, caught up in the web of her guileless innocence.

A full moon rose rapidly as night closed in on the camp. Thorne washed her hands in the stream after finishing her nightly rounds. She entered the caravan and found Dev awake.

"You look very tired," she said in greeting, "and in pain."

"You read me like a book, Gypsy."

She poured a bit of the wine into a mug and then added a pinch of opium to it. "Losing so much blood will do that."

"How long do you think before I'll regain some of my strength?" Dev asked, watching as she sat down next to him on the bed and slipped her arm beneath his shoulders.

Thorne allowed him to lean against her and pressed the mug to his cracked lips. "Tomorrow you should begin to feel much better."

Dev drank the mug's contents and then relaxed against the softness of her breast. He heard the rapid beat of her heart beneath his ear and closed his eyes. "Thank you."

She put the mug aside and then laid Dev back on the pillow, covering his chest with the blanket. "Loss of blood always makes one feel like a weakened kitten," she murmured, watching his eyes begin to close.

Blindly, Dev hunted for her hand, finding it. "Enough of this medical chatter. Come to bed, Gypsy. I need you."

She sat there in the grayness, watching Dev sink quickly into sleep, his strong fingers wrapped firmly around her smaller hand. Thorne's eyes darkened with pain as she wished that he had meant his final, whispered words. If only Dev truly did need her.

Later, after washing and slipping into a cotton gown, Thorne joined him. She blew out the taper, the silver moonlight streaming through the windows and across the bed as she lay down beside Dev. Amusement tinged her exhaustion as she rested her head in the crook of his shoulder and closed her eyes. Before, she had been frightened of sleeping with Dev. Now she looked forward to these rare moments. If this was the way her mother had welcomed her father into her bed, then they had indeed been happy.

Thorne felt a twinge of pain, realizing that she would not sleep with Dev after they left the Rom camp. He knew now that she would not try to escape, so there was no reason for them to sleep together. This last thought clung to her dreams. During the night, she crept closer to Dev until the length of her gowned body flowed against the harder planes of his, finding an edge of peace.

"*Rawni! Rawni!*" The banging at the door of the caravan jerked Thorne out of sleep. Automatically, Dev's arm tightened around her as she tried to rise. They lay in a tangle, her leg thrown across his good one. She didn't have time to feel embarrassed as Dev released her so that she could sit up.

"I'm coming," Thorne mumbled, stumbling from the bed. It was barely dawn and she held out her hand in front of her so she wouldn't bump into anything. She groped for the back door. Manuela's tense face came into view.

"Hurry, *Rawni!* It's Juan! Pilar can't do anything. We need you, we need you!"

* * *

An hour later, Thorne quietly entered their caravan. She saw Dev sitting up, the blankets pulled around his waist, his features intent and worried.

"What's wrong?" he asked quietly, watching as she shed the cloak and hung it back up on the wooden peg.

"The baby, Dev," Thorne said in a voice barely above a whisper. "He was in convulsion." She came and sat on the bed, taking in the natural strength of his features. Hot tears assailed her eyes and her voice grew wobbly. "I feel so helpless. Juan's all right now. I gave him some opium powder to quiet him." She raised her hands, burying her face in them, her voice muffled. "I was afraid he was going to die—they were all looking at me as if I knew what could cure him. I don't know how, Dev. I don't know how—"

"Come here," he said gruffly, pulling her into the safety of his arms. She came without hesitation. Dev tucked her in beside him, releasing a sigh as she rested her head beneath his jaw. "Now listen to me." His voice was gritty. "You're doing all you can. Look how many lives you've saved. Don't count the ones whose time it is to leave."

Thorne felt a jagged sob welling up from deep within her and she shut her eyes tightly, needing his care. "Oh, Dev, I love the children so much... and Juan's so tiny and so helpless. I know the bump on his head is causing his problems, but I don't know how to make it go away. I gave him opium, a sedative and painkiller. All it will do is make him sleep. I don't know if it will make the convulsions go away." A sob choked her and Thorne placed her arms around Dev. "Hold me, just hold me," she pleaded brokenly, "I feel so alone."

"Hush, Gypsy, you're never alone. You have me." Dev closed his eyes, resting his jaw against her cap of silky black hair. "I'll take care of you, I promise." He felt her begin to tremble, realizing she was trying to stop crying. "Weep, Gypsy. Weep for everything you've gone through."

He kissed her hair, inhaling her natural feminine fragrance, thinking how small and soft she felt against him.

He began to rock her back and forth in his arms and
Thorne clung to him. As each sob wracked her body, Dev
held her a little tighter, one hand against her head, the other
against her back. "It's going to be fine, Gypsy, you'll see.
The baby won't die. He'll get better because you care. Your
love will heal him, my sweet Thorne."

The sun's first rays were barely crawling over the horizon as Thorne's weeping abated. Dev's chest was wet with
her spent tears, but she made no apology, content to be
held, her head resting against the wiry mat of his hair. The
slow, even cadence of his heart restored stability to her torn
emotions and she sought only his nearness. The gentle
stroke of his trembling fingers through her hair sent an ache
of fierce love through her. He had given her what she
needed so desperately—care. New, euphoric sensations
raced through her. Was this how love felt? That feeling of
protection coupled with a spreading warmth throughout
her? Was this wonderful feeling what her mother had felt
when her father held her? No wonder they had loved each
other so much.

"You know," Dev said in a hushed voice, "when I was
a boy, I used to look forward to the times when my mother
would hold me. Even as a seven-year-old, when I broke my
toe out in the field where I was plowing, my mother's touch
was healing. I knew I wasn't supposed to cry, but I couldn't
help myself, the pain was so great. I hobbled in from the
field with tears streaming down my face. My mother was
outside our hut, peeling potatoes, when she heard me crying. I remember her running around the corner, her black
skirt flying as she came to me. I was glad Father wasn't
around, because at that moment I needed to be held and
comforted. When her arms swept around me and she
crushed me to her, the pain in my toe went away." One
corner of his mouth quirked upward and Dev gazed down
at Thorne. "I know what it means to be held when the
world has fallen apart around you, Gypsy." He leaned over,
pressing a kiss to her wrinkled brow. "And I'm glad you
came to me when you needed to be held."

Thorne stared up at Dev, drowning in the warmth of his gaze. Her lips parted and she slid her hand up his chest. "Oh, Dev..." she quavered.

He groaned, unable to resist the invitation she had placed before him, her small hand a brand against his tightening flesh. "God, Thorne," he rasped, "I need you, too." He molded his mouth gently upon her untutored lips. Heat roared through him into throbbing, hard life as he ran his mouth lightly across her soft, yielding lips. Thorne tasted of the salt of her spent tears and Dev gently kissed them away.

"Tears of life, Gypsy," he said thickly. "Tears spilled out of love for others." He framed her face with his hands, teaching her how to respond to a kiss between a man and a woman.

Thorne moaned softly as his mouth settled firmly against her own. Her heart pounded without respite and she leaned upward, wanting, needing, all that he offered her. This time, Dev was conscious. This time, he knew he was kissing her and not Shannon. A dizzying thrill swept through her and she leaned heavily against him as he deepened the kiss. The moistness of his hot breath flowed against her, and she tasted his maleness, spiraling into an ocean of new and thrilling sensations. His mouth was firm and provoking against her lips, molding and cajoling, teaching her how to respond to him in return. The seconds sped by and Thorne became enmeshed in the utter pleasure of his mouth, breath and heady masculine smell.

Gradually, ever so gradually, Dev ended the kiss. When Thorne's lashes lifted, confusion registered in her eyes. He tenderly cradled her face inches from his own. "You're as sweet and giving in your kiss as you are to those you heal, Gypsy."

His fingers tightened briefly, his brow drawing into a scowl. What had he done? Why had he done it? Those questions slammed into Dev and he reluctantly released Thorne, watching as she sat up, fingers resting upon her glistening lips. He suddenly looked away, his profile rugged and uncompromising in the light of dawn. "Damn it,

Thorne, this can't continue—shouldn't have happened," he said hoarsely. "I'm sorry. I had no right. No right at all." His nostrils flared as frustration destroyed the aching feelings in his heart.

"Wh-what are you talking about?" she asked tremulously, her eyes large and dazed.

Dev pinned her with his thunderstorm black eyes. "You. You're an earl's daughter. One of the gentry. I'm a felon wanted in England. We're as different as night and day, Thorne."

"But, Dev—"

"No, damn it! What I did was wrong." His mouth thinned into a hard line. "If I could, I'd get up right now and leave you alone. I'd sleep under this damn caravan instead of in this bed with you."

Thorne winced, her hand moving to her heart. "A-are you upset because I'm English? Is that it?"

He could barely tolerate her anguished gaze. He had to lie in order to protect Thorne from himself. He wanted Thorne as he had no other woman, not even Shannon. That thought shattered him, and Dev glared over at her. "Yes, you're English! And you're titled. And you have money. You have a home. Property. You have everything I don't, Thorne."

A sob welled up in her throat and she slowly got off the bed. "I—I see."

Grimly, Dev held her baffled expression. How in the hell could he make her realize that if he made her his woman, her entire life would be destroyed by his one selfish act? She didn't deserve that from him. Not after what she had done to help him and so many others. Frustration ate at him. He clenched his fists. "I hope you do," Dev bit out savagely. "We may have to play this charade as husband and wife while we're here, but I'll be glad when we can leave. Now get dressed. I'm hungry and I want to eat."

Stunned, Thorne stared at him. And then a flush of anger brought color to her tear-stained face. "I don't understand you," she cried. "One moment you're so kind and the next—"

"I'm Irish, Thorne. That says everything. A natural enemy to the English. Now stop trying to explain my behaviour and fix me something to eat! I want to get well as soon as possible, so we can leave this godforsaken place."

No, her heart screamed at her. Dev couldn't be serious. He had been gentle and passionate with her moments before. How could he turn into a rabid animal and snap at her like this? She trembled beneath his icy blue gaze. "No—no, I don't believe you. The way you held me when I needed comfort..."

"Damn you, woman, get it through your head. I was pretending you were Shannon."

Searing pain tore through Thorne as she took a step back, gasping. Her luminous eyes lost their anger, and shadowed bleakness filled them. Dully, she turned away, gathering up her clothes and leaving the caravan.

Dev sat there breathing hard, his chest rising and falling with exertion. Rubbing his face harshly with his hand, he cursed roundly. Damn himself! Damn life! His words had shredded Thorne. He had seen the adoration in her eyes after he'd been foolish enough to follow his instinct to kiss away her pain. The sizzling heat they had shared was far more than just a meeting of flesh. It was a meeting of hearts, of souls, tentatively reaching out to comfort each other.

"Sweet Jesus," he muttered, leaning back and closing his eyes. What was he going to do to keep her at arm's length? Thorne was a babe to the fires of passion in comparison with himself. It was his responsibility to control the situation so that his idiotic actions didn't hurt her any more than they already had. As he stared blankly out the window at the awakening camp, Dev drew in a ragged breath. How was it possible that he had fallen in love with Thorne? When had it happened? How?

As he lay back, exhausted by his emotions, the pain in his heart was far greater than that in his throbbing leg. Dev dragged his arm across his eyes, trying to blot out the whole miserable scene. The next few days would be a living hell for both of them. If he kept Thorne at bay, she would retreat from him. If he could destroy the love for him that he saw in her eyes, she would be free to find a man back in England. Someone who could give her what she deserved—a home, security and happiness.

He could give her none of those things. If he allowed her to continue to fall in love with him, she would become a felon's wife. It would be no life at all for Thorne. She was used to stability, and he had none. Unclenching his fist, Dev prayed that in the next few days he could weather Thorne's suffering. *God, give me strength. I love her too much...too much....*

Chapter Ten

It was well past the evening meal when Thorne forced herself to leave the women at the fire and take Dev his food. Since their confrontation two nights before, she dreaded going to the caravan. The apricot dusk shed a pale tint across the encampment, the evening soft and fragrant with the scents of spring. Each wooden step creaked loudly and Thorne cringed, opening the door. She stood at the entrance, allowing her eyes to adjust to the gloom.

Dev was sitting on the edge of the bed, his head bowed. Thorne swallowed hard, setting the bowl of fragrant venison stew on the cupboard. She could see the glistening sweat across his naked upper body and fought a powerful urge to place her arms around his shoulders and comfort him. Her flesh prickled as Dev slowly raised his head and pinned her with his stormy gaze. For an instant, his expression softened his face and she saw his gentler side. Just as quickly, that look disappeared.

"Your dinner," she offered lamely.

"Thank you."

Thorne turned to leave.

"Wait."

She froze. "What?"

"Don't you think the Rom are going to get suspicious because you never spend any time with me? You're never here."

Anger sizzled through Thorne and she whirled around, her eyes black. "This has been going on for two days and it never bothered you before! Why should it now?"

Dev reached for the bowl, dragging it toward him. He picked up the wooden spoon. "You need to help me stand and exercise my leg as soon as I get done eating."

Thorne wanted to flee. Even now, she ached to hear Dev ask her to stay because he cared for her. All she was to him was a pack animal, a slave to his wishes. How long she stood there watching him eat his meal, Thorne didn't know. His hair was getting long and shaggy. He needed to shave; the burgeoning beard accented the gauntness of his cheeks.

"I think you've done quite enough already," she began through clenched teeth. He had been up and walking around with old Maximoff's help three times today. "I'll help you stand tomorrow and not before that." Turning, Thorne pushed the door open.

"Thorne."

She hesitated, giving Dev an irritated look across her shoulder. "What is it?"

He set the bowl on the cupboard. "I'm going out of my mind sitting in here every evening alone."

Her heart wrenched and she tried to steel herself against Dev's admission. "Then I'll get Maximoff or some of the other men to come over here and keep you company. If I remember correctly, you hate the sight of me. I'm English."

"Don't go."

Tears blurred Thorne's vision as she tottered at the lip of the stairs. She whirled around, leapt back into the caravan and slammed the door. Her face was etched with pain and confusion as she stalked over to him. "What do you want of me?" she cried hoarsely. "One moment you curse me. The next you turn human and beg me to stay. I can't take this, Dev! The pain's too much...."

Dev winced and hung his head. He worked his mouth as if to control some invisible anguish he was experiencing. "What I'm doing is trying to protect you, Thorne."

She straightened up from her hunched position, utterly bewildered. "Protect me? From what? I don't understand."

He pushed strong, tapered fingers through his shaggy hair. "Damn it, Thorne, do I have to spell it out to you? Are you so naive that—"

"Yes! And so what if I'm naive? You have no right to play with my emotions like this." She opened her hands in supplication. "Dev, I've never hated you. As I've gotten to know you, to be near you, I began to understand so much." Her voice grew wobbly. "The feelings I hold here in my heart are new to me, and I don't pretend to understand them where you're concerned. But they are real, and you're treating me as if I'm some kind of wretch because I have them!"

Shadows played across his tense features as he stared at her taut face. His voice was low and gritty. "Thorne, you're a virgin. You've probably never been in love and have had little experience with men. God, woman, hasn't it struck you that any feelings you have for me are destructive to you? To your status? Think, will you?"

She lifted her lashes and took a long, ragged breath. "Destructive? The way you're treating me now is destructive, Dev!"

He cursed softly. She was such a creature of her emotions and yet he loved her fiercely for it. Her breasts rose and fell sharply against the white peasant blouse that dipped provocatively to tease his male senses. "I'm a felon," he ground out savagely. "Don't waste your feelings on me, Thorne. I can only hurt you."

"That isn't true!" she cried, approaching him, her fists clenched at her sides. "The feelings I hold for you are new and beautiful to me. How can you say that what I feel toward you is destructive, or that it will hurt me?"

He shut his eyes, nearly overwhelmed with desire for Thorne. "Your feelings are good, Gypsy. I don't mean to take those away from you. One of these days, you'll meet a man of your own class who will trigger these same feelings in you again, and then you can fulfill your destiny with him." He lifted his chin and opened his eyes, staring up into her tortured face. "If you come to me as a woman, think what you will be giving up. In England, you'd be shamed for our indiscretion, and your father would probably disown you from your rightful inheritance. Your friends would shut you out." He knotted his fists.

"Thorne, I can offer you nothing but misery, danger and shame. I know what your feelings are, and I don't expect you to understand or have control over them. In this instance, I'm older, more experienced in these matters, and it's up to me to make decisions that are best for you." His voice grew bleak, his eyes becoming tender. "What you feel for me hasn't been wasted, Gypsy. You've made me want to live again after Shannon's death. You've given me your heart and, in doing so, have made me believe in hope once more. Before that, my existence was one gray day after another. I threw all my hate, anger and grief over Shannon's murder into soldiering. It's all I know. It's the only way I could stop from losing my mind."

Thorne came and knelt by him, her hands resting on his. Gravely, she looked up into his suffering eyes. "I can no more take back my heart, which you hold, than stop breathing. And if England has the gallows waiting for you because you've tried to avenge Shannon's murder, then that matters not to me. My mother told me always to follow my heart, not my head. My father, once he knows all the details, will understand. He would never disown me nor disinherit me." Her voice grew sad. "And my friends in that class you speak about all look down on me, anyway. Those that love me are at the orphanage and would pass no judgment."

"Oh, Gypsy," he said thickly, framing her face, "that's not the worst of it. Did you hear me? You'd be trailing Napoleon's army all over Europe as a camp follower if you stayed with me. Did you know that the women who follow his army are whores? The children don't know who their fathers are. They scavenge off the land, stealing and looting. I could never expose you to that kind of life. I'm a soldier. I lead one of Napoleon's best cavalry squadrons and we're always called into the thick of action. My life isn't much, Gypsy. I can't provide you with a home, or land. I'll never see gray hairs on my head . . . or hold my child on my knee."

Thorne sobbed softly, sliding her red, roughened hands up his. "How can you live knowing all that? Where is your hope?"

Dev rested his brow against her hair, needing the strength and love that she gave so effortlessly to him. "I live in hope that my brother will soon be free. I have enough money to get him passage on a ship for the New World. To America. Once I see him safe, then I'll consider my responsibilities to him at an end. I can never have Shannon back, but I can give Gavin a new life filled with hope. And then I'll go after Vaughn Trayhern."

Thorne choked on her tears, clinging to Dev. "Where is the hope for yourself?" she cried softly. "You deserve to live! You deserve to hold a child of your own, and to grow old."

He managed a choked laugh, and brushed a kiss over her hair. "God surely knows what I've done or have yet to do in my life, Gypsy, but I'm afraid the scales aren't tipped in my direction. I've got the blood of so many men on my hands that I see them nightly staring at me in my sleep. I live with the cries of battles in my ears. Alyssa has her freedom and she's happy with Tray. If I can give Gavin a chance at that dream, then I'll demand no more of God. Hell is waiting for me. Every day since Shannon was killed, I've felt as if I were burning in its hot fires. That is, until I met you." Dev gently raised her tear-stained face, a tender flame in his eyes. "You've given me days filled with emotion, Gypsy, and nights of peace when you sleep near me. You're balm for my undeserving soul. How can I hurt you further by making you my woman after all you've done for me already?" His mouth curved into a smile as he brushed her tears away with his thumbs. "I love you too much to do that to you. Do you understand that, my Gypsy? I won't return what you feel for me because, in the end, when we part, it will be hard enough on you."

The moments spun between them as Thorne absorbed and digested his words. Each one was a sword slashing her heart within her breast.

"Thorne?"

"I—I understand."

"I'm sorry, Gypsy. For you. I had my chance and God saw fit to take everything away from me." He stroked her flushed cheek. "At least you have your life waiting before you. When you get back to England, you can go back and help your ailing father and work to save the children of London. Somewhere, there will be a man who will see what I see in you." He pressed a moist kiss against her cheek. "Who will love you as fiercely as I do," he murmured thickly, slowly releasing her.

She sat numbly at his feet for at least ten minutes before Dev spoke again. "I'm human, Thorne. My head knows what's right for you. For us. The man part of me wants you. All of you. I need you as I've never needed another woman. So forgive me if I weaken sometimes and reach out for you in the night to hold you close. I'm so cold inside, Thorne, and you warm me. I'll try not to touch you or…kiss you. But if I do weaken, step away from me. Help me in those moments. God knows, I'm not a saint." He ran his trembling fingers through her cap of ebony hair, then placed a finger beneath her chin, forcing Thorne to look at him. "And I owe you an apology. I never meant to hurt you." He ran the silken strands through his fingers. "Thank God it's growing back, but I want you to know that I've never felt so ashamed of myself as when I cut off your lovely hair."

Her full lips glistened with spent tears and she reached out, barely touching the shaggy strands that dropped across his brow. "If you're going to continue being a croppy, you need to get this cut."

Dev felt his heart mushroom with such love for Thorne's courage that he had to forcibly stop himself from reaching out and pulling her into his arms. Her features were pale but serene. Only her guileless gray eyes mirrored the true extent of her anguish. She was mature far beyond her years.

"Old Maximoff is good with scissors. Let him come over and cut it."

Thorne slowly got to her feet, shoulders slumped, her voice barely audible. "I'll ask him in the morning. Come, lie down and I'll change that dressing."

Dev nodded, drawing himself carefully back onto the bed. He had never told Thorne how much he looked forward to seeing her in the evening, barely able to wait until she came through the caravan door. Her touch was gentle and sure as she took the knife and slit away the old dressing.

"You've grown into your role as doctor here in camp," he told her quietly. Even in the fading light, her hair mussed, her clothes thin and wrinkled, she was a lady.

Thorne concentrated on the wound. She managed a one-cornered smile. "The last week has been quite an education for me."

Dev nodded, absorbing each butterfly touch of her hands upon his thigh as she redressed the wound. "You haven't said anything about Juan since that one night. How is he?"

"Much better," Thorne replied fervently. "The bump on his head has gone down and he feeds from Pilar's breast. He's not had another convulsion, thank God."

"Thanks to you, not God."

Thorne gave a shake of her head. "No. No one's more aware of my limitations as a doctor than myself, Dev."

"Pablo was telling me that you care for Juan at least an hour a day, sitting down by the stream with him."

A smile touched Thorne's pale features as she finished knotting the bandage. She placed her hands upon the small of her back, straightening up to reduce the strain of so many tight muscles. "Pilar is still healing from the rape, and I take Juan for a while to give her some peace."

"That's probably the highlight of your day," Dev replied, hungrily absorbing Thorne into his heart. One day she would be gone from his life. Then he would be plunged back into his living hell.

Thorne nodded and refolded the torn silk strips back into a neat bundle. "I love Juan. He's so quick and laughs so much." She wanted to say, *it's the only hour in my day that I can forget the pain of loving you, Dev,* but said nothing. Trying to mask her feelings, Thorne asked, "Has Pablo taken good care of you?"

"Pablo has been like a watchdog over me."

She rose, placing the bandages into the cupboard. "He admires you, Dev. You can see it in his eyes."

He snorted and tucked his hands behind his head. "He wants to hold my sword and knife. I keep telling him he's fortunate that his father will teach him the trade of mending tin and copper, rather than becoming a soldier like myself." Disgust tinged his voice as he looked out over the three camp fires. "I keep trying to impress upon him the loneliness it brings, the nights spent out in the mud, the odor of death in your nostrils, and the nightmares...."

Thorne moved beyond the bed to a small area where she changed nightly from her clothes into the floor-length cotton nightgown. After the nights of strained silence between them, she was starved for the sound of Dev's voice and the sharing of his thoughts. There was so much she needed to think about, to sort through from Dev's earlier conversation. More than anything, he loved her. He loved her! That admission alone sent Thorne's heart spiraling on wings of joy. But equally powerful and devastating was the realization of the harsh world in which he lived. How could she tell Dev that no matter where he went, she could go without shame? She loved him for himself. She didn't care about the country he had sold his life to or the price on his head in England. None of that mattered to her. But it did to Dev.

She slipped the gown over her head, smoothing away the wrinkled folds. Time, they still had some time left. If she could convince Dev that what she offered to him was more important than his sense of honor, he might—what? Marry her? Make her his mistress? And what about her father and the shipping business? Or her responsibility to the orphaned children?

Thorne's eyes darkened at the choices that hung before her. She touched her brow, feeling torn as never before.

Exhausted by the day's events, she padded to the bed where Dev lay deep in thought. Time...she had to have time to sort out so much. And as she lay next to Dev, his arm going around her, drawing her close, Thorne knew that this was what she wanted for the rest of her life.

Chapter Eleven

"**Y**ou're the only man who knows Devlin Kyle on sight, Captain Trayhern. And since you want my daughter's hand in marriage, I want you to bring her back to me." John Somerset gave Vaughn a weak smile and bade him to sit down.

Vaughn's blue eyes narrowed upon the frail-looking man sitting up in the feather bed, surrounded by many woven blankets to keep him warm. The fourth Earl of Somerset was in his sixties. His brown eyes had sunk deeply in their sockets and it was obvious he had suffered enormously from his wife's death and Thorne's kidnapping. "Call me Vaughn, sir." He smiled, tasting the victory of finally winning Thorne's hand in marriage, and thus access to the family fortune.

John Somerset stared at the imposing figure of the retired British cavalry officer. Vaughn Trayhern cut a dashing image, he thought, even though he used an ivory-and-gold-handled cane to get around. The old man watched as the captain sat down in the wing chair. The dark bedroom was illuminated by several lamps. "I have much to discuss with you, Vaughn."

The butler came, serving them each a glass of sherry in finely cut crystal. Somerset manor, which was located just outside London, was indeed sumptuous. Paintings by the most influential artists of the day graced the high walls of the room. "To your health," Vaughn murmured to the earl, taking a sip of the dry red sherry.

Somerset neither returned the toast nor drank the sherry as he appraised the other man. "Let us be frank with each other. My days on this earth are numbered and my speech comes and goes. I must talk while my tongue decides to cooperate with me. As you know, my daughter, Thorne, has been kidnapped by Devlin Kyle. I want her brought safely back to England." Somerset stared down at the ruby contents in the crystal glass. "Your bravery in the Irish uprising has made you a hero in England. You were a brilliant soldier until your unfortunate knee wound. We had talked earlier of your becoming a husband to my daughter. I still want that to come to pass."

A twitch at the corner of Vaughn's mustached mouth gave away his pleasure at Somerset's statement. "I had heard your lovely daughter had been abducted, my lord. I hadn't realized it was by Devlin Kyle." His voice deepened and he leaned forward, splendidly attired in a gray waistcoat and trousers with a white shirt and black silk tie. "What can I do to be of service?"

"Rescue my only, beloved daughter, Vaughn. My son, a fine officer in the British cavalry, is now dead, thanks to the Irish. Thorne is all I have left. She is my life now. If you will take this mission, you're to exchange Kyle's brother, Gavin Kyle, for my daughter. Bring Thorne back to me, and I'll give her to you in marriage."

Vaughn swallowed a burgeoning smile. After years of trying to conceal his debts, they would finally be paid off. Tray, his own half brother, had cut off his allowance, and now he lived on his gambling abilities. But even that was drawing a slow noose around his neck. Fortunately, no one in the *ton* realized that he wasn't rich any longer. That was why he courted Thorne, because her father was one of the richest shipping magnates in England. For once, he had his archenemy, Devlin Kyle, to thank for this splendid opportunity.

Somerset's silver hair was uncombed and in disarray around his pinched features. His right arm was paralyzed, as was most of his right side. Vaughn had to lean forward to hear the old man's slurred words, noting that the right half of his mouth was slack. Somerset looked frail in the voluminous folds of the white nightgown he wore.

"Since he left Ireland after your battle with him, the Irish scum went to France," the earl began. "As you may well know, Gavin Kyle is in Newgate prison. I've persuaded the authorities to have him released to your custody. They have approved his exchange for my daughter, in Madrid. One less Irish vermin to tend in prison, anyway." His hatred for the Irish blinded all reason; first his son and now his beloved daughter had suffered under them.

He raised his bony hand, pointing a finger at the captain. "Mind you, the safety of my daughter comes first. Devlin Kyle is known as Sparrowhawk over in Europe. His cavalry squadron has served under Napoleon in Italy and Egypt with honors. He's a precision-fighting instrument, a fox. Make sure you're not his hare."

"Kyle's the worst sort of blackguard," Vaughn snarled. "You say he serves Napoleon with honor? Bah! Neither the Irish nor the French know the meaning of the word. A hundred of them aren't worth one good British soldier!"

Somerset nodded. "My sources inform me that Captain Kyle will not allow any man in his squadron to rape a woman, kill a child or loot. The man may be an enemy of England, but he has an undeniable, if twisted, sense of honor, Vaughn." He raised his trembling left hand and pointed to a folded piece of parchment nearby.

Vaughn rose and picked it up, opening the missive. There, scribbled across the thick paper, were instructions as to when and where the exchange was scheduled to take place. He frowned and sat back down.

"Of course, England is at war with France. And Napoleon twists Spain around his finger. You will go on this journey with one other man besides yourself to guard the prisoner. When you meet Captain Kyle, you must go only with Gavin Kyle in hand. Do I have your word on this? I don't want any harm to come to my daughter."

Vaughn studied the scribbled note in silence. "My heart is involved in this, sir. The safety of my future wife is my utmost concern. You have my word." And then he smiled to himself, a plan already hatching in the back of his mind. "He doesn't want much money."

"Kyle wants his brother, that's all. I don't know why he's asked for such a small, specific amount. Again, the man has a twisted sense of honor. I could almost admire him, if my daughter were not in his grasp. They say he's an excellent soldier and tactician. Don't try to outsmart him, Vaughn. Simply deliver Gavin Kyle and bring Thorne home." The old man coughed violently, his frail body shaking. "Now, let us speak of more pleasant matters. I assume you're still interested in my daughter's hand in marriage?"

Vaughn sharply recalled Thorne and his disastrous attempt to woo her. She was beautiful, if a bit headstrong. A smile edged his mouth. Old Somerset was dying. The man already looked like death warmed over.

"She is as precious to me as she is to you. Nothing would make one happier to have your approval of my humble request for her hand in matrimony, my lord. You know yourself that I've entertained the idea of having her as my wife for well over a year now."

Somerset stared down at his swollen and arthritic hands. His doctors had told him he had only three or four months of life left. The urgency to find Thorne an honorable husband with the proper qualifications had suddenly become a priority to him. He couldn't leave her unmarried before his death. She needed a man to shepherd her through life. Thorne wasn't capable of running the far-flung shipping business by herself, it needed the strong hand of a man.

Hope brimmed in John Somerset's eyes. "I know you've expressed enthusiastic interest. I shall bless the union."

Finally, fortune was smiling upon him! Vaughn folded the letter, hoping his trembling hands didn't give away his elation. He put the instructions inside his coat. "Will you put that in your own writing before I leave, my lord?"

Somerset's dulled eyes brightened as he saw the wisdom of Vaughn's request. "I no longer have the movement of my right arm. However, my solicitors will deliver my wishes to your town house before you leave tomorrow for Spain."

"Very well, my lord. I assume you have my ship's passage and anything else I might need attended to?"

Somerset nodded. "Your traveling expenses, passage and four of my finest horses are already on board the *Westwind*. The captain of the ship is expecting you on board tomorrow morning at 8 a.m. to sail with the tide. My butler will give you an envelope. Inside it is the money you'll need. Then he will introduce you to my most trusted servant Eamon, who will accompany you on the journey."

Vaughn gripped the earl's hand warmly. "Very well, my lord. I'm eager to be off." *And to come back to England a rich man.* Vaughn began mental calculations of how much the Somerset shipping business and properties were worth. He'd be one of the wealthiest men in England after he married Thorne. Finally, he could pay off all his weighty gambling debts that his older half brother, Tray, had refused to pay for him.

And then there was Thorne herself. So what if she were part Gypsy? He didn't care. Those stupid society clods who ignored her were shortsighted. He would cloister her on the country estate and spend most of his time in London, pursuing the sport of gentlemen. With the kind of dowry she would bring to a marriage, Vaughn could easily overlook her tainted blood. Yes, Fortune had suddenly and unexpectedly turned his way, and he was determined to make the most of the opportunity.

As the butler handed Vaughn his hat and gloves at the door, he introduced him to a man who stood nearby. "This is the earl's head groom, Eamon Quinn."

"Irish?" Vaughn growled, settling the hat on his head.

Quinn bowed. "Yes, sir."

"The earl has instructed Mr. Quinn to accompany you to Spain," the butler informed him. "He'll be in charge of the horses and will act as your valet, sir."

Anger surged through Vaughn as he stared down at the thickset Quinn, who sported carrot red hair, freckles and intelligent blue eyes. He gritted his teeth, his nostrils flaring with indignation. "This must be a joke! The earl would never send an Irishman with me."

The butler, a tall, thin man with graying hair, drilled Vaughn with a frosty look. "Sir, Mr. Quinn is the earl's most trusted servant. His choice is final."

Although Eamon was heavyset, he was agile and pulled open the door. Vaughn limped through it and down the stairs to the awaiting coach. Two dark bays with matching white rear socks stood quietly as he climbed into the vehicle. The earl had a perverted sense of humor, sending an Irishman along with him! The coach drove away at a slow trot, the horses' shod feet clicking smartly against the cobblestoned drive.

Trayhern slowly clenched his right fist. *So, Kyle, we'll meet again, and soon. I wonder what you'll think when you see it's me delivering your felon brother to you?* A slow smile crept across his thin lips. He took the envelope from his breast pocket and opened it up. Inside were more pound notes than Vaughn had seen in a long time. He fingered them as if he were stroking a woman's flesh, and his icy blue eyes thawed.

"You're dead, Kyle," he whispered under his breath. "Dead. And so is that brother of yours. Two of you at one time. I think I'll celebrate your demise tonight."

"Señor Devlin, take me with you!" Pablo cried, running up to Dev. Dev smiled and leaned over, offering his hand to the lad. Ghazeia moved spiritedly beneath him as he helped the Rom boy up behind him on the saddle. With a laugh, Pablo fitted his small brown arms around Dev's waist. Dev urged the gray mare into a trot across the camp. The sun was almost overhead, glinting off his auburn hair. Thorne was busy scrubbing clothes at the stream with Juan nearby on a blanket, cooing happily. Several other Rom women worked beside her.

"Thorne," he called, halting the mare. He allowed Pablo to slide down. The boy grinned happily.

Thorne looked up, brushing away several strands of hair from her eyes. She sat back on her heels and rested her wet hands in her lap. "How does it feel to ride Ghazeia again?"

she asked with a smile. His smile was tender as he regarded her.

"Come for a ride with me, Gypsy." Dev held out his hand to her.

Thorne swallowed hard, staring at his long, tapered fingers. The memory of the time she rode in front of him, resting against his lean, battle-hardened body, made her go weak. A tingle raced through her, and she started to say no. But the flame in his eyes beckoned her and she placed her hand in his. In one smooth, unbroken motion, Dev lifted her in front of him. Thorne settled across the saddle, safely ensconced beneath his supportive arm.

"That's better," Dev murmured against her hair. Turning Ghazeia around, they followed the river, moving away from the encampment. But not before the Rom children caught sight of them and came running. Pablo laughed gaily, calling up to Dev, begging him to allow him to ride on the back of the saddle once again. Manuela and two other girls stooped and gathered handfuls of daisies, playfully showering them with the flowers.

Dev smiled down at the children and then met Thorne's gray eyes. "I can see why the Gypsies love their way of life. All this freedom. The children grow up knowing the land and the animals."

Thorne shivered, absorbing each of his huskily murmured words. If only this moment would never end. If only she didn't have to leave for Madrid. "Can you see the *ton*'s reaction? Barefoot children and adults? The women would swoon."

Dev nodded. "I was barefoot most of my life until I got into the military. Many people in Ireland can't afford shoes or boots."

"I like being barefoot," Thorne said, enjoying the sway of the mare beneath them and the clip-clop of her hooves. She wriggled her dirt-stained toes. Her once pale white skin had turned a golden brown. She resembled the Rom more and more each day.

"I like you barefoot, too," Dev told her in a gritty voice. "It makes you look wanton."

Thorne twisted her head, catching the amusement in his eyes. "Wanton?"

"It suits you," he said, his voice dropping to a low, intimate growl. "You're a woman who shouts of a wild, free spirit." His lips caressed her temple. "Fire burns deep within you, Gypsy. That makes you wanton."

Closing her eyes, Thorne allowed his voice to move through her like a lover's caress. She ached to be possessed by Dev, and yet she didn't know what that meant exactly.

"The *ton* would tell you a wanton woman is a bad woman. Someone who flaunts her amorous qualities without shame."

Dev guided the mare away from the stream and through a quiet grove of oak. The sunlight dappled them from overhead, and the Rom children finally returned to camp. "They would," he said, "but then, those fops who go parading around in their wigs and sporting their latest mistresses on their arms, wouldn't recognize a real woman if they saw one. You, Gypsy, have everything any man could ever dream of possessing."

She went weak in his embrace, the afternoon suddenly turning magical. "I don't understand."

"There's no pretense in you. You're honest and kind. You play no demure games, and that's only one of the many fine qualities I like about you. It wouldn't matter whether you wore a silk dress or wore nothing, you are all woman. When I saw you by the stream washing clothes, I was struck by your flexibility. I kidnapped you, put you through hell, and then you had to adjust to Rom life here. You're like a cat, Thorne, you always land on your feet, and you make the most of your situation. Instead of complaining about having to help with the daily chores in camp, you work alongside the rest of the women. You care deeply for the children and they love you." Dev pulled the mare to a halt. He dropped the reins on Ghazeia's neck and turned Thorne slightly so he could look down into her vulnerable gray eyes.

He groaned softly as he touched her mussed black hair, which was in dire need of a trim. "God help me, Gypsy, I need to kiss you. Soon you'll be gone from my life, but I find myself wanting you more and more each day." His fingers framed her face and he read the desire in her eyes. "You want it, too, don't you?" he whispered, leaning down, barely brushing her lips.

"Y-yes, oh, please, Dev... kiss me. Hold me for just a little while. I'm so scared."

He drew back, his expression darkening as he saw fear in her eyes. "Scared?"

Thorne placed her hands upon his magnificent chest, feeling the heavy beat of his heart beneath her palms. "Scared of losing you...scared that you might be killed in Madrid or—or on some lonely battlefield."

"Sweet, kind Gypsy," he murmured thickly, claiming her lips in a long, slow kiss, "touch me with your fire. Warm me. I'm so cold inside, and only you can make me feel again. Let me erase your fear." He ran his tongue across her lower lip, inviting Thorne to respond. Her mouth trembled beneath his gentle assault, and his heart soared with joy as she slid her slender arms around his neck, drawing herself to him. A smile came through his voice. "You're wanton, my Gypsy, and you're mine...all mine."

Thorne pressed inexpertly against his strong, welcoming mouth and drowned in the sensations Dev created with his lips against her own, absorbing his male essence and tasting deeply of his tender offering to her. He released her captive lips, blazing a trail of hot, moist kisses down the length of her throat, his teeth nibbling tantalizingly against her exposed collarbone. His hands slipped from her face, trailing a path of scorching fire down her shoulders and coming to rest near her aching breast. A small gasp escaped her as his large hands caressed their rounded firmness, the nipples pressing with wild insistence against the rough cotton weave of her blouse.

"God forgive me," he muttered roughly as he lifted her slightly upward, leaving her breasts easy prey to his inspection. The pebbly hardness of one rosebud nipple was drawn into the heat of his mouth, and Dev heard Thorne weep with need, her fingers digging frantically into his shoulders. How long he had wanted to taste her! It didn't matter that the thin cotton barrier was there, he only wanted to give her pleasure. Slowly, he released that perfectly formed nipple, crushing Thorne against him, holding her as she trembled violently in the awakening passion he had ignited in her young body.

"If there was any way, Gypsy," he breathed raggedly against her small, delicate ear, "I'd make you my wife, and you'd never leave my side." His mouth flattened into a single line of pain for both of them. "You're so fresh and lovely, all the woman a man could ask for." He tunneled his fingers through her hair, holding her tightly. "I find myself dreaming of teaching you how to love me. I'd teach you that a woman can enjoy the same pleasure as a man. I don't care what they taught you in the *ton* or what they would say, a woman isn't some puppet to be bedded only to have children. Those damn Englishmen believe in going to a mistress who will give him what he lusts for, instead of searching with their wives for the same passions and desires."

Thorne shut her eyes, clinging mutely to Dev, a series of explosions igniting her body. She barely heard his roughly spoken words against her ear, needing only his presence, his throaty voice and his gentleness. "I only know that I've fallen in love with you, Dev," Thorne admitted in a tremulous voice. "At first, I was frightened of you. But then my fear abated and I saw you struggle to treat me fairly. I don't know when it happened, when all these feelings for you surfaced in my heart. It was the small things you did that told me that despite your hate of the English, you really didn't hate me." Thorne opened her eyes and stared, unseeing, through the quiet oak grove. "And each day...each hour, I become more aware of you as a man, and not as an enemy of England." She swallowed, nuzzling deeply into his arms. "I don't care what kind of life I would lead in order to be at your side. I only know that I never want to leave you."

Dev pressed a series of kisses to her temple, following the delicate line of her jaw. As she lifted her head, her lips parted in invitation, he took her gently, tasting the sweetness of her mouth, of her trusting heart. Her gray eyes were fraught with sadness as he stared down at her. "And if I could, I'd take you with me, Thorne. But I can't." He closed his eyes tightly. "I won't besmirch your honor. You'll return to England a virgin. But for now, let me share other pleasures with you. Let me give back to you, my lovely Gypsy. You can take the hours we share back in your heart, your memory." He looked at her, trying to fathom if Thorne understood what he was asking. Her gray eyes were clear and luminous with offering. With love.

"Y-yes, teach me, Dev. Teach me how to love and hold you in my heart, forever."

Chapter Twelve

Dev watched the salmon-colored dawn steal silently into their caravan and across the bed. Thorne lay on her back, sleeping deeply, still in the wine-colored dress from the night before. A softened smile touched the corners of his mouth as he propped himself on one elbow above her, his hand resting against her hip. Sleeping each night with Thorne had become an exquisite agony. Last night, she had gotten drunk and danced at the camp fire. His eyes grew light with amusement as he lovingly memorized every perfect and imperfect feature of her face. Drunk . . . the little vixen.

No wonder she looked flushed. Dev hadn't realized she had consumed two mugs of the potent wine until Pilar warned him after Maximoff urged Thorne to mount Shukar Nak, her gift from the Gypsies, and ride the horse around camp. He had watched her sit unsurely in the newly fashioned saddle, weaving unsteadily on the horse. Dev smiled and gently moved several strands of hair away from Thorne's brow. She'd probably never been drunk before in her life and would pay dearly upon rising. With that thought, he leaned over, brushing a kiss on her forehead, and quietly got up, leaving her undisturbed beneath the covers.

After dressing and shaving, Dev saw Thorne stir. He squeezed out a cloth from the water basin and sat down, enjoying her soft beauty as she slowly awakened.

Thorne groaned, nausea stalking her. She dragged her hand upward, only to have it caught midair by strong fingers. Her lashes barely opened and she stared drowsily through them up into Dev's face. He brought her hand back to her side and placed the cool, damp cloth against her brow.

"This will do more good for that splitting ache in your head than your hand," he teased.

Her mouth was gummy and her voice scratchy. "How could you know how I feel?"

Dev retained her small hand within his, enjoying the warmth that effortlessly flowed between them. "As you were weaving and bobbing around on Shukar Nak last night, Pilar thought I should know just how much you had drunk before you embarrassed yourself and fell unceremoniously off your new horse." His smile widened as he wiped her cheeks and slender throat with the cloth. "That's why I put a halt to your riding activities when I did."

Thorne groaned and shut her eyes. The caravan was spinning. "I was so relieved when you pulled me off Shukar Nak." Her fingers momentarily tightened on his hand. "Thank you." And then, in a miserable voice, she moaned, "Oh, Dev, I feel so wretched."

His smile faded and he stroked her hair. "I know, Gypsy. Just lie here. I don't want to brag, but I've had a few bouts with wine myself. First I'm going to get Pilar to heat as many kettles of water as possible, and we'll use her copper tub and get you a proper bath so you can sweat out what's left in you."

"I've never felt so badly, Dev. I feel as if I'm dying...."

He placed the cloth in the basin, gave her hand a squeeze and then rose. "I know," he soothed. "While I'm gone, I want you to get out of that dress and cover up with the blanket. I'll send Pilar in to help you. A hot bath will do you good. I'll be back."

Embarrassed by her inability to help herself, Thorne was grateful for Pilar's help. The Rom woman removed all her jewelry, the dress, and then had her slip naked beneath the blanket.

Pilar chuckled indulgently. "You aren't the only one suffering from old Maximoff's wine, *rawni*. The men go staggering around camp this morning, holding their heads, begging us not to talk too loudly. I'll help Devlin prepare your bath. You just rest."

Rest? Thorne clamped her eyes shut, trying to fight off the nausea and dizziness. She protected her sensitive ears from the shrill crow of the rooster. The sound was like a gun going off inside her aching head. Why had she been foolish and drunk two cups? Delora had warned her.

Thorne had little time to dwell on her miserable condition. Dev brought in the huge copper tub and set it at the foot of the bed. Then he and Pilar began bringing bucket after bucket of hot water to fill the bottom of it. The caravan grew moist and steamy. Thorne lay curled in a ball of misery, the blanket over her head. Dev smiled and made his way around in the cramped quarters to the bed. He sat down.

"Thorne?"

"No so loud," she croaked.

He chuckled softly, peeling the blanket off her head. "We have a predicament that I don't quite know how to solve."

One eye barely opened. "What predicament?" she asked, holding her pounding head.

"I can't ask Pilar to come and help you with bathing. She would think it an odd request, since we're supposed to be married. And I know you would find it embarrassing to be naked while I bathed you."

Both eyes popped open and Thorne stared up at him. "Oh," she said lamely. Her brow wrinkled and she tried to think. "Well . . . I mean, that is . . . it hurts to think."

"I know it does. Let me carry you to the tub wrapped in the blanket. The soap and cloth are there beside it. Once I get you on your feet, I'll hold the blanket up and you can climb in."

Could she climb into a tub? Thorne wasn't at all sure. But it wasn't proper that Dev see her naked, either. She tried to arrange her scattered thoughts. "Help me up. If I can't stand, I'll just lean forward and fall in."

He grinned and slid his arms beneath her, picking her up as if she were nothing. "It's going to hurt when you stand, Gypsy," he warned her.

Thorne didn't care. She wrapped her arms around his neck and nuzzled beneath his jaw, content to be in his arms. "I can't hurt any more than I do right now," she muttered.

Taking care to walk softly, Dev proceeded to the copper tub. "Oh, yes you can," he warned her. "Ready?"

"Ready . . . I think."

The dizziness that washed over her when she uncertainly stood almost felled Thorne. She gripped Dev's arms tightly, eyes shut. The blanket was falling off her shoulders, but she didn't care. Dev halted the blanket's retreat.

"Now you have to let go of me and turn around, Thorne."

She heard the amusement in his voice, thinking that this wasn't very funny. She forced her eyes open. "You won't look?"

"I promise I won't. But if you start to fall while my eyes are closed, I won't know it."

With a grimace, Thorne pried each of her fingers from his lean, muscled arms. "Very well," she murmured, "close your eyes. I'll either step or fall into the tub." The water was heavenly as Thorne managed to clamber in without completely losing her balance.

Dev retreated to the other end of the caravan and sat down. The high walls of the copper tub effectively protected Thorne from his gaze. All he could see were her face and shoulders. "Well?" he prodded after a few minutes. "How do you feel?"

Thorne splashed the warm water across her face. "Better," she said fervently. "Thank you so much. I feel as if I've been rescued from the pit of hell."

He chuckled indulgently. "A pleasure, my lady."

"You don't have to be so prim about it," Thorne shot back, scrubbing herself with the soap.

"I wonder what your father would think of your performance with the wine?"

The quick movement cost her dearly as she turned toward Dev. Thorne winced, holding her brow. "My father's never going to find out! He'd be mortified if he knew I'd gotten drunk. Ladies simply don't get drunk. Ever."

Dev's smile deepened. God, how he would love to go and kneel beside Thorne and wash her himself. It was impossible and only magnified how much they would never be able to share together.

"Well, since your reputation is effectively besmirched, my lady, why don't I come and scrub your back for you?"

Thorne gasped and whirled back around. "Don't you dare!" And then she saw that Dev was baiting her and relaxed. "You rogue. Have you no mercy? My head feels as if it will fall off my neck."

He matched her smile, dissolving beneath her spirited return. "Not when I see a back so lovely as yours, long and beautifully sculpted."

Thorne blushed violently and tried to hurry the process of her bath. The intimacy of his tone left her shaken—and hungry for him as a man. What would it be like for Dev to wash her? That forbidden thought made her flush to the bottom of her toes.

"Are you implying that men wash their mistresses' backs?" she shot back archly.

Dev gave a lazy shrug. "I washed my wife's back. I can't speak for the fops and their mistresses."

"I—I never realized that so much existed between a man and his woman."

"That's because your parents left you outside their bedroom door," he drawled.

Thorne allowed the cloth to rest on her drawn-up knees. "I know so little of the world," she lamented. "All this wonderful intimacy. No wonder my parents loved each other so much. I never dreamed that such things took place."

Dev sobered. "Love, good love shared between the right man and woman, approaches heaven, Gypsy. Believe me," he said, a catch in his voice.

Thorne nodded sadly. "I fear I'll never know such a heaven."

He stirred, hearing the pain in her voice. "You will, Gypsy. Not with me, but with some man back in England who will appreciate you as much as I do."

She slowly turned, her face glistening with perspiration, her eyes dark and searching upon his. "And if I were yours forever, you'd wash my back?"

His body went rigid with desire as he drowned in her honest, dove gray eyes. With a groan, he muttered, "I'd wash you from head to foot, Gypsy. I'd make bathing an extension of loving you. I'd teach you to bathe me, too."

Color flamed in her cheeks as long moments of silence suspended between them. "A man and a woman bathing each other?" That was unheard-of!

Dev gave her a smoldering look that spoke volumes. "If you were my wife, I'd introduce you to a realm where fantasy would become your reality," he promised in a thickened voice. Sadness filled him. Thorne would marry someday. Probably to a stolid, proper English bastard who would leave her in her own bedroom, visit her to beget his children and have a mistress on the side. The very thought made him simmer with anger. Thorne was a young, responsive, fiery woman who would take any man's breath away. He saw loss written across her features and gently steered her in another direction, realizing love was hopeless for them. "Come on, Gypsy, finish your bath and then wrap yourself in that towel nearby. I'll close my eyes."

By late afternoon, Thorne thought she might again join the realm of the living. Dev had cajoled Pilar to make a rich, lean broth and then coaxed Thorne into sipping some of it. Grateful for his care and attention, Thorne rested her chin on her drawn-up knees, watching Dev walk through the camp. The camp was quieter than usual and even the children were subdued after last night's festivities. According to Dev, the drinking and merriment had gone on until dawn. Sleepy children stumbled from the quilts beneath the oaks to sit around the kettles of food now being prepared by the women. Her gaze returned to Dev as she watched his progress through the opened window; he was incredibly virile, dressed in his black trousers, which were tucked into his scuffed boots. He was wearing his belt, knife and the scabbard for his sword. Once again he was becoming the soldier she had first met.

The door to the caravan opened and Dev entered. The day was hot, and the white shirt clung to his powerful shoulders and chest. He made his way to the bed, his eyes never leaving her face.

"How do you feel now?" he asked, sitting down beside her.

"Better." Thorne touched her hair and then managed a sour smile. "As if I'll live," she amended.

Dev grinned, his elbows resting on his thighs. "Good. A bath always sweats out the last of a drunk. By the way, I just went over and checked on your new mare. She's a nice-looking animal. I don't suppose you noticed that last night?"

Thorne had the good grace to blush. "You know I didn't."

His teeth were even and white against his lips. "Thought so."

"Don't rub salt in the wounds, Captain. You said you've suffered a few times from being drunk, too."

He rubbed his jaw. "Spirited Gypsy now that you're recovering, aren't you?" Dev recalled with clarity how frightened and closed Thorne had been right after her capture. The woman sitting before him, hands clasped around her knees and looking like an angel in that white cotton gown, had grown and matured with the duress of her imprisonment at his hands.

"Would you prefer me to be a simpering slave?"

Dev shook his head. "Never." He reached over, grasping her hand and taking it into his. He sobered. "You've grown in many ways, Gypsy. Have you noticed?"

Warm tingles raced up her arm as his thumb gently wove patterns upon the back of her hand. "Wh-what do you mean?"

"You're more confident of yourself. More sure. I wonder what your father will think of the changes in you. Will he see them as something good and not something bad?"

Thorne held his steady gaze. "My father married my mother, remember? He reveled in her spiritedness. He loved her deeply for all that she was and was not. And he inspired that same belief in me." She chewed on her lower lip. "No, when I get back to England, my father won't think of the changes he sees in me as bad."

A load slipped from Dev's shoulders. "Good." He didn't want Thorne to be harangued by her father or friends. Releasing her hand, he got up. "I'm going to be gone for the next two days, Gypsy."

Thorne's heart slammed once to underscore her shock. "What? I mean, why?"

He smiled. "You sound just like a wife." Moved by her concern, Dev leaned over, caressing her flaming cheek. "According to Old Maximoff, there's a *pueblo* south of here. It's the last one before we have to begin to cross that desert in order to reach Madrid. I want to buy a pack-horse, supplies and extra goatskins to carry water. Maximoff has shown me a route across the desert, but with summer approaching, some of the wells may be dried up before we reach the river."

Thorne nodded. For one awful moment, she had thought Dev was going to walk out of her life. The very idea brought tears to her eyes, which she tried to blink away. "Oh . . . I see."

"Will you miss me?"

She choked down a lump in her throat. "Y-yes."

Dev sat there a long moment, taking in her suddenly drawn features. He wanted to lean over and kiss her good-bye. Before he could follow through with the driving need, Thorne drew the covers aside and threw herself into his arms. She clung tightly to him, her face buried against his neck. Dev swallowed his surprise, folding his arms instinctively around her warm, soft body.

"That's more like it," he said gruffly, nuzzling the clean strands of her hair. "God, woman, you smell so good. You feel so good against me."

"Be careful, Dev. Please be careful. Those bandits are still out there." Thorne tightened her arms around his neck, shutting her eyes, tears beading on her black lashes. "I couldn't bear the thought of you getting hurt again," she whispered, "or killed."

"Don't cry," Dev soothed, "I'm too mean to die. You've already seen that." He gently eased Thorne away from him. Nothing could have prepared Dev for the stark terror he saw in her darkened eyes. He groaned softly, leaning down, his mouth moving across her trembling lips. He tasted the salt of her tears and the honey that was Thorne. She was lush, and he became lost in the heated texture of her hungry kiss. Dev was moved beyond words by her inexperience and her honest response and dragged his mouth from hers. He framed her face, finding his breath torn from his chest by the fiery stamp of love she conveyed in the one molten moment. "I'll be careful, Gypsy," he promised huskily. "And I'll come back to you. Two days... I'll be back."

Thorne had gone to collect herbs the second day of Dev's absence just to make the time pass. In doing so, she encountered the dreaded guerrillas and had ridden hurriedly back to the camp. She saw Dev standing next to Ghazeia in the center of the camp, talking with Maximoff. The packhorse, a small bay, was loaded with supplies. A shocked sob tore from Thorne and she tried to call to them, but it was impossible.

Dev looked up as Ghazeia nickered a greeting. His exhausted features suddenly grew tense as he recognized Thorne. He dropped the reins, walking quickly forward to meet her as she wearily pulled the mare to a halt. Thorne was covered with long, bleeding scratches over her arms and hands. Her black mare had sustained cuts across her wide chest and slender legs.

"Thorne, what happened?" he demanded, coming to her side. Dev saw her lips part and heard her croak his name. He dragged her from the saddle, crushing her tightly to him.

"Oh, Dev," she choked out, "they were after me!"

Worriedly, he pushed her back, checking to see if she was injured badly. "They? Who? Who's after you?"

Maximoff came over, scowling.

"The guerrillas! They almost caught me in the meadow!" Tears glittered in her eyes as she looked up at Dev. "I was so afraid. Afraid that I'd never see you again," she said, resting wearily against his chest.

Dev held her, whispering soothing words. All the while, he and Maximoff studied the direction from which she had come. More Rom had gathered, pointing at Thorne's bloodied arms and the injuries sustained by her horse.

"Thorne, get a hold of yourself," Dev ordered tightly. "Where are they now?"

She rubbed her cheeks, trying to rid herself of the tears, smearing blood across them. "I led them away from our camp. They're at least four hills to the south of us."

"Good," he praised, giving her a tight smile, "you'd make a fine soldier. How many? Were you able to get a count?"

She absorbed the strength he offered. "A dozen... perhaps more. A-and the leader..." She shivered. "He looked angry. A-and evil."

"You're all right now, Gypsy. Maximoff?"

"Yes?"

"Lend me four of your best men. Arm them."

"No!" Thorne cried. "No, you can't go after them!"

Dev gave her a patient look, seeing the wildness and fear in her eyes. "We're not going to intercept them, Thorne. I merely want to scout and locate their position. We can't leave the camp vulnerable to possible attack. What if they come back this way?"

Miserably, she acknowledged that Dev was right. Thorne was shocked by the change in him. He was a military officer, confident, experienced and in charge. She watched as Maximoff rapidly gathered men and horses. Dev guided her toward their caravan.

"Come on, you need to sit down," he said grimly. He led her up the steps and took her inside, sitting her on the bed. Kneeling before Thorne, Dev gathered her hands in his. "Will you be all right?"

"Yes. Please be careful, Dev." Her voice was raw. "I love you so much. As I was trying to escape from them, all I asked God to do was allow me to live to come back to you. That's all I wanted or needed."

Dev squeezed her hands gently. "I know, Gypsy. I feel the same, but I'm going to have to leave. I don't know how long we'll be gone. But trust me, I'm very good at looking out for myself and my men in a situation such as this. I've many years of experience behind me. I'm going to get Pilar to tend to you. These scratches are deep and I don't want your beautiful skin marred by scars. Wait for me. I'll return, I promise."

He drew her forward, molding his mouth against her yielding lips. Fire surged through him as he discovered Thorne's ardor was as potent as his own. She pressed herself shamelessly against him, her breasts round and soft against his hard chest. A groan came from deep within Dev as she matched the bruising force of his welcoming kiss. He tore himself away from her swollen lips, suddenly contrite for having hurt her.

"I'm sorry," he gasped, soothing her lower lip with his tongue and then kissing each corner of her mouth. "I love you, Gypsy. God, how I missed you."

Thorne felt as if her heart were torn out of her breast as Dev released her and rose, walking through the caravan door. She touched her lips, wrapped in the sensations of his love and undisguised desire for her. Even the pain from the scratches and welts on her arms dulled as she floated on a euphoric cloud of desire. Getting up, her knees wobbly, she stood at the door, watching Dev and the Rom men mount and ride off at a gallop in the direction of the guerrillas.

Thorne waited restlessly by their caravan, the night shadowing her. Silvery moonlight filtered down upon a quieter than usual camp. Everyone was waiting for the return of Dev's scouting party. She fidgeted inwardly, praying for his safe return. No one had heard shots being fired, but that meant nothing. The hills swallowed up sounds. There had been little time to sit and think, because Old Maximoff ordered the horses hitched to the caravans. All the hens and roosters were put back into small wooden cages that were tied to the back of each wagon. The mares with foals at their sides were caught up and brought into the camp. All the pots and pans were cleaned and stored. Only one small fire was left burning to provide a beacon in the darkness for Dev.

Even now, Thorne's lips were tender from Dev's branding kiss. She had never been kissed with such intensity or hunger. An inner heat uncoiled like a wild explosion within her as she vividly recalled it. She had been dazed in the aftermath, only able to stare up into his strong face, wanting him . . . needing him.

Shukar was the first to nicker, warning the camp of approaching riders. Out of the gloom of the night, five men appeared. Thorne recognized Ghazeia's gray coat immediately. The Rom gathered around the dismounting party. Thorne moved through the crowd, finding Dev. His face was grim, stained with sweat and dust. As he glanced down at her, his expression thawed for a split second. Without a word, he drew Thorne to him, giving her a brief embrace before Maximoff confronted him. The Rom leader was scowling.

"What did you find?"

"We picked up their trail," Dev began, "and followed them. We rode for almost ten miles before they regrouped and went north."

Dev turned and pointed toward the shadowy hills. "Fifteen miles due north is a huge guerrilla camp. We counted almost seventy men, one hundred horses and assorted women among the troop. They are well armed and mounted." He looked down at Thorne "You were lucky you escaped. These aren't just a band of guerrillas. Whoever their leader is, he knows something of military tactics and strategy from the way his camp is set up. If I were you, I'd take the caravans due south. Tonight," he added, rubbing his bloodshot eyes. "You don't want to encounter their troop. You'd all be killed."

Murmurs rose and fell among the Rom. Thorne saw the naked fear in the eyes of the women. The children were clinging mutely to their mothers' skirts. The men were grimfaced.

"We will go in an easterly direction," Maximoff decided. "If we go south, we are in the desert. If we go east, then I can be assured of water and grass."

Dev shrugged his broad shoulders. "You go east and we'll be heading southeast to Madrid." He held out his hand to Maximoff. "I guess this is where we split up, then."

Maximoff gripped his hand tightly. "Yes. Remember, you are welcome anytime."

When Thorne realized that they, too, would be mounting up and leaving immediately, she went and hugged each of the women. Manuela cried and clung to her. Pablo tried to be brave, his small face puckered up with tears that he would not allow to fall. Thorne cried openly, thanking each and every one of the Gypsies, who had given them shelter, food and, more important, their love.

Dev was checking the supply load on the bay horse when she walked over to him. Dogs were barking, horses snorting in anticipation of leaving, while hushed orders carried across the camp. Her heart wrenched in her breast when she saw how exhausted Dev was. Thorne placed her arms around his waist, giving him a hug.

"You're tired."

He leaned over, resting his head against her hair for just a moment. "No more than you, Gypsy."

"I don't know who's more tired, us or our horses."

Mutely, Dev agreed. "I want us to put as much possible distance between us and that troop tonight, Gypsy. It means hard riding."

She mounted Shukar. "Like the night you kidnapped me?"

Dev nodded, swinging a leg over Ghazeia. "Exactly." His eyes were dark with worry. "Think you can do it?"

"Yes."

A slight smile came across his hardened features. "That's my lady. You've got mettle, Gypsy. Stay close. We'll canter and then trot, canter and then trot."

"Shukar isn't in as good condition as Ghazeia."

"I know. If she starts stumbling badly, let me know and we'll slow our pace."

Thorne nodded, suddenly exhilarated. They were together again, united against a common enemy. Dev treated her as his equal in every way, and it thrilled her. In his eyes, she wasn't some fainthearted woman who would swoon at a moment's notice. A smile suddenly crossed Thorne's lips. "We'll manage," she told him, swinging her mare around.

Chapter Thirteen

They greeted the first gray ribbon heralding dawn with bloodshot eyes. Thorne clung to the pommel of the saddle, dizzy with exhaustion. Shukar Nak stumbled again, nearly pitching her off. She heard Dev's weary voice behind her.

"We're going to stop."

Thorne closed her eyes, allowing her black mare to halt. "Thank God."

After dismounting, Dev came around his horse to Thorne. He wrapped his hands around her slender waist, lifting her from the saddle. Even in the bare hint of light, he could see the bone weariness in Thorne's dark eyes. She swayed unsteadily as her feet touched the ground, resting against Dev for support. He slid his arms around her, absorbing her natural warmth and softness. This was what he needed . . . what he wanted. Dev brushed her hair with a kiss.

"All the time that I was gone, I missed you, Gypsy."

"I couldn't sleep at night, Dev," she murmured brokenly against his chest, nuzzling against the rough weave of his cotton shirt. She heard him chuckle, his mouth trailing a series of warm, moist kisses from her brow down the delicate line of her jaw.

"Spoken like a wife who misses her husband."

Thorne lifted her chin, wanting to kiss Dev. She wasn't disappointed as his mouth settled tenderly upon her offered lips. Her hands slid up across his chest and Thorne allowed him to take her full weight, lost in the euphoria of his mouth. This time, he was achingly gentle as he ran his tongue soothingly across her lower lip, kissed each corner of her mouth and then molded her to him.

Dev reluctantly broke the kiss, staring down hungrily at Thorne. "You're so giving," he said in a gritty rush, "warm, giving and so much a woman."

With a groan, he stood her at arm's length. The gray world around them was barely beginning to wake with the encroaching wings of dawn. His gaze moved back to Thorne, who stood in his arms, her face upraised and watching him in the silence. "I missed you, too, Gypsy. I didn't sleep well at night, either."

That admission made her soul take off in joyous flight. The fleeing shadows of the night emphasized the harsh planes of Dev's face as he studied the terrain surrounding them. Thorne felt safe. More safe, more loved and more cherished than ever before in her life. She knew, standing there on the hill crowned with oak, that Dev was her life. Thorne submitted to that humbling realization. Despite Dev's hatred of the English, he was fair with others, even herself. And her womanly instincts were blossoming beneath his love. She sensed that if she could convince Dev of her love, he would gradually adjust to the idea of her staying at his side. That was all she wanted from life—Dev as her husband, and to bear his children.

Thorne returned to his arms and a soft smile crossed her lips as he folded her next to him. This was the man, Devlin Kyle, whom she loved so fiercely, whom she would die for. Not the soldier who hated the English, not the felon, but the man. Thorne rested her head on his powerful chest, content to simply be held.

"Do you think the guerrillas will follow us?" she asked, her words slurred with exhaustion.

"I don't know. It appeared their camp was fairly recent. I don't know enough about the movements of the bandits, Thorne. They may be heading in one specific direction, robbing as they go."

His face became grim as he recalled the encampment; the women there were whores who followed the troop. As he had lain on his stomach beneath an oak, hidden on the crest of the hill overlooking the camp, Dev bitterly watched the women below being treated as little more than animals, their hair filthy, their clothes in dire need of washing. He had seen a number of naked little children scurrying about like rats as one of the soldiers approached a black-haired whore. Dev had tasted bile in his mouth; the scene he observed would be similar for Thorne at the rear of Napoleon's army. He would live in constant dread that another soldier would take her against her will, thinking she was nothing but a camp follower. He closed his eyes, holding Thorne tightly.

"I'll hobble the horses and unpack."

Thorne stirred. "I can help."

He kissed her cheek. "Not this time, Gypsy. Just go over by that oak and clear away any stones and branches for a bed. We'll sleep there."

Thorne shivered at his husky statement. To sleep with Dev again...

Later, with a broken sigh, Dev lay down, bringing Thorne into his arms. He released a soft groan as she came willingly to him, the curve of her body fitting solidly against him. Shutting his eyes, he smiled.

"God, Gypsy, how I missed you...."

Thorne nestled her head on his shoulder, her arm sliding across his hard belly. "It was awful without you."

He pressed a kiss to her brow. "You were always in my dreams when I finally got to sleep."

"Were they good dreams?"

"The very best, my Gypsy. The very best. Sleep now."

She leaned up, pressing a kiss on his hard, sandpapery jaw. "I love you, Dev...."

He awoke six hours later with Thorne's last words whispering through his mind. Dev luxuriated in the feel of her body against his own. Thorne snuggled close to him like a fitted puzzle piece, her breath slow and shallow so that he knew she was still sleeping. The intoxicating scent of her, faintly reminiscent of sandalwood, filled his nostrils and Dev inhaled it hungrily. As always, he shifted his focus of awareness, having been a soldier for too long. He listened to the early afternoon sounds of birds and insects. The horses were eating grass nearby, relaxed and rested. There were no noises out of the ordinary that would cause him to rouse himself from Thorne's side.

As he opened his eyes, Dev frowned. Two days without Thorne had scored his heart until it felt like an open, bleeding wound. He never realized how much she had become a part of his life until he had left her. Dev had felt a similar loneliness after Shannon had died. That was how much he had missed Thorne. If she discovered the extent of his feelings for her, Dev knew he'd give in to her plea to allow her to go back to France with him. He shut his eyes tightly. *God in heaven, why have you done this to me? Haven't I paid enough? You took Shannon. You took my mother and father. Why have you brought Thorne into my life? To remind me of my sins? To show me what I can never have? Why have you done this?* Dev reveled in her beauty, from the careless strands of hair across her forehead to the natural flush of her cheeks to her provocative lips. He couldn't help himself, drawn to her as darkness was to the dawn. He leaned over, lightly resting his mouth against hers, willing himself to be content with such feather-light contact.

Thorne stirred, her groggy awareness focused on that mouth that gently eased her lips apart, tasting her, loving her in reverent adoration. Her mind was still asleep, but her womanly feelings and desires leapt to life, catching her off guard. She felt her nipples hardening against the shirt she wore, the blood surging like a raging tide through her lower body, her breath catching in her throat. Barely lifting her lashes, she drowned in the stormy blue of Dev's eyes. A little moan of pleasure escaped her throat as his hand ranged from her waist, up her rib cage, to come to rest on her taut breast. Tiny prickles of shock radiated outward as his thumb lazily circled her nipple, and

Thorne's eyes shuttered closed and she unconsciously arched toward him.

"Sweet," he said thickly, his voice unsteady, "my God, you're so sweet and fiery, my Gypsy...."

Thorne sobbed against his mouth as his thumb and forefinger lightly squeezed her aching nipple. He groaned as her fingers dug convulsively into his shoulders.

Her breathing grew ragged as he continued to lavish the breast with attention. Thorne tore her lips from his mouth, her eyes wide and pleading. She saw Dev smile, fire and tenderness burning in his eyes.

"This is what a man who loves his woman would do for her," he rasped. "Love between them is sharing, Gypsy, just as we're doing now." He took an unsteady breath, outlining the shape and contour of her firm breast with his hand. "I want to please you in so many ways. I want to give you back some of what you've given to me." His hand stilled over her breast and he studied her flushed face. "We don't have long before we'll have to leave each other. I promised you I would never soil your virginity, but I can love you in other ways. Ways that would please you."

Thorne could barely think, only feel. Dev's callused hand resting lightly upon her aching breast only intensified the white hotness throbbing through her. Because she lacked experience, she didn't know what he was saying, but in her heart, she had already given herself to Dev. "Please..." she quavered, "love me, Dev. Love me as your own, because I am." Her trembling fingers slid upward and she framed his hard face, drowning in his cobalt eyes. "I'm yours... for as long as you will have me, in any way that you will accept me. I'm not afraid of you." Tears gathered in her gray eyes. "I'm only afraid of life without you."

A low groan tore from him and Dev buried his head against her wildly beating heart, her breasts a soft pillow. Her held her a long, long time, crushing Thorne in his arms. And she held him in return with all her womanly strength. As he lay with his head on her breast, running his hand up and down the expanse of her thigh and hip, he knew Thorne was stronger emotionally than he was. She was offering herself to him without reserve, which shattered Dev. Now he knew just how much Thorne loved him. He followed the curve of her hip, pressing her against his hardened, hungry body.

"Listen to me," he began, his voice raw, "I love you, Thorne. As no other woman in my life. Shannon fills one part of my heart. You fill the other. I can't make you my wife. I won't turn you into a camp follower who might be raped by another soldier while I'm away at the front." He turned his head, finding the pebble of her nipple, rubbing his unshaven cheek against it and feeling her stiffen with pleasure. "For this next week that's left to us, I want to love you as much as I can. Let me introduce you to new realms, Gypsy. Let me feel your fires, your gift of life...."

Thorne sighed. She ran her fingers through his thick auburn hair, pressing his head against her breast. "Y-yes, Dev. Please . . . I've missed you . . . I need you."

With a shudder, Dev raised his head, sweeping his gaze across her innocent face. She had grown into a very desirable woman. Humbly, he realized that whatever the mysterious chemistry that bound them, it had brought out only the goodness inherent in each. He lifted his hand from her breast, carefully unbuttoning the shirt. She wore an ivory-colored chemise beneath the folds of it, and he smiled, his voice thick.

"Buttons and more buttons. Lie there, my sweet, fiery woman, and feel each touch of my fingers upon you. Reveal your beautiful breasts to me."

A ragged sigh broke from Thorne as she watched Dev through half-closed eyes. His fingers trembled imperceptibly as he eased each button free. She felt no shame as he slowly peeled the fabric away to bare her snowy breasts and pink-tipped nipples, which burned beneath his inspection. A slow column of fire spread languidly through her as he leaned down, fastening his mouth upon the first nipple, drawing it into the moist confines of his mouth and teething it.

A spasm of such intense pleasure tore through her that Thorne sank her fingers deeply into the bunched muscles of Dev's shoulder.

"Yes, feel . . . feel, my woman . . . my own."

Thorne thrashed her head from side to side, tiny jolts of pleasure radiating through her breast as he lovingly cupped it between his callused hand and his mouth. And when he peeled the chemise aside to reveal her other breast, Thorne ached for him to suckle that nipple, which screamed out for his skilled touch. Without thinking, she tunneled her fingers through his hair, guiding his mouth down upon her breast.

"Easy, my sweet Gypsy," he soothed, running his tongue around the peak. Dev was elated by her bold response. He teethed the erect pink nipple, hearing Thorne cry out with pleasure, clenching and unclenching her fingers against his shoulders. He drew the bud deep into his mouth, pulling the sweetness from her breast, easing the ache he knew she was experiencing. There was fulfillment in him as never before, a newfound sharing. Dev knew he could never culminate the act of loving Thorne. But he could pleasure her, please her, and eventually, as he made her aware of her womanliness, he could give her the ultimate release before she had to leave his side forever.

Dev raised his head and watched her flushed face and quickened breathing. "Better?" he asked, cupping her other breast.

"Y-yes . . . oh God, Dev, I feel as if I'm going to explode . . . as if . . ."

His smile was tender as he got to his knees. Thorne was like so much moldable clay in his hands as he urged her to sit in front of him. Her shirt hung open, as did the chemise, revealing her lovely breasts. "I know, Gypsy, I know," he soothed. "And for right now, this is enough. Look at me."

Thorne lifted her smoky gray eyes, lost in a world of bright, splintering explosions. "Wh-what?"

Dev cupped her small, proud breasts in his hands. "You're lovely, did you know that? I tasted the sweetness of your body through your nipples." He caressed them, watching her features go drowsy with mindless pleasure. "A man who loves his woman wants her bold, wants her to share what he's taught her. Never be ashamed of your body, Thorne. Not with me. Allow me to come and put my arms around you and hold your breasts as I'm doing now. Allow me to do this..." He leaned down, drawing one nipple into his mouth.

Thorne gasped, clutching Dev's head to her breast, shutting her eyes.

"Yes, that's it, Gypsy...invite me to you...show me how much you want to be touched."

Mindlessly, Thorne moved her body slightly, guiding Dev's questing mouth to her other nipple. A low cry of satisfaction came from her as he suckled her. His hair was thick and silky as she clung to him. After he satisfied her, a softened smile pulled at her pouty red lips.

"I never knew anything could feel so delicious," Thorne admitted in a wispy tone.

Dev smiled with her and reached over, rebuttoning her chemise and then the shirt she wore. "You take your lessons well, Gypsy." He cupped her face with his hands, loving her fiercely. "There's much we can do to please and even satisfy each other. I want to share all of that with you. What we just did was only a small part of loving."

She gave him a dazed look. "Small? How much is there?"

Dev laughed. "Much, much more. Stay here. I intend to start a small camp fire. We'll eat before we have to leave."

The Jalón River was a welcome sight to their squinting eyes. The late afternoon sun burned down upon them. For the last three hours they had ridden without shade or rest. Thorne wiped her mouth as she stared at the wide green river that flowed slowly past them. There were oak trees in abundance on each shore as the river moved sluggishly across the harsh desert and rock landscape. She turned to Dev.

"There's nothing I'd love more than to bathe."

"I'll join you."

Thorne's eyes opened wide at the huskiness in Dev's voice and the promised look in his gaze. After unsaddling and hobbling the weary horses, her mood escalated. She sat down, struggling with her dusty boots, tossing them to one side. The cooling green water beckoned her, and she longed to shed her clothes, take the bar of soap and scrub her flesh free of the dust and sweat. Thorne glanced over at Dev, who was taking his boots off.

"You have the soap?" he asked, standing.

Thorne's mouth went dry as he shed his dusty shirt, exposing his very male chest. No matter how many times she had seen him undress, her heart pounded in her breast. When he saw her expression, a pleased smile hovered around his mouth.

"Uh . . . yes, right here." She fumbled for the bar, located in her saddlebag.

The bank was grassy, and Dev took Thorne's hand, leading her into the water. The river was wide but fairly shallow. The bottom was sandy. Dev turned her around so that she faced him.

"At least take off your shirt. We can wash it later," he said, unbuttoning it.

Thorne's skin tightened beneath each of his grazing touches. She melted beneath the flame in Dev's eyes as he tossed her shirt back on the shore. She stood gripping the soap, staring wordlessly up at him, her mouth dry.

Dev saw her hesitancy. "Go on," he urged, "go for a swim."

She didn't know what he was going to do. Her body cried out for more of his knowing touch. Thorne was aware that her nipples stood tautly against her chemise as she slid down into the cooling water. For the next ten minutes, she languished in the deeper water. Dev remained where he was, soaping his magnificent body, washing his hair and then shaving. Thorne found herself mesmerized as he shaved, coming back to sit on a flat rock near him.

"I've never seen a man shave before."

Dev moved the razor carefully over his skin. "No?"

"No."

"What do you think of it?"

Thorne's eyes sparkled with laughter, her hair wet and clinging to her skull. "That I'm glad I don't have to do it. It looks dangerous!"

He smiled with her, caught up in her lilting voice. "It is." He dipped the razor in the river, using more soap across his upper lip. "Are you done?"

"Me? No. I need the soap."

He made two quick scrapes, finishing. "I want to bathe you."

Thorne's eyes widened beautifully. "Yes...I'd like that."

Dev studied her. "Sure?" She was either very fearless or very trusting. He suspected it was her trust in him that had won over the initial shock he'd seen written on her face.

Thorne licked her lower lip, not realizing the effect it had on Dev. "Yes, I'm sure."

Placing the razor beside his saddlebag on the bank, Dev led her out to the waist-deep water. The current was sluggish and it was easy to stand. He gave Thorne the soap.

"I could let you do this, but I get such pleasure out of it," he told her huskily, unbuttoning the chemise. The ivory fabric gaped open, revealing the swell of her white breasts. Dev felt his loins tighten with heat. He looked up to judge the effect his hands grazing her flesh had on Thorne. Her lips were parted and her lashes drawn down.

"No, look at me...I want to memorize your every feeling, Thorne. I want always to carry in my mind and heart the way I make you feel."

She trembled as he pulled the chemise aside, fully exposing her breasts. They ached for his touch all over again, and automatically she shed the article of clothing.

Dev tossed it to the bank and then returned his attention to Thorne.

"The soap..."

Thorne placed it in his large hand. She sucked in a deep breath as he leaned over, placing a series of feather-light kisses the length of her neck, trailing along her delicate collarbone and then... A small cry shattered her as his mouth settled over her one nipple, a shudder racking her. Thorne swayed uncertainly, and his arm went around her, drawing her to his warm, hard body. The shock of their flesh meeting and molding each other made her faint with desire. She heard Dev growl in a low, guttural tone as he spanned her narrow waist, lifting her.

She was pushed by the current against him, her hips placed against his bulging male hardness. Her fingers gripped his sinewy shoulders as he worshiped each of her taut nipples. Mindless heat exploded throughout her and Thorne threw her head back, exposing her slender throat, her body a tense bow against Dev. Each time he suckled her, a strange, warm feeling pooled between her legs.

Gently, Dev lowered her, allowing her sensitized breasts to chafe across the hair of his chest. He saw the sultry look of pleasure in her dark gray eyes, the parting of her exquisite lips.

"You like that, don't you?"

"Yes...."

He nuzzled her neck with his tongue, weaving provocative patterns on her dainty earlobes, nibbling on each of them. Thorne twisted against him, her fingers sinking deeply into his chest. "You're so hot, so much woman," he said hoarsely. Dev spanned her clean back, marveling at the curved strength of her spine. As if of their own accord, his fingers found their way beneath the waistband of her breeches. Thorne's breath became ragged as he worked the buttons free. His mind screamed at him to stop. His hungry, starving body goaded him on. Thorne lay against him, weakened by his sweet assault on her.

He splayed his hand across her slightly rounded belly, seeking, finding that carpet of silky hair below. Thorne cried out sharply, frozen in his arms. He waited, kissing her until she melted once again beneath his mouth, asking her to trust him once more. The water was cool, her skin hot, her breath moist against his taut chest. To touch her, to find out if she desired him as much as he desired her, drove him on. Gently, he worked his way between her silken thighs until her found her swollen, liquid core.

A cry was torn from Thorne as his strong fingers began to stroke her. She sagged weakly against him, faint with new sensations, new pleasures.

"It's all right, all right," he soothed raggedly against her ear. "I won't hurt you, Gypsy. Let me please you...let me..."

A sob welled up in her throat and Thorne gave herself to his ministrations, which were wreaking fire through her throbbing core. She sobbed Dev's name over and over, no longer in control.

Slowly, he removed his hand, lifting Thorne into his arms. His eyes were blue flames, his mouth set as he carried her to the grassy shore and deposited her on the blanket. She was shaking badly. He saw the confusion in her eyes as he lay down beside her.

"D-Dev?"

"Hush, my sweet Gypsy, it's all right. You're feeling the need to have me. Lie down. Trust me... trust me and I'll help you."

She was no longer ashamed of her nakedness as Dev stretched out beside her and removed her breeches. The powerful currents sweeping through her made her tremble with such a yearning that her eyes were wide, begging him to do something...anything to relieve the all-consuming ache that had centered between her thighs.

Dev leaned down, capturing one nipple, soothing her. His hand slid lightly over her slick body, across her rib cage, the flat of her belly, finding that dark triangle of her femininity again. This time...this time, she parted her thighs willingly to allow him to touch her. His heart soared with joy. Thorne trusted him completely. No matter how frightened and confused she was about what she was feeling, she trusted him.

"Ah," he murmured thickly, easing his hand downward, "you're so hot...so close, my Gypsy. Give yourself to me, move against me...yes, yes..."

Thorne arched against him, her instincts taking over. As his teeth closed over her nipple, she moved wildly against the hard palm of his hand, the friction increasing until, suddenly, an explosion of such ferocity occurred that a scream tore from her throat.

Dev watched and heard and felt Thorne enter the realm of womanhood. Tears stung his eyes as she gripped him to her in those shattering seconds, holding him, needing him. He felt her ragged breathing, the sobs of pleasure tearing from deep within her, the primitive wildness of her body. Gradually he soothed her swollen core and then ran his hand across her glistening flank and thigh, pacifying the storm that had raged within her moments before.

Thorne sobbed for breath, tears squeezing beneath her lashes. She clung to Dev, unable to understand what had occurred. The floating sensation dissolved, but a glow remained long after. Touching his damp hair, she kissed him.

"I love you," she cried softly. "I love you and I never want to leave you."

Dev groaned, taking Thorne into his arms and simply holding her. "Sh, it's going to be fine, Gypsy. Rest...just rest. We have the time." He kissed her temple, smiling tenderly into her wide, luminous eyes. "You've made me the happiest man on earth."

"I—I don't understand..."

Dev rested one hand against the silken hair above her deliciously curved thighs. "You gave me the gift of yourself, Gypsy. Something that many women never give to their men, even after years of familiarity, you've given to me by my merely touching you." His eyes darkened as he stared down at her. "God, I love you so violently that sometimes I'm afraid I won't be able to live without you."

The words were wrested from him in a moment of passion and unfulfilled yearning. "You're so responsive. Wild—" he kissed her full lips "—like that hot Gypsy blood that runs in your veins." He shuddered, longing to saturate himself within Thorne and knowing he could not. What lay ahead of him was Madrid, and losing Thorne. Dev buried his face against her breast, unable to deal with the painful moment that would soon rend them apart.

Chapter Fourteen

The sun had just set, leaving the sky a brilliant rose color as Thorne entered Madrid with Dev. La Paloma Posada, a small but clean inn made of adobe brick, sat on the northern edge of the sprawling city. The patrons were bourgeois, assuring Dev that Thorne would be safe in his absence. He purchased two rooms that adjoined each other. Dev didn't want Thorne involved in the spying activity that he'd initiate shortly. Separate rooms meant Thorne would not be openly associated with him. Earlier, he'd fed the innkeeper a story that he was a retainer for Thorne, who was to meet the rest of her family in Madrid at a pre-arranged time. That way, the owner wouldn't grow suspicious of a young woman in a room by herself. She was delighted with the wrought-iron enclosed balcony that led off her bedroom. After Dev made sure the horses were properly cared for, he joined Thorne on the balcony which faced the city. She sat with lemon water in hand, giving him a welcoming smile.

The day was fading and Thorne felt mellow, wanting to share the feeling with Dev. She roused herself from her reverie and watched as he cleaned the bridles.

"Tell me about your brother, Gavin. You've told me of Alyssa. What of him?"

Dev raised his head, drowning in her tender gray eyes. "Gavin is two years younger than me. He's the baby of our family."

"Is he a warrior like you?"

Dev grimaced. "Gavin's the adventurer, and he's an excellent swordsman. There were times in Ireland when he
saved my life. He's like a cat in many ways," he went on,
"with good night vision, and he has the nine lives of one.
Yet when a battle is over, he can relax."

"And you can't?" Thorne probed.

"No." Dev gave a slight laugh. "Gavin is more de-
tached. He lives to fight. He was never a farmer."

"Like you?"

Dev slowly rubbed the leather and frowned. "I've always been a farmer. So has Lys. Gavin was more interested
in winning a wager on a horse race, charming the women
with his good looks or using that tripping tongue of his to
get himself into and out of trouble."

Thorne smiled. "He sounds playful."

"He is . . . was." Dev scowled, staring out at the darkening sky and the silhouettes of the stucco buildings that
surrounded them. "Being in prison five years has probably changed him a great deal. Vaughn Trayhern's squadron captured him, and that bastard would sooner see us
dead than alive," he gritted out.

"It sounds as if prison life would slowly kill Gavin,"
Thorne murmured, unable to soothe Dev's anguish.

"It would kill anyone." Dev hesitated, so many old
emotions that he had kept at bay surfacing within him.
"God, I pray that he's well. I keep wondering how he'll
look when I see him. I wonder how they'll bring him to
Madrid. Or if they will. . . ."

Thorne looked up at his ravaged face. "My father will
move heaven and earth to see to my safety, Dev. If there is
any way that Gavin can be freed and brought here, he'll do
it."

He held her innocent gaze. "I wonder who's bringing
him. They can't have Gavin in chains or the Spanish would
become suspicious."

"My father will hire someone who is competent, Dev. I
pray he's sent Eamon along."

"Gavin has to be alive. All I want is his freedom."

"And then what?" Thorne asked hollowly.

"I'll take Gavin back to France with me. From there, I'll get him passage on a ship bound for America. They have just won their independence from England, so he'll be a free man over there. His past won't haunt him, and he can start a new life."

An ache began in her heart. "What about you, Dev?"

He heard the pain in Thorne's voice. "I'm going to complete Napoleon's mission. After that, I'll ask for leave." His tone turned dark. "I'm going to hunt down the man who has caused our family all this pain, Vaughn Trayhern."

"And yet his half brother, Tray, is the soul of kindness. How could the *ton* have all been fooled by Vaughn? He's popular, and thought to be rich."

"Vaughn Trayhern has spent his entire life fooling people. He's a dead man, he just doesn't know it yet."

Alarmed at the dark intent she heard in his voice, Thorne said quietly, "You mean you'll come to England?"

Dev nodded. "I promised my father that I'd take care of what was left of the Kyle family, Thorne. I also made a pact that I'd even the score with Trayhern if it was the last thing I ever did." His voice became bleak. "I can't help Shannon or my father. I was able to help save Alyssa's life because Gavin took Trayhern's other squadron on a wild chase in the opposite direction. Tray and I were able to reach Lys in time. Gavin was eventually captured and thrown in Newgate."

Tears glittered in Thorne's eyes. "Certainly Tray tried to free Gavin?"

"Yes, but Vaughn has powerful and influential friends among the *ton*, Gypsy." He managed a shrug. "Every time Tray tried to free Gavin, his attempts were blocked by a higher authority. Of course, Tray is Welsh and you know how little respect the English have for the people of Wales."

Thorne nodded glumly. Her mind was racing. If Dev was going to be in England, he could easily be discovered and killed. Agony slashed across her heart. "Dev, why couldn't you just go to America instead? Let Vaughn Trayhern go.

The past is eating you up alive. America could offer you a new start, too.''

Dev gave her a sad smile. ''My word is my bond. I live only to uphold our family honor, to see that blackguard Trayhern pay for what he's done to all of us.'' He released a painful breath. ''I have no future, Gypsy. I have only a past to atone for and rectify.''

A little more of her heart tore open. Would Dev still track down Vaughn if she became his woman? If she could drive him beyond that control of his, seduce him into taking her virginity, she might be able to thwart his plans and he would live... live to love her as much as she loved him. The reality of the situation halted her wishful thoughts. Dev was determined and he would refuse to endanger her in his hunt for Vaughn.

And then, the seed of an idea took root. If she were to conceive Dev's child, what would he do? His love of children was evident, as was his desire for a family once again. Dev thought it was a dream out of his reach, but she did not. Thorne took heart, filled with new hope. Something told her that Dev would not abandon her if she were carrying his child. Eagerly, she mulled over the idea. To have a child out of wedlock was shameful. Her father would be shamed. But he, of all people, understood love. He would forgive her.

She stole a look up at Dev's shadowed face. The risk she was taking had no guarantees. Dev could doggedly continue his revenge against Trayhern, regardless of whether she was pregnant or not. Thorne prayed that if she could force Dev to love her completely and be fortunate enough to conceive, it might turn his focus upon her...and the child she would carry lovingly in her womb. Soon, Thorne whispered silently, soon I will ask you to make me yours.

The next morning, Dev left the inn, heading south through the awakening streets of Madrid. He bought a used Spanish uniform from a shopkeeper. After bathing in the river and shaving, he dusted off the blue wool uniform. As much as possible, he had the wool material look spotless.

The shako, the heavy leather helmet, shone a bit after some polishing. He wanted to be able to walk onto the palace grounds as unobtrusively as possible. A dirty uniform was sure to catch the eye of some spit-and-polish sergeant. Dev couldn't afford that kind of attention.

He took out the black walnuts he carried in his saddle-bags and unsheathed the knife from his belt. After peeling off the pulpy exterior of the nuts, he dropped the pieces into a small tin cup. Adding a bit of river water, he watched as the liquid softened the hulls. With some kneading and squeezing, they turned the clear water a dark brown, staining his fingers.

Taking the black walnut juice, Dev spread it over the ex-posed parts of his body, most notably his face, hands and neck. In no time, his flesh took on a darker tone, the look of a Spaniard. His skin was already deeply tanned, and the stain of the black walnut enhanced the color. Taking the mirror he always carried for signaling purposes from the saddlebags, Dev was satisfied with his efforts. Now for his hair. No Spaniard had red hair. He soaked another cup of hulls. This time, instead of using the liquid, he pressed strands of his hair through the pulpy hulls. The stain turned his hair black. The final touch was his eyebrows. When finished, he viewed himself critically in the mirror. Except for the color of his eyes, he could easily pass for a Span-iard. And he knew his eyes wouldn't give him away. He'd met many Spanish soldiers who had blue, green and even gray eyes.

The sun was climbing well beyond the horizon when Dev entered the area of the palace. As he drew near, he saw peasants toiling out in the distant fields, struggling to grow their crops. Carts filled with goods ranging from tin pots to foodstuffs began to clog the cobblestoned arteries toward the many open-air markets. Dev kept alert for Spanish squadrons on horseback. Fortunately, the storekeeper from whom he bought the clothes had had a complete set of identification papers with them, saying the man was a de-serter and wanted money to escape Madrid. The papers would make it easier for Dev to move about within the palace without questions. So now he was Private Esteban Gomez.

Dev left his mare at a livery not far away to be unsaddled, rubbed down and given a generous portion of oats. Sweat trickled from his armpits as he approached one of the many gates that led to the palace grounds. At each gate there were at least two guards in resplendent red uniforms. Long ago he had discovered that the Spanish military did not have one basic color of uniform. Instead, their infantry, cavalry and artillery groups all had their own color and design for their uniforms. As he watched the main gate, the diverse and confusing colors were in evidence.

Coaches drawn by smart, high-stepping horses rumbled by him on the cobblestoned street. Dev caught sight of a lady dressed in the finest of fashion. He smiled, thinking that Thorne's natural beauty far outshone the woman's heavily made-up face in the carriage. He slowed his pace and observed the guards as they carefully checked each visitor's papers. He wiped the sweat from his jaw.

He decided to try one of the less important looking gates. Peasants and laborers trundled in and out of those gates with their various services and wares, creating constant traffic. Choosing one where men and women were clothed in thin, workday clothes, Dev made his approach. The guard at the gate was arrogant, arguing heatedly with each peasant, waving their identification papers high above his head while he delivered a stinging tirade. An old woman, her head wrapped in a white scarf the color of her hair, came next. She carried a massive load of newly pressed clothes on her bent back. They were wrapped in thick brown paper to protect them from the dust raised by the horses and carriages.

Just as she stepped up to the guard with her papers in one hand, she tripped. The entire load, carefully balanced on her back and shoulders, slipped. The paper gave a sickening rip, and at least fifteen woolen uniforms belonging to officers spilled around her. She gave a cry of alarm as she fell. Dev hurried forward to help.

"Idiot!" the guard yelled, waving his hands. "Now look what you've done! This is a mess. A mess! No one fouls the King's palace gate." Just as he lifted his highly polished boot to kick her out of the way, Dev placed himself between them.

"Let me help," he offered the guard, already wrapping his hand around the woman's pathetically thin arm.

The guard glared at him. Deciding that Dev was the answer to getting the mess cleaned up quickly, he waved his hand. He didn't want his sergeant to come over and give him a tongue-lashing. "You there, Private. I order you to take this laundress over to the palace laundry facility. Pick up her baggage!"

Dev gently pulled the woman to her feet. Blood was dripping down her fingers and soiling the black skirt she wore. "*Señora,* can you walk?"

Her black eyes were wide with shock. "You are kind, sir." Her reedlike voice trembled. "My laundry—"

Managing a slight smile, Dev urged her to one side to allow other foot traffic to pass unimpeded. "Stand over there, *señora,* and I'll pick up and carry your load. Which way to the laundry?"

With a grateful nod, she pointed. "It's not far. Come, follow me." And then she smiled, showing her toothless gums. "A slow trip it would be, Private. My knee is ailin' me from the fall."

"As soon as we deliver these goods, *señora,* I'll find someone to look at your cut hand and knee." Dev picked up the officers' uniforms. The load was incredibly heavy, and he wondered how the woman had managed to carry them any distance in the first place. "What is your name, *Señora?*" He followed her down a brick path strewn with flowers and shaded by palm trees overhead.

"They call me Maria." She tilted her head like a curious bird. "And you?"

With a slight laugh, Dev said, "Private Esteban Gomez, at your service."

Maria pressed her injured hand against her skirt to stanch the bleeding. "Kind you are, Private. I spit on all the palace guards!"

They crossed several courtyards, and Dev smiled absently. The palace guards were a far cry from their cousins, the infantry soldiers. Palace uniforms were gaudy and clean. The sabers they wore at their sides glittered in the sunlight as they moved. Noblewomen were attired in long dresses made of the finest materials, coiffed and wearing more jewels than Dev had ever seen. This was where all the toiling peasants' tax money went, Dev thought with disgust. He politely answered Maria's questions and listened attentively while she led him toward their destination.

The laundry was located at the rear of the palace. Dev saw at least a hundred women. Standing in row after row, like stalks of corn in a field, their backs were bent over washboards, each woman cleaning a huge stack of soiled clothing. The long room was hot and steamy from the kettles of water that boiled over huge, open fires. Maria motioned him down another hall that led to a series of smaller rooms. Inside the first chamber were at least twenty officer's uniforms hanging on a wire overhead. Some belonged to the infantry, others to the palace guards and a few to the cavalry.

"Private, would you hang them up for me? I'll see Master Peron about gettin' a dressin' for my hand. If I try to hang them, my blood will soil them. Then I'll not get paid for all my efforts."

"Of course, *señora,* I'll do it. Find the help you need."

Grateful, Maria gave him a shy smile. "You are a fine one, Private. Thank you."

Dev bowed. "My pleasure, *señora.* "

As soon as she left, Dev quickly hung up the pressed uniforms. He peeked out the door and, seeing no one, shut it. There was no bolt to lock it, so he'd have to change quickly. Taking down the uniform of a Queen's dragoon, he stripped off the old blue one and donned the new one. The risk he was taking was considerable. Most of the palace soldiers would know one another because it was such a small, closed community. However, he saw many young, newly commissioned lieutenants on the grounds. If anyone stopped him, he would tell them he had just been assigned to the palace today and perhaps get away with the lie. There was a major's uniform and Dev was sorely tempted to wear it. But there were few majors around and he was sure the men would spot a bogus officer of that rank. No, better to be a lowly, green lieutenant and go unnoticed.

The hall was empty when Dev made good his escape from the laundry facility. The bright yellow wool waistcoat he wore had scarlet facings. The buff-colored leather breeches were tight-fitting. A black cocked hat sat perched at a rakish angle on his hair. Dev grimaced inwardly; the knee-high black boots fitted him poorly. Whoever owned this uniform was smaller in the legs and feet than he was. A straight sword with a brass hilt in a steel scabbard completed the uniform. As a Queen's cavalry officer, he wore silver lace and piping, plus fringed epaulets of the same color on each shoulder.

He found the busy stable without much trouble. A barefoot boy in tattered trousers came racing out to him.

"Yes, sir? Your horse, sir?"

Dev looked at the long row of stalls. At least fifty well-fed and groomed horses waited at the beck and call of their owners. He scowled. "You recognize me, boy?"

The lad gulped once. "N-no, sir."

"You don't?"

Fidgeting, the boy chewed on his lower lip. "I—no, sir. But if you'll tell me which horse you want, I'll saddle him in a hurry."

Good, they didn't assign horses to the officers. Dev nodded brusquely and marched past the boy. A cooling wind floated down the immaculately clean aisle, stalls situated on either side. The fragrant smell of hay filled his nostrils. Dev's eye for good horseflesh didn't fail him. He halted in the center of the aisle and pointed.

"I want that black gelding over there saddled, boy. Have him in full gear and ready for me within the hour."

"Yes, sir!" He scampered down the aisle toward the tack room.

Turning on his heel, Dev walked back out into the bright sunlight. Now it was time to begin committing the palace to memory and more important, to count how many men and officers were present on the grounds. He walked imperiously, his body language declaring that he was not to be stopped and questioned. His heart began a ragged beat as he approached the garrison. Soldiers in every color of uniform were present. Some walked quickly, parchment in their hands, messengers for officers. At the other end of the long, two-story building, he could see high-ranking officers with their staffs gathering. Horses milled around the outer circle. What was going on? Dev perused the soldiers to make sure he didn't find another man dressed as himself. He was sure the Queen's guard was a small, tight contingent and he had no wish to meet a fellow officer for a chat. Slipping inside the first available door, he found himself in a barracks. The few enlisted men in the foyer came to attention.

"At ease," Dev growled, stalking by them, his hand on the butt of his sword. He tensed, waiting for the sergeant in the group to challenge his presence. He didn't. Relief flowed through Dev. He counted the number of beds in the two-story barracks, tucking that figure away. Going back down the stairs, he went through the next door, expecting to find more of the same.

Shock and then terror assailed him. Dev found himself standing with at least thirty other officers in a crowded room. A few lower-ranking officers turned their heads in his direction, but the generals and colonels ignored him completely. He entered and quietly shut the door behind him, remaining unobtrusive.

"Well, it's about time," an infantry captain next to him whispered hoarsely. "It's a good thing the chief minister hasn't arrived yet with the King. If he didn't strip you of your rank, the King would certainly beat you with that stick he carries."

"My horse threw a shoe, Captain, or I would have been here sooner."

The infantry captain grimaced. "You're just damned fortunate, that's all I can say. Manuel Godoy doesn't forgive lateness for any reason."

What had he walked into? The number of high-ranking military officers in the room was overwhelming. Sabers clanked and men sweated. The square room was sparsely furnished, with a number of strategic maps hung on each wall. The soldiers moved restlessly in anticipation, with a huge rectangular table of highly polished mahogany serving as the centerpiece of the milling crowd. Dev craned his neck, looking between the plumed cockades worn by the group. The King and chief minister were coming here? Was it some kind of military meeting? He began to sweat like every other man in the stuffy, unventilated room.

"What's your name?" the same infantry officer asked in undertones. "I'm Captain Alfonso of the Aragon Regiment. I just arrived yesterday. For a while, I thought I might not make it in time."

"Lieutenant Esteban Gomez, the Queen's Dragoon," Dev lied.

Alfonso's thick eyebrows moved upward in admiration. "Ah, the Queen's own. I'll wager you have a softer life than we do." He grinned from beneath his black mustache.

"No," Dev said dryly, "just the opposite. Spit and polish. Never a moment to relax."

With an understanding nod, Alfonso whispered, "I don't know about you, but this is my first staff meeting. My colonel sent me with secret papers to be given to the King."

"I'm here because I was ordered to watch, listen and learn."

Alfonso laughed. "Ah yes, they groom the young palace officers on how to run such a meeting as this. Frankly, I've never met King Charles. The colonel from our garrison has carried back many a story about the man. I've heard that he attends two masses each morning before going to workshops to assist his cabinetmakers or forgers who make pistols. Can you imagine? The King of Spain rolling up his sleeves and getting his hands dirty?"

"Amazing," Dev agreed. "I've heard he hunts every day. Perhaps he uses the pistols or muskets he has forged to shoot the animals."

Alfonso moved closer, his whisper conspiratorial. "You're with the Queen's guard. I've heard that the Prince of Peace, Godoy, is the most powerful man in the country. Is this so?"

Dev slipped his fingers beneath the stiff tunic collar and tugged on it. The material was so tight that it nearly cut off his ability to breathe. "My sworn duty is to protect the royal family, Captain. I wouldn't know about such gossip."

Effectively chastened, the captain moved away and stood silent.

There were at least three marshals in the room, from Dev's count. Somehow he had had the good fortune of walking into an important staff meeting. And then he shook his head. No guards had been posted at the doors he had entered to check his credentials. If these were Spain's finest, then Napoleon need not worry about overcoming them and claiming the country as part of the French empire. The soldiers were an indolent, lazy lot at best. Of course, he had come via the barracks, so no guards would have been posted. His Irish luck was holding.

Chapter Fifteen

Thorne masked her disappointment. How long would Dev be gone? He hadn't given her any indication of when he might return from his military duties. Was he safe? Had he been caught? Frustrated, Thorne looked up from the balcony where she sat. The weather was growing hotter, the Spanish sky bright blue and cloudless. On either side of the tree-lined inn, barefoot children played endlessly.

She had had time to think about becoming a mother, the feeling a warm, aching glow in her heart. She soberly acknowledged that if that did occur, Dev might refuse to marry her. Would he abandon her and his child in favor of revenge? What if he were killed or captured in his attempts to get to Vaughn Trayhern? The twisted web of his life made her feel helpless.

Thorne heard the inner door between their rooms open and quickly rose from the table. The mending she was going to do was forgotten as she flew into the room. A sudden gasp escaped her, rooting her to the spot. It wasn't Dev. Or was it? The man who came through the door and closed it quietly behind him was dressed as a Spanish soldier. Taking a step back, she blinked unsurely.

"Thorne?"

It was his voice. "Dev? Why are you dressed like that? And what's happened to your skin? It's so dark...I mean—"

Dev fought the urge to sweep Thorne's soft, loving body against his. With a sheepish smile, he pointed at his face.

"It's black walnut juice. I had to get into the palace without being noticed."

A maelstrom of longing surged through her and she uttered a small cry, throwing herself into his arms. "Oh, Dev," she said, her voice muffled against the wool of the uniform he wore. "I was so worried. I imagined awful things."

Laughing softly, Dev buried his face into the silken tresses of her hair. The combined smell of soap and Thorne's own special fragrance, sent a keening ache through him. He shut his eyes tightly, holding her, afraid she would evaporate into thin air if he released her. A swell of hunger exploded in his chest as he lightly kissed her hair and then her temple.

"I'm all right, Gypsy. Come, help me get out of this uniform. I want to wash the stain off my face and hair."

Thorne fought back an urge to cry and eased from his wonderful embrace. She didn't want Dev to see her tears. "I'll get a basin of water and soap for you."

After she left the room, Dev closed the folding doors leading out to the balcony. Had anyone seen him come back to the inn? Bothered by the strange look Godoy had given him, Dev had taken extra precaution in getting back to Thorne. Tomorrow morning, he had to go back to the palace. As he shrugged out of the uniform, his heart and mind centered on Thorne. Home . . . he was home. At last.

The sun was at its zenith when they walked out on the balcony. A band of Spanish peasants moved by the inn, all their worldly goods in a wooden cart drawn by a spotted ox. They eyed Dev and Thorne with envy. The children played happily in a puddle of water across the street.

"That's what I feel like doing," Thorne said, laughing softly. "Taking a bath to cool off from this awful heat."

Dev smiled absently, recalling the last time they had bathed in the river together. God knew, he was trying to keep his hands off Thorne, but it was driving him to the edge of distraction. He had felt her womanly heat, experienced her cry of elation as he had pleased her, and now he found himself wanting, more than ever, to culminate their bond with each other.

Dev noticed the sudden confusion in Thorne's expressive face. She didn't understand his actions, why he had suddenly become cool toward her when she had returned with the basin of water.

Later, after Dev had washed and changed, they went downstairs to eat. The love in Thorne's eyes only made it harder for Dev to try to combat the magical hold she had over him. After dinner, Thorne followed him in mute silence back to their room.

If she only knew how hungry he was to bury himself into her. He shut his eyes tightly, trying to ignore his rampant, scalding feelings.

Thorne's heart pounded once as she looked up to see Dev staring moodily down at her. "Are you angry with me?"

"God, no," he replied irritably, going to the table out on the balcony to sit down. Damn it! Why did Thorne have to look winsome and appealing even in the peasant clothes she wore? He knew the firmness of her small breasts and had tasted their sweetness. And he knew the curve of her belly to that silken carpet below. *Stop it! Stop it!*

Thorne stood unsurely, watching his face cloud.

"Have I done something?"

"No."

"Then why are you behaving like this, Dev? I don't understand."

His mouth tightened. The wind played with the strands of her hair; he longed to tame those tendrils from her flushed cheek. In the past few weeks, Thorne had grown from a girl into a woman. She had a right to know, he acknowledged, but he was trapped by his own good intentions. Miserably, Dev realized he hadn't handled Thorne or her situation well at all. He hadn't meant to fall in love with her, but he had. If he hadn't, it would be easy to ignore her womanly figure, her natural beauty and the pleasure she gave him.

"Things have become complicated, Thorne," he said in a growling tone, refusing to look at her.

"What things?"

He squirmed. "I don't want to talk about it."

"I do."

Grudgingly, he met her wide, probing eyes. "Say what's on your mind, then."

"You're peevish."

"I suppose I am."

"What has brought it on?"

You, he thought. No, me. He chewed down hard on his lower lip. "I'm preoccupied with military duties," he lied.

"My father's representative should be here by now," Thorne said, misunderstanding what duties he referred to.

"As soon as I get my men gathered and details worked out, I'll meet with your father's emissary."

Thorne made her way to the table and sat down opposite him. "Dev, what happens if they don't have Gavin? God forbid, but what if he's died in prison?"

He gave her a sharpened look. "My sister, Alyssa, sent me a letter last year telling me that he's alive. She's allowed to visit him once every six months."

"I see."

Dev's brows drew down. "If Gavin isn't with the emissary, it means that your father wasn't able to free him."

"He'll try, Dev."

"Yes, knowing his daughter the way I do, I'm sure he would." He held her wavering gaze. "If Gavin isn't free, then I'll give you to the emissary. You've gone through enough. I was wrong to try to use you as a lever to gain Gavin's freedom."

An unexpected rush of tears came to her eyes. Somehow, Thorne had known Dev would free her, regardless of whether his brother was in Madrid or not. It only made her love him more fiercely.

"I was English," she said thickly. "You knew nothing else of me. I don't blame you for what you did, Dev."

He snorted softly and rose. "I know."

Thorne choked down the lump in her throat. "How long will you remain in Madrid after the exchange has been made?"

"I don't know. It depends upon the information we've gathered. If my men have done their jobs correctly, I should be able to leave immediately for France after we get Gavin."

Thorne winced, feeling as if her heart were being cruelly torn apart. "I see. And then you're going to hunt down Vaughn Trayhern?"

"Yes."

"And if you survive that?"

He looked over at her. "I'm not planning on surviving it, Thorne. The odds are greatly against me. I have to slip back into England and locate the bastard."

Tears wavered in her eyes and she shut them so that Dev wouldn't see.

"I want you to go on living without me, Thorne," he told her in a strained voice. "I can see the hope in your eyes and hear it in your voice."

Dragging in a breath, Thorne opened her turbulent gray eyes, meeting his. "I'm yours, Dev. Now. Forever."

"Damn it, Thorne, don't say that!"

She clutched her hands tightly in her lap, glaring at him. "I'll say what I feel! At least I won't deny the truth of our situation!"

"Go home to England and find a man."

"I want no man except you! Do you think I could stand the Englishmen's offers after knowing you? You're nothing like them, Dev. You're natural and you're honest. I'm not a blue blood, you know that! All I want is a home, a loving husband and children. I want nothing more out of life. Do you think I care if there is little money? Or that you are a farmer? If you think I'm going back to England to marry some fop, you're mistaken!"

Dev rubbed his chest to stop the ache that centered there. "Now you're being stubborn, woman."

"Stubborn? Me, stubborn?" Thorne leapt to her feet. "Why, you—" she sputtered, then stamped her foot. "Oh! If I knew curse words like you, I'd use them right now, Devlin Kyle! You are the most addle-brained Irishman I've ever met!"

An unwilling grin tugged at his mouth. He'd never seen Thorne so temperamental before, and it only endeared her to him even more. The petulant set of her red lips made him go weak. The blazing silver in her eyes made her look like a huntress. "Sit down, Gypsy," he coaxed gently. "There are reasons for my decision and you know it."

She reluctantly sat, tense. "I'll never marry, Dev. If I can't have you, I want no one."

He sadly shook his head. "Listen to me, Gypsy."

"No, you listen! I've had a day without you. I want what's left to us to be ours."

His eyes narrowed speculatively upon her. "What are you saying?" he asked in a dangerously low tone.

Heart pounding wildly, Thorne tried to steady her voice. "Why do you try to protect my virginity when I don't want it protected? Why do you think you have the right to make that decision for me? I accept the causes and reasons for my behavior." She spread her hands in a supplicating gesture. "My heart blossomed beneath your care and love. My heart will shrivel and die once you leave me. How can you deny me these last few days we have together? How can you rob me of memories that would be as much mine as yours?" She choked back a sob. "Don't steal the dreams that will have to last me the rest of my life when I'm without you. Share all of yourself with me, Dev. Now." She closed her eyes, her voice scratchy. "I accept that you'll not marry me. I accept that you'll leave me. For God's sake, give me these last days with you, Dev."

Tears pricked the backs of Dev's eyes as he held her anguished gaze. Pain exploded violently in his chest as her honesty and the brutal reality of her statements sank into him. Abruptly, he stood and stalked through the room, leaving her.

Thorne winced as the door slammed. Dev had retreated, just as he had when she was first kidnapped by him. She remained out on the balcony, alone with her loss.

In an effort to avoid her, Dev cooled off his frustration by drinking two tankards of ale with the men who had gathered at the inn for the night. After an hour, he went back to the room. The taper on the dresser was lighted, casting soft shadows around the room. Thorne was sitting on the bed, mending one of his shirts. He deliberately glared at her, hoping to keep her at bay. Thorne's face had paled, and her golden skin stretched tautly across her high cheekbones. She left him alone as he cleaned the saddles out on the balcony of his room.

Throughout the rest of the evening, Thorne barely spoke. Dev refused to sit near her or even look at her. And all too soon, the moon rose in a thin slice above the horizon, and it was time to bed down for the night. Dev deliberately got up, dropped the saddles in his room and closed the doors to the balcony. Thorne gave him a stricken look but said nothing. If she slept with him, he would be tempted to touch her, to make her his own. A little more of his heart shrank with pain as he saw the dullness in her eyes as she stared up at him.

"I'm going to get a bath down the hall," she said softly, gathering up the mending.

"Fine," he grunted, walking back into his room. "I'm going to bed. Good night."

Thorne turned away, miserable. "G-good night..."

The night air was damp, cooling the otherwise oppressive heat. Dev stripped off his clothes and stretched out on the brass bed. He pulled a sheet across himself and waited to hear Thorne return to her room. He had purposely kept the door between the rooms open. Dev tiredly closed his eyes. He tried to escape the pain he knew he would feel when he forced Thorne to leave for England with her escort. Sweet God, but he didn't want her to go. Dev didn't want to deny her himself these last precious few days, either. It was necessary, he told himself angrily. She *will* fall in love again. She *will* marry!

Thorne padded barefoot into her room, clothed only in a clean peasant shirt. Before, she had always worn her chemise to bed. She had bathed to make herself as desirable as possible to Dev. Hesitating fractionally, Thorne went into his room. Her heart started a slow pound as he barely opened his eyes to see her standing at the side of the bed.

Dev's eyes widened, the breath torn from his chest. Thorne stood uncertainly before him, the tails of the shirt barely covering her long, beautifully curved thighs. His mouth went dry as he drank in her slender legs, dainty ankles and small feet. She was so tiny, so incredibly fiery. His gaze moved upward, across her boyish hips and narrow waist to her breasts. Her taut nipples thrust proudly against the wrinkled cotton. He felt himself harden. Her eyes were large and luminous, her lips parted. Before he could say anything, she slid beneath the sheet, fitting her body next to his.

His skin burned where she touched him. Dev clenched his teeth as she ran her cool hand across his naked chest, her fingers brushing one of his nipples. In a choked breath he turned, savagely pinning her on her back.

"Don't," he growled in a low, ominous tone.

Thorne didn't struggle as he held her wrists above her head. She saw the fever in his eyes, his anger and confusion. Licking her lips she said in a very soft voice, "I want you to love me, Dev. I want you..."

His fingers loosened from her wrists and he hung his head, valiantly trying to regain control over his body. "Sweet God, no, Thorne!"

She arched herself against him, her hip making contact with his hardness. A thrill arced through her as she saw him tense. Thorne knew then that Dev was more than susceptible to her naive advances.

"Make me yours, Dev," she begged softly, continuing to press provocatively against him.

His lips drew away from his teeth, sweat standing out on his face. Her hips were like fire against his, her skin soft and pliant. The ache for her exploded violently within him and Dev groaned. He bit out each word, his fingers tightening around her wrists. "You don't know what you're doing."

"Yes, I do!" she cried. "I love you, Dev! You give me pleasure, yet you deny yourself any. That isn't love. That isn't right. Allow me to love you in return." A soft sob caught in her throat. "I *need* to, don't you see?"

Dev forced himself to look at her. She lay helpless beneath him, her eyes wide and pleading. "It's wrong, Thorne. God, woman, you know that! If you lose your virginity—"

"I don't want it anymore."

He froze, yet wanted her to continue her sinuous movements against him. She felt so good. "Then you don't want a husband when you get back to England," he ground out harshly. "If I take you, no other man will have you."

"I don't want to be a wife to anyone else but you!" she sobbed. "I want no one's children but yours. Oh, Dev, why can't you see that? I love you. There's only you. If I go back to England, I'll die of grief or loneliness."

"You will not, damn you! You will go on living. Do you hear, Thorne?"

She thrashed her head from side to side, tears splattering her drawn cheeks. "No!"

With a curse, Dev yanked her into a sitting position. He sat inches from her, breathing hard, his chest gleaming in moonlight that filtered through the slats of the balcony doors. "Don't do this to me."

Thorne angrily wiped her tears away. "To you?" she cried. "To you? Think what you're doing to *me*. You love me, but you're willing to throw me away. You're the only man I'll ever love. When I go back to England, I'll never want marriage. I'll never want another man!"

He raked his fingers through his hair, no longer able to look at her anguished face or stand the rawness of her voice.

Thorne crawled the few inches separating them and placed her arms around his shoulders. "Oh, Dev, my beloved, I'm yours, and I want no other." She bowed her head against his tightened jaw. "I'll never love another. My loyalties are like yours—they run straight and true and honest." Lifting her face, her lashes beaded with tears, Thorne drowned in Dev's smoky blue gaze. "If you will not have me as wife, then love me and give me your baby. If I cannot have you, give me life within me so I can at least love our child."

Dev shuddered visibly and gripped her hard by the shoulders. "Damn you..."

Thorne stiffened in his iron grip, holding his watering eyes. Tears streamed down her cheeks. "Damn me to hell, then," she quavered, "for loving you. But if you must throw yourself away in the name of family honor, do it after you've given your life within me."

Thorne's face blurred and Dev choked down a sob that threatened to rend him apart. "You'll be spurned."

"I'll have your child's love."

"You'll be made a mockery of by your own people," he whispered hoarsely.

"I'll have the memory of you to keep my head held high, beloved."

Dev shook his head. "God...oh, sweet God, you don't know what you're asking of me, Thorne."

She sat very still, her breasts rising and falling sharply. "I love you enough to have your baby. At least give me that if you will give me nothing else, Dev. Do you want me to beg?"

Miserably, he lifted his head, holding her glistening eyes. He saw Thorne's lips compressed in pain, realizing too late that he was hurting her. Immediately, he loosened his grip, allowing his hands to slide downward until he captured her cool, cramped fingers. "Do you know what you'll be for the rest of your life?" he asked in a tortured voice. "You'll be an outcast. A woman of no morals. You'll be disdained. Avoided. And your father—"

"My father will take in me and our child with open arms, Dev. He loves me that much. He will love our child because I will make him understand that the baby was conceived out of love, not hate."

Her fingers were cool. Dev stared down at their slender whiteness against his dark, scarred ones. The overwhelming knowledge that Thorne loved him despite everything he had hurled at her shocked him. She would be an outcast in her own society. If she thought people mocked her now for her Gypsy blood, wait until she grew large with his child and she had no husband.

"You cannot stop me, Dev. I will use any wiles that I can to seduce you into taking me. I no longer have any pride where you're concerned. I accept that you will never marry me or allow me to follow you back to France. Are you so cruel and hate so much that you would deny me any shred of your love after you have left me? Are you? Or, perhaps, you don't love me at all."

He cowered beneath her strained voice, gently rubbing her fingers. "I love, you, Thorne," he answered quietly. She was so small. So delicate. And yet she had the backbone of a tempered steel sword. Scalding tears burned his eyes as he hung his head, holding her fingers tightly between his own. He felt humbled. Swallowing hard, he rasped, "I love you enough to give you my child." A child he would never see be born, or see grow up, hear the laughter of, or hold. And he would never see Thorne's happiness because she had given birth to the infant.

Relief flowed through Thorne. She pulled her hands from his, tenderly framing Dev's harsh face. "Then love me. You are the King of Swords in my life. You've destroyed everything as I knew it and yet, in its place, you've given me so much more." Her lips glistened with spent tears. "You've replaced what I've lost with a treasure greater than I could ever have imagined, Dev. You've given me yourself."

With a low groan, Dev swept her into his arms, his mouth crushing her lips. The instant he felt Thorne stiffen, he gentled his kiss, drinking great drafts of her warmth, her honeyed depths. Darkness surrounded them as he unbuttoned the shirt, leaving her kneeling naked before him. Dev eased Thorne down upon the sheets, sliding his hand up and across her beautiful body. He cupped her face and kissed her tenderly, drowning in her sweetness.

Thorne moaned and arched beneath his hand as he caressed her inner thigh. Her heart pounded wildly as she felt his mouth worship first one nipple and then the other. Fire, wild and uncontrolled, swept through her as he took her on a cloud of such shattering splendor that she could only gasp his name. Thorne felt his naked hardness press against the softness of her belly. Her eyes opened and she stared up at Dev. His gaze was fevered and he stroked her hair as if to calm the fear he saw in her eyes.

"I'll be as gentle as I can, Gypsy," he whispered. He parted her thighs, kneeling above her. His sun-darkened hands settled on her velvet white hips, light against darkness. Thorne closed her eyes, her lips parted, her breath lodged in her tightened throat. Her hands rested on each of his wrists.

"Yes . . . now, beloved, make me yours . . . now. . . ."

With a savage growl that reverberated through him, Dev gritted his teeth, fighting for control. He didn't want to hurt Thorne, and yet the very act itself would hurt her. The moment he touched her liquid, swollen core, a shudder passed through him, shaking him.

Thorne threw back her head as the pressure slowly mounted. Her body was screaming . . . she felt Dev's fingers tighten against her hips. Out of some elemental instinct, Thorne arched her hips upward in surrender to the hardened shaft that suddenly plunged into her. A cry tore from her lips, only to be smothered, the pain taken away by his mouth covering hers.

Dev froze, keeping most of his weight off her. Waiting. He felt her liquid tightness squeezing him and he bowed his head, kissing her. Kissing away the pain he had heard in her cry.

New sensations overwhelmed Thorne's momentary discomfort. The pressure was there, but so was an ache that began to build like a fire burning out of control. She ran her hands up his arms, opening her eyes, melting beneath his smoky gaze.

"Love me," she whispered, "love me. Show me how to love you."

Burning heat uncoiled within Dev and he moved experimentally, watching Thorne's reactions closely, monitoring every nuance of her expression. He thrust gently, feeling her give to him, her lashes lowered, a sultry look coming to her face.

"Good," he gritted thickly, "feel the pleasure, my woman, my own. Let me show you just how much I love you."

Each stroke took him a little farther into her. Each stroke created a firestorm of response within Thorne. She arched against him and felt him fill her as never before. Liquid rapture scalded her loins, and a sigh of pleasure broke from her. When Dev leaned down, capturing a nipple, Thorne automatically moved against him. He established the rhythm between them, and Thorne floated in a world of sensations. Each thrust, each motion of their sweat-slick bodies sliding against each other, increased the boiling, aching tension within her. An intense heat exploded deep within her, and her cry mingled with Dev's own as he gripped her hard to him.

Dev breathed heavily as he cradled her head between his hands in the aftermath. A trickle of perspiration wound down Thorne's cheek and he leaned down, licking it away. He smiled as she opened her eyes, which were dazed with pleasure, with satisfaction.

"You're mine," he whispered, kissing her reverently. "Mine. And God, how I love you."

Thorne closed her eyes, weak beyond belief. She could barely lift her arm to embrace Dev. How long they remained in each other's arms afterward, she could not remember. She raised her lashes as Dev gently withdrew from her. Thorne felt suddenly bereft as he knelt before her, splendid in his nakedness. He must have seen her look of loss because he reached over, caressing her hip.

"Stay there," he told her, "I'll be back."

Thorne closed her eyes, thinking she could not get up if Dev had wanted her to. She was boneless . . . floating. Automatically, she covered her belly with her hand, wanting desperately to have Dev's baby, to keep some part of him when he left her.

Sitting at her side, Dev took the wet cloth and sponged away the blood that lay pooled beneath her. He stroked her flushed cheek, watching the flame burn in her half-closed eyes. It had been good for both of them, he realized humbly. Thank God, he'd been able to control himself for her sake. She was so small.

"Dev?"

"Yes?"

"I love you."

"I know you do, Gypsy. You just showed me how much. Lie there now, we're going to sleep."

She closed her eyes, welcoming his strong, naked form against her. As he drew the blankets across her shoulders, Thorne smiled softly and came into Dev's arms. Now she was complete. She was his. There was nothing else she wanted in the world except that, and to carry his life within her.

Chapter Sixteen

Dawn filtered through the slats of the doors leading to the balcony. Thorne barely awakened as Dev left their bed. His eyes grew tender with love as he drank in her nightgowned body wrapped in a tangle of sheets, sheets they had tangled together as they had bound themselves to each other, completing the love denied them for so long. Whether he wanted to or not, he had to get back to the palace. Staining his flesh and hair again, Dev dressed quietly, his gaze always returning to the sleeping Thorne. Her lashes softly brushed her cheeks. The rose flush over her skin only emphasized her new womanly status. He trembled inwardly as he absorbed her soft lips, which were still kiss-swollen from their hungry ardor the night before. Hands trembling as he belted up the straight sword around his waist, he didn't see the leather gloves that belonged with the uniform drop to the floor near the armoire.

He carried Thorne back to her own bed, trying not to disturb her as he drew the sheet over her. He couldn't leave without caressing her mussed hair, and he leaned over to inhale the scent of her, which left his senses reeling. Chastising himself, Dev brushed a feather-light kiss against Thorne's cheek. She stirred, her lashes barely lifting, revealing languorous gray eyes softened by love.

"Dev?"

"Shh, my beautiful Gypsy. Go back to sleep." He stroked her hair and smiled tenderly down at her, wanting to stay, to slip back into that bed with her and drown within her hot, fiery sweetness once again.

"But—"

"Hush," he whispered against her lips. "I'll be back by nightfall. And then we'll be together once again."

The corners of her luscious mouth pulled upward, sending a sharp ache through Dev. Thorne reached over, her small hand resting against his chest.

"I love you," she whispered. "More than life."

It took every shred of his dissolving strength to get up and leave her. "You are my life, Gypsy. Go back to sleep, my beautiful woman. My own...."

His words fell over her like a warm coverlet, pulling her back down into sleep. Thorne did not hear the inner door quietly close or his booted footsteps move mutely along the wooden hall. Turning over, she snuggled into the pillows. Contentment lulled her back into the folds of slumber.

Later, Thorne frowned, hearing the heavy thud of boots along the hall. The clank of swords clashed with the hollow echo created by what seemed to her to be many men marching down the corridor. She heard a door open and then outraged cries, curses and harsh words exchanged. The sounds of boots came closer and closer. Her brows knit and she tossed, somewhere in the gray world of half sleep. What was going on? Was she having a nightmare?

Suddenly, the inner door was flung open and sent crashing against the wall. Thorne jerked up. She pulled the sheet up to her breast. Her eyes widened. Four Spanish soldiers in bright red uniforms entered her room. The leader, a man with a scar down the left side of his face, lunged toward her. His fingers sank deeply into her arm. He dragged Thorne toward him.

"Don't try to escape," he warned in a deep growl, then looked over at his soldiers. "Search the place!"

"Ow!" Thorne tried to pull loose. Her attention was divided between her captor and the other three men as they methodically began to search the room. The officer's fingers tightened on her arm until tears came to her eyes.

"Where is he?" the captain snarled, his face inches from hers.

Gagging on the foul smell of his breath, Thorne stopped struggling. "Who? What are you talking about?" she cried, finding her voice. "You have no right to barge in here!"

"Quiet! You have no rights. Where is the spy? I know he came to this inn last night and your room is right next to his." He shook Thorne savagely, making her head snap back. "Talk or you'll be sorry!"

Tears crowded into her eyes. The soldiers were tearing the room apart, throwing all her worldly goods to the floor, one by one. Another soldier yanked the folding doors open, searching the balcony, his musket ready to fire at anyone he might find out there. "I—I don't know what you're talking about!" Thorne's mind spun with options. With plans. Apparently, someone had followed Dev here last night, and they had meant to capture him at first light. Thank God he'd escaped! The pressure on her arm increased and the officer dragged her out of bed.

Thorne struggled to stand, but the officer deliberately hauled her against his lean body. His black eyes glittered as he perused her as if she were a piece of merchandise. Collecting her shattered thoughts, Thorne managed to get to her feet, throwing her hands flat against his chest to break contact. She raised her chin, giving him a haughty look filled with disdain.

"I don't know who you are or what you think you're doing! How dare you break in here and—"

"Captain Riviera at your service, *señorita*," he said mockingly. He shoved her away. "Get your clothes. You're coming with us."

Thorne staggered backward, hands flying to the thin cotton of the nightgown she wore. "Where are you taking me?"

"Back to the palace. The chief minister wants to have a chat with you."

Chief minister? Godoy himself? Blanching, Thorne pressed herself flatly against the wall. She shivered as all four men stood assembled in front of her, assessing her like hungry wolves. "But—that's impossible! I told you, no one is here! You have no right—"

Riviera snapped an order to one solder. "Find her a cloak!"

"Wait! Let me dress. I can't go out like—"

"The chief minister said to bring the spy. Well, he is not here, but you are." Riviera smiled savagely. "And in some ways, I think he'll almost be as pleased that it's a woman, instead."

The cloak was thrown at Thorne. Shakily, she put on the floor-length black wool cape. Barefoot, they dragged her from the room. Disgruntled and angry patrons crowded the hall and watched as the soldiers marched her through the interior of the inn.

The morning was crisp. Riviera mounted, then pulled Thorne up into his arms. Stunned, she tried to avoid contact with him.

"Now, *señorita,* you relax and I'll give you a speedy ride to the palace. Don't make the mistake of trying to escape or I promise you I'll cut up that pretty face of yours."

Shivering in terror, Thorne wrapped the cloak tightly around her. Riviera placed his arm around her waist in an iron grip. She had no choice but to lean against him as he spurred his giant chestnut gelding into a gallop. The horses clattered through the cobblestoned streets. The echo of their iron-shod hooves striking the stone careened off the adobe walls that surrounded them. The wind cut sharply across Thorne's face, and tears stung her eyes. My God, what was going to happen? Godoy was considered in England to be the power behind Spain's throne. And Dev! Dev!

The palace came into view, and Thorne was struck by myriad impressions. The guards at the gate allowed them to pass, coming smartly to attention and saluting. An old woman bearing a tremendous load on her bent back was nearly run down by Riviera's horse. He cursed at the peasant and spurred his animal through the gate. Riviera halted his hard-breathing mount at the bottom of the white marble steps that swept upward to the main palace doors. He dropped Thorne unceremoniously into the arms of two awaiting guards.

"She's the one. Take her to the chief minister."

A guard gripped each arm, hauling Thorne along. As they rapidly climbed the steps, the cloak slid free of her shoulders. With a cry, she tried to stop and retrieve it. They pushed her forward and the cloak fell into a heap, a black spot marring the pristine whiteness of the marble.

Cheeks burning with mortification, Thorne had little time to appreciate the beauty inside the palace. The highly polished tiled halls soon became a dizzying maze to her as the guards moved her down one hall and then another at a breathless pace. Few nobles were awake, but she saw servants here and there. When she could read their faces, she saw their pity for her plight, and that frightened her even more.

"Here!" one guard snapped, jerking Thorne to a halt. He stopped in front of a gilded gold-and-white door. The other opened it. "Get in there and don't think of trying to leave. We'll be standing out here guarding you."

Thorne was shoved forward. She tripped over the soiled hem of her nightgown. The door slammed shut just as she fell to the oriental carpet. Pain soared up through her hands and knees. Gasping for breath, she quickly surveyed the empty room. The silence was awesome. Shakily, Thorne got to her feet, rubbing her right wrist, which had taken the brunt of her spill. Everywhere she turned, fine paintings were hung on the wall. All were by famous European masters. A Hogarth graced one wall, and Thorne absorbed the peaceful pastoral scene.

The minutes passed with agonizing slowness. There was only one door to the windowless room, and she gave up hope of escape. Chilled, Thorne rubbed her arms and wandered about in a daze. A sound, a soft *whoosh,* caught her attention. Turning, Thorne saw what she had thought to be a solid wall move. A thickly set man whose shoulders gave him the appearance of a massive bull entered. Her heart picked up in a staccato beat. He wore a somber dark brown waistcoat, matching breeches with white stockings and black buckled shoes. His white ruffled shirt emphasized his dark features. As her gaze moved up, a coldness seeped through Thorne. His square-jawed face and merciless ebony eyes made her take a step away from him as he approached her.

"So," he began softly, stopping several feet from Thorne, "you are the *señorita* that Captain Riviera found this morning." He bowed deeply. "I am Chief Minister Manuel Godoy. And you? Who are you?"

Thorne swallowed convulsively, moving her arms protectively across her breasts as his gaze burned into her. Godoy licked his sensual lower lip in appreciation, one corner of his mouth crooking upward. Indignation swept through Thorne like a tidal wave, momentarily replacing her fear.

"Who am I? I'll tell you who I am, Chief Minister. I am the niece of the Marquis Juan de Vega! How dare you and your ruffian guards haul me about like common trash! If this is Spanish hospitality at its best, then I condemn your less than glorious and noble manners! When I tell my uncle of this inexcusable transgression on *your* part, he'll be livid." Her nostrils quivered with pent-up fury as she stood, holding his amused gaze.

Godoy managed to hide his smile. There was no doubt she was English because of her husky accent. But the niece of a marquis? Highly unlikely. Still . . . he visually roamed her proud, trembling form. Riviera had been right, she was worth a second look. And a third. Manuel scowled. There was a challenging silver flame in her eyes that proclaimed that she was a woman of substance, of elegance. And her voice was cultured, her shoulders thrown back with a pride that was inborn. Her chin tilted defiantly. No peasant or bourgeois female would dare bluff him as she was now doing. Perhaps she was a blue-blooded spy. There were ways to find out if she was an impostor.

"A thousand pardons. Perhaps you'll be kind enough to tell me your name. I'm intrigued with your English accent," he said soothingly. His smile became apologetic as he slipped off his waistcoat and held it out to her.

"Lady Thorne Somerset," she said in tight-lipped reply. "And I know very well that Spain is at war with England. I can't help it if the blood of both countries runs in my veins."

"No disrespect was intended," Godoy murmured. "Spain has signed peace treaties with Napoleon. Your presence here lends suspicion, don't you think? I merely wanted to question you about a man whom I saw in a military staff meeting here yesterday. I have spoken with Captain Riviera, and he feels you are under suspicion. Here, please put on the coat until I can get one of my servants to find you something more suitable to wear."

Stunned by the sudden change in Godoy, Thorne numbly took the coat. She shrugged it across her shoulders to protect herself from his slavering looks. At first he had appeared absolutely ruthless, and now he was the epitome of a polished gentleman. He rang a small silver bell. Immediately, a servant entered.

"Milord?" the man asked, bowing.

"Bring tea immediately, Renaldo. Then fetch Miss Somerset a proper dressing gown so that she does not stand here shivering. We wouldn't want her to catch a cold."

"*Sí*, milord." Renaldo dared to risk a look at Thorne. "What—what size?" he stammered.

With a wave of his hand, Godoy turned to the sideboard. "I'm sure the Queen has a spare dressing robe. Borrow something from one of her endless closets. God knows, she won't miss it. Quickly now!"

Paling, the servant bowed and rushed from the room. Thorne edged to a satin sofa and sat down, knuckles white as she clutched the waistcoat to her. She watched with undisguised curiosity as Godoy poured them both a brandy. Sharply, Thorne recalled her uncle telling her about him. Godoy had been a lowly guard at the palace when Queen María Luisa spotted him. She took him as her paramour. Godoy quickly rose to power after that. He controlled the Queen and usurped Charles's power by getting rid of all the King's trusted advisers. Then, like the fox Godoy was, he replaced them with his own people, over whom he had total control. When Godoy turned, his face was pleasant, a twinkle in his black eyes.

"My lady?"

Thorne stiffened as he used the proper title. She took the snifter. "What is this?"

Chuckling, Godoy paced slowly back and forth in front of her. "Only the best of our fine brandy. Drink. It will warm you like a lover caressing your flawless skin."

His voice was like dark velvet. Thorne choked down a swallow. She gasped, the liquid burning a trail of fire down her throat and into her knotted stomach. She saw Godoy smile at her. A chill raced through her.

"Now, tell me, my lady, how is it that you're here in Madrid? Not many English visit us nowadays."

Her mind whirled with choices. Thorne didn't want to involve Dev in any way. Two days from now, the exchange would take place, and more than anything she wanted to see Gavin free and with his brother. "I came by ship to Barcelona, where I visited my aunt and uncle. I'm now in Madrid waiting for my father's emissary to arrive and escort me back to London." That wasn't a lie.

"How can one so beautiful be alone in this great and magical city?"

"M-my mother died recently. I had no desire to attend gala parties or occasions, minister." She pressed on. "You see, my father is the Earl of Somerset and he was too ill to come to Spain and inform my mother's family of her death. So I came instead."

Godoy studied her upturned face. She looked so earnest and innocent. Yes, that was the word he'd been searching for—she was an innocent. With the face of an angel. He felt blood throb through his loins, he savored the sensation. Few women made him feel hot and hungry anymore. But she did. "My condolences, Lady Thorne."

Thorne avoided his sharpened gaze and stared down at the brandy. He was stalking her; she could feel it. She recalled her uncle talking angrily of Godoy, of the way the chief minister tortured his enemies in the tradition of the

Inquisition. What would he do with her? He was a huge, lethal cat, and she a mere mouse with no protection.

"Th-thank you."

Godoy resumed his pacing, occasionally taking a sip of the brandy. "So, tell me, what is a lady of your station doing at a bourgeois inn? Certainly you can afford much better."

Her heart began to leap in her breast, sending painful constrictions to her throat. "I—uh...I don't wish to squander my father's money."

"I see. Interesting. A frugal daughter of a very rich man...." Godoy motioned to the waistcoat she wore. "Search the inside right pocket."

Mystified by his request, Thorne set the snifter aside. She dug with trembling hands into the pocket and brought out a pair of leather gloves. "I don't understand, Chief Minister. Are these yours?"

Godoy gauged her expression closely. "Surely you know whose gloves those are," he whispered. "Take another look."

Thorne's hands grew damp as she turned them over. "I'm sorry. I don't own these, and I don't know who does."

"Are you very sure?"

A chill worked its way up her spine as Godoy's eyes mercilessly probed hers. Thorne opened her mouth and then closed it. Wait! She remembered that when Dev had come back in uniform, there had been a set of fawn-colored gloves in the belt at his waist. Had they fallen to the floor this morning when he dressed, and lain there unnoticed by him? The soldiers had searched the room thoroughly and found them! Heat swept her cheeks and Thorne lowered her lashes. "They aren't mine, Chief Minister." She managed a low laugh. "And they're quite large. Too large for my small hands." Thorne tossed them on the couch beside her, praying that he did not see through her bravado.

Godoy negligently picked them up, looking first at the gloves and then at her flaming red face. "How odd," he murmured, "My soldiers found them when they searched your room for that spy. These—" he waved them in front of her face "—belong to the Queen's guard."

"I—I have no idea *how* they got in my room!"

"Really?"

"Yes, really!"

"Shall I tell you a little story, Lady Thorne? A true story?"

Unnerved, Thorne couldn't meet his gaze. She clasped the snifter so tightly that she thought the fine crystal might shatter between her hands. "If you must."

Godoy cocked his head. She was a courageous woman despite her tentative circumstance, and that increased his admiration for her. "Yesterday, at a very important staff meeting between the King and his highest ranking military officers, I spotted a stranger amongst them. He wore the yellow uniform." He came and stood in front of Thorne, deliberately intimidating her. "Only one kind of soldier wears that unforgettable uniform."

Thorne glared up at him, angry because he was trying to frighten her with his bulk. "I suppose you want me to ask who wears it?" she shot back acidly.

He took her temper in stride, liking the way her eyes flared with a silver glint in their depths. "Of course I do. The Queen's guard, my dear lady. Now, I happen to be very close to the Queen. I handpick every guard that is sworn to protect her. It's a very small, elite force." His voice deepened. "I know every man's name, his background and lineage. And I know that whoever was impersonating one of her guards yesterday was a spy."

Licking her lips, Thorne glanced up at him. "If he was a spy, why didn't you arrest him then?"

Reaching out, Godoy caressed her slightly curled hair. He watched her eyes widen and then she jerked away from his trailing fingers. Smiling pleasantly, he said, "I felt it would have been premature. As it was, I had him followed. He talked for hours with a Captain Rafael Coruna at a tavern near the palace. Coruna is now in my dungeon being persuaded to give us all the information he traded with this spy.

After drinking ale at the tavern, the spy, known as Gomez, eventually stopped for the night at your inn.''

Thorne lunged to her feet, gripping the waistcoat. She whirled around, facing Godoy. ''The unspoken meaning of this is, of course, that he came to my room, is that not right?''

''Precisely.''

Shaking inside, feeling Godoy closing the trap neatly around her, Thorne called on the last reserve of her courage. ''There are twenty rooms in that inn, minister. He could have been in any of them! Why pick mine?''

''Because, Lady Thorne, the gloves were found in your room. My men searched the room next to yours, finding neither the spy nor his clothing until they found these.'' He pointed to the gloves on the sofa.

''Well . . . he must have thrown them in there while I was sleeping! To lead you off track!''

Godoy roused himself as the servant came back with a silk dressing robe and tea service. He watched as Thorne traded his waistcoat for the deep purple silk robe. It was a bit too large on her, but the color emphasized her porcelain English skin and flushed cheeks. He couldn't tear his gaze from her luscious, parted lips, and felt himself hardening with desire.

''Tea, my lady?'' He picked up a china cup and walked over to Thorne.

She took the cup and saucer, willing her hands to stop shaking. Godoy was suddenly soft and smiling again. Had she actually convinced him?

''Since I've been less than a gentleman, Lady Thorne, I insist you allow me to make proper amends for my men's behavior. Renaldo, my personal manservant, will take you to a suite nearby. A scented bath will be drawn for you, and then the Queen's own maids shall dress you as befits your rank.'' Manuel smiled to himself. She was a spy. He could smell the fear around her. And he didn't believe her story one bit. There were many European women who tried to pose as spies and failed miserably. First, he would have sport with her, and later, after he finished bedding her down, he'd get to the business at hand. Pity to mar such beautiful flesh, he thought.

Blinking unsurely, Thorne stared across the room at Godoy. "I don't understand."

"You say Marquis Juan de Vega is your uncle. I'll send a messenger immediately to confirm your story. If he verifies that you are part Spanish and the daughter of the Earl of Somerset, then I shall free you. Technically, because part of your family is of Spanish descent, you are not considered an enemy to us." He raised the cup to his lips, watching her intently over the rim. "Until then, I will make amends for the hardships you've had to endure." He set the cup down abruptly on the sideboard. To Renaldo he snapped, "See that she joins me for a carriage ride just before lunch. Tell the kitchen I want a picnic basket prepared to take along."

Renaldo bowed briskly and turned, leaving the room. Godoy watched his servant exit, then sauntered toward the same door. He looked over his shoulder at Thorne, who had shock written plainly across her winsome features. "You had better pray that what you have told me is the truth. If you haven't I'll be happy to escort you to our Inquisition dungeons, and then you will tell me all about this spy who shadows my palace."

The door shut quietly. Thorne gave a little cry, her knees going weak with relief. She sat down and buried her face in her hands. Oh, Dev! What are we going to do? If she didn't show up for the exchange... And what would Godoy do once he found out she had been abducted for ransom from her uncle? Agony overwhelmed Thorne, and she forced back the tears that wanted to fall. Godoy was lecherous. She had seen his type too often at parties back home. He was a wolf prowling the crowd for a defenseless sheep. *Dev,* she screamed silently. *Dev, you're in danger! I love you. Oh, God, please help him. Don't let him get caught!*

The guard at the laundry gate nodded to Dev as he walked the black gelding through the crowded entrance. The soldier was arguing with a troupe of dancers who were supposed to supply entertainment for a banquet later that evening. Dev guided the horse toward the laundry facility, a brown wrapped parcel beneath his right arm. He had changed uniforms at the livery where Ghazeia was stabled. Once again he was in the blue uniform of Private Esteban Gomez. It wouldn't be wise to be caught riding the horse of a Queen's guard. If anyone stopped him, he could simply say that the lieutenant had ordered him to take his horse back to the stable. The ferretlike look Godoy had given him yesterday at the military meeting placed Dev on alert. He didn't want to raise suspicions by showing up on the palace grounds in the same uniform two days in a row.

After delivering the horse, Dev went to the laundry. He carried the Queen's guard uniform back to the chamber, where he had found it. After making sure no one was around, he hung it back up. Just as he was leaving, Dev heard a familiar, reedlike voice pierce the air. Maria waved her heavily bandaged hand at him, motioning him to come to where she was sitting. Dev smiled and walked over to the bench beneath a tiled roof where Maria was mending a red uniform.

"Good morning, *señora*."

"And you, Private Gomez." Her birdlike head tilted. "Have you heard the latest?" she whispered dramatically.

Dev shook his head, dividing his attention between Maria and the servants who flowed back and forth around them. "No. What gossip circulates the palace now?" he teased her, smiling.

Maria wagged a crooked finger at him. "Not gossip! I saw it with my own eyes, I did. They came draggin' a beautiful young woman in a nightgown through the main gate this morning. She rode with Captain Riviera, Godoy's henchman. Now the palace buzzes that she's English. English! Can you imagine? They say she's a spy."

Dev's heart slammed against his ribs. "Maria, you say you saw her?"

With a cackle, she nodded. "That I did! Beautiful she was, too."

"What color of hair?" He held his breath, finding the whole conversation unreal.

"Black as a raven's wing, it was. But the oddest thing was, it was short! Can you imagine anyone cutting her hair off like that? A boy she looked like."

His hand tightened on the pommel of the sword at his side. "What color of nightgown did she wear?"

"White."

"Anything else? Did you notice anything else special about her?"

Maria thought for a moment, hand poised about the cloth, needle pinched between her fingers. "I was very close to her. That damnable Riviera almost ran me out of the way with that horse of his, he did. She wore a necklace. I'd swear it was a scarab. Gypsy she might be. I've seen many, and she had the look of one."

Dev reached out, gripping the old woman's shoulder. "A name? Did anyone get her name?"

Cackling, Maria slowly pushed the needle through the fine fabric. "A laydee, they say. I heard Godoy's own servant, Renaldo, say that she claims to be a Lady Thorne Somerset from England. Can you imagine such a lie? The girl's in trouble, I can promise you that. No maid walks away from Godoy without being deflowered. But if'n she is a spy, as they say, the minister will show her his Inquisition dungeon."

Cold-bladed terror poured through Dev. How in the hell— He quickly searched his memory. He had been so careful in making his way back to the inn. This morning he had taken even more elaborate precautions about leaving it. He had given the livery boy money the night before to saddle and lead his gelding down the street at a certain time so he wouldn't be seen leaving the inn from the stable. That look Godoy gave him yesterday had been Thorne's death sentence. Oh, God... Turning, Dev glanced across his shoulder toward the palace.

"Maria, how can I find out where this Englishwoman is being held?"

"Accordin' to Renaldo, the minister is takin' her for a carriage ride at noon. If you ask me, that's not the only ride she'll see—they say that Godoy's got designs on her body. The cooks in the kitchen have been ordered to prepare a picnic basket."

It took all his control not to panic. Dev leaned down, placing one booted foot on the bench where she sat. "Did Renaldo say where Godoy was taking this woman?"

"Why, everyone knows the minister has a favorite knoll surrounded by hedge and trees where he can do whatever he wants in private," she cackled. Maria pointed toward the rolling acres to the east. "Three miles down that carriage track is where he'll be takin' her." Maria shook her head sadly. "I feel for the girl. Godoy will mount anything with two legs. She's fragile-looking, that one. I will pray for her."

Pray for both of us, Dev thought in anguish. He patted Maria's shoulder. "Thank you, Maria."

Godoy felt his body harden to a new, painful level of intensity as he watched Captain Riviera escort the ethereal Thorne Somerset down the wide marble steps. Mother Mary, she was exquisite! The simple Grecian styled muslin gown was captured beneath her small breasts with a royal blue ribbon, emphasizing her diminutive size. His eyes roamed her, from the creamy swell of her cleavage to her slender hips and down to the apex of her thighs, hidden provocatively by the nearly transparent muslin dress. Fire ignited in him as he fantasized plunging into her moist, inexperienced depths. Yes, virginal white was the perfect color for her. Before this afternoon was out, he would see the red of her blood staining that glorious dress. And by that night, the instruments in his dungeon would be covered with the rest of her blood.

The smile that Godoy gave Thorne made her slow her step in the blue satin shoes she wore. His black eyes glimmered with an almost insane quality, and she hung back momentarily. The hot bath had unknotted her. Now, dressed in such a revealing gown, Thorne wanted to escape. She had tried to reject wearing the scandalous outfit, but the maids had insisted because they didn't want to incur Godoy's well-known wrath. Her hair had been washed, perfumed and coaxed into appealing curls. When she had looked at herself in the gilded mirror, she did not recognize herself. No longer was she a girl on the edge of womanhood. The image that stared back at her was that of a woman fulfilled by love. Dev's love. And as Thorne hesitantly made her way to the gold and gaudily embossed carriage, she knew Godoy wanted her.

Thorne sat down on the velvet cushions and tensed when he joined her. "How can I point out our many interesting sights if I do not sit near you, my lady?" he asked in a low, suggestive tone.

Shrinking away from contact with him, Thorne gripped the small fan between her icy fingers. Her throat ached with unshed tears over her fate. There was no way to escape. Riviera and his men mounted and formed a vanguard around the coach as it drew away from the palace.

"I thought a picnic was in order, my beautiful English rose." Godoy reached out, lightly stroking her bare arm with one finger. He saw her flinch. Typical of a shy, virginal maiden, he told himself, delighted with her reaction. "My cooks have prepared the finest of foods, which I shall hand-feed to you myself. Let it not be said that the Spanish do not take care of England's beautiful women properly."

The heat of his body stifled her. Thorne feigned interest in the view out the windows of the carriage as it rocked from side to side down the road. The manicured hedges and orange trees gave way to beds of carefully tended roses in full bloom. But their fragrance made no impact on Thorne, her nerves were so tightly strung.

"In England, a gentleman stays his distance, my lord minister, until he's invited to come closer by the woman in question."

Godoy removed his finger from her wrist. Her skin was so soft. Laughing, he lifted her hand, pressing a moist kiss to it. "My apologies, Thorne. I must confess, your beauty has stunned my senses. It's not often we get to entertain lovely English ladies." He maintained a hold on her hand and leaned over, his lips barely brushing the tender nape of her exposed neck. "In Spain, a gentleman is always amorous with the lady on his arm. It's expected. Applauded."

With a desperate cry, Thorne pushed Godoy away. She got up, gripped the door of the coach and settled on the opposite cushion. Nervously fanning herself, she glared at Godoy. "Sir, your manners are far from impeccable! No English gentleman would take the liberties you take! My father did not raise me to be pawed, and I resent it."

Godoy leaned back and exploded into rich, rolling laughter. He slapped his knee. "You are refreshing! Normally, any woman I want falls eagerly into my arms." The smile disappeared from his mouth, moving into an implacable line. "Don't you realize I run Spain? Queen María Luisa runs the King. I run the Queen. If you were schooled by the *ton,* then you have been taught that a man with riches and power is the one into whose arms you give yourself."

"I hate the *ton!* I hate the fops and the pretended conversations. My parents raised me to think, not to simper! The man I give myself to will be the one whom I love. No other."

"Spirit. I like that," Godoy murmured. "When I first saw you, you reminded me of a bedraggled kitten, spitting and clawing. After cleaning you up and giving you fine clothes, you still behave like one. Tell me, are you married?"

Thorne hesitated. If she lied and said yes, Godoy would take her because she was no longer a virgin. She would be just another married woman and, therefore, bedable. If she told the truth, then perhaps he would stop chasing her and respect her virginity, as all gentlemen did. But she wasn't a virgin any longer, and Thorne felt heat steal into her face. Last night, she had willingly given Dev the gift of herself. "I—no."

"What took you so long to answer?" he prodded genially. "Are you betrothed?"

"Yes," Thorne lied quickly.

"Ah, I see. So, tell me about this man who has claimed your young and innocent heart." She began to tell him about Vaughn Trayhern, emphasizing that he was a cavalry captain. Anything to slow down this bull in heat.

As the carriage rolled to a stop, Thorne's heartbeat picked up. Servants scurried down off the coach and quickly spread a huge purple blanket across the grass. The knoll was surrounded on three sides by huge trees, hedges and flowers. In Spain's unrelenting heat, they would have to be watered daily in order to survive. Yes, Godoy took very good care of this location. He coaxed Thorne from the carriage and escorted her to the blanket.

"You can appreciate the magnificent view from here," he said, gesturing proudly toward the rolling meadow filled with flowers before them. "From this knoll, we can eat, enjoy pleasantries and allow nature to work her inestimable magic."

"Chief Minister?" Riviera asked, riding up.

Frowning, Godoy looked up. "What?" he demanded, irritated by the intrusion to the flowery speech he was going to deliver to Thorne.

"I'm sorry, Chief Minister. But do you want us to wait nearby?"

"Remain a mile away. Come back in three hours." His jaw set into a bulldog line. "I want no interruptions, Captain. Is that understood?"

Riviera glanced over the knoll toward the woods, which contained many deer that the King hunted regularly. "Very well, Chief Minister. Three hours."

Thorne's mouth went dry as the coach and escort disappeared. Before them, spread out on the blanket, was an array of carefully prepared food. When Godoy turned his head to look at her, she knew she had to stall his advances in any way possible.

"I'm starved!" Thorne exclaimed, going to the blanket and kneeling down.

"So am I," he told her, coming around the blanket.

Thorne tried to escape when Godoy knelt behind her.

"Not so quickly, my timid deer," he crooned, settling his hand on her small shoulders. He brought her back against his body. "Feel how much I want you, English Thorne."

Panic shot through Thorne as she felt the huge bulge pressing insistently against her back. With a cry, she wrenched out of his arms and scrambled to her feet.

"Don't touch me!" she shouted. "You have no right! None!"

Anger exploded inside Godoy and he leapt to his feet, breathing hard. "I have *every* right. You are an accomplice to a spy. And a liar! Who knows? Perhaps even your name is false." He stalked her and they warily circled each other around the blanket.

"I am who I say I am! And I'm no spy! You leave me alone, Godoy. I don't care if you're the richest, most powerful man in Europe, you have no right to rape me."

"Rape you?" He rubbed his hands together. "Women beg me, in tears, to mount them like mares in heat."

Thorne colored fiercely over his rude description of an act she knew only as an expression of love. "You're an animal!"

His smile quirked and he nodded. "Women call me a stallion. I'm sure your father owns horses. Did he ever allow you to see a stud mate with a mare? It will be no different for you."

To Thorne's horror, he leapt across the blanket. She threw the fan at him. It struck Godoy in a glancing blow and he howled out in anger, momentarily slowed. Thorne picked up the folds of her dress, running down the slight knoll toward the meadow. She heard Godoy closing fast on her heels. Her breath became heavy. Faster! Faster! Oh God, he was going to catch up with her!

Godoy leaned out, his fingers clamping down ruthlessly on her shoulder. He spun Thorne around. Too late! He saw her raise her hand, palm open. The slap startled him, a welt burning across his cheek. Staggering backward, he released her. Again, she ran like a deer away from him. Damn her to hell! He'd fix that little vixen. Spirit was one thing, denial quite another. With a curse, he lunged after her.

Thorne chanced a look over her shoulder. Godoy's face was a mask of fury. She screamed for help, her cry shattering the meadow's silence. He would rape her. He might kill her. Her breath came in huge, ragged gulps, fire searing her bursting lungs. Each step, Thorne faltered a little more, the dress encumbering her forward motion. She heard Godoy approaching, his breath like a bull's as he charged up behind her.

Suddenly, Thorne saw a huge black horse with a blue-coated Spanish soldier riding full tilt toward them from the other end of the meadow. She screamed for help again, waving her arm frantically. Help! He had to help her!

Thorne's desperate cry strangled in her throat. As the rider approached, his sword drawn, she recognized that it was Dev. Could it be? Could it? With a sob, she pushed beyond her limits, her legs flying beneath her.

Dev savagely dug his spurs into the black gelding, hearing the animal grunt in pain. He bore down upon Godoy, who was rapidly closing the distance between himself and Thorne. He had only seconds to see if Thorne had been hurt. She was frightened, but her clothes were intact and he could see no damage done to her beautiful skin. His lips drew away from his teeth as he leaned forward, aiming the thundering black horse directly down on Godoy.

The chief minister stumbled to a halt as the soldier suddenly veered off toward him. Who the hell was this? He'd have the idiot gelded! And then his eyes widened incredulously. The face was familiar. The spy! No. It could not be. Impossible. Wildly aware that he was in mortal danger, Godoy turned and ran in the opposite direction.

Taking the flat side of the straight sword, Dev raised it about his head and brought it down with full force against the fleeing minister. The sword smacked Godoy hard from the buttocks up to the middle of his back. The sound echoed sharply in the meadow. Godoy screamed in pain. The force behind the attack sent the minister sprawling forward like an unraveling ball of yarn, his arms and legs flailing wildly.

Dev jerked the gelding to a stop, spinning him around. He galloped back toward Godoy, who was slowly getting up. The minister cowered, dropping back down on his knees and raising his arms above his head to protect himself. Halting, Dev held the mettlesome horse in one place.

"You," Dev ground out, "ought to die. Did you touch her?" He jabbed the sword point into the cloth of Godoy's waistcoat, ripping it open.

With a cry, Godoy cringed. "No! No! I swear by the Virgin Mother, I haven't touched her! Don't kill me... please, don't kill me!"

Breathing heavily, Dev glanced down at the minister. "You rotting bastard. If I had the time, I'd cut off what lies between your legs. That way, you'd leave innocent women alone forever." He took his boot out of the stirrup and kicked Godoy in the shoulder. The minister spun and fell facedown in the grass. "If you're wise, you'll not move until I've left. If I look back and see you trying to get up, I'll come back and geld you. Understand?"

Terror coursed through Godoy. He groveled in the grass, fingers digging deeply into the warm earth. "Yes, yes, I understand, I promise I won't get up! I won't even look."

Sweat streamed down Dev's tension-lined face. He had spotted the coach and soldiers no more than a mile away. After Godoy's screams, there was little time left before they came riding in this direction. He sheathed the sword. "A Spaniard's promise?" He spat. "It's worthless, Godoy. Now lie there or choose to die." He spun the sweaty, foam-flecked horse around, galloping to Thorne, who stood forlornly in the meadow.

Thorne sobbed as Dev drew up beside her. In one motion he leaned over, sweeping her into his arms.

"Oh, Dev!" She clung to him, sobbing wildly.

"It's going to be all right, Thorne. Hush. We've got to get out of here. The minute Godoy gets his men, he'll have his guards hunting all over Madrid for us." He pressed a quick kiss to her hair, momentarily dizzied by her fragrance. She was incredibly warm and soft against him.

"I love you," she cried between the tears. "I was so frightened."

He crushed Thorne against him, tears springing against his tightly shut eyes. "I died when I found out they took you, Thorne. I'm sorry, beloved. I hadn't intended this to happen."

Shaking her head, Thorne slipped her arms around Dev's neck. "Kiss me, please. I need you, need to know this is real, not some insane imagining of my mind." His mouth fitted hotly against hers and she was filled with the wild heat of knowing how very much he loved her. His lips were hungry, urgent, and she drank thirstily from his offering.

Dev tore his mouth away from hers and glanced back at Godoy, who remained motionless on the ground. Anxiously, he searched Thorne's waxen features and the darkness in her wide, tear-filled eyes.

There was a catch in his voice when he spoke. His tone was low with restrained fury. "Did he touch you?"

She tried unsuccessfully to wipe the paths of tears from her cheeks. "N-no, only scared me to death." The horse moved fractiously beneath them, sensing the danger they were in.

"Hold on, we're going to have to make good our escape."

Thorne slid her arm around his waist and gripped the pommel of the military saddle with the other hand. "How? The entire area is ringed by a high wall."

With a quick smile, Dev moved the horse into a slow gallop toward the woods. "An old laundress at the palace told me about a section of the wall that's down. Once we get off the palace grounds, we're going to have to find a new inn to stay at."

The terror that had held Thorne in its grip began to dissolve. She was safe! Dev was here, holding her tightly against him. The adrenaline that had fueled her escape from Godoy's hands left her weak and shaky. Resting her head on Dev's chest, Thorne had never felt her love for him more fiercely than in this precious, stark instant. Now they were both fugitives in Spain's eyes.

* * *

Thorne was more than happy to exchange her palace clothes for a man's dark blue wool breeches and white peasant shirt. At another stop several miles farther, after fetching Ghazeia, Dev found her a pair of knee-high boots that loosely fit her. If she appeared at first glance to be a young lad, Godoy's guards, who now prowled Madrid, would never recognize her. Dev had taken the two of them around the edge of the city through the poorest parts, trading the uniform for other clothes and selling the black horse along the way.

By siesta time, Dev found an inn that suited his needs. La Abeja de Miel Posada, The Honeybee Inn, possessed a beautiful name, but Thorne wrinkled her nose. The establishment resided among the tightly packed, ramshackle houses made of wood, tin or any material that could be patched together to make four walls and a roof over a starving family's head. Their bed, in one of the few single rooms, was merely a pallet of straw that had seen better days. A chipped pitcher stood in the corner along with a rusted tin bowl. Dev had the mattress replaced with fresh straw.

Dev saw Thorne's disappointment, and he came over, pulling her against him. He rested his jaw against her hair and nudged the bed with the toe of his boot. "I'm sorry. Besides moldy straw, I'll wager there were lice and fleas in the old pallet." He kissed her damp temple. "You deserve so much better than this, Gypsy."

In one motion, Thorne turned around in his arms and embraced Dev fiercely. "The anguish you see in my face isn't for myself, beloved. It's the poor that I feel so deeply for. No one should have to live in such squalor. The children . . ."

He smiled, running his hands across her loving, giving body, absorbing the essence of Thorne into himself. "And that's why you have the orphanages in London. I've been in those areas. I hope the children who are fed and cared by you appreciate what you've done."

"They do." Thorne nestled beneath his jaw, content simply to be held, to allow Dev's strength to fill her depleted reserves. Danger hovered with dark wings all around them. If the palace guards found any of the people that they had had dealings with, it would spell disaster.

Dev felt new tension in Thorne's body and sensed her worry. Drawing her away from him, he cradled her upturned face between his hands. Smoky gray eyes brimming with love caressed him with a warmth he'd never experienced before. "Tomorrow, I meet with my men. The day after, with your emissary. It will be over soon. You'll get out of here safely, I promise."

In less than two days they'd never see each other again. Thorne valiantly fought back tears. She forced a trembling smile. "Is it proper for a woman to ask her man to love her?"

His smile grew tender, his eyes curiously bright. "Between us it is," Dev murmured thickly, and he slowly began to undress her.

Chapter Seventeen

Vaughn Trayhern's blue eyes squinted against the bright summer sun as he stood on the balcony overlooking the crowded, cobblestoned streets of Madrid from El Toro Posada. He had chosen the inn for several reasons. First, it was only for the rich who were passing through the capital of Spain, and second, Devlin Kyle would never think to search such a place for his brother, Gavin. He glanced to the left, watching with satisfaction as Quinn placed the iron cuffs around Kyle's wrists once again.

Neither of them could be trusted, Vaughn had decided. During the journey from England and across Spain, Quinn and Kyle had grown close, almost like brothers, he thought with disgust. Twisting his blond mustache absently, he returned his attention to the people and animals that sluggishly passed on the street below. Few of Spain's soldiers had given them cause for trouble. Vaughn mentally patted himself on the back. He had concocted an elaborate lie; they were bringing back an Irish prisoner from England who had stolen some priceless Andalusian horses from a rich lord in Madrid.

Once, they had been stopped by a roving squadron of soldiers and questioned. Hearing Vaughn's decidedly English accent, they were detained for a few hours. But with a sizeable bribe and the lie, they were released.

Vaughn roused himself, realizing it was time to meet with the mercenary and his fine followers who would form the vanguard to capture Devlin Kyle once he showed up for the exchange. A smile barely twisted his mouth; yes, the Fates were certainly working for him. Four days earlier he had scoured some of the drinking establishments in the worst part of Madrid, looking for soldiers to hire. He had found a huge, hulking German sitting and drinking with a group of other mercenaries. Tossing him a gold coin, Vaughn ordered the man to follow him. In the hours to come, he knew he had picked not only a reliable soldier but a traitor, as well. Yes, Wolfe Erhard was a lucky find indeed.

"I'll be back," he told Quinn.

The Irishman bowed his head. "Very well, sir."

Vaughn glared down at Gavin Kyle, who was sitting in the straight-backed chair. "See that he's fed." And then a gloating smile came to his face. "Eat well, Kyle. It may be one of your last meals." Without another word, Vaughn shut the door behind him.

Erhard waited in the dark shadows of the inn, nursing his latest tankard of ale. He saw Trayhern limp through the opened door, resplendent in his civilian garb. As usual, the gold-handled cane was in his left hand.

"Well?" Trayhern demanded, sitting down. The serving maid came over and Vaughn irritably waved her away.

"I've paid the five men half their fee, Captain. They get the rest after they've captured Kyle."

"Good, good. And the exchange point? You've checked it out thoroughly?"

Wolfe nodded his shaggy head, taking another draft. He wiped his lips with the back of his hairy arm. "It's an abandoned hut outside the city near the peasant section. Plenty of stink and rats around, but it's empty."

"You'll have to take me to it. I want to make sure it's secluded. I don't want any nosy Spanish gendarmes around. This is between Kyle and us."

Wolfe smiled. Yes, it was. The gold weighed heavily in the pouch at his side. Gold was what sold his services to the highest bidder. He hadn't liked Kyle's sanctimonious attitude toward women, especially the English bitch. Now he would have his revenge. No...no one crossed him and lived to boast about it.

"He's meetin' two of his men, you know."

Vaughn shrugged. "That's seven against three. I'm not worried." And then he stared at Wolfe. "Unless you are the fourth."

"I've a few scores to settle. One's with a big, ugly Russian peasant called Ivan Terebenev. He's mine."

"And the other?"

"An Irishman, Lieutenant Niall Scanlon. You'd best have your pistol trained on him. He's dangerous like a snake. You never see him coming until after he's bit you first."

"You just tell that to the men you hired. I'm interested in getting Miss Somerset to safety and out of the line of fire."

Wolfe set the heavy tankard down on the oak table, watching the coming and going of local soldiers and peasants. "You want Devlin Kyle alive or dead?"

"Dead. Like his damnable younger brother. Once I get the woman clear, you have your men jump out into the open and begin firing."

The German gave him a sly look as he stroked the sides of the tankard with his large, thick fingers. "I'd make a suggestion, Captain. Send your man, Quinn, to contact Captain Kyle. Give him orders not to tell Kyle that it's you making the exchange. Kyle hates you so badly that he may disrupt the entire plan trying to get to you instead. Know what I'm sayin'?"

Erhard was right, Vaughn thought. The German was too smart and that left him wary. How could he be sure that Erhard wouldn't somehow botch the entire plan? Perhaps he was still loyal to Kyle. He would have to be watched closely.

"Very well," he said, rising. "You stay out of sight, as well. I don't want Kyle knowing you've changed sides until the last possible moment."

"I can't do that. I'm to meet with him tomorrow at noon. Besides, he'd get suspicious if I didn't meet him and the rest of his men did."

Right again, Vaughn thought sourly. He glared at Wolfe. "You had better remember which side has paid you gold, Erhard."

Wolfe grinned from beneath his full mustache, jingling the purse. "I do, Captain, I do."

"There's another pouch waiting for you once this is over and you meet me back here."

Wolfe's brows shot up in surprise. "Another purse?"

Vaughn grinned tightly, watching the German salivate at that prospect. "That's right. Just see to it that Lady Thorne and I escape unharmed and it's yours."

Wolfe laughed heartily. "If I had known before that the English were this generous, I'd have joined their redcoat army."

Vaughn rose, his eyes glittering. He didn't tell Wolfe that the English wouldn't take a hulking bastard like him. "Report to me as soon as you can after meeting with Kyle."

He limped out of the squalid establishment, taking a deep breath of fresher air as he welcomed the sunlight. The awaiting coachman opened the door and he got in. Soon, he thought, soon I'll have you, Kyle....

"Dev?"

He glanced over at Thorne as she sat down on the straw mat that had been their bed. She looked exquisite. Dev placed the sword into the sheath at his side, noting the anxiety mirrored in her lovely eyes.

"Yes?" He walked over and knelt down next to her, placing his hands on her small shoulders.

The fear was in her eyes. As it always was. But she never talked of their time together drawing to a close. Dev's heart swelled with a fierce love for Thorne as he caressed her shoulders.

"How long will you be gone?"

"I don't know," he answered. He sat down on the bed, placing his arm around her and drawing her close. Thorne's hair was freshly washed and he inhaled the sweet scent of it as she moved into his embrace. "If Ivan, Niall and Wolfe are there, we'll ride out of Madrid and find a safe spot to discuss what they've found. If they aren't all there, I have to wait."

"I see." Thorne shut her eyes tightly.

"We'll talk and then I'll come back to you. Tomorrow I'll meet the emissary over at La Plata Ave Posada."

Her heart pounded. A sense of grief pulled at Thorne and she held Dev tightly. He had made her his woman in all ways and she would never regret it. That night and early morning had overflowed with happiness turned molten by their fiery love.

Dev pressed a kiss to her temple and gave Thorne a warm smile. "You can rest up now. Get some sleep. You didn't get much last night."

She returned his caressing smile, lost in the smoky blue of his eyes. He loved her. "Yes...."

Dev rose, reluctantly leaving her side. He pointed to the pistol that sat near her. "This inn isn't safe. If anything happens, use that." He knew from long experience that poor inns such as this were often attacked by robbers and highwaymen. "I'll be back, Gypsy."

She tucked her hands in her lap. "And I'll wait," she called softly as he slipped out the door.

Thorne sat there a long time staring at the wooden door that hung on leather hinges. She shut her eyes as the tears came. They ran in silvery paths down her cheeks, plopping into her hands and across her arms. Thorne had promised herself not to cry in front of Dev. She had wanted their time to be a miracle, not a reminder that each day shortened their life together. A sob caught in her throat and she lay down, trying to sleep.

Ivan's thick brows rose. He nudged Lieutenant Scanlon in the ribs. "There he is."

Niall lifted his dark head, his green eyes narrowing. At the entrance to the cantina stood their captain. "Let's go," he told Terebenev and Wolfe Erhard, who sat with them.

Dev saw his men rise. He walked out into the cobble-stoned street and waited for them to come out of the cantina. Giving them a sharp, appraising look, he pointed to the horses tied to a nearby tree.

"Follow me" was all he said.

They rode for nearly an hour, weaving in and out of Madrid traffic. Ox- and donkey-drawn carts crawled along while carriages pulled smartly by high-stepping Andalusians in traces clattered by. They navigated in and around the peasant crowds. Dev chose a small hill that overlooked the city. It was topped with a few scraggly olive trees bent in the spring heat. He wiped the sweat from his brow after he dismounted. Scanlon gripped his hand hard, offering one of his rare smiles.

"You don't look any worse for wear. Is the girl still with you?"

Dev nodded. "Yes."

Niall stepped aside as Ivan lumbered up. The Russian's broad face split into an ear-to-ear grin, and he threw his arms around Dev, lifting him off the ground with a powerful bear hug.

"Welcome, Cap'n!" Ivan boomed. He set his captain down, slapping him heartily on the back. "We've been busy the past two weeks."

Dev acknowledged Wolfe, who remained outside the group. "Come on, let's sit down and discuss what you've all found. Wolfe, I want your report first. I don't want to stay in Madrid any longer than we have to."

Wolfe hunkered down, holding Ivan's ebony glare. The Russian hated him, but that was nothing new. He hated the Russian, too. Wolfe smiled to himself; if the captain only knew that Vaughn Trayhern had bought his services to lead Kyle like a lamb to slaughter. Yes, revenge was sweet—and financially rewarding. He plucked a piece of sparse grass, chewing on it.

"It's just as you suspected. Godoy is hated by the people."

"The poor?" Dev demanded.

"The poor, the hidalgos, and the bourgeoisie. I've been in hundreds of cantinas and scoured the different sections of Madrid. There's unrest everywhere. Men sit drinking their wine or ale, talking of little else but overthrowing Godoy. Everyone knows the King no longer runs the country—it's Godoy, the Queen's stud."

Napoleon had suspected unrest. Now it was being proven. Dev listened to the reports from his other two men for nearly an hour. The information was similar; in three major cities, there was oppression of the poor and bourgeoisie. Godoy was hated, and so was the Queen. Finally, after the reports were completed, Niall spoke up.

"What about Miss Somerset's emissary? Is he here yet?"

Dev shrugged. "I'll know tomorrow."

"And if he isn't there?"

"I wait."

Niall frowned. "What if this emissary isn't a man of his word? What if he's hired men to try and capture you?"

Dev studied his friend's lean face. Scanlon was right. He'd mulled over that possibility.

"It's a risk I take, Niall. Alone. We're here on a mission for Napoleon. Getting my brother back is personal business and my responsibility. I refuse to involve any of you in it. I can't afford to have you wounded or killed if it came to that."

Scanlon said nothing else. "We won't leave until we know the details of where this exchange will take place, Dev."

Dev got to his feet. The sun hung overhead, the heat intense. Right now, all he wanted was to return to Thorne's arms and love her once again. For the last time....

Niall rose and motioned for Dev to follow him. They walked out of earshot of the other two men. Niall's brow was furrowed as he turned to Dev.

"Wolfe is acting strangely," he said in a quiet voice.

"Oh?"

"Yes. He was asking Ivan and myself if we knew where you were staying with the woman. Of course, we didn't know. But I'd be careful what I said around him."

Dev's eyes turned icy as he considered Scanlon's warning. Niall wasn't the type of man to say much. When he did, he was usually right. "Do you think Wolfe has given information to the Spanish?"

Scanlon shrugged his broad shoulders, his left hand resting on the butt of his saber. "Ivan's growling like a proverbial bear about how Wolfe is behaving. He won't tell where *he's* staying, but he wants to know where we'll be."

Damn! Dev glanced back at the two soldiers standing beneath the olive trees. "You'll be the only one to know where I have Thorne." Dev gave him the details.

"I think we should stay around until this exchange takes place, Dev."

"I promised the emissary no other men would be involved."

Scanlon gave him a deadly look. "We know you're honorable. We don't know if Somerset can be trusted."

"His daughter can be."

"Let us wait with you. It's only a day longer," Niall counseled.

Dev was torn between Wolfe's possible change of allegiance and the safety of his men. "Very well," he muttered, turning and heading back to the crest.

"Wolfe," Dev called as he approached the German.

"Yes, sir?"

"Where are you staying? I may need to contact you."

The German glanced down at his dusty boots. "I change cantinas every night, Cap'n, to find out their mood toward the royalty." He grinned. "Besides, I can sample more women that way."

Ivan scowled. "You'd best get those brains from between your legs, German!"

Erhard glared over at him. "Keep your nose in your own business."

"Enough," Dev ordered them. He turned his attention to Erhard. "Under my command, you tell me where you'll be. Now give me the name of the inn or cantina you're staying at tonight."

Erhard chafed, barely holding on to his growing anger. He wanted to pull out his pistol and shoot that Russian peasant. Eyeing Kyle, he muttered, "Over at the Caballo Cantina, Cap'n."

Dev mounted his gray mare and bid farewell to his men. By dusk the next day they would assemble and leave for France. Entering the sprawling city of Madrid, Dev was content to allow his mare to pick her way through the narrow cobblestoned streets at a brisk walk. The city was beginning its hours of siesta, which spanned the hot afternoons. The number of foreigners in Madrid didn't surprise him. Mercenaries had been drawn to the city to sign up in the Spanish army and fight against the English. He kept a sharp eye out for soldiers, knowing that Godoy would not give up easily. There was unrest in Madrid, Dev thought. He could taste it. The peasants were oppressed, food scarce and the children running naked and dirty through the streets in the poorer sections.

Swinging his mount from a narrow street into a larger boulevard, Dev glanced back occasionally to make sure no one was following him. Almost two hours passed before he arrived back at the inn. He had an uneasy feeling about Wolfe. What was he up to? Had he made contact with Godoy's troops? Was a noose being tightened around all their necks? Grimly, Dev dismounted and gave his mare to the stable boy, who would unsaddle and brush her down.

He was a soldier once again. His gaze restlessly combed the inn, memorizing the poorly dressed patrons who lounged at the tables, drinking ale. He climbed the stairs and walked down the creaking wood hall. At the end of it, he opened the door to their room. He found Thorne standing at the opened window, her profile sharply silhouetted. He stopped, drinking in her beauty. The sunlight bathed her, giving her skin a golden glow. Thorne's once short hair was now below her ears, curling softly. All of his worries for Gavin's safety, his men and himself were ripped away in that instant. Dev felt his body turn molten with desire for Thorne once again. Softly, he called her name. She turned like a startled doe, her gray eyes huge and luminous. Throwing her arms open, she cried out his name and ran to him.

Dev groaned as she threw herself into his embrace.

"Oh, Dev," Thorne whispered, kissing his cheek, neck and, finally, his awaiting mouth. Warmth flowed through her chilled body, his mouth giving her life once again. Slowly, Dev lowered her to her feet and she looked up at him.

"I was worried."

He shut the door and lifted Thorne into his arms, carrying her to the straw mat and gently depositing her on it.

"Everything went fine," he assured her, lying next to her.

Thorne closed her eyes, sliding her hands across his capable shoulders. "I'm so glad. I had terrible thoughts."

Dev gave her a slight smile and caressed her cheek. Tomorrow, he thought in anguish, tomorrow she'll be gone forever. He winced, unable to stand the pain shearing through him. "Ivan and Niall arrived here safely."

Thorne's eyes darkened. "And Wolfe? Was he there, too?"

"Yes." Dev said nothing of Niall's suspicions. He didn't want Thorne to worry unnecessarily.

"Then you'll meet Father's emissary?"

"Tomorrow morning at ten o'clock."

She pulled Dev to her, taking his full weight, glorying in his masculinity. "That's all I've been thinking about since you were gone. I wonder if Father sent Eamon."

Dev roused himself and lay on his side, pulling Thorne close to him. "More important, can Eamon be trusted?"

"Eamon has been with the family since I was six years old. He aided and abetted my love of riding on a man's saddle. He's more like a member of our family, not just the head stableman." She glanced up at Dev, drowning in the tenderness in his eyes as he watched her. How could Dev let her go when he loved her as much as she did him?

Dev ran a strand of her black hair between his thumb and forefinger, marveling at the texture of it. "An Irishman?"

"Yes."

He shook his head. "I'd never have believed it, Gypsy. An Englishman allowing an Irishman to have so much responsibility."

Thorne framed his harsh features with her hands. "My father's a fair man, Dev."

"I'm beginning to see that." He leaned over, capturing Thorne's lips, tasting the sweetness of her. "Hungry?" he breathed against her, his hand cupping her small breast.

She shook her head, responding effortlessly to Dev's caressing hand upon her. "I'm sad and I'm scared, Dev. I—I can do nothing else but think I shall lose you soon, beloved."

The same sadness overwhelmed Dev and he gathered Thorne to him, simply holding her. "I'm sorry, Thorne," he began in a strained voice. "If I knew then what I know now, I'd never have kidnapped you."

"At least this way you'll get your brother back."

Dev buried his head in her hair, closing his eyes, needing her. Forever. "God, I keep wondering, is he well?"

"You'll know soon enough, Dev," Thorne whispered, holding him tightly, her heart breaking. "If he's anything like you, he'll survive."

He blinked back scalding tears, not wanting Thorne to see them. Despite their impending separation, she unselfishly addressed his worries about Gavin. He knew without a doubt that he'd never find another woman of Thorne's quality. Ever.

Gavin braced himself. He saw Trayhern lift his balled fist, ready to strike him for the sixth time in a row. His hands were tied tightly behind him and he could do nothing but tense his body as he lay on the floor, bound and bloodied. The side of his face exploded with pain, and then numbness. He tasted the blood in his mouth, spitting it out as he rolled to his side.

"Damned Irish cur," Vaughn snarled, walking around him. He took his cane, snapping it outward. A sharp crack of stout oak meeting bone sounded throughout the small room. Vaughn halted, watching with pleasure as the Irish felon groaned and rolled onto his stomach.

"In less than twelve hours, you'll be seeing your brother," he told him, his eyes blazing. "But I didn't want you to be in too good a condition." He scowled. "Of course, if I didn't need that Somerset woman back, I'd deliver you dead."

Gavin choked in a breath, pain radiating in sharp, jagged forays up the right side of his rib cage. He thought Trayhern might have cracked several of them. Hold on, hold on, he told himself. Don't say anything. It went against Gavin's hot-blooded nature to remain silent, but five years at Newgate had taught him much. Namely to be patient and remain silent. Patience usually got him what he wanted. Silence kept the guard's whip and fists at bay. Where was Eamon? As long as the trusted servant to John Somerset was nearby, Vaughn Trayhern left him alone. Eamon had left hours ago. Where had he gone?

"Nothing to say?"

Gavin felt sweat running down his brow, leaking into his eyes. He blinked rapidly as Vaughn leaned over him, sneering. "Nothing," he rasped.

Trayhern's smile soured. "I remember when you used to open that mouth of yours and let your temper get away from you. You've changed, Kyle."

Yes, but I'll kill you if it's the last thing I ever do. Gavin shut his eyes, nauseated from the pain. Would he live to see Dev? Five years...five long, nightmarish years since he had last seen his older brother. Knowing Trayhern, he had probably set a trap to capture Dev. Gavin had warned Eamon of the possibility and the Irishman had nodded soberly but said nothing.

Vaughn took his cane, jamming it into Kyle's shoulder and forcing him to turn over on his back. He saw the Irishman wince, his lips white and drawn away from his clenched teeth. "My meeting with your brother is going to be interesting, don't you think?"

With a guttural laugh, Vaughn limped around him and shut the door. Gavin rolled back over on his side, the rough-cut floor scraping against his flesh. It was mild discomfort compared with what he felt on his right side. Trayhern had busted up his ribs. The bastard. Gavin lay breathing heavily, trying to slow his heart. Since his unexpected release from prison, he had put more meat back on his tall, gaunt frame. Even so, the black wool trousers and dark blue shirt hung loosely on him, and the boots he wore were two sizes too big. Eamon Quinn would sneak him extra food whenever possible—beyond the amount that Trayhern had rationed out for him each evening. Clenching and unclenching his numbed fingers, Gavin closed his eyes, trying to ignore the pain and relax.

Would Dev be able to bring off the exchange? Judging from what Quinn said about Somerset's daughter, the earl wanted her back at any cost. Did Somerset know of the bad blood between the Trayherns and the Kyles? Eamon had shrugged his large, rounded shoulders, professing no knowledge of the feud. Gavin had tried to warn the servant of the impending meeting between Dev and Trayhern.

"Gavin—" Eamon Quinn stood in the doorway, his mouth slack with astonishment. "What—"

"Untie me, Eamon."

The servant hurried across the room, setting down a platter of food. Fumbling with the well-tied knots, he finally eased the harsh bonds from Gavin's bloodied wrists. "What happened?" he demanded, helping him sit up.

Gavin's hazel eyes were filled with pain as he looked up at Quinn. "Trayhern had sport with me," he rasped, holding his right side to try to ease the ache.

Eamon scowled. Ordinarily, he'd put the manacles back on Gavin. He threw them aside. "Give me your word you won't try to escape."

Gavin snorted and winced. "I'm going nowhere, Eamon. I want to get to my brother as badly as you want Thorne Somerset back." He sucked in air between his teeth. "Get me some bandages, will you? Trayhern cracked some of my ribs."

Damn Trayhern! Eamon thought as he left the room that had served as Gavin's cell the last week. He went to the adjoining room and jerked a sheet off his own bed, then came back. Shutting the door, he saw Kyle sitting where he'd left him, his face glistening with sweat.

"I'm sorry I left," Quinn muttered, tearing up long pieces of the sheet so that he could wrap Kyle's ribs. "I had to check the place where we'll be making the exchange."

Gavin glanced over at Quinn. "Does it look safe? Tell me about it."

Eamon said nothing at first, easing Gavin's soiled and bloodied shirt off his broad shoulders. He gave his fellow Irishman credit; since being taken from the bowels of Newgate prison Gavin had gotten back into remarkable condition. Kyle had been so weak that he could barely walk from the prison to the ship, and on the voyage from England to Portugal, Eamon had to tend his many cuts and sores.

Now he could see the muscle mass returning to the younger man. Kyle's black hair shone with blue highlights beneath the sputtering lamp. The trek across Spain to Madrid had browned Kyle's pale features. Eamon had watched him grow in strength a little more each day. And their friendship had also grown, whether Eamon had wanted it to or not. He couldn't help it; Gavin was a fellow Irishman. And like the Irish, he never complained once. He said little, but that was due to the prison life, Eamon surmised.

"I'll tell you about it later," he counseled. "First, let me dress your wounds."

Gavin sat still, wincing occasionally as Quinn made several very tight wraps around his chest to set the ribs in place. It hurt to breathe deeply.

"You've got to tell me what Trayhern's plan for the morrow is."

Eamon's mouth tightened. "To make the exchange, you know that." He sat back on his heels, satisfied with his job.

"Trayhern says he's going to kill us," Gavin said harshly, watching as the servant stood and retrieved the platter filled with food.

Eamon handed him the fare. "He wouldn't dare. Captain Trayhern has said nothing to me about such folly. I've seen the hut where the exchange will be made."

"Can you hire some mercenary soldiers to protect us? What's to say that he won't get rid of you, too? All he needs is that girl to take back to England with him, not you or I. And you're Irish, just as I am."

"With one major difference," Eamon corrected, sitting down on a chair. "You're a felon, and I am not."

The food was cold, but Gavin didn't care. In prison, he had learned to wolf down his meager portion lest some of his prison mates leapt upon him to take it for themselves. Despite the nausea he was experiencing from the pain, he gulped down the food. Finished, he set the plate beside him.

"I'm telling you, Eamon, Trayhern is up to no good. Your own life is not worth one whit to him."

"Sleep, my friend." He got up and helped Gavin to his feet, then guided him to the bed. Kyle was waxen, but he didn't complain as he lay down. "I'm sorry, but I've got to put the chain on you."

Gavin said nothing, closing his eyes. The servant was as gentle as possible, chaining his one leg to the bed. Amusement struck Gavin. If the inn caught on fire, he'd die. What an ignominious end to his days of soldiering that would be, hanging by a chain out the window of a inn with a bed at the other end.

Would Dev meet him at the appointed place? How was he? Was the Somerset girl alive and well? With a sigh, he threw his arm across his eyes, escaping into sleep.

Chapter Eighteen

The first gray shadows of dawn met Thorne's damp eyes. She lay against Dev, listening to his breathing, feeling the slow rise and fall of his massive chest beneath her arm. His body was hard and tightly muscled and she relished his warmth. She inhaled his scent and it spurred her senses into wakefulness. The bray of a donkey being nudged out of sleep and the crow of a cock somewhere in the distance heralded the first inkling of the day pushing back the folds of night.

Her arm tightened around Dev momentarily. Today, she would leave him. How much more pain could her breaking heart bear? They had made desperate, wild love twice in the darkness, holding each other, weeping. Thorne had never seen a man cry before, not until hours ago. And she realized as never before just how much Dev loved her. The parting was no less excruciating for him, Thorne had discovered. They had held each other, cried, love one another again and grown silent in the aftermath, wrestling with their own particular anguish.

Thorne understood the finality of Dev's quest to right the injustices to his family, but after holding him as he wept unashamedly in her arms, she also knew Dev loved her more than any woman in his life. That knowledge gave her the strength to implement a plan she had been mulling over yesterday. She would follow Dev when he went to meet with her father's representative. She was worried greatly for Dev's safety; he had told her of Wolfe's odd behavior and

Scanlon's warning. Thorne could readily believe Wolfe would turn them all in to the Spanish authorities for pieces of gold.

The plan she had would keep Dev safe and free Gavin. And her? A jagged sigh escaped her. She would make their parting this morning swift and clean. Thorne could not bear to see Dev's pain; it tore her apart. Right now, all she wanted to do was halt the suffering and misery he'd carried in his heart and soul for uncounted years.

She closed her eyes, nuzzling beneath Dev's sandpapery jaw, absorbing him into her heart. The orphanages would need her managerial guidance once again. And her father was ailing. Was he getting worse? She would nurse him back to health. Thorne knew she must keep busy in order not to go insane with the loss of Dev. Sliding her hand across her belly, Thorne prayed that she now carried a child to reflect their undying love for each other. Tears streaked down her cheeks. God had taken so much from her. At least let her have Dev's child.

Dev stirred, rolling over on his side, his arm going across Thorne's waist. He inhaled her sandalwood scent, barely opening his eyes. He drowned in the glorious splendor of her luminous gray eyes. He lifted his rough and callused hand, caressing her cheek.

Wordlessly, Thorne came to him, pressing her diminutive length against him, her lips barely touching his mouth. His hands settled on her hips and he lifted her on top of him.

"Little vixen," he murmured thickly, tunneling his fingers through her hair. "Don't tell me you want to love me again?"

Thorne felt him hardening beneath her. She ran her tongue across his lower lip, softly kissing each corner of his mouth. "I'm spent," she confided, breathless.

"And I'm sore. As you surely are, my beautiful Gypsy," he whispered, nipping her lip with a series of small, tender kisses.

"Can either of us walk?"

A chuckle rumbled through his chest as Dev ran his hands over her body, memorizing each swell and curve of her womanly softness. "I will, but only because I must meet your father's emissary." He gave her a firm pat on the rear. "You can stay in bed and rest."

Thorne withheld her grief. In a few minutes, Dev would get up, dress and leave. And she would follow him at a safe distance to find out where he was meeting the emissary. Fighting back a wall of pain, she kept her tone light to match his teasing.

"Rest, indeed," she taunted, moving sinuously against him, watching the flame of desire burn in his dark blue eyes. A thrill arced through her; Dev responded to her so easily. What power they held over each other with their love!

Dev's brow formed into a scowl. "Yes, rest. If all goes well, I intend to come back here and the exchange will be made today."

Thorne swallowed her sadness. She laid her head on his chest, allowing the heavy beat of his heart to soothe her. "I thought you would never leave the bed," she teased.

"Wench," Dev accused, rising after he had deposited her at his side. And then he sobered. Reaching over, he stroked Thorne's cheek. "I wanted last night to be very special for you, Gypsy."

Choking back a sob, Thorne placed her hand over his scarred one. "Every day and night spent with you has been special, Dev," she whispered rawly.

He kissed her with aching tenderness, his eyes curiously damp, unable to speak, only feel.

Dev was in a shadowy corner of the inn, slowly nursing a tankard of ale, when he spotted a man at the doorway who by his dress looked conspicuously out of place. Tensing, Dev allowed his hand to fall beneath the table's surface and rest on the butt of one of the pistols he carried in his belt. He had already checked an escape exit in case Somerset's plan was to capture him. Sweat stood out on his grim features as he followed the man's progress from the door. At ten in the morning, all the farmers were in the field and the only other individual, a Spanish merchant, presided at a table on the other side of the sprawling room.

Eamon Quinn flicked a glance at the two men seated in the inn. One was jowly, like a pig being readied for a feast. The other... it had to be Devlin Kyle. The man's face, his entire posture, shouted that he was a soldier. Not only that, he resembled Gavin in some respects. Heaving a sigh, Eamon made his way toward him, remembering the words that would either prove or disprove that he was Kyle. Halting at the rough-hewn table, he said in a low voice, "Spring has come."

Dev's gaze never left the man. "And the sun has set. Sit down."

"I'm unarmed," Eamon said, sitting opposite the soldier. Kyle looked like any one of the thousands of mercenaries who were in Madrid.

"I'm not."

Eamon almost smiled, but thought better of it. He folded his hands in front of him. "The Lady Thorne. Is she—"

"Safe and unharmed."

Relief flooded Eamon and he closed his eyes. "Thank God."

"No, you can thank me. The English have no god but themselves."

"Save your hatred, Captain. I'm Irish. I'm the Earl of Somerset's stable manager. He could not come because of his poor health, so he sent me."

"What about my brother?"

"He's with us. Better off than he was in prison. He's gained some weight back, but he's still not recovered entirely."

Dev leaned forward. "You said 'us.' Who else is with you?"

Eamon braced himself. "Captain, I want you to know, I bear you nor your brother ill will. In the past weeks, Gavin and I have become close. He's told me of your trials at the hand of the English and, in particular, a Captain Vaughn Trayhern."

"Trayhern is next on my list as soon as this trade is made."

"You won't have to go far, Captain. The earl hired him to bring Gavin here." Eamon saw the Irishman's eyes go wide with shock for a brief moment and then narrow dangerously.

"Trayhern is here?" Dev rasped.

"Yes, and he warned me not to tell you." Eamon shrugged. "He beat Gavin last night. He has no love for either of you. I wanted to warn you ahead of time. All I'm interested in is getting the Lady Thorne back to her ailing father. He's dying, and she's his whole life."

As she is mine, Dev thought, sudden anguish overwhelming the hatred he felt for Trayhern. "I owe you thanks—"

"Eamon Quinn, Captain. And you owe me nothing except my lady back, safely to me."

Dev remained silent several moments. "Trayhern raped my sister, Quinn. There is no way he's leaving Madrid alive. You'll be taking Thorne home alone. Can you do that?"

Quinn nodded his shaggy head. "Aye, Captain. If the truth be known, Lady Thorne is quite capable of traveling by herself."

"Yes, she is headstrong," he agreed softly. And loving. And caring. And, God, how could he part with her?

"We're to meet here at three this afternoon," Eamon said, drawing a paper from a leather pouch he carried. Spreading it across the table so that Kyle could study it, he outlined the plan.

"Is Trayhern planning a surprise for us?" Dev asked the servant, staring at him hard.

"He's divulged nothing to me, Captain, except to find a spot where the exchange can be made."

"Trayhern's not to be trusted."

"I think not, Captain, but I can't prove that."

"When we meet this afternoon, Quinn, I'll ask one favor of you."

"Yes?"

"Get Thorne to a place of safety as soon as possible. I won't shoot if she's near Trayhern. But you can rest assured, I'm going to kill that son of the devil."

"I would pray that you won't endanger her life in seeking your revenge on the captain," Quinn said gravely.

"I hold her life above my own. I will not see her placed in any danger," Dev assured him.

"Will you tell Lady Thorne of our plan, then?"

Dev slowly rose to his feet, tucking the paper into his leather belt. "I'll tell her everything." Dev thrust out his hand toward the servant. "At three."

Eamon grasped the man's hand, surprised at the strength and firmness of his grip. "Three," he agreed.

Turning, Dev left. After making sure the cobblestoned street was clear of soldiers, he mounted Ghazeia, blending into the increasing morning traffic. His mind raced with options and plans. Gavin was safe, but not in good health. What else had he expected? And Trayhern . . . the bastard had been stupid enough to volunteer his services to Somerset. Good. Dev was ready to even the score once and for all.

Taking elaborate precautions to make sure no one would follow him, Dev did not arrive back at the squalid inn until three hours later, at eleven-thirty. A heavy weight hung in his chest as he moved up the steps. This would be his last few hours with Thorne. Dev forced back a deluge of emotions that threatened to break him. He knocked once on the wooden door. There was no answer. Frowning, he opened it. Sunlight spilled into the whitewashed room from the window.

"Thorne?" Frowning, Dev looked around. Where was she? His heart began a slow pound of dread. Glancing at the straw pallet, he saw a letter on it. Sweet God, what had happened? Had Godoy found her? Snatching up the letter, he opened it with trembling hands.

My Dearest:
I followed you this morning. By the time you read this, I will be with my father's emissary. I intend to have

Gavin freed and send him back to you at the inn, so please wait here. I'm worried that there might be a trap, and I couldn't bear to see you or your brother imprisoned or killed because of Wolfe. It's safer this way for everyone concerned.

Do not be angry with me, beloved. My heart was breaking as we cried together last night. I know how much you love me and I wanted to make our parting as painless as possible. I'll love you forever....

Thorne

Dev stared down at the parchment, disbelief flaring in his watering eyes. No! She was walking like an innocent lamb to slaughter with Trayhern here! He didn't trust the bastard with any woman, especially when Vaughn found out Thorne had fallen in love with his enemy. Trayhern would easily take out his own brand of vengeance on her instead. Dev shut his eyes tightly. Sweet God of mercy! If only he knew where Quinn was staying. There was only one chance, and that was to ride back to the inn they had met at and hope Quinn or Thorne would be there.

Leaping toward the door, Dev hurled himself down the stairs. Racing past the innkeeper, he jerked the reins of his Arabian from the post, mounting in one fluid motion. Sinking his heels deeply into the horse's flanks, he galloped down the cobblestoned expanse, sparks flying each time the metal shoes struck the rocky surface.

Eamon Quinn's mouth fell open as Thorne walked out of the shadows from behind the inn. She stood quietly, her face strained. A black horse moved restively at her side. His eyes widened as he looked at her shorn hair, which barely hung below her delicate ears. And then a slow smile spread across his generous mouth; she was dressed as she always was whenever she wanted to ride, like a young lad. This was his Thorne.

"My lady!" he finally managed.

Thorne smiled sadly and came forward, throwing her arms around Eamon's rounded shoulders. "Eamon!" she whispered. "Thank God Papa sent you!"

He gave her a brisk embrace, worried that the Irish captain might discover them. Taking her back into the shadows between the stucco buildings, he asked, "Did you escape from the captain?"

"No, Eamon." Thorne gripped his arm. "Listen, there is little time. I've left a message for Dev in our room. He'll know when he arrives back to our inn where I've gone and what I've done." She gave him an anxious look. "Eamon, I know I sound addled, but I love Devlin Kyle."

"What?"

"I love him, with all my heart and soul," she said. "It's a long and complicated story that I'll tell you later."

With a groan, the servant rubbed his brow. "My lady, you're in great danger, then. Captain Vaughn Trayhern is the man your father hired to bring Gavin Kyle here."

Thorne's eyes grew large. "My God, no! Not him!"

"Aye, him."

"Then we must release Gavin immediately!"

"Captain Trayhern will forbid it, my lady."

Thorne set her lips and mounted her horse. "He doesn't dare, Eamon! After all, he'll have me back. Where is your mount? Take me to where you're keeping Gavin Kyle."

"But—"

"Quickly, Eamon! Time is precious. We dare not allow Dev to know that Trayhern is here." Justification at having left Dev washed through Thorne. He would know soon enough that Trayhern was in Madrid once Gavin got to him. She had to avoid bloodshed at all costs. The agonizing picture of Dev being mortally wounded by Trayhern danced in her mind.

Eamon walked at her side and rounded the building. "He already knows, my lady. I told him. I'll take you to the inn."

Thorne clutched the reins tightly in her hand as Eamon mounted a bay gelding. "Then speed is of the essence. I don't want Dev killed! Hurry, we must free his brother."

* * *

Gavin was sitting on the bed, his leg chained to it, when a woman in a white peasant's shirt and blue breeches burst into his room. He saw Eamon close on her heels, agitated.

"What's this all about?" he demanded as the woman strode quickly across the room toward him.

"There's little time to explain. I'm Thorne Somerset. Eamon, free him." She crouched down, gripping Gavin's hand. "Listen carefully. Dev is staying at La Abeja de Miel Posada. I want you to take the bay gelding that's waiting downstairs for you and ride there in haste." Her fingers tightened. "Once there, beg Dev to leave for France immediately. Do you understand?"

Gavin shook his head and watched as the manacle dropped free from around his ankle. "No. If you're Somerset's daughter, why should you help me? And how did you get here?"

Thorne stood, pulled out a small pouch that contained coins and thrust it into Gavin's hand. "You'll do as I say. I love your brother, Gavin. There's no time to explain. You must take my word!" She glanced apprehensively toward the door. Eamon had checked to see if Trayhern was at the inn. According to the innkeeper, he was gone.

"You love..." Gavin stared down at her as he rose. "Love Dev?" Eamon unbuckled his belt, handing it to him along with a pistol.

"Yes. It's mutual, Gavin. Hurry, put on the belt. There's enough coins in the pouch to keep you from starving. Get over to the inn. Please, for God's sake, do as I ask. Dev will confirm what I've told you." She practically shoved him toward the door.

Gavin hesitated fractionally, looking down at Thorne. Her cheeks were flushed a dark pink, her hair mussed and her gray eyes huge. He reached out, settling his hand on her small shoulder.

"What if you're lying? What if this is a trap?"

Anguished, Thorne was wracked with mounting urgency. "It's not. Please, go! Tell Dev I love him." She unclasped the chain from around her neck, giving Gavin the scarab she had worn all her life. Her voice was choked with emotion. "Give this to him. Tell him to wear it—it will keep him safe. And—" she dashed tears from her eyes "—tell him that I'll wait until the day he can give it back to me."

Gavin's eyes reflected his confusion as his fist closed around the amulet. "Very well." He glanced over his shoulder at Eamon. "May the wind always be at your back," he said softly.

Eamon smiled slightly. "And yours," he returned, the old Irish blessing warming him.

Gavin opened the door, cautiously peering down the hall. His hand settled on the butt of the pistol in his belt. Without a word, he slipped out, moving like a shadow down the hall to the stairs.

Thorne heaved a sigh of relief after she saw Gavin mount the bay and ride off. She turned and ran trembling fingers through her hair. "Thank you, Eamon," she said, coming over and hugging him.

"Don't thank me for anything, my lady. We have Captain Trayhern to deal with now," he said glumly. "He won't be happy about this. According to what Gavin overheard, Trayhern's planning on taking both Kyles prisoner and returning them to Newgate, you know."

She sank down on the edge of the bed, suddenly shaky. Dev would be furious with her. But once he saw Gavin, he would forgive her. And then, Dev would come back over to this inn and the bloodshed would be great. Pacing, she said, "Eamon, I've much to tell you. But we must flee this inn, so the telling will have to wait."

Eamon had no more taken a step toward her when the door, which was partly open, was flung back. He froze.

Vaughn halted, his nostrils flaring as he looked first at Quinn and then at Thorne. Shock rooted him momentarily. "Where's Kyle?"

Thorne gasped. There, on the heels of Trayhern, was Wolfe Erhard. "Wolfe...what are you doing here?" she demanded in a high, unsteady voice.

Trayhern glared at both of them. "One of you'd best give me an answer."

Thorne's voice was husky yet firm. "I've freed Gavin Kyle, Vaughn. I'm here, so I set him free, just as my father promised." She swallowed convulsively, her heart pounding wildly. A shiver wound through her as she felt Wolfe's eyes narrow on her. Automatically, she moved to Eamon's side.

"You what?" Vaughn cried, advancing upon her.

Thorne bit back a cry as his fingers sank deeply into her arm. He dragged her savagely to him.

"You had no right to let him go! How long since he left? Tell me!" He shook her hard.

"Captain!" Eamon launched himself at Trayhern to rescue Thorne.

Wolfe snarled an obscenity and, in one fluid movement that belied his size and bulk, halted Quinn's advance.

Gulping back her tears of rage, Thorne glared up into Trayhern's narrow face. Yes, she could see the coldness in his frigid blue eyes now. Odd that she had not discovered that before. The twisted, almost cruel smile across his mouth frightened her the most. Memory of Dev telling her how this man had raped Alyssa came back to her starkly.

"I had every right to release him! Now you let me go! I'll not be treated in such a fashion." She yanked herself out of his grasp, rubbing her arm.

Damn! Now both Kyles were loose. Vaughn's knuckles whitened around the gold handle of his cane as he studied the defiant daughter of John Somerset. Her small breasts heaved sharply against the poorly fitting peasant's blouse, displaying a great deal of her throat and the fineness of her collarbone.

"Vaughn, your business with me and my father is concluded as of this moment," Thorne began tightly. "I see no sense in wasting any time. Let us mount up and ride for England."

Vaughn stared at her. She was nervous and fretful about something. "Why the hurry?" He wanted to get Wolfe and those mercenaries to hunt down the Kyles.

Thorne walked to Eamon's side, feeling safer, although Wolfe's gaze never left her. "I insist we leave right now! I'm weary of Madrid. I want to get home to my father. Eamon says he is dying.''

Wolfe's chuckle rumbled out of his deep chest. ''What happened? Did Kyle get your sympathy so that you would help him?''

Thorne ignored the German, her eyes blazing with fury. She turned to Vaughn. ''What matters to me right now is that we leave Madrid. I'll not see any blood flow on my account. You're my father's emissary, and you must do as I request.''

''Quiet!'' Vaughn snapped. His blue eyes glittered. ''Let me think a moment.''

Thorne wet her lips. She glanced nervously at Vaughn. ''My father will pay for your services once we get home, and you'll be free once again to socialize with the *ton*.''

A viperous smile tugged at Vaughn's mouth. ''I'm afraid it's not all that simple, my lady.'' He turned to Erhard. ''Take those five men and hunt down the Kyles. Start at the inn where they met Quinn.''

''And if they're not there, Captain?''

Vaughn turned to Thorne. ''Where was he keeping you, my lady?''

Thorne's jaw jutted outward. ''I'll never tell you that.''

Trayhern flexed his fist. The snippet! There would be a time and place after they were married to punish Thorne for her rebelliousness. He would not tolerate such insolence from a man, much less a woman soon to be his property. ''Wolfe, if you can't find him, then you join back up with Kyle's band. Ride back to France with him. Somewhere along the route, I want you to kill both Kyles. Do you understand?''

With a gasp, Thorne launched herself at Trayhern. ''No! Don't you dare! You leave Dev alone!''

Chuckling, Vaughn easily dodged her poorly aimed blows, pulling her off him.

''Go on, Erhard! Once you've killed them, come to London and I'll reward you handsomely. Do you understand?''

Wolfe nodded, his grin broadening beneath his black mustache as he watched Thorne struggle without success to free herself from Trayhern's grip. "They're as good as dead now, Captain. Make sure there's plenty of gold coin waiting for me."

"More than you ever dreamed of. And one more thing, Wolfe."

The hussar turned at the door. "What?" he growled impatiently.

"I want *proof* that they're dead. Gavin Kyle has a nicked left ear. Cut it off and bring it back to me."

With a wrench, Thorne freed herself. Her breathing was harsh and labored. "Yes, Wolfe! I dare you to try to bring back the scarab amulet Dev wears around his neck that is mine. You coward!" She glared at the German defiantly. "Dev knows of your disloyalty. He won't allow you near him or Gavin!"

Vaughn controlled his own anger. "Yes, that would be ample proof. Bring her amulet back to me as evidence of Devlin Kyle's death."

Erhard smiled slightly. "With pleasure, Captain."

Once the hussar lumbered out of the room, Vaughn returned his attention to Thorne. "You shouldn't have helped a criminal like Kyle. Did you consider your responsibility to your good family name, my lady, before you erred? Where is your breeding? I'm shocked."

Thorne flared, her voice husky with emotion. "I care not one whit for what anyone might think."

He smiled pleasantly. "If you persist in clinging to this ridiculous story, your reputation will be muddied."

Thorne's mouth thinned. "I don't care about my reputation. My father will understand, even if you do not."

"You're a bigger fool than I ever gave you credit for being. Two things give a woman of your breeding importance—your virginity and your good name."

"Not necessarily in that order." Thorne glared at him. "Captain, I am Devlin Kyle's woman as much as if I were his wife. I slept with him. I wanted to. I love Dev! I don't care if you know I'm no longer a virgin!"

Trayhern went ashen. "You're soiled. Ruined..." And by that bastard Irishman. But what did Vaughn care if she wasn't a virgin any longer? It was her father's money and shipping interests he wanted.

Thorne saw Vaughn struggle with her revelation. Angered, she rasped, "Only fops count virginity and money on the same hand, Captain. I have no interest in your kind of man. Devlin Kyle is honest, gentle, and allowed me the independence to think and speak on my own. None of you would share or encourage such rapport between a man and a woman." Her voice shook. "No, I've made my choice. Our love has given us things that neither virginity nor a dowry could buy, but then, you can't understand that, can you?"

Vaughn wanted to slap her face. "If you were my wife," he growled, "I'd put you in your proper place."

"Like you did Alyssa Kyle? Don't look so shocked, Captain. I know all about your other life. You raped her, and you tortured and then murdered Dev's wife, Shannon. You're a vile animal, just like Erhard, only the clothes you wear cover up that fact. And don't worry, I'll *never* be yours!"

He smiled coldly. "Don't be too sure. Once I return you to England, safely to your father's arms, he's giving you to me in marriage. After all, when he finds you've been despoiled by an Irish criminal, he'll want to hide the shame you've brought on your powerful and influential family name. I'm sure he'll want us to marry quickly to avoid any wagging tongues." Vaughn reached out, touching her flaming cheek. Thorne pulled away from him, and he smiled. "I don't think I'd mind having you for a wife. But be assured, I'll teach you some manners."

Thorne stood there, stunned at this possibility. No, she would make her father see what a blackguard Vaughn was. Please God, let my father understand, she prayed silently. She shut her eyes, feeling the sting of tears against them. *Run, Dev, run from here! Leave me as you said you would. Flee to the safety of France with your brother.* Numb with the harsh reality, Thorne offered no further vocal resistance when she was led out to a coach that would take them far from Madrid and on a journey back to London, back to her home. Surely her father, a strong, loving man, would protect her from Vaughn's evil grasp.

John Somerset, who was merely transparent skin stretched across the bone, was distraught over his daughter's condition; her countenance was pale, grief etched in her haunted gray eyes. He pulled weakly at the covers on his chest as Vaughn completed the report.

"You've done an admirable job, Captain, under some very trying circumstances. You have my undying thanks."

Vaughn, dressed impeccably, tried to appear humble. "My lord, this may not be the proper time to discuss this, but I'm completely taken by Thorne. I believe I can offer her the strong, compassionate hand she needs to protect her during these trying times ahead. I renew my request for her hand in marriage."

Somerset raised his head and nodded. "It would be best. I want to see her happy again."

Vaughn managed a slight smile filled with hope. "Obviously, your daughter had a fleeting infatuation with this brigand, Kyle. We both know that the *ton* will take this...unfortunate incident and shred her good name." He cleared his throat. "I've had several weeks on our journey back to England to reacquaint myself with Thorne. I value her intelligence and insight. For too long I've searched for just such a woman to complete my life." Vaughn tried to look earnest when he said, "I've fallen hopelessly in love with the Lady Thorne. I think the sooner we marry the better it will be for all concerned."

John Somerset opened his eyes. His slow-functioning mind swung back to Thorne. My God, she looked like a wasted shadow of her former self! Had it been the arduous journey through Spain to Portugal and then to England by ship that had drained all her life from her beautiful eyes? He'd never seen Thorne listless, as if she didn't care whether she lived or died. Soon he would have a talk with her about this Devlin Kyle business. Kyle had raped her, Vaughn said. And Trayhern was right; Thorne's reputation would be ruined. He was desperately glad he had signed legal documents making Vaughn agree to marry his daughter. Her reputation and future would be saved.

Vaughn came from good bloodstock; his Welsh family was one of the richest and most powerful in England, due to their far-flung coal interests. Yes, perhaps it would work out after all.

Thorne lay on the huge goose-down bed in a white flannel nightshirt sprigged with tiny pink roses. The maid, Flossy, had opened the windows, the early summer breeze chasing away the stuffiness in the room. Setting the breakfast tray aside, Thorne felt her stomach roll threateningly once again. With a sigh, she sat up, burying her face in her hands. She had to get dressed and see her father. She put on a dress of soft lavender and went to his room.

John Somerset opened his eyes, a slow smile coming to his slack mouth. "I was hoping you would be up, lamb. Do you have time for a talk with a lonely old man this morning?"

A trembling smile touched Thorne's lips and she held out her hand to her father. "Of course, Papa." She brought a chair beside his bed and sat down.

"How are you feeling?" John wanted to know.

"Much the same. Sickness, sleeping late and this...this awful feeling of emptiness inside me, Papa."

"I see." He stared down at his gnarled hands. "Thorne, it's been four weeks since you've been home and I've never seen you like this before. You've lost too much weight. No matter how many doctors I bring in, you refuse their services." He met her soft gray eyes. "You've smiled only once since returning home. And I've yet to hear your laughter."

Thorne bowed her head, close to tears. "Papa, I love Devlin Kyle. Can't you understand that? He became my life, my reason to live." She placed a hand across her aching heart, her voice halting. "I have lost the will to live, Papa. I miss him terribly. I worry for him." And I worry over your health, she wanted to add. Thorne spent each day with her father. When he was awake, she would read to him. And when his solicitors came, she would read the documents to him because his eyesight was rapidly failing. Thorne would allow no one but herself and Flossy to bathe him daily. She wanted his last days filled with her care and love. An ache centered in Thorne's heart. She had no wish to burden her father with her own anguish and loss. No, he deserved to see her smile, and she promised herself that, somehow, she would once again for his benefit.

John's mouth compressed. "I've felt the same since your beautiful mother died," he admitted in a whisper, giving her an understanding look. He reached over, placing his hand over Thorne's. "I cannot accept that you truly love a criminal, Thorne. I know we've not talked on this subject before. Regardless of what you tell me, that Irish brigand raped you. You were his captive, and he forced you to sleep with him. You had no choice."

The ache widened in Thorne's breast and tears threatened to spill from her eyes. As much as she loved her father, Thorne knew he would never accept her love for Dev. Since her return home, it was as if a dark cloud had descended upon Thorne. Sleep was her only escape. In her dreams, she could be held in Dev's loving arms once again.

"I'm sorry, Papa. I don't know what to say."

John looked over at his suffering daughter. "I've made up my mind, Thorne," he began more firmly. "All the doctors feel you must get out in the sun and begin to mingle with people once again. People who care and are fond of you. I'm going to have my representative contact Captain Vaughn Trayhern and tell him that he may begin calling upon you."

Thorne shut her eyes tightly, biting back a barrage of overwhelming panic. She knew that sooner or later, her father would insist on her marrying Vaughn.

"He's agreed to marry you, and I've signed papers authorizing it in case I die before you can be wed." He gave her a long, meaningful look. "Any day now, I'm going to die. Promise me, Thorne, that you'll follow my last wishes. I want to see you happily married to Vaughn Trayhern.

He's a fine young man. Everyone thinks well of him, and he's got good breeding.''

She paled, her flesh taut across her cheekbones, the blue veins visible beneath them. The promise stuck in her throat. Tears beaded on her lashes. "C-could you wait on your decision, Papa. Just a little while?"

"The doctors feel it's best for your recovery. You need to get some fresh air and exercise. Vaughn will take you for coach rides. Picnics. He's solicitously inquired about you on a weekly basis since your return, and I've kept him informed of your condition." John frowned heavily. "I think the attention of Vaughn will dissolve this infatuation you have with Kyle, as it should. If he truly loved you, he'd have come after you, Thorne. But he hasn't. It grieves me deeply to see you sad-eyed. You barely eat. You no longer take an interest in the children at the orphanages. Something must make you want to live again." He patted her hand gently. "And I think Vaughn is just the man to do that for you. Now, let me hear your promise. Allow an old man to rest easy during his last days of life. Your mother would not forgive me if I left you without preparing for your future. I long to look into your mother's beautiful eyes . . .''

He lapsed into silence but implored Thorne with his eyes to help him finish life's task so he could go to his beloved with a light heart.

Thorne gripped her father's frail hand, unable to meet his burning, feverish gaze. "I—I promise . . ."

"I don't know," Flossy said in a conspiratorial tone to Tilly, who worked in the kitchen at Somerset manor, "there's something terribly amiss with the mistress. Cap'n Trayhern will call on her today and she's beside herself, she is!"

Tilly wiped the perspiration from her apple red cheek, pushing a gray strand of hair out of her eyes and tucking it beneath the mobcap she wore. "Ask me, the mistress is grievin' over the loss of that brigand, Kyle!"

Flossy leaned around the corner to make sure the butler, Alfred, didn't catch them gossiping. "I hear tell the mistress is distraught over having to see this captain. She hates him!''

"Why, no! I've heard he's a fine man!'' Tilly declared. "The Trayherns are the wealthiest family in Wales.''

Picking up her black skirt, Flossy saw the butler coming. "Got to leave, dearie. I'll let you know what happens after the cap'n leaves. He'll be here any minute.''

"You'd best get upstairs, then,'' Tilly scolded.

Flossy fled down the side hall and, for all her ungainly height, managed to look like a deer flying up the stairs to her mistress's quarters. Opening the door, she saw Thorne sitting at the vanity, staring blankly into the mirror, her eyes red and swollen.

"Oh, my poor lamb,'' she crooned, taking the hairbrush in hand. Earlier, Flossy had arranged Thorne's hair into soft folds around her gaunt features to give her face more fullness. "You must stop crying, lamb. Here, blot your eyes one more time.''

Thorne took a handkerchief from Flossy. "I don't want to see him. I hate him! He's a monster! Everyone thinks he's so kind and wonderful, but he isn't.''

Flossy had tried to persuade Thorne to wear a lovely burgundy dress that showed off her décolletage. Instead, Thorne had insisted upon a dull gray cotton dress with white lace around her neck and at the cuff of each sleeve. She looked little better than a maid in the prim dress.

"You have to see him, mistress. It's your father's last wish. You know how much the kind old man loves you. That's all the earl talks about—living long enough to attend your coming wedding.''

A knock on the door interrupted Flossy's inspirational talk. Another maid entered and curtsied.

"My lady, Captain Trayhern is here to call on you.'' She smiled and brought forward a huge bouquet of summer flowers. "He said these were for you, to make you smile once more.''

Thorne stared at them. "Take them away! Take them to the orphanage, where they will be appreciated, Amanda.''

Amanda gave Flossy an anxious look but curtsied. "Yes, ma'am."

"Tell him I'll meet him in the garden, Amanda."

Amanda stood there for a moment until Flossy muttered, "Off with you, now!"

Vaughn stood beneath the spreading arms of a magnificent elm tree that bordered the sumptuous flower gardens surrounding Somerset. The hedges were carefully trimmed, the flowers blooming in brilliant profusion, and the joyous songs of the birds put him in an expectant mood. He restlessly flipped his leather gloves against his thigh, his gaze pinned on the opened doors leading from the manor. He smiled to himself; the wedding announcement had appeared in all the newspapers in London. My God, but things worked out in mysterious and surprising ways!

He would get even with Kyle for bedding down with Thorne. It goaded him relentlessly that she had slept willingly with the Irish bastard. She had welcomed him into her virginal arms. Well, he'd woo her back to love him instead. No woman had ever said no to his amorous advances. Yes, he'd make Thorne want him. The way the elder Somerset was looking each day, he wasn't long for the world. Lady Luck might be fickle with him at the gaming tables, but she certainly was on his side regarding stakes of even higher value. The Somerset fortune and all its property, including Thorne, were soon going to be his.

Vaughn's eyes widened as he saw Thorne escorted from the patio by one of her maids. My God, but she looked terrible! He became worried that she might die before he could wed her, thereby squelching all his long-range plans. He immediately moved forward.

Flossy curtsied low as Vaughn limped up. She watched her mistress take a step back, disgust plainly written on every feature of her waxen face. Hurriedly, the maid took her leave, her heart bleeding for her young mistress.

Vaughn bowed, picking up Thorne's hand. "You look lovely," he lied, pressing a kiss to her flesh. Her fingers were cool and damp.

Thorne slowly raised her head, her eyes dark. She yanked her hand out of his. "Don't *ever* touch me again!" she raged, backing away from him.

A cold smile played on his mouth. "Still the spitfire, Thorne? Despite your illness, you still retain that Gypsy backbone of defiance, don't you?" He advanced upon her, watching her gray eyes widen. "You're like a horse I bought recently," he told her. "He was a big black devil who hated men."

Thorne gripped her skirts, the corners of her mouth stretched into a snarl. "No doubt you beat the poor animal into submission!"

He laughed pleasantly. "How did you know? First, I slowly gelded him. I wanted him to know just who held the power of pain and pleasure over him. And then, once he got to his feet, I had him saddled and rode him until he was in a heavy lather. Of course, he was in excruciating agony from the gelding, with blood running down his back legs. The bastard submitted to me after that ride. He fell from exhaustion and I remained mounted on him. I beat him with a whip until he stood back up on his trembling legs. From that day forward, he's obeyed me."

Thorne gasped, nauseated by the burning pleasure she saw in Trayhern's eyes. "You sicken me! You vile, cruel blackguard!"

"Just remember that story, Thorne." His voice dropped to a velvet whisper. "Because, within twenty days, you are going to be my wife. Yes, that's right. The dowry and terms of agreement have already been signed between your father and me. All that remains is sufficient time to plan a proper wedding." He reached out, caressing her cheek, finding her skin soft and pliant. "And you'll be mine, just like that big black horse is mine. Only I would never treat you like that. I know you're not feeling well. I want our marriage to be happy." He managed a forced smile. "After all, I don't think I'm ugly to look at. I shall be a good companion to you. Just give me a chance, that's all I ask."

Chapter Nineteen

"He's gone," Dr. Alex Benjamine pronounced quietly, drawing the sheet over John Somerset's head. He watched as Thorne, who had been at her father's side all morning, threw herself across her father's body, sobbing uncontrollably. Vaughn Trayhern stood by the windows, arms crossed, lips in a compressed line. The drapes were drawn, and only a few burning candles relieved the gloom of the bleak chamber.

"Thank you, Doctor," Vaughn said quietly after another five minutes. "Come, I'll walk you to your carriage."

Alex glanced over at Thorne and laid a hand on her shaking shoulder. The earl's daughter was a haggard ghost of her former self. The change in Thorne was frightening, and Alex wanted to stay long enough to talk privately with her. Somerset had made him promise to look after Thorne's deteriorating health.

"In a moment, my lord." He fiddled with his black leather case. "I think Lady Thorne may need some medicine. The death has been hard on her."

Vaughn hesitated, not wanting to appear too callous. "Very well. Thorne?" His voice was soft.

Alex frowned as he saw Thorne wince and pull her head up. Her gray eyes were wounded holes of despair.

"The doctor will see you in your bedchamber."

Alex frowned as he followed Thorne to her room. She wore a black silk gown that mirrored her grief. Her hair was coiffed to perfection, her throat unadorned. This wasn't the Thorne he knew; the carefree girl with a sparkle of life in her beautiful dove gray eyes, or a winsome smile that always hovered like sunshine around her lips. He set his bag down, watching as she went to the opened doors leading out to the balcony. She stood with her back to him, arms folded around her body.

"Thorne?" Alex walked over to her. Her shoulders shook and he pulled a silk handkerchief from his pocket and gave it to her.

"Th-thank you," Thorne murmured brokenly. She was not able to deal with the compassion in the doctor's assessing gaze.

"You're not well, Thorne. What's wrong?"

"N-nothing."

Gently, Alex forced her to turn around. "Look at me," he commanded gruffly. "I want you to get into your dressing gown," he said firmly. "I'm going to examine you."

Thorne started to protest, but she saw Alex shake his head like a shaggy mastiff and knew it was useless to argue. "Very well . . ."

After he had completed the examination, Alex held on to his shock and surprise. He saw Thorne's anxiety as he pulled her robe closed and slowly rose.

"Well, young lady," Dr. Benjamine said, closing his black leather bag, "your sickness has a cause."

Thorne walked to a chair and sat down. With trembling fingers, she rubbed her brow miserably. "What's wrong?"

The white-haired doctor managed a smile. "First of all, Thorne I want you to know that I'll hold this in confidence."

Confused, she croaked, "What's wrong with me, Doctor?"

Alex walked over to where she sat. He kept his voice very low. "You're pregnant. Almost three months along, I'd wager, from all indications."

Thorne looked up, gasping. Pregnant? And then tears flooded her eyes. "My God . . ."

He took her hand, patting it gently. "Don't swoon, my dear. There, there. It's quite all right." He poured her a small brandy, urging her to drink it before she lost all color. Obediently, Thorne took it and choked down the contents. Alex smiled as he saw color rush back to her cheeks. "The baby is fine as far as I can tell."

Thorne stared up into the doctor's kindly face. "That means," she whispered rawly, "that the baby is Dev's."

"Correct, my dear." Alex frowned. "John told me how that Irish brigand had kidnapped and then seduced you. Frankly, it's not your fault. Now, if you want to rid yourself of it—"

"No!" Thorne shot out of the chair, her hands pressed protectively to her belly. "I want this child more than life itself, Doctor." A tremulous smile fled across her wet lips. "I loved Dev, Doctor. Do you understand?"

Benjamine frowned and released her hand, slowly pacing the room. "My dear, have you given thought to what your future husband might think?"

Thorne froze, having forgotten about Vaughn. She stared at the doctor. "He won't want it." She shuddered. "He'd never forgive me, Doctor." She turned away. Vaughn would insist upon her killing the baby she carried inside her if he knew. "What can I do?"

Clearing his throat, Alex muttered, "Well, I can say that the birth was early. That sometimes happens, you know. I'm sure everyone would accept that explanation and I would gladly support it. After all, you're to be married shortly."

Fear stronger than any Thorne had ever experienced wove through her as she turned to the doctor. "And would Vaughn be able to tell whose child it was?"

"As long as the baby resembles him and not Devlin Kyle, he cannot prove that the baby is not his. All we can do is pray that he may have no cause for serious doubt."

"Which would mean he'd hate not only me but, more important, my child," Thorne concluded in despair.

"I would hope he would have compassion, my lady."

Thorne grimaced. "He's not got an ounce of that, good doctor, believe me."

Alex found her statement hard to believe and dismissed it as overreaction to her father's death. "If you are fortunate enough not to show too soon, your husband may be led into believing that the baby is his. Some women carry high and not so much outward."

"Which will I be?"

"I don't know, my lady. Thus far, your abdomen is not swollen."

Thorne tried to ignore her wildly beating heart in her breast. "If I show too soon, he'll know."

"Bed with him the first night of your wedding," Alex counseled, "and it may save you much heartache."

"I think it's time we get to the chapel, my lord," the servant told Vaughn in a mellow voice.

A knock at the study door made them both look up. The butler entered, resplendent in his black-and-white suit. "Captain Trayhern? There is a man here. A Wolfe Erhard? He demands to see you right now."

Vaughn swallowed a smile, his heart pounding once to underscore his excitement. He turned to the servant.

"Leave me."

"You have half an hour before the ceremony, my lord."

"I'll be there." Vaughn spoke briskly. "Now, be gone."

"Come in and shut the door," Vaughn commanded Wolfe. He stood behind the desk, expectant. Erhard still sported a thick mustache and his clothes shouted that he was a mercenary. "Well?" Vaughn asked impatiently. "Did you catch up with them?"

Wolfe shut the door, smiling. "The Kyles are dead. Both of them. By my own hand."

"Are you sure?"

"You gave me orders to follow and find them," Wolfe growled, tossing a leather pouch to Trayhern. "Gavin Kyle's bloodied ear and the amulet are in there."

Eagerly, Vaughn yanked open the pouch, the contents spilling out on the desk. A look of triumph gleamed in his eyes as he examined the ear, which indeed, had a nick in it. Then he picked up the amulet, smiling. "Excellent," he murmured in a pleased voice. "You've done a good job, Erhard. I couldn't have asked for a better wedding gift."

"Pay me! I'm hungry and I want a woman, in that order."

Vaughn smiled. "Before I do, tell me everything," he said, sitting down. "And be quick about it. I've thirty minutes before I marry my beautiful bride."

Thorne pulled the heavy lace veil down across her face. Her ladies-in-waiting were bravely smiling and telling her how beautiful she looked in the ivory satin wedding dress. She tried to respond, but her heart was heavy with grief. Married. She was going to be married to Vaughn Trayhern. His mother, the Lady Rowena, was present, and she was like any of the blooded *ton,* properly snobbish. Thorne took solace in a long letter penned by Alyssa Trayhern.

The envelope had arrived a week ago and inside it were two letters, one from Alyssa and the other from her husband, Tray. The letters explained in detail why they would not attend Vaughn's wedding. He had raped Alyssa and Tray had never forgiven him for the act. Vaughn was not allowed near Shadowhawk, which sat along the Irish Sea in Wales. To say that Tray, his stepbrother, did not love or respect Vaughn, was an understatement. The letter confirmed for Thorne, at least, that Vaughn was capable of great cruelty. She wept softly as she read the last lines of their letters. They bore her no ill will, and if she wanted to visit Shadowhawk alone, she would be welcomed with warmth. Tray had penned a last sentence on his letter that sent a chill down Thorne's spine. *Should you ever need sanctuary against my brother, know that we stand prepared to aid and protect you.*

Sanctuary? She needed that now. Her stomach turned threateningly and Thorne became panicky. Nearly every morning for the last month she had been ill. She couldn't be now! Fighting down the mounting nausea, Thorne concentrated on picking up the voluminous satin skirt and following her maids toward the rear of the chapel.

Later, as she walked slowly down the aisle of the chapel, which was filled to overflowing, everyone saw tears on Thorne's colorless cheeks. They assumed she was weeping with happiness. The truth was, her father had died recently and she was marrying an evil man she could never love. Vaughn waited next to the minister, attired handsomely in his black coat and trousers. The white shirt emphasized his dark blond hair and mustache.

When Vaughn touched her lace-gloved hand, Thorne shrank deep inside herself. Resigned that she had to marry him, she tried desperately to control her raging emotions. *Dev! Oh, sweet Mother Mary, give me strength to go through with this. I love Dev so much....* She focused on Dev's face, his voice, his embrace, instead of the words spoken by the minister in front of them. When she had to say the vows that would bind her for eternity to Vaughn Trayhern, they lodged sickeningly in her throat. Long seconds went by and Thorne could feel Vaughn's anger radiating toward her. Finally, she choked out in a whisper, "I do."

Her flesh burned as Vaughn placed a heavy gold and diamond-encrusted ring on her finger. Instantly, Thorne wanted to scream and fling it off her hand. And when Vaughn lifted the heavy veil to seal the bargain of their travesty of a marriage, Thorne steeled herself against his touch. She wanted no man to touch her but Dev. She had shunned Vaughn's eager advances throughout their brief courtship. As his mouth descended, Thorne tensed. She felt the bristle of his luxuriant mustache and smelled his brandy-laced breath. Mercifully, it was a chaste kiss, fleeting and without passion.

As they turned from the altar, Thorne prayed that the gala festivities planned from noon until late into the night would drag on forever. Tonight, she would have to share her bed with him. Revulsion wound through her and she felt faint, surprising Vaughn when she gripped his arm to steady herself.

* * *

Vaughn smiled as he opened the door adjoining their bedrooms. It was nearly midnight before he had cajoled Thorne away from the dancing. Her maid, Flossy, curtsied and informed him that his bride was dressed for bed and waiting for him. He remained in his wedding clothes and saw wariness written on Thorne's face as he shut the door to her bedroom behind him.

"You look lovely, my dear," he purred, advancing upon her. God, but she did! Her luxurious black hair framed her taut face and her darting gray eyes. Vaughn's gaze settled first on her full red lips and then on the thin silk gown that provocatively outlined her body. His smile deepened as he went to the end of her bed and picked up her dressing robe, handing it to her.

"Put this on, Pet."

Confused, Thorne clutched the robe in her hands. "Why?"

Vaughn caressed her chin briefly. "Remember earlier today, Pet? You promised to obey me in our vows." His teasing voice dropped to a gentler tone. "Put it on. For me. Please . . ."

Thorne slipped on the ivory dressing robe, tying it closed with a sash. She stood tensely before Vaughn, her chin raised in silent defiance.

"Much better. Now, come, stand over here by the fireplace. I have a wedding present that I want to give you."

Thorne stared at him, confused.

"Perhaps this gift will make you forget about your jaded past and look forward to a brighter, happier future with me." Vaughn swung open the door to her bedroom chamber.

Thorne gasped. Wolfe Erhard stood just inside the doorway.

"Come in, Wolfe," Vaughn invited, gesturing for him to enter.

Her heart beat painfully in her throat as she stared up at the hussar. "What is the meaning of this?" Thorne rasped, casting a wild look over at Vaughn.

"Wolfe has brought you my wedding gift. Give her the pouch you carry, Erhard."

Thorne barely caught the tossed article, her fingers burning as they closed around its stained folds.

"Now, go over to the bed and empty the contents, Pet."

A cold shudder twisted through Thorne. There was only one reason why Erhard was here. She recalled Vaughn's last orders to the mercenary. With trembling fingers, she opened the pouch. Turning it over, she shook it.

With a cry, Thorne pressed her hands against her lips. Dizziness swept through her, and she staggered back a step, eyes wide as she looked at the ear and her bloodstained amulet lying on the pristine whiteness of the coverlet.

Erhard hungrily looked at Thorne, finding her even more beautiful. He grinned beneath his drooping mustache. "You've cause to celebrate, my lady," he began in his rumbling tone. "Exactly one and a half months ago, I caught up with Captain Kyle and his brother." He touched the pistol in his belt. "Shot them both through the head while they slept."

Vaughn's smile widened. "After Kyle raped you, I had no choice, Pet. I had to defend your honor the best I could under the circumstances. Now your honor is restored and my blood feud with the Kyles is finished." He jerked his head in Erhard's direction. "Leave now! You've got your gold. I don't ever want to see your face on Somerset's property again."

Vaughn saw Thorne grow deathly pale as she clutched at the mantel to support herself. He walked toward her. "So you see, my dear wife, your past is truly dead. I will make you want me as your husband, the man whom you will eventually bed with and bear children for. Devlin Kyle is no more."

Thorne moaned and crumpled to the floor, unconscious.

"My lady," Flossy begged as she stood in the center of her bedchamber, "you must have a doctor examine you! You've been sick for the last five days and touched nothing but a little soup." The maid wrung her thin hands anxiously as she studied her mistress. Thorne lay in the bed, her eyes shut tightly.

"No."

"But . . . Lord Trayhern is greatly worried."

Thorne bit down hard on her lower lip. Since Vaughn had bludgeoned her with the news of Dev's death, her will to live had been destroyed. And surprisingly, Vaughn had not made a move to touch Thorne since then. Perhaps it was due to her illness. Thorne didn't know; nor did she care. It was only a matter of time until Vaughn took her to his bedchamber.

Flossy inched forward. "Mistress, you *must* allow a doctor to examine you." She lowered her voice to a mere whisper. "Lord Trayhern grows impatient with you. Each morning he leaves his chamber and rides the hills of Somerset. The horse comes back hours later in a lather and welt marks all over its black hide. Please, do not test my lord's temper . . . we all worry for you so."

Miserably, Thorne turned over and sat up. Her hair was mussed and in need of washing and combing. Her heart ached for the black horse that Vaughn rode. He was taking out his anger for her on the poor beast. "And how is the rest of the household faring?" she asked in a parched voice. Her old maid, who had been with her since birth, wrung her hands.

"Oh, mistress, I don't want to get in trouble with the lord. If only . . . if only you would dress and take over your duties at the manor."

Thorne rubbed her face, making an effort to think clearly. "Is he beating any of my servants?"

Flossy hesitated. "Yes."

"Why didn't you tell me about this sooner?"

"How could I, my lady? You were so sick. Lord Trayhern stalks Somerset like a vengeful ghost."

Somehow, Thorne had to pull herself together. She slowly got up. "Draw my bath, Flossy. I can no longer feel sorry for myself when so many kind and good people are suffering beneath his cruel hand."

Thorne chose a pale pink cotton dress with a high neck-line and puffed sleeves. She allowed Flossy to arrange her hair and apply a bit of makeup to her waxen features. Regardless of her personal pain and grief over Dev's death, she must try to function for the sake of Somerset's servants.

She saw hope leap to life in the workers' long features as she visited the laundry facilities, the kitchen and the stable. Everywhere she went, they bowed deeply, whispering kind words of solace for her to get well soon so that they would see her on a daily basis. Tears burned Thorne's eyes as she finished her rounds. Vaughn was never home during the day; Thorne guessed he was in London at the gaming tables.

Next, Thorne went to her father's library. Her heart ached as she entered the room where she had spent so many wonderful hours with him. The curtains had been drawn, the room dark and bleak. Thorne opened the curtains, allowing the summer sun to spill through the windows. She cracked open one of the outside doors, and the sweet scent of the country filled the place.

Vaughn threw the reins of his black gelding to the awaiting Eamon. He slapped the whip happily against his highly polished ebony boot, striding off toward the manor. It had been five days since their wedding and he had been patient with Thorne. Yes, the shock of Devlin Kyle being dead was part of her ailing, he was sure. But he knew he could eventually get her to respond warmly to him.

As he took the stairs two at a time, his blue peasant shirt clung to his hot, sweaty body. Vaughn passed the library and halted when he saw Thorne.

Thorne's head jerked up. Her fingers tightened on the book she held.

"Well, well, you're up," Vaughn greeted cheerfully, shutting the door quietly behind him. He stood there, feet apart, tapping the long, thin crop absently against his boot. "And looking much better. You've even got color in your cheeks." He smiled. "Have you decided to join the living once again? I know, it's my good looks that have inspired you, Pet.''

Thorne's throat closed with tension as she read the look in Vaughn's blue eyes. Slowly, she allowed the book to fall to the desk. ''There's little reason for me to want to live, Vaughn,'' she replied stiffly.

He languidly approached her, like a cat playing with a defenseless mouse. Taking his crop, he tapped one of her hands with it. ''You look very becoming in that dress,'' he drawled, ''although I would prefer my wife to show off her cleavage. It's the latest rage, didn't you know?''

Thorne trembled. ''I'm not interested in fashion!'' she bit out between compressed lips.

''It would make me happy if you could dress a little more fashionably, Thorne. You're beautiful and I want to show you off to the *ton*.''

She said nothing, bowing her head, refusing to look at him. ''My dressing habits should be of no concern to you, sir.''

With a chuckle, Vaughn dropped the crop and lifted Thorne's hand into his. He saw the abject terror written in her huge gray eyes. ''Since you're feeling better, I want to show you how much I truly love you.''

With a moan, Thorne tried to wrest herself from his tightening grip. She saw his smile dissolve.

''Why do you resist me, sweet wife? Could it be that you still hold some shred of love in your heart for that Irish bastard?'' Vaughn ground out savagely. ''Forget him! When you lie in my bed, you'll be mine, not his! Remember that.''

He started to pull her toward him and she fought to free herself of his grasp. Vaughn saw Thorne's hand come up, but he was too shocked to move in time. The slap resounded sharply throughout the room. Rage filled him, his cheek smarting hotly in the wake of the blow.

Thorne backed away, hands across her mouth. ''Don't do this to me, don't...''

With every fiber of his being, Vaughn controlled his urge to slap her back. He intended to wear Thorne down until she accepted him. She would become submissive to his needs and desires sooner or later. "I love you," he rasped, eyes blazing. "And I'll respect the fact that you're still ill. I want you to come willingly to me, Thorne."

"You don't love me," Thorne cried. "You don't even like me, Vaughn! Let's leave each other in peace. Get a mistress in London!"

Ominously, Vaughn walked toward her, but he did not touch her. "For your information, my dear, I already have a mistress in London. I will make you love me, Thorne. I'm not unappealing. I'm considered a fine catch, the perfect husband." His cheek stung and he captured her by the shoulders, forcing her against him.

Thorne gasped, her hands pressed against the hard warmth of his chest. She twisted her head to one side as he leaned down to kiss her.

"Come to me," he snarled softly. "Don't make me hurt you. Love me as you loved him."

"Never!" Thorne cried rawly.

Chapter Twenty

Thorne lovingly rubbed her swelling belly. She had walked out into the massive flower gardens surrounding Somerset to take advantage of the summer sun. A straw hat with a wide brim protected her from the sun's rays as she slowly made her way down a row of pink roses. Here and there, she would cup their velvet petals and lean down to inhale their special fragrance.

As she raised her head, Thorne's gray eyes darkened with a nameless fear. The last thirty days since her marriage to Vaughn had tainted everyone in the manor. The servants tiptoed down the halls, tight-lipped and cowering. Once, Somerset had been filled with laughter and lightness. With Vaughn wielding his omniscient power over all in the guise of that whip he always carried, even Thorne hid in her room whenever possible to avoid him.

Thorne sat down on a stone bench at the end of the row of roses. She had snipped one pink rose, which lay in the lap of her pale yellow cotton dress. Worriedly, she caressed her belly again, talking silently to her baby, to Dev's child. With a sigh, she closed her eyes, bowing her head. The only ray of light to her otherwise tension-filled days had been a letter delivered by messenger from Shadowhawk. Thorne had read the life-giving contents penned by Alyssa Trayhern, who gave her courage and hope.

Lifting her head, Thorne wondered what Alyssa and Tray would think of her last letter to them. In it, Thorne admitted she was with Dev's child and that Vaughn mis-

treated the servants badly. Perhaps she shouldn't have
written it, but she had no one else to confide in. If Vaughn
knew she was writing to Alyssa, he'd fly into one of his
frequent murderous rages. God knew, she'd seen the damage he could inflict with that crop of his. A number of the
servants bore telling welts and even slashing cuts from the
times they accidentally angered Vaughn. Human and animal alike lived in dread of him.

She was cold despite the warmth of the sun on her.
Thorne tried to make herself accept that Vaughn eventually would take her to his bed. What concerned her most
was the safety of her baby. The doctor had said that she
should not indulge in relations because of her pregnancy.
Protectively, Thorne pressed her hand against herself. She
was showing far more now. Would Vaughn notice? An unparalleled urge to flee struck Thorne. Vaughn would know
the child wasn't his. What would he do? She did not want
to think of that possibility.

Thorne dreaded each night as she sat alone in her room.
She barely slept at night, thinking Vaughn might stride into
her chamber and claim his rights as a husband. A ragged
sigh escaped her tightened lips. Would he come to her tonight?

Vaughn opened the door to Thorne's bedchamber. He
was clothed in a black silk robe, the riding crop lazily
hanging from his wrist. He saw Thorne jerk her head up
from the book she was reading at the desk. A smile pulled
at his mouth as he quietly closed the door and stood there,
studying her. As always, he saw the fear and disgust deep
in the recesses of her haunted eyes. Frustration thrummed
through him as he saw Thorne's disgust dissolve into unadulterated fear.

"It's been a month, Pet," he began softly, gesturing toward her bed. "I think we should begin to know each
other." He scowled as she sat frozen at the desk, the book
closed between her tense hands. "I've plied you with new
dresses, a fine coach and horses worth a king's ransom.
Show me how grateful you are."

"I'm not feeling well, Vaughn," Thorne said in a trembling voice.

"That's all I ever hear from you," he answered, strolling nonchalantly toward her. "You'll feel a great deal worse, Pet, if you don't start acting like a wife."

Thorne slowly stood up. Earlier, she had bathed and dressed in a loose-fitting gown. She screamed at herself to hold on to her anger and fear. She must not fight Vaughn, she must submit! Would he attack her anyway? And what of her baby? She could lose her child if Vaughn chose to take out his cruelty upon her. Without a word, she loosened the sash on her dressing robe and slowly took it off.

Thorne shrank back a step as Vaughn halted in front of her. Unable to tolerate his smiling face, she bowed her head, standing frozen. A small gasp escaped her lips as he reached out, cupping her breasts, which were hidden by the pink flannel nightgown she wore.

"What's this?" he murmured. "Shyness? Certainly I'm skilled enough to make you feel pleasure, not pain." Vaughn felt the rounded heaviness of her breasts and scowled. A month ago, her breasts were small and had a perfect tilt to them. Now they were like heavy globes in his exploring hands. "Are you gaining weight?" he growled. He grabbed the opened vee of the gown, forcing it down across her shoulders. In moments, Thorne stood naked before him. He quickly perused her. Nipples that were supposed to be a rosy pink were now a dusky color. Roughly, he cupped her breasts again. Thorne winced.

"What's amiss here?" he asked her in a rasp. He slid his hands down her rib cage. Where her waist had once been narrow, it was thick. And then he eyed her abdomen. He recalled how painfully flat her belly had been in those men's breeches she wore in Madrid. Now it was surprisingly swollen and there was a pearl-like luster to the flesh. With a snarl, he dragged Thorne to the bed. He stood ominously above her, breathing hard, his eyes narrowed.

"You've changed a great deal in a month, Thorne." He jabbed his finger down at her abdomen. "Now what's this?"

Thorne cowered. "I—I've gained some weight, that's all—"

Vaughn leaned over and wrapped his fingers in her hair. "Little liar," he hissed against her face as he forced her back on the bed. "Unless I miss my guess, you're knocked up like a brood mare."

She shut her eyes, pain radiating from her scalp. "N-no..."

"Liar! Now tell me the truth!"

His voice was like a slap across her face. Thorne's breath came in sobs. She had to escape! She had to! With a wrenching motion, she struck Vaughn as hard as she could.

Caught off guard, Vaughn grunted. He released her and staggered off the bed, holding his jaw.

Thorne scrambled for her dressing robe, throwing it on. She kept the bed as a barrier between them. "Leave me alone!" she shrieked.

Dumbstruck by her unexpected action, Vaughn stood there, blood dribbling from his right nostril as he stared at her. "You bitch. You conniving bitch. You're pregnant, aren't you?"

Thorne's eyes widened. "Yes, yes I am pregnant, and you're going to leave me alone! I can't stand your touch. Your cruelty to animals is only surpassed by your cruelty to people."

Vaughn's eyes glittered with feral intent. His face was livid with rage.

He picked up the crop and laughed harshly. "It's that Irish brigand's baby, isn't it? This time you've gone too far." He advanced upon Thorne, the crop raised over his head. "I won't have any wife of mine carrying a bastard!"

With a cry, Thorne leapt toward the door. Yanking it open, she scrambled out into the carpeted hall, nearly tripping over her robe. Vaughn struck at her. The crop exploded against her tender back. No! Thorne ran down the hall, screaming for help. The stairs! If only she could reach them and get to the stable. Earlier in the evening, Thorne had asked Eamon, who had been demoted to nothing more than a stable hand, to saddle Shukar Nak. She heard the whistle of the crop slice through the air again.

Pain seared her back and right shoulder as the flesh split and bled in the wake of the crop. Vaughn roared her name, a string of curses following as he caught up with her. Thorne turned unexpectedly and lunged at him. He stumbled and flailed, caught off balance as his bad knee gave way. It was enough. Turning, Thorne fled to the top of the stairs, sobbing for breath.

"No!" Vaughn cried. He reached out, his fingers sinking deeply into her shoulder.

Thorne uttered a strangled cry. She flailed wildly as he hauled her up against him. Somewhere deep within her, she knew that she must escape. The terrible glitter in Vaughn's eyes told her that he would kill her. She must fight for the life of Dev's child. For her own life. With a swift, upward jab of her knee, she caught Vaughn full between the legs. He released her, howling in pain.

Just as she got to the stairs, hand upon the banister, Vaughn lunged forward. With a curse, he struck Thorne with both hands, pushing her as hard as he could down the stairs. She screamed, teetering forward. Vaughn stood, breathing hard, and watched Thorne roll and bounce down eighty steps. The cries of servants erupted from below as Thorne sprawled lifelessly at the bottom, her face ashen.

Straightening up, Vaughn glared at Flossy, who came tearing down the hall toward him. He raised his hand. "Stand where you are!" he roared.

Flossy's eyes widened, her mobcap slipping as she halted. "B-but—my mistress!"

Vaughn stared down at where Thorne lay unmoving. "Let her stay there," he ordered. He saw two more scullery maids hovering at the door. "Anyone who touches my wife will deal with me," he thundered. "Now let her lie! She can get up and crawl on her hands and knees to her bedchamber when she wakes!"

Flossy whirled around, lifting her black skirt, flying down the hall. She went down the back stairs, sobbing.

Once out in the darkened courtyard, she rushed to the stable quarters.

"Eamon! Eamon!" she cried, opening the creaking doors. The sweet scent of newly mown hay hit her senses. Eamon appeared almost immediately, his craggy features sleep-ridden.

"What's going on, woman? Why are you shrieking like an Irish banshee?"

Flossy grabbed Eamon's arm. "Mistress Thorne!" she cried. "Master Vaughn has pushed her down the stairs... she's lying there. He won't allow any of us to aid her! God help her, but she looks dead!"

Eamon shoved his shirt into his trousers. "Trayhern won't let you call Dr. Benjamine?"

Tears flowed down Flossy's thin, parched features. "No. He's in a terrible rage, Eamon. I saw him beating Mistress Thorne with a whip," she wailed. "It was terrible! Just terrible. We all heard her screams. I ran to help, but all I saw was the master pushing her down the stairs. He pushed her, Eamon! He wanted to kill her!"

"I've no doubt of that," Eamon growled. He placed a hand on Flossy's trembling shoulders. "Now listen closely, Floss, keep a watch on Trayhern. As soon as I get the coach hitched up, I'm going to take Mistress Thorne to Dr. Benjamine. You must keep Trayhern occupied so that I can sneak in and carry her safely out of the manor." His voice deepened. "Can you do that for me?"

Flossy nodded jerkily. "Wh-what shall I do to keep the master at bay?"

"Get Alfred to take the slimy bastard some brandy," Eamon growled, lighting a lantern. "Give me twenty minutes and I'll have Mistress Thorne gone from here."

"T-twenty minutes. Very well..." Flossy turned, running full tilt back to the manor.

Vaughn sat in his bedchamber, staring moodily down at the blackened hearth of the fireplace. He was still breathing hard, his chest glistening with sweat. Throwing the crop down, he paced the length of his room. The bitch! The deceiving, lying bitch! Carrying Kyle's bastard! He raked his fingers through his blond hair. He couldn't allow that child to be born.

A timid knock at his door sent him into further rage. "Come in!"

Alfred entered. "My lord, I thought perhaps you might want some warm brandy." He closed the door and brought the silver tray over to him.

Vaughn smiled a little. Alfred's gray hair glowed like a halo about his head. The servant had the good sense to keep his face expressionless, eyes carefully downcast and voice neutral. He took the brandy.

"Set it over there and leave me."

"Yes, my lord."

Satisfaction melted through him as the fiery brandy settled in his stomach, effectively dousing his anger. Alfred was the perfect butler, always anticipating his comforts. Vaughn swirled the brandy around in his mouth, getting up and pacing. He had to get rid of Thorne's baby. There was an old woman the girls at the gaming parlors used when they found themselves pregnant with an unwanted brat. Tomorrow morning, he'd get the old woman's name and bring her to Somerset. And then Thorne would drink whatever vile concoction she made up for her, and he'd be rid of the bastard.

Vaughn poured himself more brandy and sat down, placing his bare feet up on the desk in front of him. Let Thorne crawl back to her room. It was just punishment. He smiled. That Gypsy bitch would never again disobey him, not after tonight.

Thorne slowly sat up, dizzy. She tasted the salty, metallic taste of blood in her mouth, her fingers moving to her lips. Dazed, she looked up as a heavily cloaked figure appeared silently from the side hall. It was Eamon.

"Come, my lady, I'm taking you to safety," he said huskily. Eamon threw a black wool cloak around her thinly clad body.

She tried to rise, clutching at Eamon's shoulders. Pain raced jaggedly up through Thorne and a soft cry tore from her lips. In one motion, Eamon scooped her up, carrying her quickly toward the rear of the manor beneath the shadowy lamplight.

"Eamon," she whispered brokenly.

"I'm taking you to Dr. Benjamine, my lady."

More pain throbbed through her lower body and Thorne became frightened as never before. She gripped his great-coat. "No! Vaughn will find me there! You must—"

He carried her out the scullery door, which was held open by Flossy. Several other servants ran alongside, lighting the way with lanterns so Eamon would not stumble as they made their way to the stable.

"Then where, my lady?" he rasped, out of breath. "Your safety must come first!"

Thorne sank deeply into his arms, weak and very tired. Her eyes fluttered closed. "Take me—take me to Shadowhawk, in Wales. To Tray and Alyssa...you must, Eamon. That is the only place where Vaughn will not find me. Please..."

"That's a three-day journey, my lady," Eamon huffed as he carried her to the coach. One of the servants opened the door, standing aside. The two horses stood quietly in their traces as he gently eased her onto the seat. He was shocked by the pallor of her face. Thorne huddled in the cloak, leaning back, eyes closed.

"I don't care. Don't you see? Shadowhawk is the only place Vaughn will not think to find me." Thorne pressed back a cry of pain, clutching at her belly. "Hurry, Eamon...for God's sake, hurry. No matter what happens, get me there. I'm not well. But don't stop for anything. There is a pouch of gold in Shukar's saddlebag. Get it. Buy fresh coach horses wherever you must. Take me to Tray and Alyssa...they're my only hope."

Day and night ran together for Thorne. The bumpy, swaying ride in the coach was continuous. Eamon drove the team on the whip, but he never pushed the animals beyond their stamina. At times, Thorne thought she might scream out for him to stop for just one moment when the pain became too much to bear. Desperation kept her sane. Once Vaughn discovered Eamon had taken her from Somerset, he would be on their heels like a hound from hell. No position was comfortable for Thorne. Finally, she lay down on the scratchy horsehair seat, suspended between unconsciousness and terror as the coach bumped along.

Each time Eamon changed coach horses, Thorne summoned courage from some deep part of herself to sit up. She drank the water Eamon offered to her but little else. Thorne watched in mounting horror as she saw more and more blood each time she urinated. Her belly was crampy and pain rolled through her like waves. Her flannel nightgown was soaked by the third day, and she could do nothing to escape the stench of herself. Thorne clung to the thread of hope that soon they would arrive at Shadowhawk and she would be safe . . . safe. . . .

Darkness was total as Thorne was jolted awake by the cry of Eamon's deep voice. The wheels of the coach now rolled over a smoother road. Shadowhawk? Had they finally arrived? She clutched weakly at the seat, prostrate upon it, tears rolling down her cheeks in relief.

Eamon hauled back on the horses' reins, pulling them to a halt at the entrance to the forbidding stone manor of Shadowhawk. Hastily, he climbed down off the seat, roaring for help. The door opened and a man with a decided limp came and stood out on the stone steps.

"Lord Trayhern!" Eamon gasped, running up to him.

"Yes?" His square face was drawn into a frown, gray eyes narrowed. The man took another limping step forward to get a better look at Eamon.

"My lord, the Lady Thorne is in the coach. She's gravely hurt, sir. She asked to be taken here. Please, will you give her assistance?"

Tray turned as he heard a cry behind him. His wife, Alyssa, pushed past him, attired in a burgundy dressing robe.

"It's Thorne! Oh, Tray, something terrible must have happened!" she cried, giving him a pleading look.

Eamon looked up as a third figure emerged from the shadowed light spilling from the doorway. His eyes widened. "Captain Kyle!" he whispered.

Dev moved past his sister and brother-in-law, taking the stairs two at a time. Quinn stared openmouthed as Dev headed toward the coach. Alyssa flew down the stairs, right behind her brother.

Quinn turned in shock, barely aware that the Earl of Trayhern was quietly issuing orders to several other of his servants, who had assembled around him. He looked up at the harshly carved features of one of the wealthiest men in all Wales.

"My—my lord," Quinn stammered, "we all thought Captain Kyle was dead!"

Tray frowned. "Dead?"

"Yes, my lord. Your half brother brought a man from Spain who claimed to have killed both Kyles."

Tray's face grew still. His powerfully built body tensed, radiating rage. "My brother's gone too far this time. What is your name?"

"Eamon Quinn, my lord. At your service."

"Very well, Quinn. Dev will bring the Lady Thorne inside. Does she need a doctor?"

Eamon nodded. "She's gravely hurt, sir."

Tray turned to his butler. "Get the doctor here on the whip, Craddock."

"Right away, my lord!"

Thorne closed her eyes, relaxing for the first time in three days. Finally, there was no carriage motion to tear at her. She heard a woman's voice. Alyssa, it must be Alyssa! Would she look as beautiful as she remembered? She had to thank her for helping her. Pain moved through Thorne and she took half breaths, trying to adjust to the agony. Her brow was beaded with perspiration, black hair matted around her face.

The door was yanked open. Hands. Gentle hands fell upon her shoulders. Thorne forced her eyes open. The light of a lamp was thrust in the window of the coach, illuminating the darkness.

"Thorne?" Dev's voice wavered unsurely as he maneuvered himself into the narrow confines between the seats. Anxiously, he pushed the damp black hair off her brow. "Thorne? Can you hear me? It's Dev."

A cry tore from deep within Thorne as she stared disbelievingly up into his tense, shadowed face. And then blackness engulfed her. She could endure no more.

The next time Thorne awoke, Dev was at her side. He was holding her cool hand between his warm ones. She barely lifted her lashes, thinking how distraught and sad he looked. *Alive,* her heart told her, *Dev's alive, not dead.* Her brow wrinkled. How could that be? The room was dark, save for a few lamps, the curtains drawn across windows in the unfamiliar room. Her pain was gone, and for that she was grateful. Despite her gummy mouth, Thorne forced the word "Dev?" between her cracked lips.

Dev leaned over her, stroking her unwashed hair. His eyes were red-rimmed and suspiciously bright. "Beloved?"

His voice reverberated through her, lifting her above all her misery. A broken cry stretched the corners of her mouth. "Vaughn told me Wolfe had killed you and Gavin."

"He lied, Thorne. How do you feel? Are you thirsty?"

"But the amulet... the ear..." She was so confused.

"I'll explain later, my love," Dev assured her. "Helping you heal is all that matters right now."

Her eyes burned with scalding tears of joy. "All I want... need, is to be held by you."

Dev gathered her frail form into his arms and buried his head against her neck. "God, how much I love you. I came to England for you, Thorne. I—I couldn't find you in Madrid. By the time I got back to our inn and met Gavin there, you were gone. I couldn't stand the loneliness and loss of you." He pressed kiss after kiss against her brow. "Sweet Gypsy, I got here two days ago. I came to claim you for my own."

Tears squeezed beneath Thorne's lashes and she held Dev weakly. "Vaughn..." she cried rawly.

"Shh," he remonstrated, "Eamon explained everything." Dev tried to keep the shaking rage out of his voice for her sake. "Rest, Gypsy. Let me hold you, let me tend your wounds as you once tended mine. Together we'll grow strong once again."

The emotional expenditure was too much for Thorne, and she could only weep quietly in his arms. The hurt was too great to talk about, the loneliness too deep to be adequately expressed. Finally, after Dev gave her a drink mixed with bitter-tasting herbs, she sank back into sleep.

Dev sat there, watching the tension ease from Thorne's face. His baby...their baby...was gone. *God, give me the right words to tell her that,* he prayed, holding her hand tightly within his. The doctor had done everything he could to save the child, but to no avail. Eamon wept openly because only he among the staff at Somerset had known the child was Dev's and had shared Thorne's secret joy.

Raising his head, Dev stared at the closed door. Thorne had been here one day. The doctor said her recovery would be slow because she was badly bruised and shaken by her fall down those stairs. His blue eyes became icy. Vaughn... As soon as Thorne was better, he would hunt the dog down and kill him. Vaughn would forfeit his life for the baby's.

The next time Thorne regained consciousness, she felt better. Alyssa's red hair gleamed beneath the lamplight as she sat at her bedside, stitchery in hand.

Thorne shifted her gaze and saw Tray standing tensely at the fireplace, his face profiled and drawn with anguish. Alyssa smiled warmly when she looked up to see that Thorne was awake.

"Ah, you look better," she greeted, reaching out and patting Thorne's hand. "Tray?"

Tray turned, his dark, hawklike eyes widening with relief. Dressed in leather breeches, a white peasant shirt emphasizing his barrel chest, he came to join his wife. He managed a small smile of welcome.

"Our prayers have been answered," he told her, placing his hands on his wife's small shoulders. "You look better, Thorne."

Thorne smiled weakly. "I'm just so glad you let me come here, Tray. Thank you."

Alyssa put the stitchery aside, rising, her eyes shining with tears. "Dev will want to know you're awake. We'll get him for you."

The rose-colored drapes had been pulled aside from the floor-to-ceiling french doors to allow rays of late morning sun to invade the room. Outside, Thorne could hear the shouts and laughter of several children playing in the distance. Dragging herself into a sitting position, she tried to ignore the fact that every bone in her body ached. She looked at her arms after pulling up the sleeves of the thin cotton gown. Bruises adorned her like well-earned medals from combat.

The door quietly opened and closed. Dev stood there, dressed in buckskin breeches, black polished boots and a dark blue cotton shirt that matched the color of his eyes. His hair was typically short and neatly cut. No longer was he dirty or unshaven. No, he looked like a man of the gentry instead of a peasant. Thorne gave a little cry of welcome, raising her arms as he came around the bed and sat down beside her.

This time, Thorne was fully conscious and she relaxed into Dev's welcoming embrace, content to be pulled to him. He smelled of sunshine, the tart ocean breeze and horse. He murmured her name reverently, seeking and finding her lips.

His mouth descended gently against hers, bringing tears to Thorne's eyes. As rough and hurting as Vaughn had been, Dev was caressing and worshipful. Tears streamed down her cheeks, melding their lips together as she kissed him deeply, trying to tell him just how terribly she had missed him. His fingers tunneled through her hair, his whispered endearments serving to bring her fragile emotional state to a boil. Thorne clung to Dev afterward, content to be rocked in his arms.

"I thought you were dead," she whispered, placing her hand against his hard chest. "Vaughn lied to me, Dev. He brought Wolfe Erhard to our bedchamber on our wedding night with a pouch." She shuddered. "Vaughn forced me to open it. There was a nicked ear in there, and the amulet I'd given you. He told me you and Gavin had been killed by Wolfe."

Dev stilled his anger, kissing her brow, temple and cheek. "Erhard joined us shortly after Gavin's release. I had to stay in Madrid for a week longer because of Gavin's rib injuries, which Vaughn had inflicted on him." He held her to him. "Your amulet was lying on the dresser in Gavin's room where he was recuperating. My men said it disappeared one day and so did Erhard." Dev kissed her wrinkled brow. "Erhard never returned after that, Thorne. If I hadn't tended to Gavin, I might have gone to find the bastard. Your amulet meant everything to me."

She nodded, absorbing the love that he gave effortlessly to her. "And the ear? Erhard said it was your brother's nicked ear."

Dev shrugged. "Erhard could nick any ear and lop it off the unfortunate victim, claiming it was Gavin's. No one could tell the difference."

"It was all so gruesome, Dev."

"I know, I know, beloved." As Dev pressed a series of kisses to Thorne's brow and cheeks, her dark gray eyes were fraught with the terror that Trayhern had inflicted on her.

"I—I didn't want to marry him, Dev."

"You had no choice." His voice broke. "I didn't give you a choice." Dev held her so tightly he was afraid he would crush her. "I've been an idiot, Thorne. I let my hatred of Trayhern blind me to your love. God forgive me, but you've paid tenfold for my blindness. All I wanted or ever needed was you."

Dev took a deep breath and released Thorne. He arranged the pillows behind her. His face was tortured as he gripped her small hands within his. "Listen to me, beloved. When you arrived here two days ago, you were bleeding badly."

Thorne nodded. "Our baby, Dev. The fall down the stairs did something. I felt a tearing inside me, and all I could do afterward was hold my belly."

He bowed his head, fighting back the tears. "The doctor could not save our child, Thorne. Three hours after you arrived, the baby was born. Dead."

Thorne made a mewing cry, touching her belly. Why hadn't she realized it was flatter than before? "No..."

"It wasn't your fault. The doctor tried his best, but the fall..."

With a sob, Thorne buried her face in her hands, her shoulders shaking. Dev's arms went around her and he whispered broken words of solace. She sagged against him, devastated.

How long he held Thorne, Dev had no idea. It didn't matter. The pain they shared was theirs alone. Eventually, the laughter of children, the singing of the birds and bleat of sheep in the distance impinged upon their misery. He dried Thorne's tears and kissed her longingly, wanting to erase the grief he saw so rawly etched in her wide gray eyes.

"There will be others, Gypsy," he promised her thickly, framing her face between his hands. "The doctor examined you and said there is no reason why you can't carry as many children as you want. We'll have them, Thorne. As many as you want. I promise."

Thorne looked up at Dev's anguished face. He was suffering no less than she. Just to be able to reach out and touch his long, scarred fingers, to see the love shining in his blue eyes for her alone, began to assuage her loss.

"Right now," Dev rasped, "all I want you to do is rest. Erase the worry on your brow, beloved. It's too soon to talk of other things. We're together now, that's all that matters. And each night I'm going to sleep at your side and hold you. I'm going to take away all that pain you bore for me."

As if to join in the celebration of their love for each other, the sun deigned to shine each day. Thorne, who had never been to Wales before, didn't realize the significance of the pleasant summer weather. To her great surprise, Ivan Terebenev had come with Dev. His devotion to her, and his adoration, made Thorne rally even more strongly than before. Ivan was a gentle giant of a man and she loved him despite his fierce features and gruff demeanor. She spent hours with Alyssa, Tray and their four children. Sean, their adopted Irish son of fourteen, took it upon himself to remain with Thorne wherever she went, whether it was to the lush flower gardens, the herb garden, the stable or to the huge holding pens filled with sheep being prepared to be shorn for their valuable wool.

Thorne saw the love between Tray and Alyssa, knowing that she and Dev possessed a similar bond. Today she had worn a simple peasant skirt of bright red and a white blouse with puffed sleeves, intent upon gathering a basket of herbs for the kitchen. The sun beat down warmly upon her skin as she crouched between the rows of basil and rosemary, plucking the bright green leaves in the late morning after the dew had disappeared. Dev had been sleeping soundly when she rose earlier and completed her toilet. Of late, he had been staying up into the long hours of the night with Tray. What they discussed remained unknown to her.

Never once had Dev addressed the fact that she was still married to Vaughn. Or that she was sure Vaughn was trying to locate her. Hearing the full story behind Vaughn's treachery to Tray from Alyssa, Thorne realized he would never dare step foot upon Shadowhawk property. Whatever love had existed between the two half brothers had been killed when Vaughn tried to get rid of Alyssa.

Thorne was so busy mulling over those facts that she didn't hear Dev's approach. He stood there, dressed in the usual breeches, boots and shirt, his hands resting on his hips, watching her. The last ten days at Shadowhawk had worked a miracle on her, Dev thought. Her flesh, once pasty and pale, was taking on a golden hue, as it had in Spain. Her black hair, once short as a man's, was now swinging loose and heavy around her shoulders. Even her cheeks proclaimed a new bloom of health, and for that he was grateful.

Although he slept with Thorne each night, Dev had made no move to love her. The doctor had sternly warned him to allow her to rest for a good month after the loss of their baby. His blue eyes grew warm as he watched each of her graceful movements. This was his Gypsy once again, the child-woman who was like the earth itself, fertile, steady and loving. Despite Thorne's recovery, there was a great sadness in her eyes, and he knew she was grieving over their lost child. No matter how much she tried to smile when in the presence of Tray and his family, Dev always saw the haunted look deep in her telling gray gaze.

He walked quietly to where Thorne was crouched and leaned down, placing a quick kiss on her damp temple. With a startled exclamation, Thorne turned. Her shock turned into a dazzling smile that sent longing through every fiber of his body.

"Good morning," he said huskily, lifting her into his embrace.

"It is," she said breathlessly, throwing her arms around his broad, capable shoulders. Tilting her head, Thorne waited for his welcoming kiss. She wasn't disappointed as he molded his mouth gently to her lips. The taste of coffee and his maleness filled her senses, and Thorne languished within the fire his mouth was wreaking upon her.

"Mmm, nectar from the flowers," he rasped against her. "You're sweet life itself, Gypsy."

Thorne stood in his arms, thinking how handsome Dev was. Lines creased his brow, and she wondered what was bothering him. "You're worried," she said, easing from his arms and placing the last of the basil in the basket.

Dev took it from her, linking arms with Thorne as they made their way out of the garden. "We need to discuss some things," he said. He led her to a carved stone bench that stood near the center of the flower garden. He motioned for Thorne to sit down.

Thorne's heart began a painful beat against her ribs. "What is it, Dev?"

He crouched before her, his hands resting on her tightly clasped ones. "I'm going to leave tonight, Gypsy. I have some unfinished business to take care of." He frowned. "I didn't want to go until I was assured of your recovery."

"You're going after Vaughn, aren't you?"

Dev nodded. "I have no choice now, Thorne. Not that I ever needed one. He'd done enough damage to my family before he injured you and murdered our child."

Fear raced through Thorne. "Dev, please don't go! Didn't you come to England with the intent of claiming me? You said you'd released yourself from your vendetta!"

Dev's mouth worked into a grim line. "Thorne, that was before you arrived at Shadowhawk. My God, you bear the scars of his whip on your back. He deliberately shoved you down a flight of stairs to rid you of our child." His voice came out flat and harsh. "He's going to pay for what he's done. Perhaps no judge in England would convict him, but I will."

"No!" The cry tore from her soul. "Please don't go! Why can't we go away from Vaughn and England? You're what is important to me, Dev. Oh, please, heart of my heart, don't seek revenge."

He gently pulled her hands free of his shoulders. "Gypsy, I love you more than I've ever loved any woman in my life. If I don't challenge Trayhern and finish this business off between us, he'll be a shadow stalking us no matter where we go. Don't you see that?"

"I see that you can be killed."

Dev stroked her flaming cheek, trying to soothe her. "Vaughn thinks I'm dead."

Thorne moaned, clinging to his callused hand, which rested against her cheek. She shut her eyes tightly. "Have you thought what will happen if you are killed?"

"I've already made arrangements with Tray and his solicitors," Dev told her quietly. "Look at me, Gypsy."

She opened her eyes, agony moving through her.

"Tray has agreed to allow you to stay at Shadowhawk for the rest of your life, if that's what you want. If I am killed, he will contact your father's solicitors in London to press legal charges against Vaughn. One way or another, Tray will

see to it that Vaughn's power is stripped from him with re-
gard to you and Somerset. If you want a divorce, Tray will
help you to secure one. Then, after that, if you want to return to Somerset, you may.''

Thorne shook her head, blocking out the gruesome details. ''I want none of that! All I'll ever need or want is you,
Dev. I don't care if we're poor! I would rather eke out a
living tending the soil than lose you!''

Thorne's pleading tore at him and Dev couldn't draw his
gaze from her. He felt her hands grip his, hands that were
so small and slender in comparison to his own. He heard
Thorne choke back a sob. He hung his head. What was he
doing to her? To them? His mouth worked into an uneven
line, and he tried to control his own wildly seesawing emotions.

''How can a god let someone like Vaughn live after what
he's done to you? To so many people I've loved,'' he
rasped, unable to hold her gaze. Dev held her hands tightly
between his own. ''I love you more than anything,
Thorne.''

She pressed her brow against his cheek. ''Love must
outdistance hate. You've lived so many years on hatred and
revenge, Dev, you're accustomed to nothing else.'' Her
lower lip trembled and the words exploded from deep inside her. ''Please . . . if you love me, call off this revenge. I
believe God will take care of Vaughn. He'll be punished,
Dev, I know he will. But not by you.'' She blindly pressed
a kiss to his damp cheek, shaken by the discovery that he
was crying. With trembling hands, she framed his face,
forcing him to look at her. ''We have each other, that's all
we'll need. We had a child, that was proof of our love—''

Dev felt helpless rage well up within him. ''A child murdered by Vaughn.''

''That's over! It's past, beloved. Dev, look at me, look
with me to our future. In a few more weeks, we'll sail to
America. Together. Isn't that more important?''

He swallowed hard, cradling her delicate face between his
hands. ''You're more important than anything in my world,
Thorne. All right, I'll forget about going after Vaughn. But

I don't believe God will punish the bastard. Men like him live to create more misery for others, that's all.''

An incredible surge of relief flooded Thorne. Long moments passed before she found her voice. "I love you so much," she quavered.

With a sob, Dev crushed her against him. "I can't conceive of life without you, Gypsy. I want you happy. I want to see that smile back in your eyes again."

She wept with him, relieved that he was finally going to give up his quest for revenge. "When we sail for America, you'll see that smile again," she promised him softly, kissing him repeatedly.

With a shaky laugh, Dev kissed her in return. Suddenly, the dark load he'd carried for so many years slid off his shoulders, and it was all because of Thorne, her goodness, the life she infused into him. Each time she looked, touched or loved him, she gave one more piece of his soul back to him. "You're my life," Dev rasped thickly. "My life...."

Chapter Twenty-One

Fog swirled and eddied in and around the grove of trees near Shadowhawk. Silent white fingers wound between the trunks of the oak and ash, the gray light evidence that another morning was dawning.

In the distance, a muffled bark of a dog sounded twice. The birds within the grove tried out their songs for the first time as daylight gained a foothold on the awakening world.

A rider on a black horse appeared like a ghost out of the swirling fog. The horse's nostrils were flared, his ebony coat shining with sweat and foam covering his opened mouth as the rider urged him on at full speed. Vaughn Trayhern rode like a man possessed, using his crop against the horse, beating welts into the animal's glistening hide.

His eyes were narrowed as he pushed the horse to the edge of his physical limits. Three days ago, he had finally found out where Thorne had gone. Shadowhawk and Tray's warning never to step foot on it be damned! He was going to get his wife back! Rage, hurt and wounded pride had kept Vaughn awake as he rode from England to Wales. He stopped only long enough to buy fresh mounts at coach stations. The *ton* was alive with rumors about Thorne and himself. He would not allow his good name to be blackened by the Irish-loving whore! One way or another, he was taking her back to Somerset with him.

* * *

Thorne leaned down, pressing a kiss to Dev's unshaven cheek as he slept. A tremulous smile caught the corners of her mouth as she watched him turn over. His thick lashes barely moved.

Dev stared up into Thorne's flushed face. Her dove gray eyes danced with love. He groaned, reaching for her hand. "What time is it?" he asked, his voice thick with sleep.

"Eight in the morning."

Dev groaned again. Thorne was dressed in a lovely pink skirt and blouse, and she looked fresh and natural. Love welled fiercely within his chest. "Eight? Why are you up so early? The entire household's still sleeping."

Laughing lightly, Thorne kissed him on the brow and slipped from his grasp. "Remember? I was going to take Sean with me down to the beach and pick some coltsfoot along the cliffs. It grows well there, and it has to be collected with the dew still on the leaves. He wanted me to teach him all I knew about herbs, so I promised he could go with me this morning. The horses are saddled and he's waiting in the stable yard for me."

Scowling, Dev rubbed his sleep-ridden eyes and turned on his side toward Thorne. The beach. The horrible story of the day that Tray's half sister was killed by pirates on that lonely beach came back to him. He had shot Tray on that same beach years ago, thinking that Alyssa was his prisoner. The place was stained with violence and grief. "Do you have to go there? Surely there's coltsfoot elsewhere."

Picking up her basket, Thorne slipped it over her arm. She gave him a winsome smile, walking to the door. "The largest leaves grow in the most inhospitable places. We'll be back in time for breakfast."

"Well, as long as Sean is with you, but be back in an hour."

"Just one hour," she promised, blowing him a kiss. "Go back to sleep, beloved. I'll wake you with a kiss when I return."

With a lazy grin, Dev slowly sank back down, pulling the sheet up to his waist. "Is that a promise, wench?"

Her eyes sparkled with happiness. "A promise, my beautiful man."

Dev snorted and threw an arm across his eyes. "Beautiful! Women are beautiful, men are handsome."

The room rang with her lilting laughter. "Your face and body are beautiful in my eyes. That's a compliment!"

A grin edged his mouth. "Get out of here, wench, or I may decide to keep you in my bed and acquaint you with my beautiful body."

Thorne chuckled and shut the door quietly behind her. Humming softly, she skipped down the carpeted hall toward the stable. Sean would be impatiently waiting to be off on their next adventure together. Her heart spilled over with happiness. Was it possible to savor such continuous joy without her heart exploding?

Sean sat on his white Welsh pony, watching as Thorne dismounted. At fourteen, he was long and lanky, almost too big for the small animal. Behind them, small breakers broke upon the sandy beach, the brisk sea beyond it a dark green. Fog hung over the cliffs that slanted a hundred feet above them.

Thorne smiled up at Sean. "Well, aren't you going to get down and help me?" she teased, moving carefully among the fallen rocks that hid the broad-leafed coltsfoot.

Sean's serious face broke into one of his winning smiles, his green eyes lighting up. "Go ahead . . . I'll watch."

Thorne laughed and took the basket, lifting her skirts and maneuvering around several boulders up the slight incline. "So much for me believing you wanted to learn about herbs. Are you sure your father didn't tell you to come along to be my guard dog?"

With a slight shrug, Sean muttered, "Naw, he didn't."

Thorne gave him a sidelong glance that spoke volumes. "I see . . ."

"Well, no one should ride down to this beach alone. You know the stories—"

"Not today, Sean Trayhern! It's a glorious day and all I want is to hear laughter, see your wonderful smile and listen to the gulls sing to us."

Sean lifted his dark head, searching the cliffs above them. "All right, I can do that for you. Stay here, I'll be right back!" He urged his pony into a canter toward a path that led off the beach.

"Hey—wait!" Thorne waved her hand. She scowled for only a moment and then shook her head. If she knew Sean, he'd probably spotted some white daisies on the lip of the cliff and was going to fetch her a bouquet. Like his adopted father, Tray, he was forever thoughtful. Smiling, Thorne concentrated on picking the dew-laden coltsfoot and placed the leaves in the basket.

Gulls skimmed the Irish Sea behind her, their cries echoing off the cliff where she worked untiringly. Thorne had ceased to miss Sean's presence, concentrating instead on the herb she hunted for. When she heard the distinct sound of hoofbeats in the distance, she straightened up. Wiping her damp brow, she squinted. It wasn't Sean. Someone was galloping up on a black horse. And then Thorne raised her hand in greeting. It was Dev! The brigand! He'd gotten out of bed after all, to come and share the newly awakened day with her.

The basket nearly full, Thorne quickly picked her way down from the slope to the sand. The hoofbeats grew louder. She released her skirt and lifted her head to greet Dev. Thorne's eyes widened as fear shot through her. She dropped the basket, the coltsfoot scattering about her feet. No! Oh God, no! It was Vaughn!

The heavy snort of the horse drawing closer shocked her into action. With a cry, Thorne spun around, tripping over her skirt, nearly losing her balance. Running for her mare, she labored through the sucking sand. Half-crazy with fear, she lunged for the reins.

Vaughn lifted his whip, slashing it downward. The black mare squealed, leaping away from Thorne. He jerked his horse to a stop in front of her. His eyes blazed with an awful light and the crop trembled in his outstretched hand.

"I ought to use this on you," he ground out in a bare whisper. A cutting smile slashed across his maniacal features. He saw Thorne go waxen, her hand pressed against her lips. "Did you think I'd let you go this easily, wife of mine?" He kicked the horse so it jumped forward, nearly striking Thorne. She cried out, dodging the powerful beast that was barely held in check by Vaughn's gloved hand.

Shaking violently, Thorne stared up at Vaughn. He looked insane, his hair unkempt, lips pulled away from his teeth, eyes burning with a hatred that went clear to his soul. "I won't go back to Somerset, Vaughn," she said.

"I think you will. You're legally mine, and I won't be the butt of jokes!"

Trying desperately to think of an escape route, Thorne glanced around. This was her first foray to the beach. Even Tray had tried to dissuade her from coming here, where so much Trayhern blood had been spilled before. A knot formed in her throat, and her voice was strained. "I intend to divorce you, Vaughn. I'd rather die than go back and live with you."

His smile turned to a cutting sneer. "I tried to be good to you, Thorne. I've never had a woman spurn my good looks. I thought I could eventually woo you with my charm." His voice dropped to a low grate, vibrating with hatred. "But you never let go of your love for that Irish brigand, did you? And you hid the fact that you were pregnant by him from me. By God's blood, woman, don't you think you deserved what you got? I see you're no longer pregnant. That fall you took evened things out between you and me. Now the slate's clean. You'll come back with me and take your rightful place at my side."

Tears splattered down Thorne's cheeks. She clenched her fists, taking a step toward him. "You rotten, sick thing! You murdered my baby! You did it on purpose! What makes you think I'd ever come back and live with an insane animal like you?"

Vaughn slowly raised the crop and pointed it at her heaving breast. "Get over here and mount behind me. Do it, or I swear you'll regret your decision."

Thorne backed away from him. "You've made me regret enough already!" she raged. "Carry out your threats, Vaughn, because I'll never come willingly to you. Never!"

His eyes turned ruthless. "Very well. I'd just as soon bed you here on this beach as at the manor. It makes no difference to me. I want a son, damn you. And you will bear me one." He took his booted foot out of the stirrup.

With a cry, Thorne leaned down, grabbing a fist-size rock. She hurled it at Vaughn. The horse jumped sideways, struck by the missile. Vaughn cursed, nearly unseated.

Spinning away, Thorne lifted her skirts and raced up the rocky incline. Sobbing for breath, she fell several times, cutting her hands and bruising her knees as she scrambled to escape. Hysteria claimed Thorne as she heard Vaughn scream her name, his cry echoing off the cliff face. And then she heard another shout.

Jerking her head to the left, Thorne saw another rider careening down the rocky path to the beach. She blinked back the tears, trying to see who it was. Oh God, it was Sean! Vaughn would kill him! Ragged gasps tore from her as she straightened up, squinting. The horse was gray. No, wait! A trickle of hope flared to life within Thorne. And then, absolute terror. It was Ghazeia! She'd recognize the mare's long, flaglike tail anywhere. Dev! It was Dev! She whispered his name, an aching prayer on her contorted lips. Had Sean seen Vaughn and ridden back to Shadowhawk to warn Dev? He must have, he must have!

Vaughn turned and watched the rapidly approaching rider. His lips twisted into a snarl. Devlin Kyle. Shock momentarily shattered his fury. Erhard had tricked him! The hussar had lied! Wrenching his gelding around, Vaughn put the spurs to him. It didn't matter. It was better this way. He could kill the Irish brigand himself.

They raced toward each other through the sand. Dev drew his sword, preparing to do battle. In the split second before they met, he saw Vaughn's insane eyes. He was a man gone mad with revenge. Blood pounded hard through Dev as he girded himself, feeling the undeniable surge of adrenaline pumping through his body. His battle-hardened mare lengthened her pounding stride, ears laid flat against her head as she hurtled toward a horse twice her size. Dev expected no quarter from Trayhern. Both had been in many skirmishes, and the rules of war applied then as now. At the last moment, he spurred his mare straight toward the black. He prepared himself for the coming collision, sword upraised.

The gelding tried to avoid the charge. Dropping to his rear legs, the stunned animal went berserk, unused to a battle of any form. Vaughn cursed and was thrown over the animal's head. With a grunt, he landed hard on the sand and rolled away from the flailing feet of his downed horse. His face was contorted with shock as he stood. Vaughn uttered a cry of rage as Devlin Kyle turned the nimble gray mare and galloped back toward him.

Staggering to regain his balance, Vaughn reached inside his waistcoat, pulling out a small pistol. He saw Kyle's eyes widen. He quickly lifted the pistol, aiming it at the brigand. Satisfaction claimed Vaughn as he pulled the trigger. The pop of the pistol was muffled by the screams of the disturbed gulls around them.

Ghazeia reared skyward. A groan came from deep within Dev as the lead ball slammed through his boot, embedding itself deeply into his calf. Automatically, Dev urged his mare forward. In seconds, he knocked Trayhern off his feet, dislodging the gun. Pain radiated smartly from Dev's leg as he dismounted. Vaughn wrenched his sword from its sheath, stalking him.

"You're a poor shot," Dev snarled.

Sweat covered Vaughn's face. "Thorne's mine! I'm taking her back with me!"

Dev limped toward Trayhern, flicking the tip of his nicked and scarred blade at the Englishman. "She was never yours, Trayhern, and you know it." He halted, his voice turning deadly. "Before you die this day, I want you to know that you murdered the child she carried." He held up his sword, the blade gleaming dully as sunlight pierced through the fog. "An eye for an eye. Your life for our child's life. An even trade."

Vaughn's grip tightened on the pommel of the sword. "You treacherous Irish beggar. She carried your bastard, and I wouldn't have it! She's married to me!"

"Prepare to die, Trayhern. We're evenly matched now, you with your busted knee and me with a lead ball in my leg," Dev taunted softly, beginning to circle him.

"You're wrong!" Vaughn rasped, lunging at Kyle, the blade missing his chest by a scant inch. "When this is over with, you'll be the one to die!" He looked at Thorne, who stood a hundred feet away from them, her eyes wide with agony.

Dev shook his head. "I should have killed you in Ireland, when I had the chance. Instead, I let Alyssa sway me into allowing you to live. And in doing so, you've hurt the second woman I've loved in my life. You killed my first wife. You've killed Thorne's baby. This time, Trayhern, you'll answer to me a final time for all those sins."

With a cry of fury, Vaughn launched himself forward, his sword cutting through the air. Satisfaction soared through him. The leg wound he had inflicted upon Kyle was more than a mere flesh wound. Each time the Irishman moved, he limped badly. Blood was leaking heavily from the wound and Vaughn knew if he could tire Kyle out, he could easily finish him off and emerge the victor. Despite his knee injury, he moved with surprising agility and speed.

Steel rang against steel as they bit savagely into each other, the air charged with their anger. Vaughn grinned, sensing he had the upper hand. Kyle's face had drained of color, his mouth quirking with pain each time he pressed an attack against him. So, Kyle thought he could win against him in sword combat! He, Vaughn Trayhern, who had been in the King's cavalry!

"You're nothing but rabble, Kyle," Vaughn rasped, attacking him and then feinting. "You're as poor with a blade as a beginner!"

Dev smiled mirthlessly, the pain in his leg forgotten. His blue eyes glimmered with ruthless intensity. "This rabble

will be the death of you, Trayhern.'' He lunged forward.
The point of his blade slashed across Vaughn's shirted
chest, drawing a thin streak of blood across it.

With a cry of surprise, Vaughn leapt back. "You vile
filth," he snarled, then pushed another attack against Kyle.

Parrying rapidly, Dev retreated beneath the savage on-
slaught, steel meeting steel in a wild flurry of action. Trayhern's face was crazed, his eyes squinted, a cry tearing from
him as he pressed relentlessly forward. Pain shot up
through Dev, and his wounded leg gave out beneath his retreat. Unable to stop from falling backward, Dev threw his
blade up over his head to protect himself from the coming
blow. He heard Thorne scream out in warning to him.

Dev hit the ground hard, the air knocked from him. He
locked his elbow as Trayhern's blade hurtled down upon
him. Sparks flew as the blades exploded against each other.
Vaughn grunted, bringing the sword up, both hands around
the pommel. Dev rolled away. The point slashed into the
sand, inches from Dev.

A veil of grit flew upward as Vaughn jerked the blade
free, sprinting for a third attack before Kyle could get to his
feet. He had him! He had him! Vaughn lifted the blade high
over his head, his eyes glittering with triumph. Sweat
streaked his taut face as he prepared to deal a death blow
to the Irishman. As he launched forward, bringing the
blade down with all his power, he saw Kyle twist from his
position on the ground, thrusting his blade directly up at
him. A sob ripped through Vaughn when he realized with
terrible finality that he could not stop his forward motion.
The triumph that had been his only split seconds before
turned to terror.

Dev jammed the sword upward. He felt the point strike
bone and then glance off into the softness of Trayhern's
inner organs. Rolling aside, Dev escaped Vaughn's blade as
it fell from his hands. Trayhern dropped to the ground beside him. Panting hard, Dev dragged himself to his knees,
black dots dancing before his eyes. He crawled over to the
dying Englishman. Sweat stung Dev's eyes, making them
smart as he leaned over Trayhern. Vaughn's eyes were nar-

rowed with hatred, his breath coming in loud, labored gasps.

"Rot . . . in hell, Kyle . . ."

Dev gulped for air as he watched Trayhern die. "*You will*," he rasped harshly, and then pitched forward, unconscious.

Bleating filled the air. The huge holding pens at Shadowhawk contained hundreds of sheep awaiting shearing. The afternoon was warm, the tang of salt in the air strong as a breeze wafted off the moody Irish Sea beyond the cliffs where the manor stood. Thorne stood beside Shukar Nak, the reins in her hands. The sea was a deep emerald color, the sunlight bright between puffs of white clouds above her. A perfect day, Thorne decided. The black mare raised her head, nickering. Thorne turned. It was Ivan on his small steppe pony. He grinned widely in greeting and dismounted.

"I've been looking everywhere for you, *malenki ptitsa*."

Thorne warmed to his pet name, little bird, for her. "Why?"

Ivan lumbered up, thoughtfully scratching his black, wiry beard. He was still dressed in his baggy gray trousers, and a voluminous white peasant shirt was stretched to its limits by his massive, hairy chest. His eyes sparkled with amusement as he looked down at Thorne. "That grouch of an Irishman won't take no for an answer. *You* tell him that I cannot go to America with you. He won't believe me!" Ivan thumped his hand against his chest, creating a sound like a drum being struck. "I told him, 'I'm not a farmer, I'm a soldier.' A good Russian soldier. What good would I be, coming along with you? Ptah! I'd only be underfoot!"

Thorne's eyes took on a look of sadness. "But—you said earlier that you would come with us, Ivan."

Ivan winced at the sudden wobble in her voice. How easily touched she was. He patted her shoulder awkwardly. "You know me better than anyone."

"Yes, and Dev and I agree that America is the only place for you, Ivan. You can't stay here in England after what has happened." Thorne gripped his huge arm, which seemed to have the circumference of a small oak tree. "I know how loyal you are to Dev. You've fought at each other's side for so many years." Tears came to her gray eyes as she searched his generous features. "And I love you, too, Ivan. I—I couldn't stand the thought that you might not be going with us. We'd both worry for you."

Shyly, Ivan hung his head, staring down restively at his booted feet. "Ah, *Malenki Ptitsa,* you'd melt the ice around the hardest man's heart," he mumbled.

Her grip on his arm tightened. "Then you'll come?" she breathed, hardly daring to believe her ears.

Ivan muttered something in his mother tongue and then cocked one bushy eyebrow in her direction. "I'm not good with a plow!"

"Then care for our horses, Ivan. We need someone who will be good with them. Tray wants us to take over some of his Welsh mares so that we can begin a new breed in America. You're so good with animals."

With a groan, Ivan raised his eyes heavenward. "I knew when the cap'n ordered me to come and talk to you about my decision, I was lost. That Irish husband of yours isn't stupid. He knows I have a weak spot in my heart for women." He pinched her flushed cheek. "And especially for you."

With a cry of joy, Thorne threw her arms around Ivan's thick neck, hugging him as hard as she could. "Oh, Ivan! You're wonderful! Wonderful!"

Overwhelmed by her effusive display of affection, he placed his massive hands around her narrow waist and hoisted her up on the black mare. "What am I going to do with you?" he rumbled. "You're such a child..."

Thorne leaned over, giving him a peck on his fully bearded cheek. "You won't regret your decision, Ivan. I promise you," she said excitedly.

Ivan stepped back, blushing furiously. "Go! Go tell that clever husband of yours that I've changed my mind... again!"

* * *

Dev was watching the shearing of the sheep when Thorne rode up. He turned, a slow smile of welcome pulling on his mouth. The last three weeks had been a miracle. True, he still limped around with his leg wound, but with time, it would heal completely. He watched with pleasure as Thorne dismounted, her light blue cotton dress outlining the feminine shape of her ripe, young body. Although they had been married a week ago, Dev remembered the doctor's earlier warning about Thorne needing the time to heal physically from the loss of her baby.

He ached to bring her in communion with himself, but he was almost afraid to touch her. So much had happened since Ivan had carried him home on his steppe pony after the sword fight with Vaughn.

"Dev!" Thorne cried, picking up her skirts and hurrying up to him. Her cheeks were flushed the color of ripe apples, her full, expressive lips parted in a breathless smile.

He leaned over, placing a kiss on her damp temple, and then took her into his arms. "What is it?"

"Ivan," she gasped, "Ivan's changed his mind! He'll go to America with us!"

With a chuckle, Dev gently embraced her. God knew, he wanted to crush her in his arms, make love with her all night long and show her just how much he loved her. "I knew you could do it, Gypsy." And then he sobered, removing a strand of hair from her brow. "Thank you."

Thorne tilted her head, confused. Every time she looked into Dev's blue eyes, she saw that same hungry yearning. And yet he barely touched or held her. The doctor had pronounced her fit once again. Now she waited impatiently until Dev's leg healed. Sliding her hands up his arms, she wrapped them around his neck.

"There is only one way to thank me," she whispered wickedly.

Dev enjoyed the sultry look in her half-closed eyes. "And that is?"

Her heart pounded, underscoring her fear of Dev rejecting her. Was it proper for a wife to ask her husband to make

love with her? Would Dev think her wanton? Licking her
lower lip, she stole a glance up at him.

"Tonight . . . love me? Please . . ."

Dev stared down at her, shocked and yet pleased beyond
words. He stroked her unbound hair. "Are you sure,
Thorne?"

"Yes."

"But the doctor—"

She stamped her foot impatiently. "The doctor said I've
been fine for a week now!" And then she blushed furiously, unable to look at him.

A slow grin pulled at his mouth. "If that's what you
want."

"Yes," she muttered, wildly aware of the heat in her
face.

"I like your boldness, Gypsy," he told her in a gritty
voice.

Thorne's head snapped up. "You do?"

"Very much. I want my wife bold and unafraid to discuss how she feels or when she wants me."

A shiver of expectancy quivered through Thorne and a
tremulous smile touched her lips. "I—I was afraid you'd
think me wanton . . . something a good wife shouldn't be."

With a roar of laughter, Dev turned, walking with her
back toward Shadowhawk. "Wanton?" he teased. "Isn't
that the only way a Gypsy can be? I think we had this very
conversation in Spain, didn't we?"

Again, Thorne blushed. "Gypsies are not wanton! How
dare you."

Still chuckling, Dev led her up the stone steps. "Tonight
we'll explore what wanton means, my beautiful young
bride." He gave her a heated look filled with promise. "I'll
teach you a new meaning to wanton and you'll understand
what a beautiful word it is."

Thorne came to him dressed in a floor-length ivory silk
nightgown, the slender curves of her body lovingly outlined. Dev stood in the near darkness, a lone candle burning above the mantel of the fireplace. As she walked slowly

toward him, her hair recently washed and combed until blue highlights shone in it, Dev thought of how far they had come together since the kidnapping.

She stopped within a foot of him, suddenly shy and demure as only Thorne could be. He offered her a slight smile of encouragement as he shed his robe, standing naked before her. Silence hung fragilely between them, and Dev saw her gray eyes widen as she looked at him. He felt at once the most powerful man on earth, and the most humble. She looked at him with shining adoration and love in her eyes. This would be the first time they had come together since Madrid . . . so many lonely months without each other.

As Dev stepped forward, he reminded himself of the brutality Thorne had endured because of Vaughn. Skimming his hands across Thorne's warm, pliant shoulders, he brought her lightly against him.

"For what it's worth," he breathed against her offered lips, "I'll be as gentle as possible with you, beloved."

"I'm not afraid."

A rapturous sigh escaped Thorne as his mouth captured her lips. She melted against his tall, hard frame. The male fragrance of his body filled her and she hungrily responded to his exploring kiss. Her knees weakened as his callused palms enclosed her breasts and his thumbs stroked the hardened nipples. In one smooth motion, Dev picked her up, carrying her to their bed.

Dev laid Thorne down and moved beside her, running his hand lightly across her belly. Meeting her slumberous gray eyes filled with the silver fire of desire, he whispered, "I love you, Thorne," and laid his head upon her breast, holding her tightly for a moment, content with her womanly nearness. Her small hands moved across his naked shoulders and he felt fire uncoiling, thick and turgid, within him. Raising his head, Dev propped himself up on one elbow and captured a budding nipple beneath the shimmering material. A ribbon of pleasure sizzled through him as he heard Thorne gasp and then press her silken form against him.

He slid his hand beneath the gown, following the curve of her thigh, pushing the material up across her belly. Her skin was lustrous beneath the candlelight, softly blurred with shadow, emphasizing her gentle curves. Urging the gown off her, Dev contented himself with simply drinking Thorne into him.

"You're a feast for my eyes," Dev told her thickly, pressing small kisses to the corners of her lips. "Your mouth is honey..." He ran his tongue across hers, feeling and tasting each curve of her. Lowering his head, he captured the dusky nipple of one breast, drawing it deep into the heat of his mouth. Thorne arched and cried out, her fingers winding through his hair. "Ripe, red berries to be sampled..." Dev cupped her breasts. "Beautiful, small white globes, so perfectly round and soft..." Trailing a path of fire down Thorne, he nuzzled the ebony carpet above her thighs, inhaling her female scent, aching to claim her. "The fragrance of a wanton woman who loves her man," he rasped huskily, following the juncture where her thighs met. He kissed her silken mound, feeling her strain against him, sobbing for breath, sobbing out his name as if it were a prayer, begging him to claim her.

He got to his knees, gently parting her long, curved thighs, sliding his hand over their lush, velvet expanse, watching Thorne closely. She tossed her head from side to side, crying out his name again and again as he stroked her swollen, fiery core. She was ready for him, he realized humbly. In that moment, he loved her more fiercely than ever before. She had placed herself without reservation into his hands, trusting him, giving to him....

Thorne moaned as she saw him lower his head. He lifted her hips slightly, kissing her intimately, his mouth wreaking sensual havoc upon her reeling senses. She could stand no more, an ache more primal than she had ever experienced driving her to meld with Dev. Thorne watched dazedly as he, as if sensing her needs, drew her to him. Then she closed her eyes, waiting...waiting...

His warm hardness entering her was welcomed and joyous. Thorne drew in a deep breath, opening her arms to

Dev. He lay still, barely within her. Thorne forced her eyes open, confused, needing—wanting—all of him. She saw the beads of moisture upon his pained brow, the hunger in his narrowed midnight eyes, and she whimpered. Her lips parted in a pleading gesture to complete the union, and she instinctively lifted her hips.

A groan tore from Dev as her body met his. His fists knotted into the bedding on either side of her halo of hair as he fought to contain his explosive need of her. Again, she moved, pulling him deeper and deeper into her hot, womanly core. He clenched his teeth, drawing air between them.

"God...Thorne..." She wrapped her slender legs about his hips, joining them deeply, forever together. Whatever chains had held him in check were shattered by her knowing movement. Dev twisted his hips forward and heard a gasp escape her, but it was a joyful sound filled with pleasure, and he buried himself within her, reveling in their love.

An uncontrollable fire burned fiercely within Thorne. Each thrust of his body brought her closer and closer to that white-hot core that threatened to explode within her. She felt his hands settle on her hips, and her eyes closed. Her hoarse cry was captured by his mouth and he shared the sound of her fulfillment with her. Thorne floated in a state of gauzy bliss, barely aware that Dev clutched her and groaned, finding rich relief within her.

They lay in each other's arms long moments afterward. Dev brought Thorne to his side, holding her, stroking her damp back until it dried beneath his ministrations. As he lay above her on one elbow, Dev absorbed her into his soul. Her lips were slightly swollen from the power of their kisses, her breasts pressed to the wall of his chest, the curve of her hip still melded to his.

"You were wanton," he told her raggedly, kissing her temple and then running his tongue around her ear lobe. "Wanton, earthy, giving and taking, my Gypsy. You make me burn and die each time you touch me. But it's a sweet death I'd gladly give my life for."

Thorne murmured his name, kissing his damp, salty shoulder. "I'm glad I'm wanton for you," she admitted weakly, still caught in the languor of their lovemaking.

He gently eased Thorne to her back and splayed his fingers across her belly. "You and I," he told her huskily, "will create another child from our love."

Tears made her gray eyes luminous as she looked up at him. "Children who will be born in a free land, Dev."

Nodding, he stretched out, holding her, his hand protective against the roundness of her stomach. "A land that has no memory of our past or of where we came from, only where we're going." Dev kissed her brow, eyes, nose and, finally, her lips. "We deserve America. We've proven our courage and our strength for each other."

Thorne buried her fingers in his hair, thinking how vulnerable Dev looked in that moment. His harsh features were softened and his blue eyes, usually hard and measuring, were filled with hope. That discovery shook her deeply. She'd never seen hope in his eyes before, or heard it in his gritty voice.

"My King of Swords," she murmured. "Just as the tarot cards I laid out in Spain had promised, you carried me out of danger and into the light."

Dev managed a slight smile, his heart mushrooming with such love for her that he thought he might die of happiness in that shared moment. "I'm the King of Swords no longer. I'm trading my sword in for a plowshare, Gypsy. I was once a farmer and I'll be one again."

She ran her fingers lightly across one of the many white, puckered scars caused by sword wounds garnered throughout his hard life. "I'm glad," she admitted. "I want our children to know peace, not war."

"They'll know our love first," Dev promised her, his eyes growing misty, "and I'll have your love, Gypsy. I want nothing more out of life than you."

* * * * *

Harlequin Historicals®

COMING NEXT MONTH

#127 THE LADY AND THE LAIRD—Maura Seger
Forced by her grandfather's will to live in an eerie Scottish castle
for six months or lose the crumbling keep to rogue Angus Wyndham,
beautiful Katlin Sinclair discovered a tormented ghost, hidden
treasure and burning passion in the arms of the one man she could
not trust.

#128 SWEET SUSPICIONS—Julie Tetel
Intent on reentering society, Richard Worth planned to find a well-
connected wife. But he hadn't expected the murder of a stranger to
revive his scandalous past—or that his marriage of convenience to
lovely Caroline Hutton would awaken his passion and heal his
anguished soul.

#129 THE CLAIM—Lucy Elliot
A confrontation was inevitable when determined Sarah Meade and
formidable mountain man Zeke Brownell both claimed ownership of
the same land. Yet underneath their stubborn facades and cultural
differences there lay a mutual attraction neither could deny.

#130 PIRATE BRIDE—Elizabeth August
Pirate captive Kathleen James impetuously married prisoner
John Ashford to save him from certain death. But although
freedom and happiness were only a breath away, a daring escape
brought them further danger in the New World.

AVAILABLE NOW:

⬧ Harlequin®
JANELLE TAYLOR
Valley of Fire

HARLEQUIN IS PROUD TO PRESENT *VALLEY OF FIRE* BY JANELLE TAYLOR—AUTHOR OF TWENTY-TWO BOOKS, INCLUDING SIX *NEW YORK TIMES* BESTSELLERS

VALLEY OF FIRE—the warm and passionate story of Kathy Alexander, a famous romance author, and Steven Winngate, entrepreneur and owner of the magazine that intended to expose the real Kathy ''Brandy'' Alexander to her fans.

Don't miss VALLEY OF FIRE, available in May.

HARLEQUIN Temptation

Rebels & Rogues

Quinn: He was a real-life hero to everyone except himself.

THE MIGHTY QUINN
by Candace Schuler
Temptation #397, June 1992

All men are not created equal. Some are rough around the edges. Tough-minded but tenderhearted. Incredibly sexy. The tempting fulfillment of every woman's fantasy.

When it's time to fight for what they believe in, to win that special woman, our Rebels and Rogues are heroes at heart. Twelve Rebels and Rogues, one each month in 1992, only from Harlequin Temptation!

BIG SUMMER READ

Summer Reading At Its Best

In July, Harlequin and Silhouette bring readers the Big Summer Read Program. Heat up your summer with these four exciting new novels by top Harlequin and Silhouette authors.

SOMEWHERE IN TIME by Barbara Bretton
YESTERDAY COMES TOMORROW by Rebecca Flanders
A DAY IN APRIL by Mary Lynn Baxter
LOVE CHILD by Patricia Coughlin

From time travel to fame and fortune, this program offers something for everyone.

Available at your favorite retail outlet.

BSR

H A R L E Q U I N
American Romance®

Be a part of American Romance's year-long celebration of love and the holidays of 1992. Celebrate those special times each month with your favorite authors.

Next month, we pay tribute to the *first* man in your life—your father—with a special Father's Day romance:

JUNE

S	M	T			S
	1				
7	8				13
14					20
21	22				27
28	29				

FATHER'S DAY

**#441
DADDY'S GIRL
by Barbara Bretton**

Read all the books in *A Calendar of Romance*, coming to you one per month all year, only in American Romance.